DEATH'S DANCER

PRAISE FOR JASMINE SILVERA

"DEATH'S DANCER weaves suspense and romance into a story as smart as it is sensual…Silvera deftly choreographs the action using lush depictions of Prague's storied scenery and deliciously dark humor. A thrilling debut." -Camille Griep, *Letters to Zell, New Charity Blues*

"A spirited, sexy paranormal romance." -Kirkus Reviews (Death's Dancer)

ALSO BY JASMINE SILVERA

Dancer's Flame (Grace Bloods #2)

Best Served Cold (Short Story)

DEATH'S DANCER

GRACE BLOODS BOOK ONE

JASMINE SILVERA

This is a work of fiction. Names, characters, organizations, events, places and incidents are the product of the author's imagination or used fictitiously.

First publishing date 2016

No Inside Voice

ISBN: 978-0-9976582-0-0

Cover dancer photo by Richard Calmes

Cover design by Damon Freeman

Book Design by No Inside Voice

Printed in the United States

To Kam,
Sister. Reader. Friend.

CHAPTER ONE

Isela Vogel danced for gods, no longer convinced anyone was listening. She pressed the ball of her bare left foot into the polished wooden floorboards. As she exhaled, her right leg floated with extraordinary control from the floor. Her fingers flared: palms out, thumbs turned down and in to present the backs of her hands. With a slight bend of her elbows, she pushed her hands away from her body. Her right arm twisted down from the shoulder blade as her left fingertips arched toward the sky.

In every movement, every breath, she danced, demanding their attention anyway.

The scent of cardamom, oranges, and cinnamon permeated the air from the pots of scented water hanging around the hexagonal ring. There was no evidence dancing in a ring was more or less effective than anywhere else. A tradition of performers dictated a dedicated space, properly lit, with good ventilation and solid flooring, was a necessity. Each academy had its own ring style, but for Isela, the Praha Academy was home.

The domed skylight bathed the room in an aura of hued light from the sea glass soft panes. Although the practice studios in the floors below were mirrored, the walls of the performance ring bore the original Mucha murals. On sunny days, the room warmed nicely. This close to winter, radiators behind elegant, gilded grates provided heat.

Isela bowed her back, the muscles of her abdomen contracting to support her upper body as it cascaded behind her until the sweep of her dark hair dusted the floor. She hated dancing with her hair unbound, but some patrons insisted on it. In some corners, the belief existed that the value and effectiveness of the dance was due to its beauty. Since a majority of dancers were women, she thought there might be some credence to that.

But beauty was not what made dance a language. Each movement had a name, and when strung together in choreographed sequence, they became a request from her patron to the gods themselves. She knew them all. Of the entities they called gods, she knew less.

Powerful, inexplicable forces with their own priorities had existed among humanity since the beginning. Without knowing better, humans labeled them gods and turned to worship, attempting to appease and gain favor. The lack of interest in communication from the gods didn't stop humanity from trying.

Dancing saved humanity, or nearly doomed it.

Her right palm met the floor before the left. Her belly contracted, drawing first the extended right leg and then the trailing left over her head. She found a moment of balance in inversion, with all four limbs pressing out in opposite directions. It was hard not to feel proud of her skill in these instances. Even knowing her body had already begun to fail her.

She held the last pose for a few breaths. The sensation of the world around her returned as the air rushed into her lungs. Sweat rolled down her skin, pooling at her feet. Adrenaline and endorphins kept the coming ache in her hip at bay, but she knew from experience that the reprieve would not last long. At last she palmed her hands together at her heart, closed her eyes, and floated through a curtsey. The chime sounded, signaling the completion of the dance.

The old Sanskrit invocation whispered across her lips, *"Om bolo sat guru maharaja ki, jai!"* She danced for gods for a living, but she worshipped nothing. Everything divine was in the dance itself, not the entities she moved for.

Finished, she lifted her head and left the ring.

At the edge of the room, a woman waited patiently, towel in hand. Even at average height, Isela dwarfed her visitor.

"Director Sauvageau." Isela took the offered towel, dabbing at her forehead. "To what do I owe this pleasure?"

"I have a new assignment for you," the older woman said. "Urgent and extremely sensitive. Come with me."

"Do I have time for a shower?"

Divya shook her head. "Later."

Descended from the godsdancing founder, Corinne Divya Sauvageau had been a dancer in her youth. She still moved with a lithe grace, though silver streaked the tidy chignon at the base of her skull. The students had long ago given up trying to guess her age. Isela joked that Divya was impossible to pin down because she was everywhere at once. In spite of her notoriously hectic schedule, she seemed to know everything that went on inside the walls of the Academy.

Her tailored pantsuit, suitable for a full day of meetings with clients, looked out of place in the ring she had once commanded. That didn't stop Isela from feeling joyfully humbled by the older woman's unexpected presence.

Taking the slippers Divya offered, Isela hooked them onto her bare feet before tossing a light wrap across her shoulders.

"Your third warrior transition is sloppy." Divya changed the subject to avoid further inquiry.

Isela inclined her head. It had been a long time since she feared her teacher. "Perhaps you should give me some pointers, old lady."

The tiniest collection of wrinkles creased Divya's almond skin around her mouth and eyes. Her laughter startled the custodian mopping the floor. When her gaze fell on him, he hurried back to his task.

"Come to my office," Divya said. "Before you ruin my reputation as a fire-breathing dragon."

Her eyebrow rose when Isela left an extra tip on the offering tray beside the door. "Bribery?"

Isela shouldered her bag and faced Sauvageau. "An expression of gratitude."

Divya had handpicked Isela from a school performance nineteen years earlier, overcoming resistance from the Academy officials to enroll the unknown child of American refugees. Theirs wasn't the only resistance she had to overcome. The director made her plea in person on the doorstep of the family home, promising to take personal responsibility for the gangly eleven-year-old.

The invitation was a privilege that existed on a knife's edge. To be a dancer would bring the girl uncomfortably close to the powers that had led the world to the brink of destruction. Though the godswar had ended and dancing was now rigidly sanctioned, those who danced served as a reminder of the peril and promise of human communication with the gods.

These days, the most successful dancers lived comfortable lives, performing primarily for business deals and the personal issues of the wealthy.

Isela shivered in the cool air of the hall, aware of the students moving past her. Their stares itched at her skin like the drying sweat. She resisted the urge to look down or away. She was no longer a girl, plucked from the stage of a poorly lit community center to walk in these shining halls among more well-connected, well-regarded peers. The stares no longer judged and found her wanting.

She no longer lived in constant awareness of her differences. She would never be as lean as the classical prima ballerinas. If she needed a more supportive top than the thin-strapped leotards provided for her full breasts it was no longer a source of shame. That her body veered toward curves over the long, corded muscles developed by years of training no longer brought embarrassment.

She'd conditioned her body to master the most demanding maneuvers, mastering the inversions and acrobatics that made her renowned among her peers. More than half her life had been devoted to study and performance. She made dance her purpose, stripping it down to the bones and reassembling it as her own. She was what many of them aspired to become. Or feared enough to give wide berth. She had earned her place.

"Your every move is the dance," Divya cast her stern expression about, discouraging those who contemplated approach. "Even the First Years can see it."

Humbled by praise, Isela's gaze went to the floor. "I have you to thank for that."

What would be left for her, she wondered, when she could no longer dance? The clock had begun to tick; each performance brought her closer to the end of her career. She no longer knew herself without it.

The director's phone chimed, and they paused while she checked the screen. Divya's mouth twitched again. This time Isela thought the smile held a hint of sadness.

"That was an exceptional performance," Divya said. "Your patron added a nice bonus to your check."

Isela spoke to cover her discomfort at her mentor's unusually liberal praise. "So what's the job? If you're sending me to Sur Americas again, I need to get my shots. I was sick for weeks last time."

"Closer to home."

The equivocation soured Isela's curiosity as they continued the walk in silence to the director's office.

The broad oak door opened smoothly as they approached. Divya never hesitated. Isela hung back a step, marveling as she always did at the door, which never failed to open at the right moment. On the other side, a stocky man, with the hands and ruddy neck of a laborer and fringes of white hair kept carefully combed around the base of his skull, held the handle.

Divya greeted him with a nod. "We'll take tea, Niles."

Niles oversaw the Academy's security in his capacity as Divya's personal assistant. He didn't exactly look the part, in spite of the expensive suit and impeccable manners, but Isela had seen both his handwriting and his combat skills. She had no doubts about his qualifications for the position.

Always effortlessly formal, he bowed. "Miss Vogel."

"Don't you think we're past all that?" She smiled as he closed the door behind them. "You make it sound like I'm twelve and getting busted for mouthing off in Salle's class. Again."

"Apologies, Miss Vogel," he said without breaking his stern expression. "Madame Salle sends her regards."

Divya pinched her lips closed on a smile.

Divya's personal sanctuary always surprised Isela. Something about the woman's suits, clean lines, and rigid demeanor always made Isela think she would be more at home in the ultramodern official suite used to welcome patrons. But this room of carved wood and bright fabrics, with its overstuffed chairs and cozy nooks, had her personal touch in every corner. Divya gestured toward the reading chair close to the fire as Niles followed with the tea service.

"That will be all."

Isela frowned. Divya never spoke to her staff so curtly. Niles bowed and retreated to his desk in the outer room.

Divya served the tea herself, handing over the delicate porcelain cup.

Isela resisted the urge to run her hand over her hip as endorphins and adrenaline faded, leaving a throbbing discomfort in their wake. The fewer people who knew about the damage, the better. If Divya knew, she'd force Isela to retire or cut back her schedule. Isela may have needed the money less than she had as a young dancer, but she had never needed dance more than she did now.

Her stomach grumbled audibly, and Divya offered up a tray of biscuits. At heart a performer, the director would not be rushed.

"The client is… unusual." Divya grappled with the word.

Reaching for a third biscuit, Isela paused. Divya was patient, yes, dramatic perhaps, but it wasn't her habit to hedge.

"If it's the nude thing again…" Isela withdrew her hand, rolling her eyes. "I don't care how many times they ask, I am not taking off my clothes for art, faith, or anything else."

Divya smiled with such wistful sadness it was as though she was recalling memories of an old friend, or perhaps someone she had lost.

What in Hades was going on? Isela shifted uncomfortably.

"Know that we have ways to protect you," Divya assured her. "And your family, if you decide not to take the job."

Isela focused on her breath as her heart raced against her ribs. "What kind of job is this?"

She'd heard of terrible things happening to dancers, back in the old days.

Following World War II, the discovery of godsdancing changed humanity forever. A young ballerina drew on her culture's tradition as a great synthesizer—a land where thousands of gods existed not as separate entities but facets of one—and crafted a language by combining them. She linked moves, added accents from one discipline to the base of another. She commanded the attention of the gods and learned to bend their will to human desire. She trained others, and the dance began to evolve into its current form: a combination of moves drawn from hundreds of traditions around the globe.

At first there was success: crops flourished, illnesses retreated. But pettiness and greed began to color human requests. Governments collected dancers for their arsenals, rewarding families with bribes or manipulating them with thinly veiled threats to gain their cooperation.

The result: a two-week international conflict known as the godswar left the world ravaged and on the edge of chaos. Fifty years later, it was still recovering.

The director set down her teacup, bringing Isela out of her thoughts. "You must know that I tried to decline, but the necromancer can be very… persuasive. I reminded him you must be willing for your dancing to be effective."

But Isela's brain had stopped. "*The* necromancer?"

The one thing humans learned to fear more than the power of gods was the only thing that saved them from annihilation: necromancers. Unlike the gods, the Allegiance of Necromancers announced and named itself. Within hours of declaring their world takeover, sightings of the vicious forces, capricious storms, and indiscriminate destruction vanished. Without arms, the war ended quickly.

The eight members of the allegiance carved up the globe and assigned satraps to smaller regions within. The shells of human governments remained, but it was no secret who kept them in line.

The necromancers' powers extended beyond human laws, controlling the life and death of their subjects. With their ability to suspend death, some doubted they had ever been human at all. As far as anyone could tell, they were immortal, or at least impervious to human weapons, and mortals who pissed them off had a way of turning up dead, or worse.

Unlike other major cities, Prague was not held by the satrap of a distant power. The European necromancer, Azrael, was so fond of the city he made it his base.

"He requested you specifically," Divya finished.

"He wants me to dance?" Isela asked. "For what? An earache?"

The joke, intended as a distraction from the worst-case scenario, fell flat.

"For him," Divya answered, ignoring her jibe. "He wants you to dance for him."

After the war ended, the allegiance stated the intention to maintain a new world order, namely, an enforced peace. Though they put a stop to government recruitment of dancers, necromancers permitted their continued existence by sanctioning academies for training and managing dancer solicitation. The regional satrap was responsible for approving all requests. Dancing outside the regulation led to swift and harsh punishment.

In recent times, most dances were for exclusively mortal concerns: restoring health, securing business deals, good marriages. Hiring dancers was becoming an antiquated ritual; the wealthy version of lighting incense in a temple or paying an indulgence, with somewhat better returns.

Isela put down her tea to keep from splashing it all over her shaking hands. Divya met her eyes, and Isela knew the time for jokes was finished.

Isela kept her voice steady. "He supports the Academy, and he's a good one—right?"

"He's a necromancer, Isela," Divya said evenly. "Some say he personally nailed that man's eyes to the door of his shop."

Isela's stomach lurched. It had been all over the feeds. The eyes had continually moved—pupils opening and closing—for days. A guard had been assigned to the door to ensure they weren't tampered with. What had become of the rest of the man was a mystery.

Even when the allegiance united to put the pieces of the world back together—keeping the fallout of the godswar from becoming a full-scale apocalypse—some of the individual necromancers proved to be tyrants to their own people.

"They have hired dancers for intercessions before," Isela went on, bent on talking herself out of panic. "Look at Leonora. She was able to retire after dancing for the Sur American necro. This could be my ticket."

To where, she had no idea. What was there for her outside the Academy? But her hip was failing. If the doctors were right, she should worry less about the future of her career than her ability to walk when it was over. How much longer did she have?

"Leonora danced in the ring." Divya's words came slowly.

That was it. The thing that was making the older woman nervous. No, Isela corrected, scared.

"He wants me to dance… where?"

Divya spread her hands. "At his discretion. It's an unusual request these days, but it has been done before. Once. I suppose it's a matter of security. You know how zealously they guard information about themselves."

Divya shook her head, catapulting herself from her chair with uncharacteristic violence. "You're not going to take it." She paced a small circuit near the bookcase, her hands clenched at her sides. "I didn't bring you here and train you to become fodder for a necromancer. We have a network, from the old days. It's rusty, but we protect our own. I can get you and your family out of here today."

And go where? There was no place on Earth she could go where the allegiance would not find her. What would he do to her, or her family, when he did? She thought about her parents. They were much older than when they had left the United States. And her brothers had families of their own now. What of the Academy? It wouldn't take Azrael long to figure out Divya had helped her. How many would pay the price because she ran away?

If anything, she was the expendable one. All she had was a philodendron slowly taking over her apartment. The knowledge didn't stop her throat from choking with despair. Her passion, her skill, her life—the one she had worked so hard to shape for herself—was now being offered up. And she would have to hold the platter.

If it meant protecting everyone she loved, she would do it. "I won't run."

Divya sank into her chair, and Isela saw her age in the slump of her shoulders and the deep lines carved by her frown. Isela folded herself onto the floor beside her mentor. She reached out tentatively and laid her fingertips on the older woman's hand. The skin was soft and paper-thin.

She could feel Divya's pulse racing. The faintest twinge of sweat and fear came through her usual scent of spicy peppers and warm chocolate.

"Hey, I'm the best, remember?" Isela forced cheer into her tone that sounded maniacal to her own ear. "Of course he wants me."

Divya's haunted eyes stared at her. "When you were eleven, I promised your mother that this life, the Academy, was a way of giving you security."

"And you have," Isela said firmly. "You gave me… everything. Now let me use it."

She was a performer. She made herself smile.

Divya collected herself. "He asked for you. Make it your advantage."

"Oh, I can be a diva." Isela waved her hand with a stilted laugh. "I better be getting paid for this."

Divya looked almost her old self again when the corner of her mouth twitched faintly. "My dear, the paycheck alone makes Leonora's wealth a pittance."

The godsdance was a job, a way to provide for herself and take care of her family in a troubled world. A job that would one day—sooner rather than later, in her case—end. She stared into the fire as her eyes blurred. One big job would set her family up for life.

"He would like to meet with you this afternoon," Divya said. "To discuss the choreography."

"And the petition?"

"You'll have to talk to him about that," Divya said, a hint of annoyance in her voice. "I am not permitted to know."

Closing her eyes, Isela took a breath. She held it, sipped a bit more air, and exhaled. When she opened her eyes, Divya was waiting.

"I'm going to shower and change." Isela rose from her chair. She was proud of how steady her voice sounded. Casual, even. "Then I'll just run over to the castle."

Like that was something she did every day.

"Niles will take you."

The gesture touched Isela more than she expected. "He'll never—"

"He insisted." Divya interrupted, her voice coarse with emotion. "I insist. I'm still in charge."

Isela collected her bag and rose from her chair. Niles held the door as she passed, deferring her gratitude for the tea as though it was any other day.

"We all have a job to do, Miss Vogel."

CHAPTER TWO

A monument to Art Nouveau design and Czech pride, the Municipal House had served as a center for Prague's community, culture, and gathering since the beginning of the twentieth century. Recognized as being state of the art for its day, it had seen countless concerts, balls, and been the backdrop for history-making events—none so important as the necromancer's claim to Prague as the capital of his territory.

Left in shambles after the wars, the restoration of the Municipal House was his gift to the Praha Dance Academy. Great pains had been taken to preserve the original interiors and decor. These days, only the first floor and front halls, housing a museum and a few of the old ballrooms, were open to the public. The students and faculty of the Academy occupied the rest.

Isela barely remembered life before Prague. Once she began training, the Academy became home. When she graduated and accepted the offer to become an Academy principal, the only thing she had insisted on in her contract was it be as a *resident* principal dancer.

As she crossed the threshold of the attic turned apartment in the southwest wing, her body relaxed out of habit. The spacious, breezy room with slanted ceilings and windows overlooking the city was her sanctuary. Only there did she allow herself to sag against the wall beside the door and succumb to tears.

She wiped them away quickly. Years of hard work had given her little appreciation for self-pity.

It was almost noon. Her hip had begun to ache, a dull throb that spiked as she climbed the five stairs into the main floor of the apartment. She had rushed to the ring this morning, leaving the place a mess. Training taught her the value of routine, so she threw herself into an abbreviated version of her post-dance cleaning ritual to steady her mind.

She tidied as she went, plumping the ample cushions on the couch facing the view of Old Town and folding a throw blanket into a neat square on the arm of the reading chair next to the antique bookshelf.

In the living room, she drew the drapes away from the floor-to-ceiling windows; cloud-diffused light filled the space. It had rained earlier, but the clouds were lighter now, and forecasts called for snow before the end of the week. She longed to stretch out on the long mat by the window, but moving through sun salutations would have to wait.

She ordered the dance theory books stacked haphazardly on the nightstand and scooped up scattered earrings, depositing them on a framed screen atop the dresser where she kept all her jewelry neatly hung. By the time she finished making the bed, she almost felt calm.

At the end of the long room, she paused to strip before the glass-walled shower surrounding the tiled depression in the floor. Beside it, the massive claw-foot tub hunkered closer to the window with a view of the city roofs. The apartment ended in the walled-off water closet with its own separate sink and vanity.

Isela adored how her room felt expansive without interior walls. The philodendron's tendrils crawling across the entire length of the windowed wall seemed to agree.

Under the flow of hot water, she took her time working conditioner from the roots to the tips of her sweat-snarled curls. Detangled, she gathered the mass of her hair on the top of her head, then soaped and scrubbed her face. A final rinse and she shut off the water. She wrapped her hair in an old T-shirt, squeezing the moisture carefully out to keep the curls smooth as she contemplated how to present herself for her new patron.

Most new patron meetings took place in Divya's public office at the Academy. Presentation was part of the performance: she'd dress to emphasize her dancer's body. Curvy as it was, there was no arguing she was at her physical peak. As she gained fame, there was less need to show off. Most patrons were repeats or booked her on reputation alone.

However, the thought of facing one of the most powerful necromancers in the world made her want to camouflage herself. She dressed modestly in a rose-colored wrap dress that cascaded off her hips to swirl around her calves. She wrangled her curls into twin braids, pinning them to the crown of her head. Tiny ringlets around her brow and neck sprang free defiantly. She hung teardrop-shaped silver hoops from her earlobes and kept her makeup subdued.

As an afterthought, she buckled a low-profile holster to her thigh. What good a pair of knives would do against an immortal, she had no idea, but they made her feel better. She wound a scarf around her neck and cast one final glance over her treasured space.

There was no time to waste. She had a date with death.

* * *

NILES MET her outside as she passed through the glass doors. Her eyes went to the elaborate stained-glass canopy that had always been her favorite part of the building's exterior. Greens and peaches colored the muted light refracting through the glass. Niles unfurled a crimson umbrella edged with gold in anticipation of her leaving the shelter of the building. The colors the Academy shared with its home city bloomed against the rain-sodden day, and a small gasp went up among the passersby as they recognized her.

He guided her toward the waiting Tesla sedan. His arms spread wide, providing a physical barrier between her and the curious onlookers. No one dared approach. He opened the rear door before she could reach for the handle. With her hand on the doorframe, she paused to fill her lungs with the petrichor that followed fresh rain and slid into the car.

The door shut behind her with the solid vacuum-sealed sound

of a space shuttle cockpit, tinted windows obscuring the light. She leaned back onto the eggshell leather seats—only the best for Director Sauvageau.

"All right then, Miss Vogel?" Niles glanced over his shoulder at her.

"Ready as I'll ever be."

The car pulled away from the curb in eerie silence, triggering memories of the scents and sounds of the gasoline-powered cars of her youth. Under strict regulation by the allegiance, combustion-driven engines were rare these days.

The suspension muted the jarring effect of the cobblestone streets, and for that, she was grateful. She was so busy replaying her conversation with Divya for clues to what lay in store it took her a moment to notice the speed of travel. This late in the afternoon, the traffic in the heart of Old Town should have been monstrous. They breezed through another green light.

Isela met Niles's eyes in the rearview mirror. "VIP treatment?"

"It appears so."

The car crossed the Mánes Bridge and climbed the hill toward the castle that dominated the city skyline. Never needing to stop for a light, she watched the traffic part ahead of them. Did the necromancer do it himself, she wondered, or did he have underlings to redirect traffic?

Gallows humor will get you nowhere, she thought with a smile as the car pulled off the main road and descended to the castle gates. Especially if they really could read minds.

Her phone buzzed in her purse. She checked the caller ID and grimaced at the image of the familiar smiling face, cheek to cheek with her own. "Kyle."

He'd probably come by her flat to work on her hip. She wouldn't be able to lie to him about where she was. He would hear the nerves in her voice. She sent it to voice mail. She met Niles's eyes briefly in the rearview mirror.

"He worries."

Niles nodded. "Can I give him a message for you?"

"Just that I'll be home," she said, taking a deep breath to steady herself with the promise. "Soon."

The Prague Castle was a complex of buildings framing an

increasingly narrowing street leading toward the main grounds. While an architectural student might have admired the enormous range of styles represented by the individual palaces, Isela felt like livestock being funneled down a chute.

As they reached the castle proper, the gates rolled open soundlessly. The car continued between the columns topped with statues of battling Titans. Isela was unable to shake the impression that the two muscle-bound demigods peered hungrily into the car as she passed.

Niles drove through the first courtyard and into a second, to a door lit subtly by recessed lighting. Positioned at the handle, a man in a dark suit stood, a silk tie knotted expertly at his throat.

When Niles opened her door, she swung her legs out, flowing to a standing position under the umbrella. She started forward, but his hand on her arm stopped her. She could count the times on one hand Niles had touched her, three of them being helping her up from the sparring floor after a particularly brutal takedown. This was just too much to bear for one day. She faced him, eyes shining.

"You'll pardon my forwardness, miss," he said. "You are the best godsdancer the world has ever seen. Don't let him forget it."

Isela inclined her head, blinking once, and the tears were gone.

"Wish me luck," she said with what she hoped was a confident grin.

"You don't need it, miss."

No, she thought, turning away. *I need a miracle.*

CHAPTER THREE

The man at the door appeared to be a few years Isela's junior and, up close, looked like a boy playing dress-up in his father's suit.

"Miss Vogel, welcome," he said. "This way, if you would."

As he took her coat, she snuck glances at the foyer. The entire complex had been closed to the public since Azrael named the castle as his seat. Renovations and restorations—rumored in the billions—returned it to its former glory after centuries of hard use and little maintenance.

Contrary to the dark rooms and smoky halls she expected, the façade appeared like something out of an architectural history magazine. The minimalist decor was tasteful, a refined mix of old and new, well suited to this, one of the youngest buildings in the complex. Every angle could have been the backdrop for a publicity photo.

She half expected armed guards or earpiece-wearing, dark-suited security teams to be prowling the grounds. And where was the mess of obedient zombie servants going about their master's business? She chastised herself; she had to get the word "zombie" out of her head. Using the derogatory street name for the necromancer's dead subjects would not earn her any favors.

Little more than brainless automatons, or an example of what happened when you crossed a necromancer, the undead earned the comparison. It was all much more civilized than flesh-eating and rotting corpses. When the length of the punishment had been served, they were released to die, and their bodies returned to any remaining family for burial.

The kicker was, some humans, craving the comforts of power after the godswar, offered themselves in servitude under a contract. They retained more of their personalities, serving in more senior roles.

As far as she could tell, she was alone with her guide. Up close, there was something not quite right about him. He was too pale, his eyes too bright. And he wasn't breathing. She had never seen a Contract before. This one could have been a young analyst headed to work. He was clearly not a brainless servant.

"It's an honor, Miss Vogel," he said. "I'd never thought I'd meet a godsdancer, especially one of your stature."

Isela knew she was staring but couldn't think of anything to say, except, "Thank you."

He wasn't wearing an earpiece, but with the distant facial expression and head tilt, it seemed as if he were listening to someone. When his attention returned, his expression was fixed. She thought she saw the hurt in his eyes like someone, or something, unseen, had chastised him.

"I apologize for delaying you. Right this way."

He moved quickly down the long hall, and Isela was glad she had chosen kitten heels instead of the sexier ones she might have picked for an ordinary client. With any other client, she might not have expected to have to run—or fight—for her life at some point. They clicked across the stone floor with the proper sound of authority though, and she liked that. It was a good reminder, as Niles had said, she wasn't some human lackey, called to heel at the feet of the necromancer. She was the *best* damn godsdancing human lackey in the world.

The long hall led into an even larger space that could have been a museum gallery. It was, in a manner of speaking.

Isela's chest constricted as they walked the path laid out between sculptures. She eyed the paintings lining the walls. Each one belonged in a museum. There were no guardrails, plastic boxes, or video cameras. Maybe it all was safer here than it would ever be in the halls of the Louvre or the Met. Part of her mourned as she passed what she was sure was a *Rodin*. Ordinary people would never again stand in the same room as these treasures. Or, like her, they would be too worried about what lay beyond to give them the proper attention.

The manservant stopped at the end of the hall beside a pair of enormous wooden doors, which were beginning to open. Isela tried to slow her heartbeat with her breath but couldn't stop it from racing on.

Here she was. At the door of the home of the most feared man in Europe, if he could be considered a man at all.

The undead gestured with an open palm to proceed. Isela started forward and glanced back to find her guide standing still. Apparently, this was where his journey ended. When she looked into the third courtyard beyond, one of the most handsome men she'd ever laid eyes on strode toward her, hands clasped behind his back.

"Miss Vogel." He stopped with military precision and folded at the waist in a courtly gesture. "I am Gregor, head of security."

She recognized the German accent, but only because after almost twenty years of practice, her father had never quite been able to shake the slight hint of his origin. This man's accent was just as faint.

The smirk on his face was anything but courtly. It was knowing and sensual, with lips no man should have a right to and eyes an electric shade of blue. Pale skin swept over refined cheekbones into cropped black hair.

His smirk tilted the slightest bit under her scrutiny. She sealed her mouth shut. At the Academy, she trained among some of the most attractive human specimens in the world. Isela was not about to be cowed by this one's looks.

"I understand this is a matter of some urgency," she spoke in German, keeping her tone brisk and formal.

Her mother often joked it was a good thing her father also spoke Italian, for all the romance of his native tongue.

"At your pleasure, Fräulein," he responded in kind. Gregor turned. "You will follow me."

Her mother was wrong; it was possible for German to sound sexy as hell.

Without eye contact, Isela found it was much easier to breathe. And concentrate. He wasn't a zom— an undead, but he wasn't quite human either. For one thing, he was breathing. But his unironic use of the German title given to young women made him seem generations older than his appearance.

Necromancers and their courts were more secretive than any government agency had ever been. What little anyone knew was crafted by the PR teams a few bothered to employ. Who knew what other creatures they were capable of creating or manipulating.

They moved through the largest of the three courtyards, awash in shadows cast by the enclosed cathedral and the falling darkness. The imposing exterior of St. Vitus loomed over them in all of its neo-Gothic glory.

Isela didn't realize she had slowed down until her guide paused a few steps ahead. He angled his head toward her.

"The cathedral has been closed for some time," he stated. "Restoration."

"I've just… never seen it so close," she uttered finally, unable to hide her awe.

She didn't assume a necromancer had much interest in a church even if it was the grandest in all of Prague. However, she'd heard stories and seen old pictures of the stained-glass windows by Mucha and Svabinsky. She longed to see the light shining through them.

Isela's guide paused, sparing the cathedral a glance, before giving a disinterested shrug. He picked up the pace. "If you please."

She hurried after him.

"St. George's Basilica, to your left," her guide offered after a moment. "Also a former convent."

She made a thoughtful sound, but her eyes were on the statue of the saint impaling the dragon coiled below his mount's hooves. "Has it all been restored?"

"Of course," her guide said without pause.

Isela bit her lip on an apology, bristling at the arrogance in his tone. It shocked her out of her reverie. Whatever he was, he didn't think much of her; that was abundantly clear.

They entered a set of buildings she thought might be the Old

Royal Palace. Nothing to do but get it done. She sighed as they paused before what she hoped was the final set of doors. A pair of hulking men guarded this one. Their suits did nothing to disguise the fact that they were clearly there for brute force. Identical, grimly fixed faces stared ahead as they waited.

At some unheard signal, the guard on the left nodded and spun to open the door.

"You will address them as 'sir' or 'madam' at all times," her cold-eyed escort informed her, no longer quite so aloof. "Remember that you go before your betters, for your own sake."

Isela swallowed her retort at the expression on his face. This was not the time to be cheeky.

Wait a minute, she thought. *Them?*

Her stomach missed its landing and crashed into her racing heart. Her escort looked back at her curiously.

She lifted her chin and met his eyes. "I am ready."

Who walks into a wolf's den and comes out alive? Her father's old joke came unbidden as she stepped forward. *A wolf.*

* * *

IN THE ROOM's perfect silence, burning wood crackled in the enormous fireplace like thunder, but Isela sensed she had walked in on an argument. Cloaked in darkness, punctuated with lamplight and the glow of flame, the cavernous space was thick with tension. Her skin hummed with it, nerves sending a message to her hindbrain that only had one interpretation: run.

Instead, Isela made herself stand very still and measured her breathing. As her eyes adjusted to the dim light, she realized she was flanked. Assembled in a single room were the eight most powerful necromancers in the world. She sealed her lips shut and forced a slow, quiet exhale out her nostrils.

To her left, a dark-skinned woman sat queenlike at the head of a table, wearing elegant batik robes of the western African tribes of former Senegal and Nigeria. Her companions were a fine-boned Japanese man in an exquisitely tailored suit, and a slight woman tattooed on every visible inch of flesh. A curl of smoke rose from a brown-wrapped cigarette between her knobby fingers. Curiously, it had no scent.

She exhaled as she spoke, smoke curling around the hint of aboriginal lilt in her voice. "Small, but the record cannot be a lie."

Across the room, a sloe-eyed woman with the poise of a pharaoh and the beauty of a runway model shifted her attention to Isela. Deep, kohl-lined eyes, so dark they appeared pupil-less, sought to peel Isela's skin away to stare into her skull.

"You've frightened her," she purred, smiling. "Come, Paolo, get on with it."

"*Bem-vindo*, pretty dancer. We have a job for you."

Isela jumped at the voice directly behind her. She reeled back from the wide caramel face framed by curly, gold-streaked hair. *How had he gotten so close?* She tripped, stumbling over her heel, and felt her balance give.

Shit, she was going to go down, in front of a room full of necromancers. A part of her brain screamed relief; let them pick another dancer! But pride shouted louder as she recovered in an effective, if less than elegant, plié.

Strong, feverishly warm hands caught her elbow, tipped her upright. Isela turned and came face-to-face with her very own necromancer, Azrael. She'd seen him once but at a great distance and obscured by a crowd. He had been darkness and movement then, a smudge in the scene, like a thumbprint on a photograph.

His eyes are silver, Isela's startled brain coughed up as she stared into his face with the helpless rapture of a rodent before a cobra strike. It was replaced quickly with *gorgeous*, which came from another part of her anatomy entirely. She flushed.

He had a face like one of the sculptures in the hall: strong forehead, with a heavy brow and a broad, formidable jaw. A bow-shaped mouth plumped deliciously in all the right places, though the lips were firmly fixed. Skin dusted with gold hinted that he had not been born in the city he now claimed as his home. His eyes, lifted at the corners and framed with full lashes, bore into her as though her every thought was ink on a page for his exploration.

And judging by the sharp tilt of his eyebrow, he found them utterly inane.

That shocked her into motion. Released, Isela put her back to the fireplace. That put all the necromancers between her and the door, but she had no hope of escape anyway. From the moment she entered the room, she'd been at their mercy.

Each of them captivated her attention. Isela longed to study each but was terrified to be caught staring. Worst was Azrael, who made breathing feel like effort.

You have value to them; show them why they asked for you.

She swept her leg behind her in an elegant curtsey. "Isela Vogel, Principal Godsdancer, Praha Academy. How may I serve you?"

Isela aimed her words at the Sur American necromancer, who seemed the least terrifying of this group. He reminded her of her youngest brother: a handsome, cocky male with an easy smile.

"At least she knows her place. Unlike most of them." Isela jerked in surprise at the Russian-accented voice of a stunning redhead draped over a curule chair beside the fireplace.

The redhead picked at her nails with a jewel-hilted dagger. At Isela's sustained gaze, she showed teeth that had been filed to points. "You'll do what we tell you and be grateful you are useful."

The elegant man at the table shook his head, distaste on his face. "Gods, Vanka. Control yourself."

The redhead's snarl melted the bones in Isela's body, and she fought the urge to run.

Stay put, she told herself. *No sudden moves.*

"You are American." Paolo spoke again when the tension had ebbed.

"I was born there," Isela said evenly. "After the godsquake, we moved to California. The tech industry was saturated, so when Czech opened citizenship to people with development skills, we came."

"You cost me good talent when you opened your borders, Azrael." A male in a white T-shirt and a motorcycle jacket uncrossed his jean-clad legs and rose from his chair.

His heavy leather boots moved soundlessly across the floor as he approached. His was a rough sort of handsome, with a face from a sepia-toned daguerreotype and the sort of broken-hip swagger that reminded her of an old Western movie. Isela steeled herself not to flinch at the proximity as he approached, but he walked past to the fire with only a fleeting glance.

What was left of North America belonged to him. Rumor had it he was busy trying to recover the East Coast from its status as a nuclear wasteland and stayed out of most allegiance business.

"They needed jobs," the European necromancer shrugged. "I needed expertise. Opportunity."

When Azrael folded his arms, his chest and biceps pulled against the black dress shirt tucked into slim-cut trousers. Isela caught herself staring and reined her gaze back to the crest over the door. With mouths open and wings spread, the eagles and lions that made up the four quadrants of the Czech coat of arms looked as though they wanted escape this room as desperately as she did.

"You speak fluent German." Paolo ignored them, making a slow circle of her.

Isela kept her attention on the crest, her words careful. "My father was born in Berlin. My mother learned when my brothers were kids. We spoke it at home."

"Not an only child?" Paolo said.

"Third of four," Isela said, fighting the clutching feeling in her chest at the mention of her family. "I don't see them much. I live and work at the Academy."

She glanced at Azrael, convinced her first impression of his eyes had been wrong. He had moved casually to the side of the fireplace opposite the redhead, Vanka. He occupied space like a shadow. Absolute stillness coupled with a roving attention made him fill the room. His eyes were not a bright gray but actual silver; the color a cat's eyes shone when light reflected on them in the dark. None of the others had that gleam. It was an inhuman gaze. Any expectation she might have had that he would protect her from the others evaporated. She stared back at the crest, feeling his silver eyes fix on her.

Another voice spoke up from the table. "You were the youngest student in the history of the Praha Academy."

Isela redirected her attention, responding to the elegant woman in batik directly. "Director Sauvageau recruited me when I was eleven."

"A child of refugees," the suited man mused. "The Praha Academy is one of the most respected in the world. Three times the number of auditions as there are openings. What did she see in you?"

Isela knew what she was. Still, it grated her to hear her background reduced to points on a dossier.

She fought to keep her voice even. "I wish I could say. I started dancing late because of our circumstances and had inconsistent formal training, at best, until the Academy. I was offered a partial scholarship. My parents scraped up the rest so that I could attend as a resident student and complete my schooling and dance training simultaneously. I planned to be a ballet dancer, maybe teach."

"Like your mother," he said lightly. "Yoga, is it? Quaint."

"Godsdancing called me," Isela said sharply to draw the conversation back to herself. "I was given an opportunity. I earned my place."

The fire crackled.

"This one has teeth," the tattooed woman chuckled, a low, threatening sound.

"You remember the war?" Paolo asked, cocking his head with that same inviting smile.

Isela shook her head. Back straight, head up, shoulders down, she ran through her checklist, ignoring the ache in her hip. They hadn't so much as offered her a chair, but she wasn't about to ask.

"We heard stories," she said carefully. "My parents tried to keep our lives as normal as possible."

"And the gods?" the suited man asked.

Oh, the beings who almost destroyed the entire world? Were they just crazy and oblivious not to know what they were doing? Or were they just selfish enough not to care?

No one knew the exact relationship between gods and necromancers. If necromancers were their children, that would make a strong argument for insanity.

"I'm not sure what you're asking." Isela forced her voice to be indifferent.

"Are you a believer?" The tattooed woman had a singsong way of speaking. Only it sounded less comforting and more like the lure of a siren.

"Do I believe in the gods?"

Stay on message, Vogel. Don't get lost in the details.

"I believe humans didn't know what else to call them," Isela began. "I believe, for whatever reason, they're drawn to creativity—

dancing—and that our intention was good when we first tried to communicate with them. I believe we made a mistake thinking they would behave like the gods we believed in. That kind of power is dangerous, to be respected and not taken, or used, frivolously."

"And yet, you danced for a real estate deal this morning." The suited man laughed.

Isela's face burned, but she did not back down.

"I dance because of how it feels to disappear in movement," she said pointedly. "To lose the sense of myself and become something larger. *You* approve the requests."

And if you knew what the gods could do, why didn't you stop them before they wrecked the world? She bit her tongue to avoid snapping. Radical groups speculated the war had all been a front to move the necromancers into power.

The fire popped in the weighted silence. Isela was sure they were talking around her, telepathically.

Clearing her throat, she composed herself. "May I ask what this has to do with the job?"

"What do you know of Luther Voss?" the suited man asked.

"Who?"

"Indeed," he said with a final sigh that let her know this had all been a game to him. "Paolo, you've read the dossier. She comes highly recommended. Top of her class at the Academy. Ten years as a professional. Her success rate is quite remarkable, considering the decline."

Isela's interest piqued. Outcome data was kept closely guarded. But this was evidence of something she had long suspected: the gods' interest in humanity was waning.

"You'll forgive our curiosity." Paolo took over the conversation again, but his smooth smile and friendly demeanor no longer relaxed her. "But you are something of a, how do they say in America, Raymond, an underdog?" He did nothing to hide the taunt in his words.

"We are simply dying to know what your secret is," the sloe-eyed beauty in the window spoke up. Her voice was like velvet, beguiling, but Isela felt as if a heavy weight was pressing against her forehead.

"My… secret?"

"To your success," she continued, rising from her seat.

There were monuments to this woman all over the Middle East. Her people loved and worshipped her as the incarnation of a god. Isela felt the compulsion toward awe, but beneath it was a terror that made the hairs rise on the back of her neck.

"I don't know..." Isela faltered. Her head pounded.

"What is so special about you?" The woman smiled. "What stories do you whisper when you dance for them?"

"I have no secrets." Isela felt ill. She wavered on her feet, feeling the words spill out of her. "There are one hundred and eight postures and maneuvers. I simply arrange them according to the request."

"Kadijah." Azrael's voice cut through the haze shrouding her brain like a lick of flame. The pressure eased, leaving only the ache of an old burn. "You have forgotten the tenants of our allegiance."

Isela gasped, looking between them. The woman was already sauntering away, resuming her throne beside the window. But the expression of pure loathing she cast Azrael would have flayed the skin from the bones of a mortal.

"We all have secrets, my dear," she said, eyes switching to Isela with a look that no doubt made her subjects fall down in worship. "You may keep yours, for now."

Isela felt sick. And angry. Angry she had been brought here, made to stand before them and defend herself as they picked at her past and used their powers to prod her like a lab rat.

"We have a certain problem that requires your services," Paolo went on.

"I've danced to resolve many issues, sir." She forced the words between gritted teeth. "It would help to know what the issue is, for my choreography."

"You'll know when we tell you, insolent bitch." Vanka's snarl was Isela's only warning. The jeweled blade came out of nowhere, arrowing toward her. Isela spun, crouching to avoid it. Her hand slipped under the pooling material of her skirt and freed the knife on her thigh.

Rage burned clean through fear and prudence. She threw before thinking, aiming for the redhead's heart. Her own blade went through the redheaded necromancer, embedding itself in the chair's back. The image of the necromancer wavered as it passed through and reformed, unharmed. Only now, the Vanka's face held naked outrage.

Isela felt the breath leave her lungs in the face of that anger. It was over. She had revealed herself, and she would die now. Or be turned into a zombie and made to pay for her indiscretion over and over again.

Vanka rose, speaking words in a language Isela had never heard. Isela was frozen in her crouch.

Azrael paced into Vanka's path, one hand lifted.

"You dare cast in my territory," he snarled. "You overreach your bounds."

From her crouch, Isela felt the sudden wave of heat roll off his back. His legs braced against an unseen force.

Between his calves, Isela watched the redhead fold back into her chair, her face growing pale as her mouth clamped shut.

"You started it," the tattooed woman sang from across the room. "He finished it."

It was a childish retort, laced with so much power and animosity Isela cringed.

Then Azrael inclined his head to look at Isela out of the corner of one eye. He never turned his back on the redhead.

"Forgive me," Isela murmured, rising from a crouch with head bowed. "It was an instinctive response."

"Are all dancers so… instinctive?" the suited man asked, his light tone belying his interest.

"No," she said, adding, "sir."

"Punishment, Azrael," Vanka shrieked.

"Can we get on with it?" The sloe-eyed necromancer sighed. "I tire of this harpy's screeching."

How this group had managed to piece the world back together amazed Isela. Half of them seemed certifiable, and they certainly didn't like one another.

"Death closed the eyes of its lords," the tattooed woman sang.

"Five necromancers have been murdered," the batik-draped woman elaborated with a little exhale of annoyance.

"She must know something." The North American necromancer aimed his words at Vanka. The redhead stared at Isela as though she wanted to make a rug of her skin. "The last one was in the news."

Isela remembered the report, a prominent necromancer found dead in Tokyo. As far as anyone knew, only necromancers could kill one another. Isela had brushed it aside as none of her concern. But now it appeared it was her business.

"None of the others have been leaked?" Azrael asked.

"No," the Japanese necromancer said. "And the reporter who broke the embargo has been… reprimanded."

"Good," Paolo said as something far older and more deadly than his dashing young male appearance moved behind his eyes. "Even the lesser of us must be protected from human speculation."

Isela tried not to trip over the tumble of thoughts that came next. Five murders had left the most powerful necromancers in the world so troubled they were driven to bring in a human gods-dancer. For what? She still didn't understand what they hoped to get out of her.

"You will work with Azrael," Paolo said, turning his attention back to her. "He will be your exclusive client until this issue is resolved. It has been arranged with your agent. You will be compensated handsomely."

"Why?" Isela immediately wished she had kept her mouth shut as all eyes went to her.

Vanka muttered something uncharitable about the lack of necessity for a tongue as a dancer. Clearly, this group wasn't used to having to explain themselves to anyone. Or being asked questions.

"Why do you need me?" Isela finished against her better judgment.

"Azrael will explain what you need to know," Paolo said finally.

She had a feeling the conversation continued without her. She had been judged and found sufficient for their needs.

She looked to the door, hoping that her escort would reappear. Apparently, she wasn't the only one.

"How is that Hessian of yours, Azrael?" Vanka said from the chair, her voice taking on a covetous tone.

"Gregor sends his regards," Azrael said without a hint of emotion, but Isela felt the sudden waft of heat. It was a warning.

"You are too protective of him," Vanka mused.

Azrael said, “He belongs to me, and you will remember that.”

“So possessive with your toys.”

“It would serve you well not to forget it.”

And that was it. Meeting adjourned. Vanka vanished from the chair like heat waves fading off pavement, leaving only Isela’s blade buried in the back. The others went in their own fashion, disappearing, dissolving, or simply winking out, as though they had never been there at all.

Except one. Azrael.

CHAPTER FOUR

Being alone with Azrael made Isela feel like she was in more danger than ever. There was nothing to distract him now. Of course, they had been alone all along.

"They weren't really here, were they?" she asked as he plucked her blade from the chair back.

"We rarely meet in person, for obvious reasons," he murmured without shifting his gaze from the blade. "Hence the lighting. Our presence can have peculiar effects on technology."

He waved a hand, and lights came on, making her blink. She heard the faint hum of electricity, noticeable only because of its previous absence. Even fully illuminated, the enormous room maintained a dim, firelit quality.

"Weighted nicely," Azrael said. "This is a good blade. Are all dancers so well armed?"

Her throat went dry as he crossed the room to stand in front of her, filling her vision. She stared at his collarbone. Eventually Isela forced her eyes upward, the smug arrogance on his face making her skin prickle with irritation.

"Lie to me at your peril," Azrael said, one eyebrow rising. "Vanka expects you to be punished."

Indignation raced up her spine at the sensation of being a ball of yarn for a very large, very bored, cat.

"Some are even better armed." Isela squared her shoulders.

That's it, Vogel, she told herself, *when—if—we make it home, I am putting you on suicide watch for continuing to mouth off to a necromancer.*

Azrael made a sound that might have been a laugh. The corner of his mouth twisted upward, again making her feel as though he knew her every thought. Only this time he found her amusing. "For all the good it did you."

Without looking, Azrael held out the blade, handle first. For a moment she wondered what he would do if she sliced down and opened up a couple of his fingers with it. That would show the arrogant bastard.

Azrael's hand moved faster than her eye, grabbing Isela's wrist as she took the blade. He pinned her arm, twisting it behind her back and bringing her closer. She found herself encircled by an amazing amount of heat coming off his body. Her free hand splayed defensively against his pectorals.

The intoxicating scent of agarwood and toasted cinnamon coated in molasses bewitched her nose. He didn't even smell like a normal man. He lowered his head, inhaling deeply. Her nostrils flared as, for a moment, those shining silver eyes met hers. The heat in them put the fire to shame. This close, his irises were not a uniform molten shade but variegated by tiny ridges of texture, like any other human eye.

Beautiful. Isela couldn't stop the thought.

Azrael's lowered eyelids hooded his silver irises, the long fringes of lash as dark and silky as fur. His smile hovered inches from her mouth.

"Careful, dancer." His breath brushed her lips. "Accidents happen."

Get a grip, Vogel. The man makes puppets out of corpses.

Between gritted teeth, she muttered, "Somehow, I doubt that."

Another noise—humor? Surprise? And he released her. Isela skittered out of reach and sheathed her blade before she did something else stupid. Having a knife in her hand gave her a false sense of security.

"The allegiance believes your dancing may provide the increase of power I need to successfully summon one of the victims," Azrael said idly. "Something none of us have been able to do so far."

That was news to her. Dancing for gods worked one way; she petitioned and they answered, or not. It wasn't like plugging a bulb into a socket. She was about to tell him so, when he spoke again.

"You've danced for athletes before, correct?"

"Yes, I—"

"The choreography should be similar, I imagine," he went on, oblivious to her objections. "I need increased strength. Stamina. I need more time in between than I can get on my own."

Isela chafed. *In between* what? "But I—"

"The latest victim will arrive in a matter of days." Azrael interrupted with quiet finality. "Until then, it would be good for you to prepare."

"How do you—"

"I'll call you when your services are required." The way he said it was a mockery of her earlier deference.

Isela paused, surprised. After everything she'd seen, he would just let her leave?

"You'll not speak of it to anyone," he said.

"How do you—"

"Trust me," he said, showing rows of beautiful white teeth.

* * *

OUTSIDE, Isela fought the urge to collapse against the nearest wall and let her knees go to jelly. Her heart threatened to explode with each new beat. Cold night air flooded her lungs, and she drank it greedily. Her senses were sharp, her entire body primed to run. And then she felt a hand on her arm.

Isela grabbed the assailant's wrist, twisting and spinning before the little cry of surprise could leave her own mouth. It was a boy in a fine suit who landed on his back on the paving stones, her short blade drawn and at his throat.

Her zombie guide was a new shade of pale. Shock opened his mouth to a wide *O* as his eyes strained to see the blade at his throat. She hadn't known the undead could be afraid of a weapon. That was useful information.

"Sorry, Miss Vogel," he breathed, words coming in a high-pitched stammer. "I just thought—you looked—I wanted to help! Please!"

Isela made herself let him go, stand up, and sheathe her blade. The courtyard might be under surveillance. She didn't know how Azrael would feel about her threatening his pets. More so, she didn't want to reveal her training any more than she already had.

"Forgive me," she said.

Isela could not make herself offer a hand, but she backed well away as he leaped up, patting down his suit and ordering his tie.

"I've called your driver," he said, all business, though the color was still out of his cheeks and he couldn't meet her eyes.

"Yes, thank you."

It was all she could do to follow him through the rest of the castle to the first courtyard. She took her own coat, and he backed away sheepishly. Niles held the door to the car. If he noted the trembling in her limbs or breath, he was sage enough to keep his own countenance. But she might have sworn she heard relief when he uttered her name in greeting. "Miss Vogel."

"Can't you just call me Isela, for once in my life?" she muttered as she climbed in the back.

The door shut behind her without comment.

Isela wiped her palms on her dress and tried to relax against the seat. Her whole system was disturbed, as though someone had run a current through her just to see what might happen. She tried to forget the flash of cat-eye silver on her own.

She fidgeted with the seat belt, unable to sit still.

"Let me out." Isela hadn't realized she'd spoken aloud until she saw Niles's eyes on hers in the rearview mirror. "Please. I need to walk."

Without question, he pulled the car over and put on the hazards. She had the door open before he could open his own, and she flung herself out before leaning back in.

"I just need to stretch my legs." Isela forced a smile.

"Shall I wait for you here?"

"I'll walk home. Let Director Sauvageau know that everything went better than expected." *I'm still alive.* "I'll brief her in the morning."

"Understood."

Though the rain had stopped, she shivered a little in the damp breeze.

"There's a hat and gloves in the trunk," Niles said. "An umbrella also."

Gratefully, Isela closed her door as the trunk popped open. She knew it must have taken all his willpower not to get out and help her.

The hat and gloves must have been Divya's. They smelled of her; a subtle mixture of spicy peppers and bittersweet chocolate. The gloves were too small, but the knitted cap was a welcome addition. She took the umbrella, closed the trunk, and started walking. The Tesla slid past her, and she allowed herself to be swept up in the crowds thronging the tiny streets in the growing darkness.

Prague had always drawn tourists, and the necromancer's presence in the city only swelled the numbers year round. With a few weeks until Christmas, the streets were thronged and festive. Isela didn't pretend to understand humanity's ability to live in apparent contradiction: terrified of necromancers but fascinated and drawn to their power. Brought to the brink of annihilation by gods and still celebrating old religious holidays faithfully. A tour group pushed through the crowd, hurrying to follow the guide, wearing a "Streets of the Necromancer—Tours Daily" smock over her winter coat.

Isela shook her head, moving through a rainbow of faces, all bundled up against the cold.

The area of Mala Strana, or Lesser Town, had always been affluent due to its proximity to the castle. Now, it was also one of the most touristy. The narrow streets were lined with shops below exclusive boutique hotels and flats. Out of the shops drifted the scent of mulled wine and coffee, the hot pastry rolls coated in sugar, and the ubiquitous crêpes folded around everything from cheese to Nutella. Restaurants advertised daily menus and authentic cuisine, mostly goulash, on signs outside the door. Warmly dressed hosts and hostesses made a personal appeal to the passersby.

Isela kept her chin tucked, blending into the crowd. In spite of her renown as a godsdancer, she found she still enjoyed a blissful level of anonymity in public. No one expected her to be walking around alone in the streets.

In the press of people moving toward the Charles Bridge, she felt herself slowly coming down from whatever panic response the necromancers had incited. When she found herself disgruntled by an oblivious couple that cut her off on their way to dinner, she knew she was firmly grounded in humanity again.

Isela's thoughts drifted back to Azrael.

That she could have thought for a moment she was attracted to him was a sure sign of emotional distress. All eight of the allegiance were visually arresting—even if their looks didn't conform to human standards of attractiveness. She thought of the plump, batik-clad woman, who looked like she could be someone's kindly grandmother, until you met her bronze eyes, full of power. *Was it the power that made them so compelling? Or had they used it to somehow transform themselves?*

And Azrael was the most striking of all. If not for his eyes, she would have thought him a few years her senior. They were ageless and inhuman. As for the rest of him—

Handsome was so mild it was almost insulting. Other words—*powerful, dangerous, sexy*—made her question her sanity and her libido.

Isela stopped, leaning her weight against the wall of a building and letting the cold of the bare stone temper the heat rising in her core. She didn't feel distressed. She felt magnetized.

Relationships had always been something of a conundrum. The work to maintain one took valuable effort from dance, but Isela had needs, so she'd tried once or twice. In the end, she'd happily given up the effort. After all, she had friends for companionship, and everything else could be taken care of with a small device she kept in her nightstand table, which was a lot less complicated than an actual partner.

Until it couldn't be, Isela admitted. It had been an appallingly long time since she'd been with anyone.

She was attracted to him. So what? What breathing woman with an active heartbeat wouldn't be? There was masculine, and then there was male. The former could be acquired, molded, cultivated. The latter was pure, essential being. Azrael had that in spades.

The cold made her shiver, and she pushed herself off the wall, tucking her hands into the pockets of her coat. She focused on what she now knew about necromancers. They had an intricate code of rules, but what held them to the code was a mystery. Beyond controlling death, they could appear by projection and disappear at will. And they weren't all knowing—even if they did have some sort of extrasensory communication abilities. They could be taken by surprise—murdered, it appeared. They were vulnerable to something other than each other. And most disturbingly, there was something in the world capable of putting the eight most powerful necromancers in the world on alert.

Now she was caught up in it. She thought of Azrael's response to her surprise that she would be allowed to leave after all that she'd witnessed.

They knew everything about her and everyone she cared about. There was no need to say more to imply the threat.

Isela paused to catch her breath, stepping out of the flow of tourists. It would do no good to spend too much time dwelling on things she could not control. She had a job to do. The sooner it was done, the sooner she would be free.

The hair prickled on the back of her neck and with it came the sensation that she was being watched. She stepped into a line for a hot-wine seller and scanned the crowd. Her gaze paused at a figure motionless in the crowd on the other side of the street.

Gregor wasn't even trying to blend in. In a black wool coat and a brilliant, crimson silk scarf around his throat, he attracted glances left and right as the wave of people simply parted around him. Not that he paid them any mind. His eyes were only for her. His full mouth rounded up at the corners in a way that would have brought blood to her cheeks if they were not already flushed with cold.

Instead, Isela steeled her gaze and tipped her chin. Gregor inclined his head and winked at her. A nudge from behind drew her attention. The vendor waited, an impatient line stamping behind her.

Isela ordered her wine, fumbled for her change, and conducted the exchange in practiced if not fluent Czech. She scooped up the little Styrofoam cup and hurried away.

So she had a tail. And not just any tail. Azrael's head of security.

The same one that homicidal maniac Vanka wanted. *To fight or fuck?* Isela wondered.

She sipped her wine, letting the heat warm her belly as the sugar and the alcohol went to her head. A twisted smile wrinkled her mouth. Might as well keep him busy.

Isela hadn't bothered to do her Christmas shopping. She dipped into the next shop, pushed back her hood, and smiled beguilingly at the shopkeeper.

"*Paní* Vogel," the woman said with a little gasp as other customers glanced up. "It's our pleasure."

Twenty minutes later, Isela emerged with a bag draped over her arm. She made her way through the shops before the Charles Bridge, buying at least a little trinket from each and attracting a small crowd of followers.

On her second cup of hot wine, she reached the Charles Bridge with an entourage and second thoughts about the intelligence calling this much attention to herself. A crowd this size could get dangerous, quickly. The effort it took to avoid limping turned the distant throb in her hip into a steady ache. She hurried on, packages dangling from either elbow. As she stepped into a hole made by a missing cobblestone, her hip buckled.

Damn it, not again, she thought.

A strong arm caught her around the waist, another hand finding the small of her back for support.

Isela glanced up into chill blue eyes. His smile cut like ice, but that didn't make him any less gorgeous.

"*Fräulein* Vogel," Gregor chided cheerfully. "You must be careful. It is too easy to take a wrong step in these old streets."

The crowd had drawn away, and when she glanced past him, she could see the rest of Gregor's men had formed a loose circle around them. Not all men, she noted. A woman almost Gregor's height dipped her chin once, giving an all clear. She was sleek and fierce in a leather jacket lined with bright fur that stood out against the dark skin of her square jaw.

Isela clamped her mouth shut and tried not to stare.

Exposed now, there was no mistaking who they belonged to. The crowd began to disperse; her popularity could not diffuse their fear of anything close to the necromancer.

"Shall we?" Gregor withdrew to take her elbow, keeping his other at the small of her back.

Isela shifted the bags on the crook of her arm. The woman canted her head, and a six-and-a-half-foot tall Nordic blond with impressive facial hair stepped forward, taking the load from her. She flushed with embarrassment.

The dense crowds on the bridge parted as they crossed, the pressure of so many eyes on her like a physical weight. Three quarters of the way across, she stopped. Curious, Gregor raised an elegant eyebrow at her.

"Just a moment." Isela sighed, ignoring the shift in his expression to amused disbelief as he realized where she was headed.

Usually she made sure only to cross the bridge in odd hours so she had the most likely chance of slipping in to touch the gold plaque without having to wait. Her father had instilled the tradition when they first arrived in Prague, and it stuck with her, no matter how illogical it was in this age of necromancers and gods.

It was rare for the statue of St. John of Nepomunk to not be thronged with people. Tonight was no different, but as she slipped through her escort, the crowd peeled back. Isela found herself face-to-face with the statue and the little plaque, bronze polished with the touch of so many hands.

Tradition dictated touching the plaque of St. John would grant luck and a certain return to Prague. She dusted her fingers lightly over the plaque, then walked on a few meters to the bronze cross embedded in the stone. She was dimly aware of the flashes going off from a hundred little devices as she closed her eyes, touched the cross, and made a wish. When she rejoined Gregor, there was something else in his smile now, and the ice seemed to melt a little from his eyes.

"Well, that's a shot for the rags, if I've ever seen one," he said in a droll tone that managed to capture amusement and annoyance in the same breath. "Godsdancer wishes for reprieve."

"You don't know what I wished for," Isela snapped as they moved on.

"I suppose I'll have to wait a year and a day to see if it comes true," he said lightly, unable to be baited.

Isela huffed as the rain began again. Gregor slipped the umbrella from her grasp and opened it in a single deft move.

"I hope you'll have something far more interesting capturing your attention by then," she said and meant it.

"You don't give yourself enough credit." His icy blue eyes glinted at her. "I find you fascinating."

* * *

On the other side of the bridge, the familiar cadet blue Tesla sedan was waiting at the curb. Niles opened the door as she approached, taking the umbrella from Gregor when offered. She bridled at being loaded in the car like one of her packages; however, nobody seemed to be paying attention to her anymore. The door shut, and she saw, but could not hear, the exchange between Niles and Gregor.

As they pulled away from the curb, Isela exhaled and sank into the seat, all her restless energy spent and a slight wine-induced headache buzzing behind her ears.

"How did you know?" she asked.

"Divya received a call."

Isela rested her forehead in her hands, wondering what other stupidity she might be capable of committing in the next few hours.

"I'm sorry, Niles," she said, though she didn't know if she was sorry for dragging him back out to rescue her or for putting everyone she loved at risk just to irritate Azrael's head of security.

Silence answered her from the front seat. They entered the subterranean parking garage across from the academy.

"I'm glad you were able to get your Christmas shopping done at least," Niles said mildly as he helped her load packages into the elevator.

Isela glanced at him to see an almost smile on his weathered face.

"Want to know what I got you?" she asked mischievously.

"I wouldn't dare presume."

CHAPTER FIVE

Isela closed her apartment door behind Niles, resting her forehead against the solid wood.

"Next time you intend to spend all day in a black hole, do you think you could warn me first, Vogel?"

Isela jumped with a little scream at the sound of the voice overhead. She jammed her palm to her chest to reinforce her ribcage against her hammering heart and glared up at the six-foot-tall danseur staring down at her.

"Kyle, you scared the shit out of me," she muttered, climbing the stairs as her heart rate returned to normal.

"My, we're high-strung," he said, drifting into the kitchen behind her.

"It's been a long day."

"No shit. It's almost ten."

Isela glanced at the clock, amazed. No wonder she was exhausted. She brushed past him without meeting his eyes, flipped the switch of the kettle, and the water begin to boil almost immediately. His key, on the chain she'd given him in the shape of a pair of red wayfarer sunglasses, sat next to the kettle.

"Should be hot, I just made a cup," he said.

When she turned around, Kyle lifted a cup of tea in one hand, free hand crossed in the crook of his folded elbow. He was doing his best to look irritated. But with brown eyes turned down at the edges in a perpetually rueful expression, he resembled nothing so much as a wet Labrador puppy.

"You had a massage today," he said. "After your dance. I waited around for twenty. I came back this afternoon, and you had obviously been here and left again."

"I'm so sorry." She sighed.

In all the commotion, Isela had forgotten. Her body began to twinge with the usual aches and pains from dancing, not to mention the tension from the last few hours.

Because godsdancing was drawn from so many traditions, academies became known as the great repository of knowledge for dance all over the world, attracting an international student body. Each of the academies had its specialty. Praha students who did not go on to be godsdancers often found careers in ballet companies and modern dance troupes.

Kyle had been sent to the Academy for ballet but had converted to godsdancing a year later. As the only other American in their class, they'd bonded. They were both outsiders.

"I had a meeting with the director," she said. "You know the old lady. Duty first."

Kyle set down his cup and retrieved a second one, returning to the hunk of fresh ginger and a few slices of lemons waiting on the cutting board. "I *know* that. Who do you think the first person was I went to?"

"And you managed to find her?" Isela said, trying to lighten the mood.

"I have my ways," Kyle said with a little smirk, before a deep furrow carved his brow. "Actually, I badgered Niles while he was trying to finish Divya's correspondence. He said you'd be home 'soon' and absolutely nothing else. So I brought my book and made myself comfy."

She could see the place where he'd curled up on the couch with a throw blanket and the latest in a series of steamy murder mysteries he was addicted to. Kyle was a Luddite when it came to technology. Isela had given him a reader for his last birthday, but he hated the pop-up ads and insisted on old paperbacks. That might work in her favor. No doubt pictures of her little shopping expedition with Gregor was all over the web. If she could just make it until tomorrow, she could come up with a good cover story—

Isela forced a little smile. "You figured you'd camp out here and drink my tea as payback?"

"Your mom sent me a message, for the gods' sakes." Kyle looked up, and she could see the concern in his eyes. "I promised I would wait here until you got home."

Her family had always been tight-knit. Like most refugees, they relied heavily on one another during the first years of their new life and only a little less so as they settled in. Leaving to go to the Academy may have limited their relationship in some ways, but it hadn't severed their connection. Beryl Gilman-Vogel always seemed to know when her daughter was in a tight spot and called or came by to see her.

Isela fixed her eyes on the steam rising from her cup as he poured the water. Of course her mom would reach out to Kyle if she couldn't track down her daughter. He'd been a fixture at Sunday dinners for years. He'd even helped with the remodel of the downstairs studio. He was family too. She should have warned him.

Kyle gave her a long look, then, based on whatever he saw, opened the jar of honey and put a good dollop in the steaming cup. It would be difficult to keep secrets from Kyle, but if it kept him from the danger of being involved in the necromancer's job, she would break his heart.

"I had to meet a new patron," Isela said, sliding her fingers around the cup when he offered it.

"Right after a dance?"

She shrugged and blew gently on the tea.

"Who was it?"

"Some hoi polloi friend of Divya's," Isela shrugged again, drifting toward the window.

"You're using that word wrong." Kyle sucked his teeth. "Hoi polloi was a reference to common people, not the elites."

"Originally." She grinned. "But once the common people got ahold of it, it was over."

Kyle laughed, and she was relieved when he let the subject change stand even if the new one didn't make her feel any better.

"Your hip is bothering you. I can see it from here. Lay down, I'll give you quick once over, and we can reschedule your full."

"Kyle, you don't have to," Isela protested as he herded her to the bed.

"Just a few minutes," he said. "Do it or else, Vogel."

"Yes, Doctor."

Isela only feigned reluctance. Kyle gave better massages than the Academy's therapist.

She handed over her mug and flopped gracelessly on the bed. Kyle pressed long, dexterous fingers into the flesh above her hip bones. She whimpered.

"See," he said. "I told you. Now breathe and be still."

Isela obeyed. But her mind drifted immediately back to the necromancer's study. How was *she* supposed to help Azrael?

When Isela closed her eyes, she saw his face. She'd never been attracted to cocky men. Growing up with brothers, she recognized most male bluster immediately as a way of covering up insecurity. But Azrael's arrogance lacked bluster. Instead, it seemed backed by a level of self-possession she had never known. He knew exactly what he was capable of. She wondered if he was that confident in bed.

Isela shivered.

"You gotta keep ahead of this, Issy." Kyle broke into her thoughts. "If you don't want to take the doctor's advice on surgery."

"And thereby end my career."

"You don't know that," he chided. "Anyway. If you're not going to at least entertain the idea, you have to keep up on your massages, especially after a job. The body is going to try to support you, even though it can't do it properly, and you'll pay for it."

"Yes, Doctor Bradshaw," she teased. "How's Jiří?"

His thumb found a knot that made her wince.

"He still won't see me," Kyle said, an audible smile in his voice. "Such a drama queen."

"I thought you had that covered?"

"Trust me, Vogel." He laughed outright. "This man has me outclassed and outgunned in that department. All because of one picture."

"Of you wrapped around that sexy Flamenco dancer from Sevilla?" Her raised brows pressed into the pillow.

"He was a guest lecturer," Kyle insisted. "And he was demonstrating a hold."

"Is that what they're calling it these days?"

"Don't be such a prude."

"Jiří's just mad because you're not spending enough time wrapped around him," Isela pronounced. "You could fix that easily, but you won't, stubborn man."

They were quiet for a long minute.

Isela felt the words fighting their way up her throat, thoughts of the stunning heat of Azrael's gaze. She swallowed to keep herself from wondering aloud how it was possible Azrael's eyes actually *glowed* silver.

Kyle gave one last expert pass before sitting back on the edge of the bed. "I like Jiří a lot but…"

Isela sat up, laying a hand on his knee. "Life is too short for buts."

"Thanks for the love advice, Doctor Nun." Kyle bumped her shoulder with his. "Feel better?"

"Worlds." And she truly meant it. "You are a magician." She stood, sipped her tea, and contemplated the quickest way to get rid of him. She yawned and stretched out an arm.

The door chime rang.

"Christ, what now?" she muttered, earning one of Kyle's trademark side-eyes.

"Yana was down in the lounge earlier when I was looking for you." He laughed. "You know how quick everybody knows everything around here. Come in!"

In true principal ballerina form, Yana Petrova sprung up the stairs like a gazelle and skipped across the hardwood floor. She pirouetted before the bed, ending in a curtsey the lead dancer of every ballet company in the known universe would have envied.

Only when her little performance was complete did she toss the thick black bangs out of her eyes and gaze up at them with her more familiar, mischievous expression. Born in Prague to a Russian family, Yana overcame the weight of her powerful family connections to earn her place as a principal in the Academy ballet troupe.

"And I'm the drama queen." Kyle laughed standing up to kiss her cheeks. "Show-off."

Yana was a moonlit night to his sunny day—all pale skin and etched cheekbones with pouty, bee-stung lips and the bluest eyes Isela had ever seen before Gregor's had bored into her. Yana's height *en pointe* was a match for his. With complementary lines and contrasting coloring, they made a perfect pair for *pas de deux*.

They'd even dated for a couple of weeks as teenagers, before Kyle had come out. "*Da*," Yana accepted the news nonchalantly. "I only mourn what a beautiful couple we made. We will remain heart-to-heart, yes?"

She was dating a handsome young Formula One driver within the week.

"Gods' tears." Kyle had laughed. He broke the news to Isela while they stretched during a class break. "I love her, but I'm glad I'm not *in love* with her. She would destroy me. And have you seen the guy? Those cheekbones. I could die!"

They still danced together occasionally, and Yana became one of his most loyal friends in the Academy, which earned her a special place in the pantheon of Isela's heart.

"You're here, butternut." Yana had a half dozen pet names for her favorite people.

"Where else would I be?" Isela sighed.

The ballerina clucked, her eyes narrowing. "With Azrael's head of security. It's all over in the news. I came to tell *you*, Kyle."

Kyle scowled, and the heat rose in Isela's cheeks.

Yana produced a little tablet and flipped the screen to show them images from the latest entertainment newsfeed: Isela walking across the Charles Bridge while arm in arm with Gregor.

Isela stared at Kyle, watching the assumption that Gregor was her new patron light up his eyes. It was foolish to think she could have hidden it from him. Yana pinned them both with a look.

"What are you two up here caballing about?" she scowled.

"Caballing..." Isela began.

"That isn't a word, Yana," Kyle finished, fixing Isela with a look that said her secrets were safe, for now. "Issy just got back, and she's tired. Maybe we should pester her tomorrow."

Isela could have wept with relief. The last thing she needed was a debriefing—with two people who knew her as well as family—

about a meeting she couldn't talk about and her response to a man she had no words for.

They all looked up at the sound of knocking. A key jingled in the door. Apparently, her apartment was Grand Central Station.

Yana smiled, crossing her arms over her chest, and answered before Isela could. "Come up."

Kyle shrugged helplessly at Isela. "*In*, Yana. Come in."

"You are American, yet you school *me* in English?" Yana sucked her teeth at him.

Isela sighed. The new arrival, a petite woman with sparkling eyes and bronzed, freckle-dotted skin skipped up the steps.

"Trinh, you're back!" Isela couldn't hide her joy. "How was Vietnam?"

"I have the worst jet lag." The smaller woman yawned and hoisted a bottle of wine. "But I got this beauty, along with my fee, for dancing this morning, yesterday morning. Whenever. The floods have been terrible at home. I just wanted to come up and see you before I crashed. And confirm the rumor you have a mysterious new patron?"

Isela squirmed as three sets of eyes went to her.

"A '61 Bordeaux!" She snagged the bottle of wine and headed to the kitchen. "Most of these were lost in the war. Right, Kyle? I'll get some glasses."

"Riiiiight." Kyle's expression stated his verdict on her clumsy attempt to divert the conversation.

She clenched her teeth and waited for Yana to put two and two together.

"The necromancer's head of security is your patron?" Yana asked.

Isela sighed. Well it was better than the truth. "His name is Gregor."

When she looked back, Yana turned the tablet toward Trinh.

Incredibly, Trinh gasped, mock-clutching her chest, and staged an elaborate spiraling swoon onto the nearest chair. "He has a name."

"And you can have him," Isela muttered, popping the cork and fighting the urge to put the bottle to her lips. "He's an arrogant peacock of a man."

"Sounds like an affair for the ages." Kyle winked, handing over glasses.

"Was this a meeting with a new patron or a date?" Trinh asked suspiciously as she and Yana swiped through pictures. "Cause it kind of looks like—"

"I know how it looks." Isela focused on pouring, ignoring the traitorous heat in her belly at the thought of Azrael's hands on her arm. "And I can't talk about it."

"You know how it is," Kyle said. "Some of the patrons are weird about hiring dancers. We've all had to hold our tongues. It's not fair to ask Issy to tell—"

"*Mein Bitte-Pferd*," Yana said skeptically, appraising the glasses. "Just one sip. French wine is overrated."

Kyle flapped his lips in disbelief. When Isela poured his glass, he waved his hand to indicate more.

"There is *nothing* to worry about." Isela sighed, handing off glasses. "Yana, you just called me a 'please horse.'"

The self-proclaimed student of language seized every opportunity to practice. She picked up key words—mostly swears—and made up the rest.

Yana scowled. "I do not like this. I have friends who can take care of this person for you, little pony."

"Thank you for offering to sic your dad's people on him, I think." Isela waved off her concerns and lifted her glass. "It's a job. You all know the drill."

"Except Yana." Kyle laughed, bumping her shoulder as he lifted his glass. "She's too good to dance for gods."

Yana sniffed but raised her glass. "This man bothers you, you say the word. He will disappear like that." She snapped her fingers.

"Whatever. He's smoking hot." Trinh winked and brought her glass up. "I'd totally tap that."

Kyle rolled his eyes. "T, you are shameless."

"How's the view from your glass house, Bradshaw?" Their glasses clinked.

Kyle grit his teeth. "For the last time, I was demonstrating a *hold*."

Trinh's full brows arched in response, but she returned the

conversation to Isela and Gregor with a sigh. "All that danger is kind of sexy."

In spite of herself, Isela wanted to laugh. Surrounded by her friends in the safety of her own home, it was almost possible to forget she'd stood before the Allegiance of Necromancers a few hours prior, drenched in a cold sweat.

Isela toasted with them but set her cup down after a sip. Wine loosened her tongue easily, and there were things she didn't want to say. She needed to keep it together.

Trinh teased her for a bit longer about the image of her shopping with the 'tall, German hunk of handsome' that was sure to be on the society pages the next day. Yana sulked until the car arrived to escort her back to her palatial flat overlooking the river.

Isela found herself curled up on the couch with Kyle, his arm tucked around her and her head pillowed on his chest. A silence as warm and comforting as down settled between them. She blew out a long breath of air, and he squeezed her shoulders.

"It's not that guy, Gregor," he said after a long moment. "Your new patron."

Isela jerked her eyes up to him, mute with both relief and horror. She knew she should say something—evade, joke, lie outright if she had to. But he spoke first.

"Don't bother," he said with a sad little smile. "You're a terrible liar. It's him, the patron, isn't it? The necromancer."

Her chin ducked into her chest, and she felt his lips press against her hair.

"I won't say anything," Kyle murmured. "But I'm here for you. You know you can tell me anything."

The shock wore off, leaving only the realization she alone had been trusted with an impossible task that might cost her everything even if she succeeded. She already knew too much about necromancer politics and how far they were willing to go to protect their own. What would keep them from making her disappear when this was all over to hide their vulnerabilities? After watching Azrael among the others, his promise to Divya seemed laughable. Who would enforce it? It was suddenly too much. If there was anyone she could trust, it was Kyle. He would understand the need for secrecy. And having someone to share the burden with would make it less heavy.

Isela opened her mouth to speak, and nothing came out.

She tried again. The words bubbled up in her chest. She knew what she wanted to say, but nothing escaped her throat. She gasped, choking on impotent breath. Kyle stared at her wide-eyed, watching her struggle with words that twisted in her mouth and forced themselves back down her throat.

"What is it?" he said.

Stricken, her eyes met his.

Isela opened her mouth once more to speak, understanding Azrael's words to her had not been a threat at all. He'd done something to her. Something that prevented her from speaking of their agreement to anyone. What else was he capable of?

"I can't." She choked. "I want to, but the words won't..."

Kyle slipped a second arm around her as she broke down. Tears came when words would not, and she gave in to them. He held her silently. Outside, the first snow of the winter began to fall.

CHAPTER SIX

Isela woke on the couch under her comforter with a stuffy nose and a headache. Kyle had washed the wineglasses and filled the water kettle. She unfurled herself from a fetal ball, peeling off the previous day's clothes and smelling the faint odor of her own fear. Slipping into salwar pants and a halter top, Isela turned up the heat in the apartment. She stepped onto the unrolled mat beside the biggest window like a drowning woman climbing onto a raft. Outside, the first snowfall had left the world dusted in a thin layer of white. It might all melt by noon, but she loved the sight of the early light through air that sparkled, heavy with frozen moisture.

Isela didn't bother with music, folding her body into a seated position and tuning in to the sound of her own breath. After a few moments of stillness and measured breathing, she unfolded her limbs and moved into a sequence of postures as familiar as the feel of the mat beneath her feet.

Her mother would chide her that sun salutations should be done facing the east, but she loved the occasional view of the waking city before her. After a dozen or more progressions, her warming body began to release some of the tension that had crept into her muscles and joints overnight. Her breath deepened as her ribs expanded, and she moved into more difficult postures. She flowed between them, feeling the edges of dance creep into her movements, giving the transitions grace and fluidity.

In the midst of a transition, Isela had the sensation of being watched. She brushed it aside as impossible; no one, not even Kyle, intruded on her morning sessions. Irritated that paranoia had crept into her practice, she redoubled her attention with a few extra breaths. Balancing on one leg, she hooked her free ankle in her hand, extending the leg above and behind her as she controlled the counterbalance of her upper body lowering toward the floor. She reached her other hand behind her to catch her toes and flexed both elbows away from the foot so that her upper body and leg formed a teardrop shape balanced on the standing leg.

Out of the corner of her eye, something flickered—a flash of gold like the glint of sun off metal. The feeling of being watched increased. But now there was also a smell. Cardamom and rose hips. She breathed deeply, letting the scent fill her lungs. An unearthly chime echoed inside her skull, and for a moment she simply was not there. The weight of her limbs disappeared, and there was empty space where the world around her should be.

Isela came back into her body, startled and panting, suddenly exhausted. She could barely lower herself out of the posture without falling down. She glanced at the clock. Five minutes had passed.

What the hell was that all about?

What else had Azrael, or one of the other necromancers, done to her?

Isela glanced around. Still alone, the smell and sound were gone, as well as the sensation of being watched. The hair rose on her arms and neck, and a slow, subtle warmth circulated in her body.

She repeated the posture on the opposite leg, unable to hold it for anywhere near as long, and went into her resting state.

The phone buzzed once from her bag. She scanned the text from her mother. *It's been almost two months—see you on Sunday? Dinner at seven.*

It was less an invitation than a command.

"Shit." Isela thumbed a quick response. *Of course. Crazy busy!*

She allowed herself the vague hope Azrael would be finished

with her by then. How long could a necromancer take to solve a couple of murders? Even if it required her to boost his powers.

This was not going to be like any other dance, no matter how Azrael tried to bluster his way into her easy compliance. She wasn't going to let the inability to speak to anyone stop her from figuring out how to do her job.

Isela showered, ate, and headed down to the library. She logged into the network, checking her personal and business mailboxes. Her jaw dropped when she saw her bank balance.

"Too many zeroes," she murmured. "Fuck me."

That earned a stern glare from the librarian. She checked her calendar. It had been cleared, and her profile blocked off as indefinitely retained.

The library was mostly empty at this hour, save for a few students cramming for winter exams, but those nearest to her were staring.

One whispered, "Necromancer," and the other paled.

"Sorry," she whispered with a little wave. "Hi."

Isela logged out and crossed the room to the door near the back. The main library had long ago been digitized, but upstairs was reserved for instructors and professionals. It was full of old books that were not in the digital system. Receiving a security code had been a rite of passage when she'd graduated.

Isela keyed herself in and paused for the retinal scan before hearing the door lock click open. The door slid shut behind her as she climbed the stone steps to the top floor. The smell of old books hit her first. Most of the manuscripts were dated obscure references, irrelevant except to those doing in-depth study of a specific area. The cataloguing system was just as dated.

That was why they had Madeline. The keeper of the Academy's restricted library sat at a huge elevated desk in the center of the room.

"Bonjour, Isela. You've been a stranger, *petit.*"

"Bonjour, Miss Maddy." As broad as she was tall, Madeline moved with a gentle rolling motion on her way down the three steps to the main floor to give Isela a hug. Isela's nose twitched with the familiar scent of lilacs and vellum.

"I heard you got a big job, girl." Madeline squeezed Isela's shoulders with surprising strength. "I've been told to give you any help you need. Sit yourself down."

Isela had the inner library to herself. Shelves lined the hexagonal-shaped room, two stories tall, the tops reachable by ladder, which was kept on a brass track. Beneath the scent of ink and old paper, she caught a whiff of cedar. Books, some of them appearing centuries old, were packed into the shelves by no discernable system. She had long suspected there was a reason it was kept visibly uncategorized. Only Madeline seemed to be able to locate anything in a reasonable amount of time. There was no computer on her desk, not even a card catalogue.

"Say the word, and I will bring you every book with any reference to any subject," she chimed. "Where do we begin?"

Isela wanted to laugh and cry. Divya had done this. Madeline was the gatekeeper to every bit of the most secret wisdom in the Academy. Now she had unlimited access. If only she could figure out how to ask for what she needed without triggering the spell Azrael had put on her.

Isela tested out a few words.

"Dancing and necromancers?"

Madeline gave her a helpless look. It wasn't enough to go on.

Drawing powers from dancers didn't come out at all. Neither did *killing a necromancer*. Frustration made her eyes well up. Madeline patted her on the shoulders.

Isela gritted her teeth and tried again. She might be able to approach it indirectly.

"Dancers helping necromancers," Isela said. "Power transfer."

Madeline nodded a few times, her sharp eyes taking on a distant look as though she were somewhere else entirely. Isela had another idea.

"The necromancer's security." She could talk about the others without restriction. *What had Vanka called him?* "What's a Hessian?"

Madeline filled the room with laughter. "They were German mercenaries, known for being hired to fight the patriots in the American Revolutionary War. They were fierce in battle and had the reputation of having supernatural strength and abilities. But after the Brits were defeated in the revolution, they went out of vogue. Where'd you hear that?"

"Gregor," Isela barked. "His head of security. The necromancer called him that."

"Is he undead?"

He didn't have the lackey boy's paleness or lack of respiration. "I don't think so," she said. "But he's—different somehow. Like how he talks, he's so formal and nobody uses *fräulein* anymore."

Madeline gave her a peculiar look. "If you think necromancers and false gods are the only strange things in this world, *chéri*, you've got an education coming. Wait here. Let me get started."

She ignored Isela's offers to help, returning with an armload of books, moving quickly for someone who had to be approaching her seventies. Many of the titles were in other languages or simply faded away; most of the books Madeline had brought to her predated the godswar.

Madeline set down a tablet, flicking the screen on with a tap and bringing up a series of images. Isela recognized the German in photo after photo. Gregor had been at Azrael's side since the allegiance had come forward, and neither one seemed to have aged in the last thirty years. If they weren't immortal, they were close enough to it.

Isela noticed a familiar woman among the group that comprised Azrael's security team. She was as tall as any of the men, with full, handsome features and dark, ropy curls.

"Looks like an Amazon," Madeline said when she saw Isela's finger hover over the image. "If I was assembling an Aegis, you'd believe I'd recruit a few of those."

Isela's head came up. "Aegis? What's that?"

Madeline hesitated, drifting away from the table to tidy a nearby shelf. "The breastplate of Zeus? That fearsome sigil bearing the countenance of the Gorgon's scaly crown and worn on the left arm of Athena? A word perhaps stolen from the Libyans by the Greeks, claimed by the necromancers to name the men and women they've chosen to accompany them through time."

Isela scanned the photos again. Hessians and Amazons. She spotted the two giant twins that had guarded the door in the faded sepia images, looking fierce in Polynesian garb. Just how long *had* Azrael and his cronies been around?

"This is fucking weird," she muttered before catching herself. She glanced at Madeline, chagrined.

"Call it like you see it." The older woman shrugged and strolled away. "Want some coffee?"

Isela brightened. She'd never liked coffee, but Madeline's was a singular experience. "Café Touba?"

Madeline splayed her palm on her ample bosom, the rich, deep brown of her skin a contrast to her bold yellow-and-red-patterned dress and called out something in creole too fast for Isela to catch before finishing. "Is there any other worth drinking?"

Isela started with the first few books about necromancers but emerged with only unsubstantiated rumors and stories. She pushed them aside and clapped her hands as Madeline presented a steaming cup of coffee infused with cloves and black pepper.

"Miss Maddy," Isela hesitated after delighting her nose with a long inhale. "How old are you? Really?"

Madeline taught the library studies course to all First Years. As a late enrollee at the Academy, Isela had been the oldest in her group and stood aside self-consciously until Madeline took her hand and pulled her close. "No excuse for not learning, *petit*."

In all that time, the librarian seemed unchanged. Isela had attributed it to genetics, but with everything she'd seen in the last twenty-four hours, she couldn't help but wonder.

Madeline shook her head, sucking her teeth lightly. "A lady never tells her age, *petit*. Especially not to nosy little girls."

She chucked Isela under the chin and winked before returning to her stacks. Isela flushed, embarrassed by her own rudeness. Dancing was her skill. It was what Azrael wanted her for. She needed to stop looking for mysteries and stay focused on doing the job she had been hired for. The allegiance had promised a generous payment. The only way her life was in danger was if she couldn't figure out how to do what they wanted. She hoped.

Like most dancers had been taught, she assumed it worked one way: patrons asked, she danced, the gods delivered, or didn't, as it pleased them. The allegiance seemed convinced Azrael could draw on the power of a god directly through her dancing.

Isela scanned the books on the history of dancing in religion until her eyeballs ached, sipping gratefully at the coffee. There were plenty of references to mortals communicating with gods through dance—from Greek oracles to voodoo priests—but nothing about amplifying power.

Antsy, Isela stood up to pace and tipped over her cup.

"Shit!"

She shoved the books out of the coffee's path. One tumbled to the floor. Madeline hurried over with rags.

Isela knelt to retrieve the book, carefully unfolding a page that had been wrinkled in the fall. She fingered the old dog-ear thoughtfully, her eyes drawn to the words.

Make no mistake: to dance is not a one-way transfer. An open door is also an invitation.

Isela shuddered, dropping to the floor and dragging the book onto her lap. She was distantly aware of Madeline sopping up the mess. When she tried to help, Madeline waved her away. She paged through the book, careful of the deteriorating binding.

The language was archaic, Byzantine sentences twisting around one another until she forgot where the paragraph started by the time it ended. She grabbed her notepad and scribbled a few things. When her eyes began to itch, she looked up at the clock to find another two hours had passed. She glanced at her notes. More questions than answers.

With a sigh, she carefully refolded the dog-ear before closing the book and setting it on the stack.

"I need to take a break," Isela announced. "I don't know how you manage in here all the time."

"Old habits," Madeline's laugh followed her to the door. "I'll leave everything as you have it."

* * *

"AGAIN!"

At the barked command, Isela dragged her body off the padded wooden floor. Sweat stung her eyes, and she shook the wet hair out of her face to look at the short figure in wide-legged black pants standing a few feet away. Trinh had already turned to address the students seated around the edges of the room, describing the attack and the defense—and its faults. Petite and soft-spoken in person, in class her voice was clear and direct, punctuated by gesture.

Finally she returned her attention to Isela, resting her fist in her palm. She kept her face still for the sake of her students, but Isela had known her long enough to recognize the wicked gleam in her dark eyes. Trinh was enjoying herself.

Isela had three inches and twenty pounds on the woman, but Trinh had earned the master's belt that closed her jacket. Barefoot and calm as a metro busker at rush hour, she held out a hand.

"Christ on a crutch," Isela muttered under her breath as she lowered into a preparatory stance.

"Wasting the breath on talk," Trinh barked.

Isela's eyebrow rose. Her back to her students, Trinh winked.

If Isela had thought she would just drop in and spar with a couple of the students to burn off some extra energy, someone hadn't told Trinh. Of course, that was part of the reason she loved Trinh's classes; she never took it easy on Isela. There was no favored dancer status on this padded wooden floor. That meant she could let go too. Mostly.

Isela inhaled, focusing on the last bit of breath entering her lungs. She sipped deeper and unleashed her body on the exhale, marching across the floor with strikes that Trinh evaded and countered. Isela slipped loose of a hold, rolled under a grab, and swept Trinh's knees from beneath her. She made herself smooth and elastic, each strike coming with a punctuated exhale.

In these moments, Isela was aware of how much fighting and dancing had in common. And this particular style was much like godsdancing: a blend of defense-based martial training that graduated to assault and immobilize.

Trinh fell to the floor but managed to wriggle free, getting her feet under Isela and tossing her across the mat. Isela tucked into a roll, pushing out her heels in time to keep herself from sliding into the sparring weapons rack. Without thinking, she reached back and wrapped her fingers around a staff.

"Improvisation." Trinh nodded, still empty-handed. "Good. See if you can keep it."

Isela came on swinging. She used the staff to keep Trinh at a distance, and it worked, until she stumbled. Trinh directed her fall by the wrist, spun, and slipped the staff from her grip. Now it was her turn to dodge and run.

She was no match for the martial instructor. She wound up on her back, panting against the end of the staff at her throat.

"Yield," Isela croaked, smiling.

Trinh brought the staff down and offered a hand. The students were applauding furiously, even before Trinh stepped back and gave a formal bow. Isela palmed her fist and bowed in response.

"One of you may reach the level of Isela and take your chances in open spar with me," Trinh addressed her students. "Until then, up! Everyone, partners. Defense three and four, attack one and nine."

Isela followed her to the weapons rack, exchanging the staff for a towel. Their backs to the sparring students, Trinh kept her voice low.

"It's always a pleasure to have you," Trinh said. "But you were intense today. Does this have something to do with the job—"

"I just feel like I need all the help I can get right now," Isela said.

"Well, you have mine, always, but that stumble was your hip, wasn't it?"

Isela had schooled herself long ago not to draw attention to it, so it was easy not to bring a hand to the sore joint, but she winced a little.

"It's getting worse," Trinh admonished gently.

"Yoga helps, and Kyle's massages," Isela said before admitting, "It's not getting better."

"And now a job that requires you to brush up on your combat skills?" Trinh shook her head.

"Just working off a little steam."

Trinh harrumphed. "Hit the showers. We can get lunch after and talk about what you need to work on."

CHAPTER SEVEN

Isela walked into the sterile room, her bag slung over her shoulder, not knowing what to expect. Two days of waiting and preparing ended with Gregor's chilly voice on the line, announcing she would be needed in three hours for a summoning.

It gave her just enough time to walk through the choreography once more as a warm-up and follow the rest of her instructions.

Gregor had said to dress for a night out. She'd done her best, with a little help. Taking a cue from his outfit on the bridge, Yana'd paired a black pencil skirt that tapered sharply at the knee with a gauzy crimson blouse tucked into the high waist of the skirt. The blouse obscured a floral lace bralette designed to be hinted at. Peep-toe stilettos clung to her feet by thin ankle straps. It took both of them and a dozen pins to sweep her hair up in a voluminous imitation of a dancer's bun. Yana highlighted her subtle makeup with Afghan red lips to match the top. Over it all, a cropped, merino cape draped her shoulders, pinned at the collar. Her dancing gear was stashed in a giant purse from Yana's own extensive collection.

Her buzzer went off as they finished. It was Niles calling on behalf of her newly arrived escort.

Yana appraised her at the door. "Not so bad, as Kyle was too busy courting his little man to fix you up."

Isela sighed. "I couldn't ask him to blow off date night."

She was grateful for Kyle's absence. Every time they saw each other during the week, the line of worry seemed to settle deeper between his brows. She hated knowing it was her fault. By the time he found out she'd been called to the castle, she'd be on her way home. Safe. She hoped.

Isela said. "Anyway, I look amazing, thanks to you."

Yana affirmed her judgment with a scowl. "This is too good for that *Scheisse Baum* of a man."

Shit tree. Well, Gregor was tall. Isela wanted to throw her arms around Yana, but she restrained herself to air kisses to either cheek. Yana looked grateful for that reserve as she folded her arms over her chest and smiled dangerously. "Go now. Make him lose his mind, yes?"

The first and second year students mysteriously loitering around the halls couldn't keep from staring as she walked by.

Isela hoped all the research she'd done in preparation would pay off. She tried not to think about what might happen if she was unsuccessful. Maybe Azrael would pick someone else.

The thought left her curiously cold. She wouldn't wish the responsibility, or the danger, on another dancer. The security guard hurried to open the door ahead of her.

The flashes and calls from the crowd momentarily disoriented Isela as she stepped through the door. Niles had cleared a path to the curb with academy security, and she felt exposed in front of so many eyes. She pasted on her performance smile, searching for the necromancer's escort.

To her surprise, Gregor himself emerged from a midnight-colored Audi roadster with enormous wheel wells that resembled the muscular haunches of a predator and an engine that definitely rumbled with gasoline combustion.

He ignored the gawkers to take her arm, dusting kisses on both cheeks. His black suit complimented the predatory vibe of his vehicle.

"You should have warned me you were wearing red," he said approvingly as he cast a toothy smile at the press photographer. "I would have matched my tie."

"So we're going public as a couple now, eh?" Isela murmured through a frozen smile.

Gregor's eyebrow rose as he guided her to the passenger side.

"Apparently, PR thinks it's a suitable ruse to distract the public and an opportunity to—humanize—the necromancer's security force."

Humanize, she thought, slipping into the car and tucking up her heels. Saddling Gregor with a wife, two kids, and diaper duty wouldn't be enough to gloss over the impression that he was a thinly sheathed blade. No wonder he needed a PR overhaul.

The mental image made her smile.

Known as Azrael's enforcer, the most brutal acts of the necromancer's rule not attributed to Azrael himself were often credited to Gregor. According to Trinh, it was Gregor who guarded the eyes Azrael had nailed to the door. Rumor had it the eyes belonged to a necromancer who had challenged Azrael. The thought killed her smile.

"So how long have we been… seeing each other?" she questioned carefully. "Just to get my story straight."

Gregor shifted into gear and peeled away from the curb, sending the crowd scrambling out of his way. She winced as he bared his teeth in a smile.

"Since the fall gala at the Academy. If you recall, I escorted Azrael there and remained with him at the social event following the performance." His voice was emotionless. Calculated. He didn't like this idea much either.

Isela remembered the night. Kept busy with introductions to donors and patrons, she hadn't even seen the necromancer. Trinh, however, had spent the next few days gushing over the "devastatingly hot guy" that shadowed the necromancer the entire night. Mystery solved.

The touch of his finger moving up the back of her hand to the wrist brought her back to the present. It was all Isela could do not to jerk away. If Gregor got his thrills being the scariest fucker in the room, she wasn't going to give him the satisfaction of knowing he'd gotten to her.

Gregor glanced from the road as he darted through traffic, the stiffer suspension pounding the cobblestones into her back and seat. She fought the urge to brace herself on the door and center console. His eyes slid up her body, and the enclosed space of the car felt stifling.

"You did well on short notice," he complimented.

"You don't clean up too bad yourself." She drew her hand away with calculated slowness and rested it primly on her lap.

He chuckled. "So American, your way of speaking."

"My mom," she said after a pause. "People say I talk like my mom sometimes."

"It's amazing how some habits become so ingrained in us at such a young age. We're barely aware of them anymore. My accent, as you noted."

Isela was so surprised at the admission and the attempt to empathize that she really looked at him for the first time since entering the car. Again, Gregor cast that dangerous smile her way.

"I was born," he quipped. "I had a family. Parents. Siblings. Once."

"I never would have guessed," she retorted. "You seem like a pretty self-made man."

Gregor chuckled. "No need to be nervous, dancer. I'm not the one you need to worry about."

"That's exactly what I'm afraid of," she muttered before she could catch herself.

His smile faded. "That's good. A little fear is healthy. You might live longer."

* * *

A LITTLE FEAR, she thought, following Gregor down the long hall into what appeared to be a medical facility below the castle. She would choke herself on it if she wasn't careful. The facility had been a surprise from the moment they'd entered from the garage. She hadn't spent much time contemplating a necromancer's basement, but this high-tech setup of bright lights and stainless steel was unexpected.

Isela kept her breathing slow and steady. They passed a few white-coated technicians on the way. All gave the pair wide berth. If their incongruent clothing stood out, the techs gave no sign.

Finally Gregor opened a door to a room that resembled a medical theater. On one wall were cabinets and a counter of instruments. Another wall was filled with rectangular, stainless steel squares. On a large table—a gurney, she realized—was a figure draped in sheeting. The stench of charred flesh invaded her nostrils. A morgue.

Who has a morgue in their basement? Oh, wait.

Isela came up short, distantly aware of Gregor's arm sliding around her until it was too late to escape. His fingers curled onto her hip. It was a casual gesture, one that might have fit in with the ruse of their being a couple, but the firmness revealed his true purpose. She could not run.

Isela tore her eyes away from the sheet to see the necromancer Azrael flanked by the Amazon and one of the enormous Polynesians from the door. Another man, white coated—doctor, lab tech, undead minion?—carefully cleaned and arranged instruments at the counter, his back to them.

Azrael's eyes locked on her. She took a half step back into the wall that was Gregor's chest. She wasn't sure what rose in her throat —a scream or vomit—but she sealed her lips shut and concentrated on her breathing. She made herself be perfectly still, aware of the man across the room eyeing her with the gaze of a hunting animal.

Gregor moved away, and the cold air at her back made Isela shiver.

"Master," he bowed. "The dancer."

Isela could not look away from Azrael. He filled the room with presence. Even Gregor was dampened by it. She wondered briefly if he was compelling her in some way—like whatever spell he'd put on her to keep her from talking.

"Will you have enough space to dance?" Azrael was speaking. To her. She forced herself to consider the question.

"You want me to dance… here?"

Silence. His face was a collection of brutal lines and hard angles. It felt like the temperature of the room dropped another few degrees.

Ok, no more stupid questions. Just do your job, and get the fuck out of here. Alive.

Isela glanced around, fixing her eyes on the space she would need and ignoring everything else.

"I need this side of the room cleared," she ordered. "About a twelve-by-twelve area. It's small, but it will do."

Azrael nodded. "Gregor, Rory."

Her escort and the Polynesian began moving empty tables and an instrument stand out of the way.

Silver eyes fixed on her again. "Anything else?"

It was impossible not to look at him, so she compromised by studying the brush of dark hair against his collar when she spoke. "I need to change."

Isela chanced a look into his face to see his eyes flash again. She realized instinctively it was an emotion of some sort. Anger? Irritation? But he didn't speak.

"My clothes," she clarified.

He might be used to being surrounded by mindless automatons of his own creation, but she wasn't a zombie, never mind an impossibly immortal soldier. She was human, and he needed her cooperation. He was going to have to give something to get something.

"I will do what you ask." Isela forced calm into her voice. "I'm going along with this arrangement, aren't I?" She gestured at herself and Gregor. "But I would like a little privacy to change my clothes, please."

The silence rivaled a tomb; it was so complete she imagined hearing the whisper of dead skin cells hitting the floor.

Gregor exhaled—a laugh?—and the sound of furniture being rearranged resumed.

Azrael nodded again. The Amazon stepped around him and approached. Sleek and muscled as a hunting hound, her black jeans and fitted turtleneck were interrupted only by the gun holster buckled to her chest. She paused, beckoned and walked on, opening the door. Isela's forced herself to walk, albeit stiffly, after the woman.

She opened the door to a small antechamber. "You can change here."

She followed Isela inside and closed the door behind them, standing with her back to the door.

Isela set down her bag. She bit back a frustrated sigh. She'd changed in front of other dancers but never under guard. As if she had any idea where to go even if she did run. She focused on peeling off her skirt and neatly folding the top with it. She undid her hose and gratefully relieved her feet from the stilettos. On went leggings, long enough to slip under her heels, and a fitted tank top with internal support. Considering the temperature of the room, she pulled on toeless socks and a sleeved wrap that tied snugly around her waist. She secured her hair with a few extra pins and repacked her bag.

The Amazon opened the door when she nodded.

If she expected Azrael to be waiting for her to return, she would have been disappointed. The sheet had been removed, and she glimpsed raised arms with hands curled into burned claws. Her stomach turned, and she averted her eyes.

The white-coated man was explaining they hadn't been able to recover either the brain or the organs.

Isela had never seen a summoning—a necromancer calling spirit to dead flesh—but she knew it involved the physical matter of the dead body, preferably a heart or brain. *Was this why he needed her, because the body was incomplete?*

"Mind your task, dancer," the Amazon said, startling her.

Isela met her gaze and nodded.

She set down her bag and occupied the newly cleared space, walking a few times around its circumference to orient her body. It was smaller than usual, but it would do. She always choreographed for a small area when performing in a new ring, not knowing what she would be given. It was easier to expand a dance in the moment, than contract one.

Mentally reviewing the choreography she'd prepared based on Azrael's request and her research, Isela warmed her body with a methodical sequence of stretches beginning at the toes and going all the way to her head and neck. She used the same sequence every time. Like a mantra, it combed her mind into the meditative state she needed to be in to dance.

The room fell away. She lost track of everything, including that wretched burned flesh smell, letting a deep bubble of stillness expand around her. The quiet was so complete she barely heard the call for her attention until the necromancer himself spoke it. His voice sliced through but did not break the bubble, filling the space with a husky timbre.

"Ready, dancer?"

Isela acknowledged him with a nod and felt him retreat, so

swiftly and expertly the space was undisturbed by his passing. A shiver moved through her. She closed her eyes and began to dance.

She had designed this routine to be performed without sight. It lacked multiple spins or long balances that would require a fixed gaze. Grateful for the foresight, it relieved her from having to see what the necromancer was doing to the corpse. Though her curiosity was piqued, she knew she would have never been able to focus if she had tried to watch.

Isela could smell his work; a strange, burned orange-and-sugar scent not entirely unpleasant banished the char. In the absence of sight, her mind became active, her eyelids a screen on which bursts of light and color flared. She breathed deeply, losing herself in the motion.

A bright flare of gold behind her eyelids almost broke her concentration. It flashed warm, the opposite of Azrael's cold silver glare. After a moment, she realized it was taking the shape of a figure—a woman—mimicking her movements exactly. It hovered just out of reach like an image in a mirror.

A thrill of excitement raced up her spine. Isela tested the theory with her fingers, twitching them slightly. The gold figure responded in kind but with her left hand, not the right. A mirror. But not quite. The body was slimmer, taller, and leaner than Isela's. After a turn, it became curvier, fuller-breasted and thicker-hipped. Every time she turned, it changed. Once, Isela swore she made out extra arms and a tail. Improvising, she experimented with a spin and another, startled to find her balance held so long as she focused on the gold shape.

She envied Yana and Kyle their ability to dance with a partner. She struggled to maintain the level of awareness on her surroundings it required. It went against her nature of surrendering entirely to dance. But this was effortless. It was as if the gold figure was her shadow.

"You can stop now."

The voice cut through the dance that had now become a *pas de deux*, and the gold shadow vanished. Inexplicable loss welled up in her chest from a bottomless place.

Isela came back into awareness of her body to find it exhausted, dripping with sweat. Her tongue, thick in her mouth, was as dry as an old blanket. She blinked to find all eyes in the room on her. Her knees buckled. She barely caught herself as she fell to the floor, hands taking some of the impact from her knees and shins.

The cold air enveloped her; her sweat-soaked clothes did nothing to keep the chill at bay. She shuddered hard, searching the faces for succor. Gregor's was openly captivated. The others were unreadable. She stopped at Azrael. He was watching, his lips set in a firm line, his jaw locked. He was furious.

"What happened?" Isela croaked before she passed out.

* * *

"Nothing at all?"

She woke in the castle proper, wrapped in a blanket softer than cashmere. The Amazon crouched beside her chair, assessing her. After a moment, she pressed a cup of something hot into Isela's hands.

Isela drank, smelling ginger and mint before the taste left the lingering sweet sour of lemon and honey in her mouth.

"Little sips." The woman stilled her with a hand on Isela's wrist when she tried to drink too deeply. "Don't make yourself sick."

With restraint she didn't know she possessed, Isela pulled the cup away from her mouth. Her tongue cried out for more, but she felt her belly contract and knew the woman was right. Her awareness stretched, beyond the chair and the cup, to the room around them. A fire was crackling in the hearth a few feet away, but she still felt the cold of the morgue in her bones.

Azrael leaned over an impossibly large book resting on one of two enormous tables. She shivered. He was like negative space in the room, where light could not reach. Gregor stood by the door. His eyes met hers briefly, and she saw none of his previous flirtation. Her heart buckled. Without a word, he turned from his place and left the room.

The Amazon seemed to linger only long enough to make sure Isela didn't drop the cup on the priceless Persian rug beneath her chair before she rose. When she saw Isela's gaze, she hesitated but walked toward the door. Isela had the feeling her dawdling at the door took powerful effort. No words were spoken, but after a moment, the Amazon left, closing the door softly behind her.

Isela found herself alone with Azrael. This time she felt even more defenseless than the last, if that could be possible. She finished her tea and set down the cup to avoid betraying her trembling hands. He seemed absorbed in his book. His back to her.

Not dead yet, she reminded herself, straightening up and tugging the blanket around her shoulders. "The summoning didn't work?"

Azrael turned to face her, leaning against the table and crossing his arms over his chest.

"You've won over my Amazon," he said without answering her question. "For that alone, you've earned my respect."

My Amazon. As in, she belongs to me. Slave? Employee? Lover? Isela tugged her thoughts away from sussing out the relationship. He was still speaking. "If you think that gives you the right to question me…"

Isela exhaled sharply. "I'm not—you—I'm trying to figure out what happened. I'm not exactly *there* when I'm dancing, and I need to know what happened so I can fix it. Next time."

If there is a next time.

The density of the silence made it difficult to breathe. She concentrated on his clothes to avoid his eyes: all black, the cut elegant in its simplicity.

"The summoning worked," he said finally. "But the dancing did nothing to improve it, as the others had hoped."

That was it. *She'd* failed. No, Isela corrected swiftly. She had done what she was asked to do, without knowing how or why or even *what* to do. And it hadn't worked. She was too exhausted for diplomacy.

"And you're surprised?" she said, plowing on heedless into the silence. "You tell me nothing about how this works, expect me to dance in a *morgue*, and it didn't do anything, and this is surprising?"

Azrael spun and crossed the room so fast the movement blurred. When her vision resolved, he was on one knee before her chair and his silver eyes peered directly into hers. There was nothing penitent about his positioning. Instead, she felt like she was staring down a panther crouched, ready to spring.

Maybe she ought to learn to get ahold of her mouth after all. Isela shrunk as far as the chair back would allow but refused to let her eyes fall.

"You speak too freely, human." His eyes traced the shape of her mouth.

"Then get yourself a zombie."

The blood left her face as a slow smile grew across his.

"You think I haven't thought of that," he murmured.

"I think if you could, you would have already." Isela was proud of herself for sounding so calm while all her instincts screamed *flee.*

Azrael sat back on his haunches, a calculating expression creasing the handsome face. "It doesn't work that way."

Wonder of wonders, she thought. She was right.

"How unfortunate for both of us," her voice squeaked.

One eyebrow arched. "Indeed."

This close, she confirmed it wasn't just an absence of heat or light about him. She sensed a complete stillness, as though laws of matter and energy ceased in his presence. It was the kind of quiet she spent years training as a dancer to possess. No wasted energy, nothing unintentional.

Azrael was as complete a being as she had ever met. Powerful and self-contained in ways she could only imagine. He just *was*. It was terrifying to behold and impossibly magnetic. He was the most beautiful thing she had ever seen.

He was not human. Not touched with empathy or compassion, but neither with vindictiveness or cruelty for its own sake. What she had mistaken as disdain for her humanity was disregard for it. As if he had forgotten—or never known—what it was to be surrounded by beings more powerful and mysterious than he.

He reached up to take one of her sweat-stiffened curls between his fingers.

Isela's pulse bounded under her skin, despite the tension in her balled fists. Azrael provoked more than just "fight or flight" in her. Had it been so long since she'd felt desire that she'd forgotten the tingling sensations racing from the center of her body to the edges?

As if reading her mind, the finger released her curl and drifted to her mouth. She stayed motionless but felt a surge of heat. She was glad she wasn't on her feet, or her knees might have gone to water. Instead, as his fingertip traced the line of her lower lip, she only had to fight the urge to part her mouth and taste him with her tongue.

What the fuck?

A small, knowing smile pulled his full lips taut inches from hers. Damn, it wasn't fair for him to have a mouth like that.

Isela felt the groan in her chest, barely catching it before it escaped her throat. His index finger traced her cheekbone, thumb pressed into the pad of her lower lip. Broad, surprisingly callused fingertips flared against her neck and jaw. Silver eyes fixed on her, studying, finding, deciding.

The morgue cold had vanished: whatever he was doing to her had forced it out of her bones. If she wasn't already dehydrated, she would have broken a sweat.

"I don't…" She closed her eyes. The words came stronger now. "This isn't… no."

When she opened her eyes again, surprise colored his face.

"That's not part of the deal." Isela glanced down at his wrist. "*This* is not part of the deal."

Azrael withdrew, and her body ached at the loss of contact.

Fucking traitor libido, she accused.

"You want me." That bold, masculine confidence cut through the languid stupor of arousal. It was not a question. And she was not a swooning first year. Defiance steeled her spine and narrowed her eyes.

"Is being seduced by a necromancer supposed to flatter me?" Isela said, ignoring the niggling bit of truth that begged the contrary. "I mean, why bother when you can wiggle your eyebrow and make me drop my panties?"

He jerked back as if her words had been a blow.

No, she thought, startled. *Worse than a blow.*

She'd actually offended him.

That dangerous, seductive heat growing between them vanished, replaced by a deadly cold. A snarling grin cut his face. "I have no need to coerce a woman into my bed."

His bed. An instant image of black satin sheets and an abundance of pillows. Four posts with silk straps for wrists and ankles. She gave herself a mental slap. *Snap out of it, Issy. He can turn you into a zombie. That is not sexy.*

"I'm sure you don't," she said lightly. "When you could have a mindless automaton."

He leaned toward her, hands on either arm of the chair. She reeled backward. When she could go no farther, she struck out instinctively. He caught her wrist before she could make contact. She clawed at his forearm with her free hand. It was like trying to scratch stone.

He rose to his feet, and though he only held her wrist, her entire body followed as though scooped out of the chair. She dangled like a puppy by the scruff, feet kicking impotently. A little scream escaped her.

In the background, Isela heard the door open, but her entire frame of vision was filled with his monstrously beautiful face. He shook his head, without taking his eyes from her, and it closed. Who had it been? Gregor? The Amazon? Not that it mattered. She had no allies here.

"You cover your own attraction by accusing me of compulsion." His voice never rose from the dangerous purr.

"You can control the words that come out of my mouth," she countered. "Why wouldn't you be able to make me think I want you? You told us necromancy was about biological control. 'Scientists, not magicians,' wasn't that the line your allegiance used?"

Azrael gave her a little shake. "You insult me with your loose tongue and your base insinuations."

"I'm not the one ripping out eyeballs and leaving them nailed to doors because someone said something I didn't like."

Cold silence. A calm settled over her. Now she'd done it.

Azrael released her. Isela's feet hit the floor a moment before she knew she was going to fall into the hearth. She reached out to break her fall as her hip gave and would have put a hand in the fire if he had not caught it first. He stabilized her, pinching her wrist.

"If you were any of my people," he said emotionlessly, "I would remind you of your maker and your vow. Then again, were you any of my people, you would never speak so against me. But you are not one of mine," he said, turning cold eyes on her. "You are mortal. You are weak, foolish, and impetuous. Knowing what your kind has done throughout history, I should not be so surprised you are incapable of something as simple as being circumspect in your words."

He let her go.

Isela stumbled backward, gasping as she held her hand to her chest as if it had been burned after all. Tears clouded her eyes, and her consciousness swirled toward the darkness that edged her vision. Relief won the battle with shame. All she knew was she had to get out of there.

Heedless of the fact he could have caught her before she reached the door, she ran, throwing it open. She bumbled past the twins, bolting for the front doors, and no one stopped her. Outside, she paused.

Dawn was creeping into an inky, dark sky. She had been here all night. The blue Tesla waited silently in the courtyard. Once she was inside, Niles pulled away from the curb with speed that earned her gratitude. She tore one of the water bottles from the storage space between the seats and drank it down. Her throat felt raw and hot.

They didn't speak. She glanced back once as they crossed the Vltava, heading toward the Academy. Behind the car, a black, two-door Audi with tinted windows kept a discreet distance. It followed them all the way to the turnoff for the garage, before racing into the dawn.

CHAPTER EIGHT

Azrael watched the Academy driver bundle a terrified Isela into the car from the window of his private study. He'd retreated there after she fled the drawing room.

She'd surprised him.

When he came to his senses, with her wrist in his hand and terror in her earthy grey eyes, he realized how close he'd come to losing the control he'd so carefully constructed to contain his power. And that wasn't the first time.

When Vanka tried to curse her, it had been easy to rationalize stepping between them, as a desire to preserve the code of the allegiance.

In truth, seeing her draw her little blade against one of the most powerful necromancers in the world intrigued him. It was apparent she was afraid from the moment she stepped into the room. Based on his experience with other mortals, even the most blustering were eventually reduced to helpless capitulation under the weight of their own terror in his presence. And that was without the rest of the allegiance in attendance.

Instead, Isela faced them as composed and self-possessed as any of the members of his Aegis: the warriors chosen to be his shield and council. She was afraid, but she refused to be cowed by it. Her courage, despite the fear, was foolish. In that room, it should have been deadly. He told himself he was forceful with Vanka to prove a point. At best, that was a partial truth.

Her mere presence had an uncanny way of destabilizing him.

When she arrived with Gregor, the sight of her disrupted his concentration. The brown skin on her calves below the skirt and above the neck of her blouse shimmered like fine velvet. Beneath it the suggested curves of her breasts and ribcage were second only to the slope of her fully covered hips in the fitted skirt. Her mouth, tantalizingly full, beckoned in a shade of pouty red. The tiny coils escaping from her upswept hair bounced at the back of her neck when she strode away from him.

When Gregor touched her, Azrael almost snapped. He'd agreed to the ruse, even insisted when Gregor balked. But the moment he saw the man's hands on her body, he wanted to tear Gregor's arms from his sockets. Gregor, who served, without question, for centuries. Azrael would have broken every bone in his hand if it had wandered even a centimeter lower.

And, by the gods, Gregor knew it and held her anyway. He had to, or she would have tried to run. Azrael was able to regain control with that knowledge, but that didn't stop the feeling he was gradually being unwound every time her storm cloud eyes swept over him.

At last she'd left the room. Trading revealing eveningwear for leggings and a bodysuit made her inexplicably more alluring. She moved with ease and surety through the warm-up, limbering her body with attention to detail and sensitivity. She had them all captivated, even before she began to dance.

He'd watched clips of her before but nothing compared to seeing her dance in person. When Azrael caught a glimpse of her dancing, she had almost thrown him off course.

She moved with grace that was her very nature, like water pouring down a rock, fire racing through a forest, an avalanche slicing down a mountain. She moved with fierce strength and a stark, unself-conscious beauty. She wasn't trying to be, or do, anything. She simply was. No wonder even the gods ceased their senseless bickering to mark her move.

Perhaps the failure of the summoning hadn't been her fault. It had been a lost cause to begin with. Most summonings were conducted at the site of death for a reason. He had thought it safer to bring the body back to castle where his wards could provide protection if anything went wrong.

The murderer had known what they'd been doing—by obliterating all traces of the brain and organs, they'd blocked his attempt to recall the victim. Luckily, no snares this time. Only the wall: a powerful block that expanded in all directions, ice-cold and shuddering with a force matching his own.

This time—likely thanks to Isela's dancing—he'd gotten close enough to batter himself against it for hours. His inability to break through the wall made him even more uneasy than when he'd accepted the task of finding the killer. Eluding snares and overcoming other necromancers' defenses was his specialty. The kind of power and skill it took to block him was beyond a minor necromancer. Not for the first time, he considered whether the killer might be among the allegiance.

Well, he had volunteered, he reminded himself.

And not one of the other members of the allegiance had protested his enlistment. He'd never known them to agree unilaterally on anything. As the newest member of their group, he had the distinct impression he'd been set up.

And saddling him with a dancer like Isela. Why couldn't they have picked anyone less… tempting.

He rubbed his hand over his eyes as the door opened behind him in response to his telepathic summons.

"Have Gregor follow them," he said. "Make sure she gets home safely. We'll need her again soon, I'm afraid."

"Done." Hesitation emanated from the long pause that followed.

"Yes, Lys?" he queried carefully.

"She has a fierce heart." If anyone would know, it would be Lysippe, the first of his Aegis. He trusted her judgment when his own was clouded.

"I know." Even dangling from his hand, Isela had been unrepentant.

"But she's not a warrior," Lysippe said, troubled. "And something is wrong with her. She hides it well, unless she's tired. Then she limps."

When the door closed, Azrael thought back on the moment in the library. She had danced for hours without wavering. No wonder she had collapsed. Exhausted and confused, the physical drain on her body reminded him of how fragile she was. And he had fallen on her like an animal in heat.

The combination of sweat and her natural scent was an aphrodisiac stronger than any perfume. Azrael hadn't known why he'd touched her, or exactly when, only that he did. He couldn't stop himself once he had the sensation of her skin against his fingertips.

He read the subtle response of her body to him and discounted the strength of her will. She pricked his pride by insinuating he would coerce her. Twisting her mind to keep her from speaking the wrong words to the wrong people was for the security of their mission and her own safety. The thought of having her come to him under duress or spell for his own pleasure disgusted him.

Azrael was not as handsome or charming as Paolo, but he had never had a problem seducing women. They came gladly, and he never took from them without giving amply in return.

He was out of practice, he realized shamefully. And this little dancer drew him, even when she was putting him at arm's length. It would be a nice diversion from the gravity of his assignment. The allegiance made it very clear what the consequences would be if she showed any signs of following the steps of the ill-fated Luther Voss.

Azrael wanted Isela to come to him willingly out of desire that overrode her fear. He resolved to show her another kind of dance, one ending with her sweaty and satisfied, longing for his touch. That, he would enjoy immensely.

* * *

"HIDING up here in your dusty old attic won't save you. We have the keys."

Isela rolled herself awake, peering at the clock on the bedside table. It was almost four in the afternoon. She barely remembered staggering into bed. She hadn't even bothered with a shower. She dragged her aching body from the thrashed pile of pillows and blankets and pulled an old terry robe around her shoulders.

"How did it go? I saw reports. You looked stunning, naturally." Yana bounded up the stairs, followed by Kyle and Trinh.

"My gods," Kyle said as they reached the top. "You two must have had some night."

Yana slammed her elbow into his ribcage as Trinh pushed around them both.

"I can't believe you kept this from us for so long," she cackled gleefully. "You should see the gossip sites. You are all over them." She paused. "What the hell happened to you?"

"That bad, eh?" Isela winced, pushing the tangled mat of her hair off her face.

"Sweet sugar patties," Yana whispered. "Have you seen yourself?"

They followed her to the mirror. The face that stared back was a stranger's: hollow cheekbones and dark circles under her eyes.

"Well, who doesn't want to lose an extra pound or two?" she said, trying to keep her voice light.

"More like ten," Kyle said, earning another jab in the ribs. He pulled a square, black box made of heavyweight board that must have come from a jeweler from behind his back. "Surprise. I guess this must be a makeup present for whatever happened last night?"

"Makeup present?" she echoed, glancing at the box, then the mirror.

Hours of dancing couldn't have done this to her. Maybe she was coming down with something.

Necromancer fever?

Kyle cut into her thoughts. "Tall, dark, and Teutonic delivered this a couple of hours ago—"

Trinh interrupted. "What the hell did he do to you?"

"I will have this man killed, butternut." Yana pounded her palm with her fist.

"He told Niles not to disturb you," Kyle finished, furious. "If we had known—"

"Nothing happened. I'm fine. I had to dance, and it was… bizarre, but no one hurt me. I promise." Tears smarted her eyes as relief swept visibly through her friends.

Isela set the box on the dresser, ignoring their dismay. If it was from the necromancer, she wasn't sure she was ready to know what was inside.

Yana looked indignant at the idea that a token from an admirer wasn't given some sort of priority. "You won't open it now?"

"After I shower and eat," Isela said. "And drink another gallon of water. I'm starving. Please tell me I smell croissants in that bag."

"Gods, you have a nose like a bloodhound." Trinh shook her head, lifting the paper sack from her favorite bakery. "Go on then."

Trinh emptied the fridge of a half dozen, almost-empty jam jars, and Kyle scrambled eggs while Isela showered. Isela loitered over their breakfast-for-dinner, accepting the crumb-filled plate of baked goods Kyle pushed across the table at her.

While Yana retrieved the box, Isela busied herself slathering the last croissant in jam, taking her time with every bite until Trinh impatiently removed her plate.

"You godsdancers eat like herds of starving elephants." Yana sniffed, poking three-quarters of a muffin on her plate. "I would never fit in my tights."

"I think she could use it," Trinh said.

"She's not even hungry anymore," Yana snapped. "She's delaying. Open the box already."

Isela wiped her hands and eased the lid off, dreading what lay inside.

Inside was a smaller velvet box. The hinge creaked softly as she opened it, revealing a hair brooch the size of her hand. Rows of cranberry-red jewels of varying sizes set in a plain metal base created elegant lines and whiplash curves evoking the wings of a songbird. It was an unmistakably old piece, commanding and delicate.

"I guess he liked that shirt," Kyle murmured, his voice hushed.

"What's not to like." Yana scowled. "Isela has lovely breasts. It left nothing to the imagination."

Isela choked on her water.

Yana sniffed. "Those aren't rubies—is that even gold? I don't see the fuss."

"No, you beautiful thing, it's worth much more." Kyle said, kissing her cheek. "They're bohemian garnets. This is turn of the century. Probably around the same time as the Municipal House itself. Wonder if this is Franta Anyz? He did commissions in the dining hall downstairs you know…"

Glimpsing something else in the bottom of the box, Isela hurried to take it back before they could see it. She closed it, shuddering dramatically. "Pretty. Well, what did I miss around here?"

Between the three of them, she got caught up on the usual assortment of Academy drama. She was amazed how much could be churned up in less than twenty-four hours. At last Yana and Kyle left to get drinks with some of the other troupe members, dragging a reluctant Trinh with them.

When they were gone, she dumped out the hair brooch and fished for the slim black rectangle she'd seen earlier. A data stick. She booted up her laptop. After the retinal scan and security clearance warnings, she clicked through folder after folder of scanned documents. One appeared to be the notes of a dancer. Not unusual, as most dancers kept records of their choreography, searching for patterns and successful sequences to incorporate in jobs. Madeline had pulled all the stored notes of former dancers in the library, but she had never seen these. She made out initials: LV. Recognition thrummed at the edge of her awareness, along with excitement.

Her phone buzzed. She set down her computer and raced across the room. She didn't recognize the number, but she was certain of the caller's identity, even before she answered.

"I apologize if I treated you briskly last night," Azrael began without preamble. "Your dancing was, in a way, successful. I was able to get closer than before to the answers we seek."

A bit of righteous pride surged in her, but she was too stunned by his admission to pay it much mind.

"Please accept the token and my regrets for my actions," he said.

"You can't buy me with a hairpin." Isela came to her senses.

"I should hope not," Azrael said evenly. "But I trust it provided a convenient cover for the real delivery, which you have just accessed on your computer."

Isela flushed. *Stupid, stupid, stupid mouth.*

"Yes," she admitted finally. "It was. Thank you. The information is—well, there's a lot of it, and I think it will be helpful, but it will take some time to go through and try to understand it all. Will we try again?"

A long pause followed her question. She thought some people might have been made anxious by those pauses, but she found herself soothed by the steadiness of them. Unlike the last time, when he had rushed through her concerns, she got the impression he was actually considering her words.

"Not with this one," Azrael said finally. "But yes, we will try again. I expect we'll have another opportunity soon."

So Isela didn't have much time. But at least she had better leads.

"I don't think I need to tell you that the information on that device will not be readable by anyone but you," he went on.

"This message will self-destruct, yeah, yeah, yeah."

Silence.

She cleared her throat. "I understand."

"Good."

"Azrael?" The name felt foreign in her mouth, like she was speaking in the tongue of a long-silenced language. Did the quiet grow that much more still on the other end of the line? Should she have called him 'sir' as Gregor advised? Too late now. She plowed on.

"I wasn't very diplomatic last night," she said haltingly. "But it's always a bad idea for dancers to become—involved—with their patrons. Professional boundaries and all that."

"Of course," Azrael said smoothly. His next words brought a flash of heat to her core, taking her right back to the drawing room the night before. "Deny your attraction to me if it makes you feel safe, Isela Vogel. But you will beg for me before we are done."

The air went out of her lungs. Despite her intention to start off on a better foot, Isela hung up on him.

CHAPTER NINE

Isela spent the rest of the week cross-referencing information from Azrael's data and Madeline's library. His research validated her suspicion that the gods were not morally superior beings, responsible for the creation of humanity. According to the necromancers, the beings known as gods were attracted to humans out of simple curiosity—lacking mortality or corporeal form, they were drawn to interfere in the short lives of those with physical bodies. The human body in motion proved an irresistible lure.

This was what the allegiance needed her for—her dancing could be used to attract a god so that Azrael could syphon off the greater power to boost his own.

According to the dancer's notes, it had been done. Dancers coded their notes to prevent exact replication, but with a little experimentation, she was able to grasp the basics of the sequences. Divya had designated a practice studio for her, removing it from the availability schedule of the school. Isela spent her afternoons there, tearing up her old choreography and incorporating what she had learned.

Claims of possession by gods ran rife in every religion in which dance played a part. But those were human exaggeration. Something in Azrael's data confirmed the dog-eared page she'd found in Madeline's library: gods had possessed mortals who opened themselves. Dancing for Azrael's intention was opening herself up in ways she hadn't before. It explained the time loss and what she thought of as the "bubble" she disappeared into when she was dancing. If the bubble was her ability to turn herself into a conduit for the gods' power, maintaining her awareness of it and controlling how far she went was critical.

On Sunday, Isela broke her self-imposed isolation. She donned old blue jeans, mud boots, and layers of long-sleeved T-shirts under a down jacket, tucked an old Ford baseball cap over her pigtails, and snuck out of the Academy.

At least she tried to.

By the time she reached the ground floor, word had spread and the hallways were mysteriously clustered with young dancers. She debated facing the mob versus fleeing when Divya clapped her hands sharply.

"What is this?" Without raising her voice, she sent the entire assembly retreating against the walls. "You have nothing better to do than create a fire hazard in my halls?" Her dark eyes pinned Isela where she stood. "Miss Vogel, my office. You're late."

"Ma'am." Isela bit back a smile as she hurried through the dispersing crowd.

She had to jog to keep up with Divya's pace. They passed the office and headed down the halls to the kitchens.

"Ma'am, where are we—"

"Don't 'ma'am' me." Divya cut her off. "You haven't ever before, don't start now. You think what's in the hallway is bad, what's outside will straighten your hair. Take the back entrance. Call Niles if you need a ride home."

Divya hustled her out the kitchen, and she slipped into the snow, unwatched and unnoticed. Isela skirted wide of the Academy's front doors where an army of photographers was camped out.

Isela wanted to throttle Gregor, Azrael, and the bloody PR person who had come up with this crazy idea. She wanted her life back.

She hopped on a tram that ran along the Vltava heading south. Leaving Old Town behind, the frenetic pace of holiday tourists quieted within a stop or two, and she was able to find a window seat facing the direction she'd come. She let the announcements of stops in muffled Czech lull her as an early sunset turned the gray sky pink around the edges. At a glimpse of the castle, framed by rose gold, she wondered what Azrael was up to at this hour.

Popular myth claimed that necromancers were creatures of the night. She thought Azrael might fit that description better than most, with his carved-from-marble face and luminous eyes. Maybe he didn't even get up until dusk. The image of him rising from a tomb like Dracula made the corners of her mouth twitch.

But his last words echoed in her head, sobering her. A little chill raced up her spine, and it had nothing to do with fear. He was beautiful, in the dangerous way of a predator whose survival hinged on its ability to strike without notice. His quiet demeanor was mesmerizing. He was like a hooded cobra, with eyes that could hold its prey captive until it struck.

To entertain the idea of that man in her bed was insanity.

It was how Azrael said it that had wormed the possibility into her head. There would be no awkward conversation afterward in which she blamed her focus on her career for her lack of ongoing interest in a relationship. There would be a beginning and an ending.

Isela didn't miss the implied pleasure either. Begging was a pretty bold claim. From a normal man, she would assume it was, at best, an empty boast. It sparked the defiant intention to resist him, but lurking curiosity tugged at her. She was a fool if she thought a man who'd been around for a couple hundred years hadn't picked up a few tricks.

Holy shit, she was considering fucking a necromancer.

Isela tucked her head onto her knees and almost missed her stop. She had just enough time to fling herself out of her seat and dive between the closing doors. Outside, she slipped on the snow-slicked cobblestones and landed in a slushy puddle. Her hip complained, and she was forced to sit still until the wave of pain passed. The startled onlookers gasped, but she waved them off.

"All part of the show," she grumbled, accepting the hand of an elderly gentleman with a surprisingly strong grip.

He winked one bright blue eye at her, and his neatly trimmed silver beard quirked up in a smile. The scent of tobacco and old books drifted from his flapping lapel. When he spoke, his thickly accented English was a comfortable second language. "And a fine one. May I suggest avoiding an encore performance? I don't believe your trousers can withstand more abuse."

Isela reached around to find she'd split her pants in the fall and groaned. The jeans were an old pair and her favorite. She swore in three languages, and the man chuckled.

When she looked up, he had unwound the scarf around his throat and held it out to her. She started to protest.

"Go on now," he said. "Take it."

Isela demurred, switching to Czech, which clearly delighted him. "But I can't."

Most people assumed at a glance that as a foreigner, she could not speak Czech. But her mother had insisted on mastery of the difficult tongue to make their new country home, and as her celebrity grew, it endeared her to her adoptive city.

"It's so rare I get to play the gentleman." His Czech was the most formal she had ever heard. He leaned in, sharing a confidence. "And to a renowned dancer of the gods, no less. I insist." He reached into his breast pocket and fumbled out a business card. She noted, beneath his heavy winter coat, his tweed suit and a vest with a dangling pocket watch chain. "If it is convenient, you can have the scarf sent to my business, payment on delivery."

The split in Isela's pants was letting in cold air. She took the card. The scarf unfolded to reveal a lovely strip of black fabric embroidered with red and gold roses. It wrapped tidily around her hips, blocking the draft.

"*Děkujeme*." She thanked him with a little curtsey.

He tipped his cap.

The next tram sent a gust of wind onto the platform, and he hooked the umbrella to his forearm. "That's my tram. Good evening, young lady."

When the tram was gone, she slipped between cars to cross the street.

* * *

Isela's family lived in an old neighborhood at the foot of Vysehrad; the ruins of a medieval fortress turned park at the south edge of the city. When they'd come to Prague, property had been cheap. Her father bought not just one flat but an entire building—a shabby, old, art nouveau thing that needed as much repair as it was worth. It had given him something to do in the first few years when work had been inconsistent, and it kept the boys out of trouble.

Her mother joked that her three sons were rambunctious, rebellious, and handsome—a terrible combination for a mother. The two eldest were two years apart, and though Isela had been close to her youngest brother, all three were closer in personality.

Once the eldest, Mark, hit puberty, her parents had bought a small cabin in the Czech forest where her mother took the boys most weekends to let them run wild, leaving Isela and her father to play card games and work on the building. It was impossible not to feel a little abandoned. Once she'd been accepted to the Academy, the demanding studies had solidified the space adolescence had built between them.

Initially, the family lived on the top floor of the eight-unit building, and the lower units provided rental income. Later, they converted the ground floor shop into a studio where her mother could teach yoga.

These days, her mother referred to the building as the "Vogel Compound." Two of her brothers lived with their families in units below the family flat. The youngest was working on renovations of another with the help of his girlfriend.

Isela loved her brothers without question, but their wives had earned their spots in her heart. After all, any woman who could break through the pack loyalty to isolate and win the heart of one of the Vogel boys had to be more than average. One by one, they turned the bachelors into responsible alphas, heads of their own households.

Her sisters-in-law were cautious around her at first—she spent so little time at the house that she was mostly family legend. She envied their bonds with one another and her mother. She'd been away from home for so long, in the most important ways, she'd almost forgotten her place.

And then one year, Isela received a pair of teardrop silver hoop earrings as a birthday present, signed, "your Sisters." The first time she wore the earrings home, she saw the pleasure in their eyes. They dragged her into the kitchen, plied her with margaritas, and begged her to tell them old stories of the boys. When she came down with the flu, they brought soup to her apartment. They dragged her along on enough girls'-night outings that she stopped being reluctant to intrude.

The Sisters had closed the distance the Academy had created and assured her that the safety net of the family would always catch her too.

Now it was up to her to protect them. That cooled any thoughts of itch scratching with the necromancer.

Isela let herself into the building with her key, following the long hall to the stairs. An elevator had been installed at some point, but old habits died hard. On the way up, she greeted Mrs. Simpson, another North American refugee, who had lived in the building since Isela was a kid.

Lukas Vogel was the kind of landlord that made tenants stick around. Only one apartment in the building wasn't held by a long-time resident: a shoebox studio he kept "for emergencies." At any point in time, it was occupied by a single person or a family in need. Sometimes they were students from her mom's free weekly community classes. Once or twice, it was somebody her father met on the street on his way home from work. In any case, they had a free place to stay until they were back on their feet. The apartment was on Mrs. Simpson's floor, and she kept an eye on the tenant.

The heavy aroma of a home-cooked meal reached her before Isela got to the top floor. The door was cracked, and the sound of laughter and conversation drifted out. She let herself in as the steamy wave of food-scented air blasted her nostrils. She paused in the entryway to peel off her boots and coat and call out a greeting.

A petite woman with a halo of curly hair rounded the corner: her middle brother's wife, Bebe. "Just in time! You can settle a debate. Mark says Chris lost his virginity to a Russian hooker, who he thought was his girlfriend for a week and a half before someone let him in on the fact she was a working girl."

From the kitchen behind her came peals of laughter and male voices raised in protest or agreement.

Isela sighed, a smile rising unbidden. Just another family dinner in the Vogel house. She hugged Bebe with all her strength.

"Oof, what's that for?" Bebe pushed her back after a moment. "And what are you wearing?"

Evie drifted into the entryway: taller, thinner, with wispy blond hair tied back in a loose ponytail and a flushed face from the heat of the kitchen. One of her twins, Thyme, snuggled contentedly on her hip. Evie flipped up the hastily tied scarf to reveal the grimy slush marks from her fall. "Ach, your pants!"

"You know me," Isela shrugged. "Clumsy to the last." She raised her voice to be heard in the kitchen. "And I think the lady you speak of was actually Ukra—"

Evie cut her off. "This is not a conversation for little ones with big ears to be hearing."

"Sorry, Evie." Isela tweaked her niece's nose.

The taller woman kissed her on both cheeks. "Bebe, get Issy some pants. Those are ruined."

Bebe dashed out the door before Isela could stop her, trotting down the stairs to her own flat on the floor below.

"Come, come." Evie herded her inside. "You're freezing."

Isela squeezed her niece's nose. "Hallo, Thyme."

"Hi, Tante Issy." The four-year-old slid down from her mother's hip.

"Now go play with Lil, Tavy, and the boys," Evie insisted. "Big people are being inappropriate… again."

The girl wrinkled her nose. "I don't want to play with the babies."

Evie rolled her eyes at Isela but took her daughter's hand. "Come. I'll play with you for a while."

They went their separate ways, her eldest sister-in-law following the sound of kids in the living room. After Evie and Markus' twins, Bebe and Tobias' three had come in quick succession. Her mother, Beryl, joked if they kept up, they'd be able to field a family football team. The din, Isela considered, was rivaled only by the adults in the kitchen.

In the humid, packed room, preparation and conversation immediately swallowed Isela. Markus, with his hickory-brown skin and coiled dark hair, was standing at the stove, stirring something that gave off mouthwatering aromas of onions, garlic, and venison. Tobias, the second son and the mirror image of their father's lanky build and oversized features, chopped tomatoes for salad, making a mess of it. The youngest, Christof, teased for his shockingly handsome face under a fringe of tawny hair, lounged with a beer beside the fridge. His arm cradled a lanky, cinnamon-skinned woman with an easy grin that everyone had high hopes would pin him down.

"Hey, sis." Christof slid his arm free to greet Isela.

"Little brother," Isela elbowed him out of the way to hug his girlfriend. "Chris, if she hasn't run away by now, I think you can keep your paws off her for five minutes. Hi, Fifi—"

Her mother interrupted. "Fifi is a small poodle."

"Yes, Ma," Isela said, smiling conspiratorially at the younger woman. "Good evening, Ofelia."

Presiding over it all, Beryl Gilman-Vogel cradled a glass of wine in one hand, looking like a queen from the top of the silver-threaded dreadlocks piled neatly on her crown to the fuzzy yellow and black bee slippers that had been a birthday gift from her grandchildren.

She never claimed to be a good cook, and the quality of the meals had vastly improved with the addition of the Sisters. Still, Sunday dinners had been a tradition since Isela was in diapers and continued after she'd left for the Academy. With the demands of her studies and dance training, getting home even once a week had been tough. After graduation, Isela made an effort at least once a month, but this had been a longer gap than usual, with rehearsing her demo performance for the gala and doing publicity work for the Academy in addition to her normal schedule of dancing.

Her mother put down her glass to embrace Isela. It was the kind of hug only a mother could deliver, and Isela felt her whole being settle. Thoughts of the necromancer and his kind vanished.

Beryl smelled like lilacs and the incense she used in her studio. Her flawless, walnut skin was smooth and warm against Isela's cheek. She was stronger than most women half her age. The hug wrung Isela out, cleansing her of all the accumulated worry, reminding her who she was and that she was home.

"Missed you, Little Bird," her mother murmured in her ear.

"Missed you too, Mom." She heard her own voice crack.

"Papa's in the library." Beryl let her go. "Go say hi before dinner. Said he had a headache."

Isela nodded, taking the glass of wine Mark offered.

At the end of the long hall was a small room their father had converted into a library. In it were a few books but mostly his machines. He'd been into computers as long as she'd been alive, working as a software engineer until his retirement.

"Caught you nappin'," she said, tapping the lowered newspaper spread on his lap.

She folded to her knees at the foot of his chair beside the window.

Startled, her father looked down at her, and her eyes met their match. Once, their hair had been the same color too—a shade of dark chocolate feathered with caramel—but now his was mostly gray. How long had it been since she had been home? Her schedule had been full, and she'd missed a few Sunday dinners. But no more than a few months, surely. He appeared older. Her memories were of a strong man that hefted her as easily as a bucket of paint. She noted how the paper trembled when he put it down to greet her.

"Little Bird."

Unlike her mother's hug, her father's left her worried. His arms didn't close completely, and she detected the faintest tremor in his hands. His sweater, an old favorite her mother had been begging him to toss out for years, hung from his frame. His usual scent, dry and warm, like beach sand with the hint of hazelnuts he always snacked on while he worked, had a curious and slightly unpleasant tang. He looked frail.

But his mind was still as quick as ever. When she sat back, he tapped his paper. "Tell me about this boy of yours."

Isela groaned, glancing at the photo on the front of the society section. The montage featured shots of her on the bridge, arm in arm with Gregor, and slipping into the black sports car.

"Oh, Papa." She sighed.

* * *

IT WAS no better at dinner.

Bebe fixed Isela up with a pair of flare-legged corduroy pants in her own signature style: hippie bohemian. Isela promised to return them next week, but Toby shook his head.

"She can't even button them anymore, sis." Toby tossed a fore-lock of wavy brown hair out of his eyes as he pushed his glasses up his nose. "Keep them."

Bebe's glare would have sliced a brick in half. "Three beautiful children and you're disappointed I don't fit in my college cords anymore?"

"Baby, you're even more beautiful than you were in college," Toby said and refilled her wineglass. Isela nodded approvingly, and he winked. "I'm slow, but I catch on."

"Psst, Issy," Fifi said when Beryl was distracted. "Tell me about this guy, Gregor."

The Hessian? She almost said in response.

"What about him?" Isela queried slowly as she tried to decide how much they knew and what would be safe to tell them.

Fifi rolled her eyes, giving Bebe one of those "do you believe this one" expressions she must have picked up from Evie. She fit right in. If Chris didn't marry her, Beryl was surely going to adopt her.

"He's a total hunk." Fifi wagged her eyebrows.

"Excuse me?" Chris chimed in, tugging at her elbow.

She pushed him away. "How long have you been dating, really? You never mentioned him. And is he as scary in real life as he is in the pictures?"

"Scary?" Isela peeped, suddenly aware that all eyes were on her. She dragged her fork through the remnants of her goulash.

"You know he ripped out some guy's eyeballs and stuck them to the guy's door for disobeying his boss." Mark jabbed his fork into his last dumpling for emphasis.

"Mark, the girls." Evie glared as their daughters' eyes fixed on their father.

Mark lifted his weighted fork, waving it in their direction. "Which is what happens to people who don't follow orders, like when it's time to brush teeth and go to bed."

"Mark!" Evie smacked his bicep as two pairs of eyes saucered.

"No, I—" Isela said, shaking her head. "I don't think he… did that."

"You don't *think*…" Toby pushed his glasses up his nose.

"Well, it hasn't exactly come up in conversation." Isela sighed, exasperated.

Maybe coming to a family dinner before this was all over had been a bad idea.

"Yeah, that's not the kind of thing you mention over dessert, Tobias," Mark said, pitching his voice high to mimic Isela. "So, the eyeballs, were they squishy, or did they pop?"

"Markus Garvey Vogel!" Beryl barked.

"Sorry, Ma," he said as he stuck his tongue out at Isela.

"Not my fault you are a total blockhead." Isela wagged hers back at him. "Lilach, Thyme, your papa is a Cro-Magnon. Can you say that?"

Thyme shrieked laughter and tumbled out of her chair, throwing herself into Isela's arms. Lilach still looked to be losing her war with tears.

Isela scooped up her nieces, inhaling the smell of sweet nutmeg and crayons, and cradling their warm bodies against her own. Even the jab of bony elbows and knees as they settled more comfortably against her felt right.

"Seriously, Issy," Chris pressed. "This guy, Gregor, he's good to you?"

Isela tried not to think of how terrified she'd been when he led her to the basement morgue. "Yeah, he gave me an incredible hundred-year-old hair clasp."

The defensive lie came easily to protect her family. The Sisters cooed. Evie gave Mark an elbow, and he glared at Isela.

"I mean, he treats you *right*?" Chris asked, one eyebrow raised.

Of all her siblings, she was the closest to him. They'd shared a room until she'd left home. Mark and Toby were older, tougher, and it wasn't until she and Chris formed an alliance that they were able to keep the older boys from ganging up on them. But she'd gone to the Academy to study, and he'd hit puberty and become one of the pack.

"He's a good guy," Isela reassured them. "Loyal. And he's not the guy to mess around with either. I'm safe with him."

That was true, she thought. Mostly.

Chris didn't look satisfied, but Isela saw the tender way Fifi put a hand on his forearm. He shifted, going still.

Their secret language made her heart twinge. She was happy for them. Of the three brothers, Chris had always been the best-looking and taken the least seriously. He'd been mocked for the girls that fawned over him, even as his heart repeatedly led him astray. He deserved to be loved, and Fifi had been better than anyone Isela could have picked for him. Isela had never seen him so quietly confident as he was with Fifi. She seemed to ground him in a way he desperately needed. Her eye caught the sparkle on Fifi's slim finger, and she grinned.

"Baby brother, you didn't!" she scolded teasingly, mock glaring at them both as she grabbed for Fifi's hand. "Since when?"

Ofelia flushed, a beautiful rosy glow in her cheeks, and Chris snugged his arm around her shoulders. "It should have been the other way around, but…"

Isela cocked her head, finally noticing the slight fleshiness in the girl's cheeks. "You're pregnant."

Chris expression widened to that big, male, self-satisfied grin she recognized well after three nieces and two nephews.

"And the Vogel fertility once again asserts itself," Beryl grumbled.

The whole table dissolved into laughter.

"I'm due in June," Fifi answered her next question. "We're getting married over New Year's. It's going to be a bit of a shotgun affair. Can you be there?"

Isela smiled and answered without thinking, "Of course! With bells on." The next thought came before she could check it. *If I'm still alive.*

After dinner, she found herself banished to the living room with the women and children while the men took over cleanup and dishes.

"Mom," Isela said, looking up from playing a game of Memory with Thyme. "Is Papa all right?"

Her mother smiled but did not look up from her book. "Of course he is. He's just tired. I thought when he'd retired, he would wander down the studio for a class or start coaching the Vogel football club. But your father is your father. He doesn't change—still fixing up this old place and tinkering with boxes."

Isela nodded, unsatisfied with the answer.

"What about you, Isela?" Beryl turned the tables, fixing her in a gaze that missed little. "Are you all right, really?"

Isela felt herself flush as the Sisters looked up as one.

"Everything is good." Isela shrugged. "I'm staying super busy with work."

"And Gregor," Bebe added.

"And Gregor," Isela said, "is definitely taking up a lot of time right now."

Beryl frowned, and Isela knew her mother saw right through her. Always had, always would.

"Isela Rose Vogel."

In the ensuing silence, a persistent buzzing caught everyone's attention.

"Phone," Evie said.

"That's me." Isela levered herself off the floor, racing to the hooks by the door where she'd left her purse.

She fished out her phone, and her stomach fell as Gregor's name and image flashed on the screen. She recognized the tie from their night "out," so he must have added it when she was unconscious in the study. She hit dismiss and silenced the phone. According to the history, he had called twice. *Shit.* When she returned to the living room, she felt like she was walking into a wake. Who did she think she was fooling? This had been a terrible idea.

"Who was it?"

"The Academy," Isela lied anyway. "Kyle probably. He always forgets Sunday dinners."

Beryl smiled. "Ah yes, he's a good boy. Why didn't you bring him? You know he's always welcome here."

"He was…" Isela began. *Why didn't she?* That would have been the smart move. Kyle would have distracted everyone with his stories and sense of humor. Her brothers liked Kyle. Kyle would have covered for her.

Her phone buzzed again. Insistently. *Hadn't she switched it to silent?*

"Do you need to take that?" Bebe looked at her strangely.

"No, it's fine," Isela said, clearing her throat. "He can leave a message."

"So does this Gregor fellow eat?" Beryl asked.

"Food?" Isela echoed.

"You should bring him to dinner sometime." Evie clarified the hint as a suggestion. She passed Bebe a worried look.

"Yeah!" Fifi chirped, looking up from her bridal magazine. "I would love to meet him."

"We all would," Mark finished from the doorway.

Isela wanted to melt into a puddle on the floor.

"Tante Issy." Thyme tugged her arm. "Tante Issy, who is *him*?"

She was saved—or damned—by the sound at the door. With panic, she realized it wasn't the buzzer of the downstairs door but a knocking on the door to the flat. The room went silent.

CHAPTER TEN

Azrael looked out over the city. The snowfall had increased steadily over the past few hours. As daylight waned, thick, round flakes settled into sticky piles. He felt the coming of night in his bones, as he always did, the tug of darkness as welcoming as a blanket. His senses expanded with its coming.

The whole city flared to life from the dullness of its daytime existence. Millions of lives, busy with their own concerns, envies, fears created an endless background droning during the day. Some of which he knew involved him—predominantly fear. His mentor, guiding him as he grew into his powers, insisted it was better to be feared than to be loved. It certainly made ruling them easier. As the majority of minds surrendered to sleep, he could more easily tap into the deeper sense of the city itself and the earth beneath it.

He remembered, seemingly lifetimes ago, when his powers had only come to him at night. It was that way with all necromancers. Many remained bound to the darkness for their power. But a few, like him, evolved. It was the first sign he was to become something more. The most powerful were rare; it was almost a decade before he met another who could manipulate energy to the same degree he could and more than a century before meeting the one who would become his mentor and shepherd him into his full power. Still, they all had their small differences, unique talents that made no two the same.

They kept those differences hidden from humans. Let it be believed that their powers extended only to communication with and raising of the dead, mind reading, and thought control. Let them believe that necromancers controlled the entities humans insisted on calling gods. It was enough to keep mortals from once again dabbling in a world they knew nothing about.

The door opened, and Gregor entered. Azrael could sense the blood and death that clung to the Hessian before the man spoke.

"There's been another," Azrael said, without turning.

The susurrus of fabric accompanied Gregor's bow. "It seems to fit the pattern, master."

"Who discovered it?"

"The apprentice." Gregor stood in the shaft of light from the door, his features cast in darkness.

"You left it as it was found." Azrael felt anticipation growing in him, the shift from waiting inertia to movement. He found himself excited by the prospect of a challenge. His thoughts flashed to the dancer. Isela. It had been almost a week since she stood trembling before him, meeting his eyes despite her fear. Another challenge.

"As you commanded," Gregor said, breaking his thoughts, taking a careful pause. "Azrael, are you certain it's not best to retrieve the body. You mean to do this… there?"

Gregor served willingly, but he knew enough of gods and necromancers to be cautious.

"I do," Azrael said. "Bring the dancer, and call in the rest of the Aegis. We may need them."

CHAPTER ELEVEN

The knock came again. Resonant. Insistent.

"Expecting anyone, Ma?" Mark asked.

Toby appeared in the kitchen doorway beside his brother. Chris was a step behind.

On the other side of the door was a—sure to be furious—solider. *Fuck.* Isela took a breath.

"What is everyone standing around for?" Lukas Vogel pushed past his sons, a dishrag in hand. "Even I can hear the door. Has everyone forgotten their manners?"

"Lukas," Beryl cautioned, watching her daughter's face, as Isela called, "Papa, wait."

But he was already at the door. Isela hurried forward, not sure what she would do, only that she would put herself between her family and death if it was required.

Gregor stood on the other side. Tonight he wore a suit, with a white shirt and no tie. The knee-length, wool coat and loose scarf around his neck completed the look of a casual executive, fresh from a late dinner meeting. A red kerchief was folded in his breast pocket. He was wearing his most easygoing smile, but Isela saw the ice when his eyes flashed on her.

"*Guten Abend, Herr Vogel.*" He spoke formally, ignoring her to address her father. "I apologize for disturbing your family at such an hour, but I have been trying to reach your daughter."

Blinking, Lukas glanced from the man to skim the four young women. It seemed to take him a moment to find Isela.

"Well, with all the commotion, I'm not surprised Issy didn't hear her phone," he said, finally offering his hand. "Lukas Vogel."

"Gregor Schwarz." He took her father's hand and gave a little bow. If he'd added Prince of Darkness as a title, she wouldn't have blinked.

"Please come in," Lukas said, pleased.

His sons had other ideas. Moving together, they blocked the entrance to the living room.

Gregor came up short. "My, my, the legendary Vogel boys."

That was how she'd always thought of them: the Vogel boys. But looking at them now, she saw the men they'd become while she spent her life learning to dance for gods. It wasn't just that they had families of their own now. Assembled and on guard, they seemed formidable in a way she had never considered. Not one of them stood under six foot tall. All inhabited their broad shoulders and deep chests with functional ease. Even Toby, in his glasses and cardigan—so much like their father in his easygoing, if occasionally inept, way—was not to be dismissed in stature. Young wolves, all.

Isela darted around Chris to stand between Gregor and her family.

"Ahh, everyone," she said. "This is Gregor, Gregor, this is everyone."

Her brothers stood between Gregor and the rest of the room, and the Sisters clustered their respective broods behind them. In the No Man's Land between, Lukas seemed puzzled by his family's behavior while Beryl watched with hawk eyes and a stiff spine.

"My mom, Beryl." Isela coughed.

"Frau Vogel." Another crisp bow.

"Gregor, these are my brothers," she said. "Mark, Toby, Chris—this is..."

"We heard," Toby said.

"Gregor Schwarz," Mark finished.

"And these, I assume, are the lovely ladies Vogel?"

"Evie, Bebe, and Fifi," Isela rushed.

"What is everyone standing around for?" Lukas queried. In

German, he added, "Please, Mr. Schwarz. We were just about to serve tea, or would you like coffee?"

Everyone started talking at once.

Isela: "We really have to go."

Beryl: "I'm sure you have a moment."

Mark: "Pop, maybe they have a date."

Fifi: "Yeah, come in. We want to hear all about life in the castle."

Finally, Gregor: "Of course we have a few minutes for coffee. I would not be so rude as to snatch your daughter away."

Isela craned her neck to look at him in surprise. The smile was as casually charming as ever, but the glint in his eye suggested snatching her was exactly what he'd like to do, preferably by the hair.

"Papa, we really have to go." She shook her head. "I completely forgot this *thing* we have. I was going to go right after dinner, but..."

But Lukas was already taking Gregor's coat, complimenting the fine construction of it.

"We really should get these little munchkins to bed," Evie said, moving slowly under the weight of a daughter on each hip.

Bebe followed, herding Isaac and Octavia in front of her, Philip in her arms. "It was... nice to meet you, Mr. Schwarz."

"Gregor, please," he said. Isela wanted to kick him, but was positive it wouldn't even register.

Bebe and Evie gave him wide berth, scooting the gaping kids out the door.

"Home soon, Eves," Mark called.

Evie sent him a long look, one of those bits of intimate couple conversation.

Isela detected one-part plea and another part warning. She wanted to implode and erase her presence from the universe. How could Gregor not see this for what it was? Her mom looked like she wanted to jump across the entryway and rip out his throat with her bare hands.

This was not going well.

She found herself on the love seat beside Gregor, balancing a cup of untouched coffee on her knee to keep her hands busy while he and Lukas talked about the old country, and her brothers looked on as if they were deciding on an angle of attack. Only Fifi, cheery and oblivious, prattled on excitedly about the newspaper reports chronicling their relationship and begging for details. Isela haltingly manufactured stories while hoping Gregor was listening with half an ear to corroborate, if needed.

"No, no, darling," he paused in his conversation, switching to English as he smiled at Fifi. "You were dissatisfied with the prawns at Čtyři Růže. She complained about this all the way to my flat."

Fifi looked charmed. Beside her, Chris gently edged her behind his shoulder.

"So, Greg," Chris said, eyes glinting with an expression Isela recognized immediately. "I can call you that, can't I?"

Isela glared at him. *Shut up*. She nudged him with her foot.

"Please," Gregor nodded. "I find the Vogel nicknames charming."

"For which of my sister's best qualities did you fall for first?" Chris questioned.

Gregor's hand slid onto her knee, fingertips gently resting on her inner thigh. The air went out of the room. Isela fought the urge to smash her coffee cup into his perfect face.

"Why her legs, of course," he said, and now his smile resembled nothing so much as bared teeth. He laughed softly and inclined his head. "You'll forgive me for not having the gentleman's answer. But I am only a man and so flawed. It wasn't until I was lucky enough to meet her in person that I discovered her sparkling personality and… inner fortitude."

Toby gripped Chris' shoulder before the younger man could lunge. Isela gave him credit that it looked enough like a casual touch to be passable. But she had reached her limit. She set down her cup and stood, knocking Gregor's hand away in passing.

"We really have to go," she said. "*Now*."

Gregor smiled apologetically at her family, spreading his hands. "As my lady commands. My dear, what are you wearing?"

"Pants," Isela snapped.

Back in the entryway, Isela found their coats. Gregor helped her into her coat as her father promised to show him his full collection of seventeenth century German family crests on his next visit.

Isela slipped away to hug the boys and Fifi. Chris held her the longest.

"If he—" he began in her ear, threateningly.

"You'll do what?" She sighed. "Gods, Chris, don't be stupid. Promise me."

He hugged her again. "Doesn't matter, Issy. We'll kill him."

Tears stung her eyes. "You guys have the Sisters and Mom and Papa to take care of. I can handle this."

She turned to face her mother. Beryl didn't look happy.

"It's fine, Mom," she assured. "Please. The boys…"

Beryl squeezed her so tightly the air left her lungs. "I'm not worried about them, Little Bird."

Isela swallowed the knot of emotion in her voice. She hugged her dad, and finally they were in the hallway, headed down the stairs.

* * *

For the first time since Gregor walked in the door, Isela was able to draw a deep breath as she led him away from her family. On the second floor, the door opened, and she almost crashed into Mrs. Simpson.

The old woman took one look at Gregor and jerked into her apartment, slamming the door. The locks clicked.

Gregor's smile flared. "That little old woman has more sense than all your brothers put together."

Isela glared at him. "You came into their home, with their families around them, bearing your teeth and pawing at me. What did you expect them to do, roll over and show their bellies?"

He snorted, following her down the long hall to the front door.

Isela spun on him, full of rage and anguish. "I took this job willingly. I will do what he asks, if it kills me, but you stay the fuck away from my family. Do you understand? Or so help me—"

"You'll what?" Amused, Gregor pulled the heavy door open easily.

She growled, hands fisted in impotent rage, and marched past him into the night.

"That's what I thought," he said. The lights on his black Audi flashed as the doors unlocked. "And if you had answered your phone, like a good little dancer, that whole scene could have been avoided."

He opened the door before she could grab the handle. She flung herself into the car with such violence it rocked. One perfectly groomed eyebrow rose.

"You did hear it ring," he said evenly as he leaned into the open door.

She flushed and looked away.

"Azrael's wards ensured it would always stay with you and you would always be drawn to our calls," Gregor explained casually. "The night you fled the castle, you neglected to bring your bag but somehow held on to your phone, did you not?"

He closed the door behind her, leaving her to think about it. When he climbed in the driver's side, his smile was gone.

"Yes, but—" she began.

"But nothing," he said, starting the engine with a roar. "You flirt with danger when you keep the necromancer waiting for even an hour. You have him to thank for that little *tête-à-tête* upstairs. If it had been up to me, I would have broken down doors and dragged you out by your nape. Over the bodies of your precious brothers, if need be."

The image pushed Isela dangerously close to tears. Her voice was gravelly with emotion when she spoke, but it did not shake. "A *tête-à-tête* is an intimate conversation between *two* people."

Gregor's hands flexed on the steering wheel. She wondered if she could get to the blade strapped to her calf. If he was going to snap her in two, she didn't have to make it easy.

When he started to laugh, she flinched. He relaxed into the seat, and the car picked up speed. He glanced at her, his expression full of homicidal mirth.

"I'm beginning to like you, dancer." He chuckled, switching his eyes again to the road. "You're spunky. Now put on your seat belt. Even if you succeeded in cutting me, the doors are electronically secured, so you won't get far. We've wasted enough of the master's precious time as it is playing this game."

"He's your master, not mine," she grumbled, drawing the belt across her chest.

Gregor smiled again, patting her knee as if she were an obedient child. She jerked her knee away.

"Eyes on the road." Isela gasped as headlights shone in the windshield.

He nimbly directed the car through traffic, handling the loss of traction without sacrificing speed.

"You're a fucking sociopath," she said, her breath coming back reluctantly.

"Name calling, Little Bird?"

"Don't call me that!"

He grinned at her.

Isela needed a subject change before she tried to stab him anyway. She glanced out the window. They'd turned away from the river, leaving Old Town and the castle behind them.

"Where are we going?"

That did it. His maniacally jovial mood was replaced with the overtly dangerous one she knew best.

"There's been another."

She glanced out the window. "Shouldn't we be headed to the Academy? I can't dance in this."

"Your bag is in the trunk," he said. "Director Sauvageau was good enough to pack for you and provide me with your location. After a little persuasion, of course."

"Did you hurt her?"

He sucked his teeth. "You think so little of me."

"You just threatened to kill my family because I didn't pick up my phone."

"Only the adult males, according to the hunter's code," he clarified. "And no, I didn't hurt your mentor. Azrael prefers more diplomatic techniques. As his servant, I oblige whenever possible."

He sounded disappointed.

"Why aren't we going to the castle?"

"The body is not at the castle."

"Why wouldn't it be in the morgue?" she drilled, still processing what she had heard. Azrael preferred diplomacy. At what point had diplomacy been exhausted and he'd decided to remove that man's eyes and nail them to his front door?

"Since the last attempt was unsuccessful, Azrael thought it best to return to the traditional way of summoning," Gregor said, interrupting her thoughts.

She understood that much from her reading. "At the place of death?"

"Prepare yourself, dancer," he murmured, whipping the car off the main road into a dingy neighborhood south of the fortress. "As they say in America, things are about to get very interesting."

Gregor pulled the car into an open slot in front of a shabby, functionalist building covered in graffiti. Isela recognized the bearded Viking look-alike from the night on the bridge and one of the stern-faced Polynesians out front. Otherwise, the street was quiet. If there was a murder here, she would have expected the police, at least out of an appearance of duty. But the street was silent as any other.

"That's not really an American saying," she muttered, climbing out of the car. "Most people do it with your accent—*à la* Freud."

Gregor sucked his teeth again, pulling a familiar bag out of the trunk. "Freud was Austrian and a fool. I am German."

"And an ass," Isela muttered, slamming the door so hard his smile flattened into a thin line.

"Such a filthy mouth, for a pretty little bird."

Isela shouldered her bag and let him lead her through the snow to the door of the ground-level store. Over the door hung a sign, *Antikvariat*. She took a deep breath and walked into hell.

CHAPTER TWELVE

Something about the address and book-lined walls, interrupted only by dusty antiques, tugged at Isela's memory. She had never been there, but she knew this place. The shop was quiet as only a bookstore could be. The ground floor was a warren of twisting halls and side rooms. She followed Gregor to the stockroom and down a short hallway.

A tangy, burnt metallic stench grew stronger as they moved deeper into the building. It had been the same at the morgue but fainter, more sterile.

The hair rose on the back of her neck. She almost collided with Gregor's back.

"Eager to dance with the dead, are we?" he murmured. "Stay here."

Gregor opened the door on a small room at the end of the hall.

She peered around his arm. The room was a tiny apartment: kitchenette, sofa, reading chair, and a small TV. It had been tidily kept, done in earthy fabrics that made the windowless room feel more like the den of some small animal.

"Rory." Gregor greeted the second of the Polynesian twins standing guard just inside.

"He's waiting." The bigger man grunted.

Gregor beckoned Isela forward.

She stepped through the doorway to his side. Because of the

darkness and the colors, it took her a moment to recognize the source of the pervasive odor.

She had no idea how much blood a human body contained, but she was certain whoever had lost this much hadn't survived. Knowing academically that someone had died at her destination was one thing. Being confronted with the blood all over the walls and floor, pooling and congealing into dark puddles, shocked the breath out of her body.

"Exhale." Gregor's voice came as if from a great distance. "You must exhale."

She shook her head doggedly, because inhaling again meant taking in more of the smell. A hand forced her chin around. Gregor's blue eyes stared into her face as her own eyes darted back to the room around him.

"Look at me," he whispered. "Dancer. Look at me and exhale."

She jerked her gaze into his, and the breath left her at once. She followed it with an inhale, then a slow, steady exhale.

"You're much better at following orders when you're frightened," he said, smiling cheerily. "Now keep breathing. Nasal fatigue will take over soon."

She tried to nod, but he held her fast.

"Are you going to vomit?" When she didn't answer, he repeated his question, giving her a little shake. "It's going to get worse from here, better to do it now."

She shook her head, swallowing hard. "No, I'm fine. Let go."

"Follow me," he ordered as he removed his hand. "Watch your feet."

The bigger man stepped aside to let them pass. Isela didn't want to go any farther, but she followed anyway, tiptoeing around the red on the floor. At a second doorway, Gregor paused. When he looked back, he was careful to block her view.

"Put your arms around my neck," he ordered.

The only thing worse than walking through a room-turned-abattoir might be that command, she considered. She sighed and obeyed anyway. He slid one arm around her waist, lifting her easily, and took a leap. She looked back at the pool of blood they'd crossed, and her stomach quivered. She buried her face in his shoulder, and his hand swept behind her knees. He smelled like sun-soaked earth with an edge of steel. She breathed in deep and closed her eyes.

"Master, I've brought the dancer." Gregor's voice rolled through her chest, bringing her head upright fast.

The dark warren opened up into an enormous space, much bigger than should have been possible from the shop outside. One wall was lined with cabinets, the countertop full of bowls and vials. The smell was worse here.

Impossibly, there was more blood, and there were pieces. Body parts. In the center of it all, with the cat-eye shine in his gaze, stood Azrael. He wore a long black duster that had to be leather but moved with a velvet softness and absolute lack of reflection as he turned to them.

Suddenly aware of how intimate it must look to have her hands wrapped in Gregor's lapels and her face in his neck, she tried to let go. His arms locked around her like metal bands. She wriggled, but it did no good. She knew that shine in Azrael's eyes now for what it was: hunger.

And Gregor—who must have known what kind of game he was playing—was enjoying himself. He ducked his head casually and took a deep sniff of the skin behind her ear. A shiver went through her, and the light in Azrael's eyes flared.

She sensed being between them might not be a good idea.

Abruptly, Azrael turned his back on them.

"I've cleared you a space in that corner of the room. Will it do?"

Gregor dumped her unceremoniously on her feet and fastidiously tugged at his lapels. Isela stared.

"An answer," Azrael barked. His voice sheared through the jumble of thoughts as she struggled to reconcile all the pieces, trying to make a man out of the parts scattered around the room.

She jerked her eyes away from the mess to follow his gaze. "Yes—it will, I can—yes."

Isela tiptoed across the room, trying not to look, but a bit of shine on the floor caught her attention. It was a gold chain, attached to an ornately carved pocket watch from another century. Her mouth began to form words, even as her stomach roiled.

Gregor took a step toward her. "Dancer."

Her eyes darted between him, Azrael, and the floor as she

fumbled through her jacket, withdrawing a small blue rectangle of paper. All the elements came together: the address, the pocket watch, the smell of tobacco and old books. The intelligent, mischievous eyes. Oh gods, were those his eyes in the corner? She saw Gregor moving toward her through a blur of her own tears, and she held up her hands to ward him off. Darkness crept around the edges of her vision.

"Fuck, she's going to blow," Gregor said.

Some small part of her brain was pleased she'd annoyed him.

"I know him," she said, her gaze careening around the room one more time.

Both men stilled. Azrael's shoulders snapped up, his nostrils flaring, and he held out a hand to stop Gregor.

"I mean, I just met him, tonight," she murmured. "He loaned me his scarf when I fell getting off the tram. He was a nice old man. He recognized me—most people don't if I'm dressed… like this."

The worlds tumbled out of her, and her stomach won the battle.

Gregor was fast, she gave him that. He had an antique pot under her face and an arm around her waist before her stomach clenched. He slipped the card from her fingers as he eased her to a clean spot. She braced her palms on the floor, shoulders hunched, letting her body give up its recent meal.

It was going to be a long night.

* * *

Azrael watched Gregor crouch over her as she emptied her stomach, supporting her weight easily with one hand. He tucked a stray curl behind her ear, murmuring a few comforting words in German. It came naturally to him, even though he'd buried the last of his bloodline when old age took them a century before.

That was when he'd truly gone cold, Azrael considered. Gregor's family had been all that tethered him to humanity. After that, he'd become a purer solider than even Azrael had intended. In the last hundred years, Azrael had begun to wonder if Gregor had become too detached, too dangerous.

He should have been relieved to see this sign of his old humanity. Instead, that insensible, possessive fury threatened his calm. He felt Gregor's eyes on him but was helpless to quiet his rage. When Gregor smiled, Azrael realized he knew exactly what danger he was in. Just as when he'd entered, he taunted Azrael by continuing to stroke her hair. Maybe Gregor really was losing his mind.

"Can you stand?" the Hessian asked her, the edge returning to his voice.

Isela bobbed her head, wiping her mouth with the back of one hand. Leaning on his arm, she clambered to her feet. She withdrew herself from Gregor's support as quickly as possible. The color had drained from her face, save for two flushed spots under eyes shining with moisture. She didn't seem to be aware she was shaking so hard her teeth chattered. Gregor shed his coat, draping it over her shoulders. He examined the card and crossed the distance, passing it casually to Azrael.

"Havel Zeman," Azrael murmured. "Antique books and curiosities."

"That was Zeman's cover." Gregor nodded. "He's been licensed to practice in the city for almost fifty years. Scrying and past-life recollection mostly."

"He was a psychic?" Isela chimed in hesitantly.

"Tell us everything," Gregor ordered.

Isela took a breath, relating the story. When she was done speaking, her voice had stopped trembling, and some color had come back into her face.

"He touched you," Azrael said.

Isela misread the tone of his question for jealousy, frowning as she glared at him. "He helped me up. I fell…"

Zeman needed physical contact to read minds, Gregor said telepathically.

Telepathy was a simple matter of projecting thoughts and emotions. Mind reading was more complex. The ability to read minds varied by the strength of the reader and the mind of the subject: weak readers could pick up the occasional stray thought or emotion, but it took a strong reader to view memories without the subject's participation. A much stronger reader than Zeman had been.

Azrael shook his head. *Isela's mind is too strong to be picked apart with a brief touch.*

Willpower tempered human minds against casual exploration. He knew from experience Isela's mind was strong, hardened likely by the discipline it took to master dance.

He recognized her, Gregor pushed. *If there is chance that Zeman picked up that she's working for the allegiance.*

For him. The ties between them were growing tighter, drawing Isela deeper into association with him. He'd assumed only one dance would be needed to break down the barrier preventing him from identifying the killer. Then the allegiance would pay the balance of her fee, releasing her from service, and he would hunt down the killer with his Aegis.

But did our killer bother to read Zeman, Azrael countered. *Or did they get what they came for already?*

We can't know that. Gregor thought grimly.

There's one way to find out.

Isela's gaze swung between them and Azrael felt her frustration building at the apparent silence. "Am I… Did someone kill him because I'm helping you?"

"No," Gregor snapped, distractedly.

Azrael weighed telling her the truth against keeping his suspicions secret.

"I don't think so," Azrael said, ignoring Gregor's scowl of disapproval. "But he may have learned you were brought on by the allegiance to assist me when he touched you."

"If the killer knows we're onto him," she said. "Because Zeman read my mind…"

He watched the realization solidify on her face. For a moment her eyes grew wide and wet as shock went to horror. Azrael needed to get her dancing—occupied.

"I'm going to find out exactly what Zeman knew when he was killed," he said. "And what killed him."

Isela nodded, rolling her shoulders back and lifting her chin as determination hardened her face. "And I need to dance."

"Lysippe and Dory will keep anything outside from coming in,"

Azrael said to Gregor. "You and Rory hold the next room. I want the others on alert."

When Gregor was gone, he faced her. She stared up at him, jaw clenched.

"If you are going to vomit again, do it now," he advised. "Once we begin, we can't stop until it's done."

Her cheek twitched, but she shook her head.

"I can't let you change elsewhere," he said, gesturing to her bag. "But I will turn my back, if it pleases you."

"Thank you."

He listened to the whisper of fabric, contemplating the mess before him. As before, the brain and offal were gone. But this time the killer had been in a hurry and hadn't competed the immolation. If he was lucky, he or she hadn't been able to construct the barrier that had blocked Azrael from the other victims. He might gain some information that would lead him to the assailant.

"So what does that mean?" Her voice broke through his concentration. "Licensed to practice?"

"Necromancers are regulated," he said with the hope that giving her information would keep her from focusing on the carnage. "We track who and how many are in each territory."

"How many are there?" she asked.

"A few thousand," he said. "Minors, mostly. Their powers are limited and always will be."

"Not all of them are as powerful—"

"As the allegiance?" he said, beginning to craft the sequence for summoning in his mind. "No. Some of them may, in time. If they live that long. But most will never be more than fortune-tellers and readers. It's how we survived for so long among humans."

"So you mean the psychic hotlines?" she quipped, a thin element of humor returning to her voice.

He laughed softly. "A few, yes. But they're mostly just bored housewives who know how to tell people what they want to hear."

"Is there a high death rate among necromancers?"

"Are you finished?" he asked, turning.

She pulled the sleeved sweater wrap around her chest, covering the swell of her breasts in the thin leotard beneath. "Yes."

"Among the most powerful, existence can be"—he paused, searching for the word—"cutthroat. The weak don't survive."

"And Havel was—"

"Just collateral damage," he said. "I believe. But old enough to be able to defend himself against most attacks."

Her nipples jutted against the fabric as she stepped quickly through what looked like a stripped version of a dance. She nodded to herself and began the process of limbering up.

Azrael could just make out the outline of the low profile blades she kept on her thigh as she moved. Little help against what might come for them here, but if they made her feel confident, so be it.

She closed her eyes and came to a stillness at once profound yet pregnant with potential movement. Thought escaped him. He'd never seen a human capable of so much centeredness, so quickly.

"I'm ready." She opened one eye, and he realized he had been quiet too long. She was waiting for him.

"Let's begin," he said finally.

Isela closed her eyes and, this time, began to move, slowly unfurling her arms as her spine snaked. He watched her for a few moments. It was a very different dance than the previous one: less elegant and acrobatic and more powerful, intentional. She moved in the four directions, stamping her feet and snapping her wrists in time to a beat only she could hear. The movements were more primal, less controlled. She grew tall, tightened, and writhed side to side. Every movement seemed bigger and more pronounced. Her braids came apart, sending dark hair flying this way and that, making her seem even more vast and alluring. This wasn't a lure, this was a summons. He could not look away.

Without having to reach for it, the power surged against him like hounds before the hunt. He spread his fingers as if to catch it all, and it clung to him, racing over his skin leaving behind the sensation of a million tiny sparks.

Azrael sucked in a breath. Summoning at the location of the death made connecting to the soul easier but did not have this effect of drawing power. This was Isela. Whatever she had learned, whatever she was doing differently, it was working.

He spoke the final incantation to push his spirit into that gray space he called the In Between. It was an echo of the present world, superimposed over the slaughtered necromancer's aedis, the hidden room where he practiced his craft. Immediately the wall blocked Azrael from the scene. But this time it was not opaque. Beyond it, he could see the flickering form of Zeman as he had been, whole.

Azrael examined the wall, extending in all directions between them. He had tried before to break it down by force, to batter it with will and power. Now he placed his hands on it, felt the energy coursing under his palms, and listened closely to the way it flowed. He heard the sound of the weaving that created it and, after a moment, sensed the slight ripple of a gap. He sought out that opening, thrusting his awareness through the break in the weave. Like a snag in a scarf, he plucked at the loose threads until they began to unravel. Finally the hole was big enough to slide through.

The prudent thing to do would be to break down the wall entirely or bring the spirit to him. But it would also take more time, and they didn't have that. Already he sensed movement around the edges of the summoning and sent a warning to his guard.

He dove in head first, sending himself through the space.

On the other side was a room identical to the one his physical self occupied. He sent his awareness backward in time, watching the contents of the room reset to how it had been, before the carnage. Havel Zeman moved around his aedis, a book of magic open on the center counter as he assembled his spell. The book itself was a masterpiece. Azrael possessed only a few grimoires so old and none in such immaculate condition. He wondered briefly where Zeman had come upon something like this. Most of the oldest books were in the hands of the allegiance.

Zeman looked up, his attention caught by something just over Azrael's shoulder. Azrael spun, but there was nothing behind him but the wall, the loose threads and rapidly growing hole, waving in an unfelt breeze.

When he turned back, Zeman was inches from his face. Azrael flinched. The dead rarely acknowledged him until he brought himself to their attention. Zeman was clearly waiting for him. The old man's mouth moved, but only the dull roar of white noise came out. Azrael tried to read his lips even as he twisted his power in an attempt to bring the white noise into some semblance of a voice.

"The Queen of Diamonds," Zeman's static resolved in broken bits. "Cuts with a blade of ice—"

At a familiar shout, Azrael looked behind him again. He turned in time to see the old man's face contort into something inhuman. Broad, spiral horns sprouted from his brows, and in his clenched fist was a knife, gleaming gold with a serrated blade. Azrael had enough time to bring up a guard. The knife caught him in the ribs instead of the heart.

Agony radiated from the blade's point of entry. He had known pain before but none that rendered him so entirely useless. His body arced as his head rocked back, leaving him vulnerable. An old memory came to him: his mentor's voice as he prepared for his first journey into the In Between.

"Remember, Goat Boy,"—the nickname lacked the derision it had once held—"what happens there echoes into this plane."

"You mean if I die there—"

"I will raise a pyre for your body."

Azrael screamed.

CHAPTER THIRTEEN

Isela gasped at the flash of gold. This time she didn't flinch, and it darted forward. They danced together, she and her sparking shadow, and the memories of the blood-drenched room and ruined flesh faded away. She laughed, twisting with joy.

And then it touched her.

A jolt raced through her system. Her heart froze for a few beats too long, then jumped to restart. The shock brought her out of her bubble and into the knowledge that something was very, very wrong.

The room was dark, the only light coming from Azrael's body. The rich glimmering around the edges of his skin and hair cast the room in an emerald glow. He stood stiffly, his eyes fixed on some unseen point. A flicker of a shadow across the room caught her eye.

"Gregor?" she whispered, reaching for her blade.

She made out a shape forming as the shadow became something out of a nightmare. She screamed Azrael's name—a warning—and everything went wrong.

Azrael grunted, and folded at the waist. He went down to one knee with a groaning cry. The shadow slid from the wall into physical form. It had the shape of an impossible four-legged beast; the combination of features unnatural and terrifying. Its horned, canine head swung toward the necromancer. Without thinking, she sprang from her circle, blade in hand. The thing that had been shadow leaped at Azrael. She rolled, sliding beneath it across the blood-slicked floor, and felt the blade connect. The blade turned to ice in her hand, clattering to the ground. The grotesque shadow emitted an inhuman shriek, buckling midleap and wheeled away from its target.

It stumbled across the room on its haunches, trailing black, viscous liquid that turned to vapor and dissolved. She crouched beside Azrael, tearing her eyes off the creature to frantically search his face. Her left hand ached all the way to the elbow, but she was too busy feeling his body for injury to register her own pain. At his ribs, something warm and wet filled her palm. When she withdrew her hand, it was slick with blood. From the walls of the room around them, more unnaturally shaped shadows began to coalesce, wrinkling with their own movement.

"Gregor!" She shouted for help.

On the other side of the door, thumping and howling was her only response. Her hand encountered the hilt of a blade tucked into Azrael's coat, and she drew it to replace her missing one.

His eyes flickered open, silver meeting gray with a look of such surprise, her stomach dropped. "Isela?"

She focused on the creature.

The wounded shadow snarled and paced but stayed out of her reach as she brandished the borrowed blade, moving to a crouch over Azrael. Her hip burned with the effort. She braced one knee on the floor.

The door behind them exploded, and Gregor strode through in a swath of light. At the sight of her—crouched over Azrael with blood on one hand and a knife in the other—Gregor's expression changed from concern to kill.

Great, of course he thought she stabbed Azrael.

She had just a moment to point her knife behind him and manage a garbled warning before another one of the shadow grotesques leaped into corporeal form at his back.

Gregor ducked, spinning faster than anything mortal could have. He drew a black sword from the sheath on his back before it had fully formed from a coalescence of curling smoke. The partially translucent sword proved solid enough; he caught the creature on the backswing, severing it in half.

The first grotesque renewed its attack. Solid now, Gregor's black blade came down again, severing its horned head. While Isela froze, Azrael dragged himself to one knee and pushed her behind him. In his bloodied hand was something that looked like an emerald the size of a fist. It glowed so brightly her eyes stung. He flung it past her, and an inhuman shrieking filled the space as emerald light bathed the room in sparks.

The gold shape flickered in the corner of her eye, and Isela shouted a warning. Gregor met the creature with the 9mm that had appeared in his free hand, emptying a clip in its spiral-horned head. She darted across the room to her bag, fighting the urge to curl up into a ball until it was all over.

She looked at Azrael. He was fighting, but even she could see the wound taking a toll. For every one they killed between them, there were two more. Three more bled through the walls into form as she watched.

Azrael met her eyes, his back to the center island, breath coming in gasps that betrayed how much pain he was in. He mouthed a single word. "Run."

She froze as if bolted to the floor. His mouth set in a line, and she felt a jolt of something hot and energizing burst into her chest. He pointed his palm at her. The command replaced her fear.

Run.

She grabbed Gregor's coat from her bag and sprinted for the door.

Outside the room, she knew immediately why no one had come to her aid sooner. Lysippe, Rory, and Dory battled a rising wave of the same shadow grotesques alongside the Viking and a pair of fighters she didn't recognize. She leaped over the big blood puddle, heel skittering at the edge, and paused, trying to find a path as Azrael's command pulsed through her.

Lysippe fought to Isela's side. "With me."

The shadows crowded the room, books and shelves flying in the conflict. Lysippe led, cutting through the fray. Rory and Dory, she noted, were using their bare hands and machetes the size of her thigh, twisting horned heads and chopping necks fearlessly, but Azrael's forces were outnumbered. As long as there were shadows, there were fresh creatures to fight. Lysippe got tangled up in a two-headed, frog-shaped shadow with a scorpion tail, but Isela saw her opening.

She ran for it. Outside the front door, she paused, breathing. The faint sound of combat coming from inside reached her on the pavement: flashes of light punctuated by gunfire and the occasional inhuman roar of a dying creature. She stumbled backward, away from the violence. She didn't belong in there; this world wasn't hers.

The door opened a crack, strained against its hinges by an ebon, snarling, pig snout. The nostrils flared as it scented her. Isela fisted her hand in the coat over the rectangular Audi key. She skidded across the frozen cobblestones, clicking the lock as the shadow pushed hard enough to twist the hinges and shatter the glass in the door. It clambered behind her.

She flung herself into the passenger side, slamming the door shut as the shadow hit the car with a solid thud. The car rocked, then went still. The scrape of nails on the chassis and glass as it searched for entry made her skin prickle.

She maneuvered into the driver's seat, searching frantically. Too many dials and not a key slot in sight. The car rocked again as the grotesque bashed into it repeatedly, circling the car.

Isela pounded the dash when she realized the rectangular fob that had opened the doors didn't even have a key.

"Start godsdammit!"

The car came to life with a roar. The lights flashed, illuminating the dashboard. The center screen flared. Ignoring the polite, female voice that greeted, "Herr Schwarz," Isela put the car in reverse and slammed on the gas. The back bumper connected with something solid that gave a shrieking howl. The pig-nosed shadow skidded across the hood, reflection-less eyes meeting hers for one hungry second as it jawed the windshield wiper. She found first gear and yanked the wheel away from the curb.

She hit the gas, and the force drove the creature sideways, sending it scrabbling off the hood. The car arrowed down the street, fishtailing, before its wheels steadied in the slush. She checked the mirror; the thing was on its feet, yowling, before giving chase. She upshifted and whipped around the corner.

Isela hadn't been behind the wheel in years—there was no reason to in a city with this much public transport—and this car wasn't the average sedan. The car lunged at the slightest touch on the gas, wheels sliding in the snow. At least the brakes were good, she considered, as it dropped speed sharply for her quick turn down a narrow side street.

She heard gears grind as she struggled for third, then it bucked and gained speed again. It didn't help that her left hand was growing numb from the elbow down. She buckled her seat belt.

She slammed on the brakes as the street dead-ended into a construction zone. She checked the mirror as one of the two grotesques slid to a stop at the open end of the street. It looked bigger out in the open, more savage. It had to be the size of a full-grown bull. Had it always had a tail with a stinger, or was that new?

It lowered its horned head, shaking it.

"Toro yourself, motherfucker." Isela slammed the car in reverse and hit the gas.

They met with a sickening crunch. She gasped as her body jerked against the seat belt robbing her of breath. Still, she kept her foot on the gas and felt the car's rear end lift slightly against the resistance.

"Come on, Gregor," she begged. "Tell me you didn't skimp on power."

The car began to force its way backward. As soon as she was in the intersection, she jerked the wheel, shifted, and hit the gas again. When she checked her mirror, the grotesque was gone. Isela made her way up the road toward the old fortress, the snowy streets untouched by tracks from lack of traffic. She missed the turn and had to double back. The engine gave an unhealthy rattle when she upshifted again. As she came around the fortress, she allowed herself to pick up a little speed, pushing into the curve.

The car hit a patch of ice, and the steering wheel slipped loose of her numb left fingers. Spinning out of control, the Audi jumped the barrier and tumbled down the hill. Isela lost consciousness surrounded by the rippling fabric of airbags.

* * *

She came to upside down, hanging from her seat belt, and

trying to remember her own name. The only thing that was perfectly clear was Azrael's command compelling her to motion.

Run.

She scrambled out of her seat belt, dropping to the roof of the car. Using the folded sleeve of the coat wrapped around her arm, she cleared the window of broken glass. Grunting with effort, she dragged herself out into the snow, pausing on her back to look at the ruin of the coupé.

Keep moving, she told herself, rising to her hands and knees, then working her legs beneath her.

The bushes at the top of the hill rustled. A pair of animal eyes shone in the headlights before vanishing in a flash of white and gray fur. She thought it was a dog. A big one. A little sob caught in her throat.

"Time to go, Issy, move your ass," she commanded.

She left the car in the ditch, climbing up and trying to orient herself. She was near the entrance to the fortress. To the right was an old canal turned walkway. She had spent enough time here as a child to know it led down to the river. If she could get to the river, she could follow the road and catch a tram.

She started to walk. Her hip burned as adrenaline cooled, sending shooting pain down her leg, but she forced herself to move faster. The darkness was complete, broken only by the occasional streetlamp casting circles of light in the snow. Mist curled off the ground, thickening to a low, hovering fog. She realized she was not alone when the bushes to her left rattled. The movement sounded like an animal. She leaped away, picking up her pace and dropping her remaining blade into her right hand.

The cold began to seep into her clothes—the light-soled dance shoes and leggings providing no barrier against the ice. Shivering, she forced herself on. Or the animal forced her. Every time she slowed, there would be motion from the darkness, the sound of paws in snow. She was being herded, she realized, through the park and to the hill on the east side of the fortress. Nothing showed itself, but she knew it wasn't the creature from the bookstore, or she would have been dead.

Faltering now with pain and cold, she fought her way down the hill, oblivious to where she was going, only knowing that she had to keep moving.

"Run," he'd said.

Azrael, the most feared necromancer in Europe, had told her to run. Her chest clenched at the thought of him, bloodied and fighting for his life. And when everything went bad, he tried to get her to safety.

Whatever power he had infused faded with her body heat. She tripped and came down hard on one knee, sobbing as pain reverberated up her leg into her hip. Something brushed her side, big and furred with a musky animal scent, disappearing into the dark. She lurched to her feet, brandishing the blade. Had she seen a tail whip before vanishing into the shadows?

Nothing came.

She limped on, moving downhill now, barely sentient. She saw a flicker of gold out of the corner of her eye and spun on one heel, sliding in the snow and falling backward as the solid, lightless mass of the shadow grotesque passed where she had been standing. One taloned hoof slapped her as she fell, sending her skidding sideways in a snowdrift. She lurched to her hands and knees as it tumbled to the ground opposite her and rolled to its feet.

Its front hoof dangled, the scorpion tail broken and dragging. An oily liquid, which she assumed was blood, seeped from its side, melting snow before vaporizing into the growing fog.

Her left arm gave, and she slid to her elbow, right arm extended.

"Come on, you ugly son of a bitch," she snarled, coiling her legs to lurch away.

The grotesque swung its head at her and gibbered. It lowered its horns.

A second blur of fur and snarls charged from the undergrowth. It was too big to be a dog, and its shaggy coat was silver gray, fringed with longer black guard hairs. Against the shadow monster, it looked like a paltry thing. But it hooked onto the bigger creature's lower jaw, shaking its head with bone-snapping fury.

The grotesque howled, spinning as it tried to dislodge its new opponent.

A second animal came from behind, leaping on to the shadow's back and biting savagely at the neck.

Her frozen brain stumbled over the visuals she was receiving—wolves—in the Vysehrad Park? On her knees, she stared, unable to move, as the two smaller, fiercer beasts tore into their larger opponent.

Then a third wolf, white and gray, appeared in front of her. It stared at her with big, glaucous eyes that weren't very wolflike at all and snapped its jaws.

Isela got the hint. Summoning one last burst of strength, she stumbled away, breaking into a lurching run. She felt the pale wolf keeping pace; its thick coat pressing against her leg. She stumbled once, reached out, and found its shoulder under her hand, bracing her. The smell of animal—earth and musk—was thick but not unpleasant. She tumbled down the hill, bursting through the trees alone on a street that was suddenly familiar. She was home.

She spun; the wolf was gone.

Under the streetlamps, the neighborhood was quiet. She felt the tears coming, even as she limped down the street to the familiar art nouveau façade. The front door opened, bathing the sidewalk in a square of light so soft and warm she wanted to lie down in it and sleep. Instead, she picked up her speed, hurtling her body forward out of the darkness and into her mother's arms.

CHAPTER FOURTEEN

Isela fought back the sobs, forcing herself to breathe. "He's hurt, and he gave me the strength to run."

"Hush," Beryl said, stroking her hair and face. "Come on, let's get you inside."

"It's done," Evie said quietly from behind them, nodding at the open doorway. "The boys are home."

Isela turned in her mother's arms, and a cry escaped her.

Three wolves emerged from the park through the snow. The larger two—one all black, the other black and gray—moved in an easy jog. Their heads came up to the side mirrors of the cars parked along the curb.

The smallest was lean and less broad in the chest than the other two. He cavorted in the snow that matched his pale coat, bucking and snapping. He transformed first, shaking his head and his fur like a wet dog as he bounded toward the house. Between one stride and the next, four legs became two with arms swinging easily alongside as Christof trotted down the street, naked as the day he was born. Fifi ran out to meet him, a blanket in her hands. She swaddled it around his hips before he lifted her off her feet, tossing her easily over his shoulder. Barefoot, he spun in circles, impervious to the cold, as she shrieked and beat at his shoulders with her fists.

"We showed that son of a bitch," he barked, throwing up his head with a wild howl. "Didn't we, boys?"

Markus and Tobias came next, with more dignified transitions. Bebe and Evie met them with blankets.

"Last time I checked, it was Toby who did the work." Mark rolled his eyes.

Toby spat into the snow a few times. "I'm never going to get that taste out of my mouth. Next time, you're on jugular."

"Fair enough." Mark picked at something in his teeth. "Oily bastard."

Chris bounced Fifi on his shoulder until she squealed.

"Well, sis, you sure have some taste in men." Chris laughed.

Fifi wriggled down, and he nipped at her neck and chin with little barking noises.

"Bad dog," she chided, prying herself loose.

"I'll show you a bad dog," he bared his teeth, chasing her back into the house.

Bebe rolled her eyes and handed her husband his glasses. "My gods, were we ever that bad?"

"Worse." Toby sighed. "You were disappointed I couldn't keep my tail."

Isela tried not to let her mind linger on that image.

"Really, Issy." Toby went on. "What were you thinking? You can't play with the necromancer's toys and not get your hands dirty."

"Young wolves," Isela stammered as their eyes went to her.

It was how she'd always thought of them; from the time they were kids, they had operated like a pack. Even Chris, once he'd hit puberty, had been theirs, more than hers. She looked at her mother in question.

"It's your father's fault," Beryl said with a little shrug.

"Papa is one too?" Isela could barely bring herself to ask it.

Beryl shook her head. "It's a recessive gene. I don't have it, so it shouldn't have manifested, but—" she shrugged. "What could I do? Puberty came, and it was either teach them to survive, or let them get themselves killed."

"The cottage?" Isela said.

"I had to get them out of the city," she said apologetically. "I wanted to tell you so many times, but we decided it was best…"

A look passed between Mark and their mother. Beryl nodded

and returned her attention to rubbing her daughter's left forearm. Something in her touch brought sensation back to the numbed out places and, with it, pain.

"Come on, you're bleeding," she said. "You need to get inside."

Isela thought of Azrael and resisted.

"Gregor Schwarz can handle himself, Issy," Mark snarled. "I should have taken him outside earlier this evening, and maybe he wouldn't have gotten you into this stupidity."

"It's not Gregor's fault," she found herself arguing as Beryl herded them all inside. "He's just following orders."

"Do you hear yourself?" Mark asked. "Following orders? Sound familiar?"

"Shh, you are going to wake the girls," Evie chided above them on the stairs.

Hissing, Isela snapped. "I can't believe you would go there."

"I can't believe you are defending him," Mark growled.

"I'm not," she said. "It's just not his fault we were there. What were we supposed to do, tell Azrael to fuck off?"

The whole party went silent at the mention of the necromancer. Above them on the stairs, Chris abruptly let go of Fifi and turned. Isela flushed. She was tired and angry, and she'd said too much. Where was that damned silencing spell when she needed it? She had never seen her mother so furious. Or focused.

"Girls, downstairs," she ordered. "We're going to need something stronger than our usual wards. Fifi, get Lukas, the kids, and Mrs. Simpson to the safe house. Boys, find something to eat and get ready."

"Ready?" Isela looked between them. "For what?"

"Let's hope he doesn't survive whatever he called up tonight," Beryl said. "Because I'm not going to let him put you in danger again."

They split up, Beryl leading her downstairs flanked by the Sisters. She took them through the studio, past the serenely smiling Buddha at his altar, to the door that opened to her private office. Inside, the back wall opened up to reveal an inner passage.

"Where are we going?" Isela asked. "What's going on, Mom? What *are you*?"

"There are many ways for a coven to form," Beryl explained

patiently as they walked. "In my case, I bore sons that drew other women with the ability together. In the old days there were sons for protection, four wives for the directions, and a coven formed."

Isela hesitated. "But you didn't have four sons."

"No," Beryl said softly, a smile lighting her face. "I had three boys with a recessive Were gene and one daughter who talks to gods when she dances."

Isela wondered if she was passed out in the snow in the park somewhere and this was all some strange dream. But everything was real, from the feel of her mother's arms, to the familiar smell of the studio. The hall opened up into a bigger room, and a sense of déjà vu swept Isela as she entered the second secret room of the night. Her stomach turned with the memory of carnage in the first, but this one was empty of blood, and when Bebe swept on the lights to reveal a clean, bright, walled space, the feeling passed. The furniture was colorful and startlingly modern. Bebe put on the electric kettle and busied herself with the rack of herbs and a book on an angled pedestal.

"You're witches?" Isela said as Evie guided her into a reading chair beside a lamp and table.

"It only takes three to make a coven," Bebe chimed in. "The rule of fours is old school."

"And once Ofelia grows out of her awkward-love-spells phase, she's going to be a force to be reckoned with," Beryl added.

"*If*," Evie murmured, taking a damp washcloth to Isela's face. "That girl. She took herself to Chanel after that latest spell. For maternity clothes. I didn't know Chanel *made* maternity clothes.

Beryl waved her off. "She's young."

"It's hard to argue with her when she's making money hand over fist with love potions and charms," Evie said wryly. "Hold still, Issy."

Isela winced as painful sensation began to return to her left fingertips.

"Let me see," Evie said, gently cradling her palm. The fingers were an angry pink, but the tips were black. "It's like frostbite. Bebe."

When the kettle finished, Bebe brought over a mug full of something that smelled of mint and herbs Isela had no name for.

"Just breathe this in for a bit," she said. "It will warm you up and take the edge off the pain. Mark said they tasted cold. Did you have metal in your hand?"

"My blade." Isela nodded. Evie turned her palm over and ran a fingertip over the black edge imprint of a slim hilt.

She rummaged through her little basket and found a paste that went on smelly and oily but absorbed quickly into her skin.

"Is that magic?" Isela asked as the feeling came back into her fingertips and the black mark faded.

Evie laughed softly. "It's herbs that will help speed the healing, in a lanolin base."

"And something extra." Bebe winked.

"But are you licensed?" Isela asked.

All three women looked at her sharply.

"Azrael said the necromancers are licensed to do the things they do," she said.

A coded look passed between them. Bebe went back to the counter and her mixing.

"Don't you worry about us," Evie said firmly, squeezing her good hand.

Isela began to shake so hard she spilled hot tea over her hands, and Evie had to take the cup.

"If he finds out," Isela said with fearful certainty. "If you get caught practicing…"

"Necromancers owe all they are to witches," Beryl stated. "I would like to see him try."

Isela's head spun. She sat back in her chair. A few hours ago, she was protecting her ordinary family from a dangerous world of power. Now she was being protected from a necromancer by werewolves and witches. Her family.

She must have dozed off, because she was startled awake by a glimmer of light in the corner of her eye, which she had come to recognize as prescience, a warning. "He's here," she breathed.

The numbness and pain in her arm was gone. She glanced at her hand; the marks on her fingertips had faded. Her sisters-in-law were witches, she reminded herself.

"Need more time," Bebe muttered from the countertop, surrounded by books and herbs.

Beryl cocked her head as if she were listening to a sound only she could hear. A curious smile curled her lips.

"I can handle this one," she said, grabbing a little box from the table beside Isela's chair. "Isela, come."

Isela lurched to her feet, surprised to find the pain in her hip no longer so sharp. They went back through the studio to the front door of the building.

A limo was parked out front. Before the buzzer could ring, Beryl Gilman-Vogel swung the door open and stared up into Gregor's unsmiling face.

His blade was no longer visible, but Isela knew it was there—as if the image of him drawing a smoky hilt from between his shoulder blades was a negative imprinted on her brain. He looked polished as always, as if a few hours ago he hadn't been slicing his way through a pack of creatures too bizarre to be real. It was almost dawn.

"I'm pleased to see that you are in better condition than my car," he said to Isela.

Her mother held up a hand. "You are not permitted here, creature."

A smile quirked the corner of his lips. "Forgive me, Frau Vogel. Isela must come with me. For her own protection."

"My daughter returned here bloodied and chased by demons four hours after you took her away," Beryl said. "I think we'll take over from here."

Gregor's sword was beginning to fuse together at his back, shadow taking form.

"Mom—" She tugged at Beryl's arm.

Gregor lunged for her, and Isela flinched away before she realized an invisible wall had stopped him. She would remember the flummoxed look on his face forever as he tried again, pushing up against the barrier with one hand. He drew his blade and swiped at it. The blade bounced off. He snarled.

Beryl crossed her arms over her chest and lifted her right hand. Pinched between her finger and thumb was something so small Isela barely recognized it. A hair.

"You left something," Beryl said quietly. "You ought to be more careful."

"Witch," he said, a curse and a realization.

"My grandmother taught me a few things," she said without an ounce of smugness. "Tell your master to find another dancer. Ours is not for him."

Gregor swept backward, his coat flaring out like a cloak. She saw him as he had once been, when the blade was steel and not made of consolidated power. "No one defies the necromancer."

From the shadows beyond the lamplight came low, thunderous growling. The hairs on Isela's arms stood on end.

Gregor turned, laughing, as he lowered his sword to face the three wolves stalking slowly into the light. They outnumbered him, but Isela had seen him in battle. And the boys were itching for a fight.

She tugged her mother's sleeve. "You have to stop them. You don't know what he can do."

Beryl put a hand on her arm. "The boys can look after themselves."

"I have my instructions," Gregor promised them all. "The dancer comes with me."

The black wolf lowered his head, ears pinned to his skull, and slipped between Gregor and the limo. Isela remembered Toby teasing Mark about it being his turn to take the dangerous job—going for the jugular.

"It's been ages since I've had a wolf pelage," Gregor mused, not the least bit concerned by being flanked. "Markus, is that you? I will wear your pelt to your funeral."

Markus snarled, canines flashing. Isela heard Evie's sharp breath and thought of Lilach and Thyme growing up fatherless.

Gregor's cold blue eyes fixed on Isela, full of warning.

You have something Azrael needs, Isela reminded herself. *Use it to protect them.*

Isela ignored the cries of the Sisters and started down the stairs.

Tobias, the black and gray, inched closer to Gregor, saliva dripping from his open jaws. He snapped with devastating power, and the hackles on his back flared. When Isela grew close, he hesitated, crowding against her thigh.

"Gregor," Isela lowered her voice. "Please."

"No harm will come to them from my blade," Gregor said. "If you go with me."

"Not good enough," Isela said, shaking her head. "Make Azrael promise. Make him *swear.* I go back with you. I will keep helping him, but no harm comes to any of them."

Gregor's raised brow told her how incredulous he found her demand.

Isela insisted. "I know you can communicate with Azrael, tell him. Call him if you have to. If you don't, I'll help my brothers rip your throat out or die trying."

He cocked his head, hesitating for the first time. Isela kept an eye on the wolves. She slid beside Christof, her hand settling in his hackles.

"Fifi needs a wedding, not a funeral," she whispered. "Don't do this."

The wolf dropped his head but did not back down. Isela was close enough now. When the bargain was struck, she knew what she had to do.

"All right," Gregor said finally. "You have a deal."

"Isela, no," her mother shouted.

Isela threw herself between Markus and the sword as the black wolf lunged. Markus twisted midleap to avoid crashing into her, jaws snapping shut inches from her face. Snow crunched beneath him, breaking his fall. He scrambled to his paws, snapping and snarling. Tobias was at his side, ready to defend him while he recovered his footing. She heard Christof growl and swept to the other side, putting herself between the youngest wolf and Gregor, and their backs to the limo.

Gregor laughed, sheathing his sword.

Isela's eyes found her oldest sister-in-law. "Evie. Don't let them fight this. Please. I can't live with myself if…"

She thought her sister-in-law nodded. It was enough. Evie took Beryl's hand and Bebe's. The wolves fell back, pacing and furious.

Gregor opened the limo door. Isela hesitated.

Christof whined, sinking belly down in the snow, and looked miserable as only a young animal could. Markus growled and turned his back on Isela, trotting toward the house.

Only Tobias remained, silent and watchful, as she slid inside. Her last sight before the door closed between them was of her middle brother's ashen eyes. He lifted his head and let out a long, low howl of mourning.

CHAPTER FIFTEEN

"Here."

Inside the limo, she'd moved as far away from Gregor as possible, drawing her knees beneath her on the seat. She jumped when he flicked his wrist, tossing a small, black, rectangular bit of plastic on the seat beside her. She reached for it a moment before she recognized the Audi logo: the key fob to Gregor's car. Her hand withdrew.

"I thought you might like a souvenir," he muttered. "I am not sure exactly what part of the word *run* involved the word *drive*."

"I'm sorry about your car," she said, then added defiantly, "Sorry it didn't burst into flames and explode after I wrecked it."

"I will have another one made," he remarked casually as if they had been talking about the weather. "It will take time. I have nothing but that."

"Can I at least stop by the Academy first?" She asked tiredly as the city blurred outside the window. *For a bite to eat and the chance to lock myself in a room and scream until my lungs burst.*

Her clothes were damp and bloody. She reeked of that particular tangy metallic odor she now associated with blood and demons. Her braid had come undone, and the bulk of her hair floated in tangled wisps. She must have looked awful.

Gregor's satisfied smirk was her confirmation. He had apparently found time to shower and change into fresh clothes before taking up the task of retrieving her. He adjusted his lapels, brushing off imaginary lint.

"My master would like to confirm certain events of tonight."

Isela bit back a sigh. Azrael wanted to do a postmortem right away. Of course he would want to figure out what had been powerful enough to catch him by surprise.

"I have been advised not to delay any more than absolutely necessary," he said. "Hence my lack of a new cape."

"I should have let Mark rip your throat out."

He laughed. "Perhaps one of these days, you will get to watch him try."

The limo passed beneath the battling titans at the castle gates, and Isela looked away from the brawny men. She'd had enough violence for one night. The limo came to a stop in the inner courtyard before a familiar illuminated door. Ignoring the driver—a stern-looking undead man—Isela flung herself out. The door opened, revealing a familiar sheepish young man in the expensive suit.

"Miss Vogel," he said, his voice warbling between delight and concern. "Good to see you again—so soon."

Isela didn't trust herself to be civil, so she kept her mouth shut.

Gregor strolled a step or two behind her. "Tyler."

At the sound of his name the younger man leapt as if goosed. "Mr. Schwarz."

She waited as Gregor took his time removing his coat and scarf, shaking them out neatly before leaving them with the young man.

"Lord Azrael asked you to bring Miss Vogel directly." Tyler's voice cracked. "To his quarters."

Gregor's mouth set in a long, hard line, but he gestured down the hall. It ended in a set of doors disguising an elevator, which took them deep below the castle to a long passageway lined with stone.

"Azrael's personal quarters are by the gardens," he said with a little sniff that indicated his disapproval. "In the former riding school."

"He lives in a *barn*?"

Gregor ignored her as they boarded a second elevator.

"Why didn't you just have the car take us there?"

He forced the next words between gritted teeth. "Azrael's preference is to keep up the belief that the main building of the castle is his home in every sense. We use the tunnels for coming and going to make it more difficult to track our movements on the grounds."

The elevator spat them out in a building that, compared to the castle, felt almost cozy, with soaring ceilings and enormous windows looking into the vast night-cloaked gardens. Even in semi-darkness, she felt the enormity of the space. The building might have once been a stable, but now it was a carefully designed retreat. The ghosts of elegant, modern furniture edged from the shadows. They crossed hardwood floors so dark they were almost black.

As she lagged behind on the stairs, Gregor cast a glance over his shoulder, his eyes wandering to her hip.

"Lysippe was right," he said idly. "You are defective."

"It's not a defect," she snapped. "And it's only bad because I spent most of the night running for my life. I can still do the job I was brought here for."

"How unfortunate for you." Gregor paused before an enormous, black wooden door to give her one long stare full of warning. "Do your job too well, and he will have to kill you."

* * *

AZRAEL COULD FEEL the tension between them before the door opened. Isela limped into the room, a half step behind Gregor. She came up short with a sharp exhale.

Azrael hadn't bothered to change from the carnage of the battle in the bookstore, and what was left of his shirt did little to cover the stark white bandage wrapped around his waist and lower ribs. Even his undead servants had balked at their master's insistence that he would wait before ridding himself of the stench of demons and old blood. He dismissed them all after sending Gregor to retrieve Isela. He needed time alone to think and to wait for her.

He took pride in the knowledge that he had the most

formidable Aegis of all the allegiance. His first, Lysippe hand-picked each over hundreds of years. He had given each near immortality and preternatural fighting skills in exchange for their vow of service. Another one of the allegiance necromancers might have fallen tonight, wounded and overwhelmed by the enemy's minions. But his Aegis fought until he was able to gather the strength to close the opening to the In Between and prevent any more demons from spilling through. His pride in them was unmatched.

And what was he to make of Isela?

Coming out of the summoning on the floor, dragging himself back from the ocean of pain, the first thing he saw was her taut body crouched over him. She'd brandished his knife, even as she stared disbelieving at the creature gathering strength across the room.

Still, he considered with the ghost of a smile, she refused to be cowed.

In hindsight, he should have ignored the PR team's recommendation that she be seen publicly only with Gregor and sent Lysippe to retrieve her. He'd seen the entire exchange at the house through Gregor's eyes. Gregor had seemed so calm, even after the discovery of the wreckage of his prized automobile. Azrael thought he could trust the Hessian to use diplomacy to retrieve her. But the witch's spell blocking Gregor from the house had pushed him over the edge.

It was Azrael that had kept him from doing battle with the wolves. Gregor had drawn his blade so fast Azrael almost missed the opportunity. Even as he'd snatched mental control of the man's hand, he'd admired Gregor's will and strength.

He heard Isela's demands through Gregor's ears. He'd agreed to them, as much to prove a point to Gregor as a gesture of goodwill to her. The night had been full of surprises. Not only the revelation of the witches and their familiars, but the title of the powerful necromancer thought lost to madness: the Queen of Diamonds.

Dancers had never been effective when coerced, and what Isela had done tonight—willingly, surrounded by the gore of a violent murder—spoke to her strength. If keeping her family safe motivated her to do the job, all the better.

Gregor had gone too far tonight. It was unfortunate, but he had to be reminded of his responsiblity.

Cultivating a cohort of soldiers who would fight to the death for him had taken centuries. He'd learned how to create the balance of trust and respect without destroying their spirits. He didn't want broken men and women obeying out of fear. He wanted warriors: intelligent, confident, and unafraid to challenge him when he needed it. But also capable of following an order.

It was a fine balance.

Discipline, Gregor could respect. And what did Isela need?

She stood before him now, a wreck in tattered clothes and injuries old and new. She was terrified and exhausted, but the rage she should have suppressed before him rose anyway. Her spine was erect.

Instead of reacting, as he had the first time she let her anger overwhelm her, he read her mind, seeing her indignation at her family's treatment and all her worry—for him.

Azrael faltered. She had been afraid. The last she had seen, he was bleeding out on the floor of a basement surrounded by the carnage of another necromancer. The attack had surprised him, and without knowing any better, his surprise had added to her terror. She'd never been trained as a fighter beyond that martial class the Academy thought it kept hidden from him. Still, her instinct under attack had been to protect him.

He expected as much from Gregor or Lysippe. But Isela, wielding her laughable little knife against a hellhound, was a revelation. She'd even struck a blow, wounding herself in the process. The damage would not be permanent, thanks to the witches.

Perhaps he shouldn't have been surprised at all by her actions, considering what Gregor had encountered at the Vogel house. She came from a combination of bloodlines that could have only resulted from the modern age of a world in chaos. Witch blood and wolf heart and trained to dance for gods.

He remembered the warning from the allegiance: *watch her carefully, the dancing may open her up to forces that cannot be allowed to come into this world.* At the first sight of possession, she must be put down to maintain the equilibrium of the world they'd built.

He'd just started to like her. He'd hate to have to kill her.

"Will you sit?" he asked.

Isela shook her head doggedly. "I'll stand."

Gregor growled. She flinched but did not obey.

Fine, Azrael decided. *First thing's first.*

He rose, still stiff with pain.

He'd hoped to include Gregor in the conversation, but the information would have to come to him secondhand. Azrael had taxed himself in the basement and needed to recover his strength, but an example must be made—for both of them. He strode across the room, gathering power in his hand.

"I didn't give you the sword on your back to be wielded against innocents," Azrael snarled.

He felt Isela's startled gaze on him as he moved faster than her human eyes would be able to track.

Gregor paled as he collapsed, his chest caving with the blow that sent his crushed ribs into his heart and lungs. He went to his knees on the floor, wheezing as blood trickled from the corner of his mouth. The door opened, and Lysippe entered silently, summoned by Azrael's telepathic call.

Azrael went to one knee beside his second, his words a thunderous murmur just loud enough for Isela to hear. "The next time I give an order, it will be obeyed. Second guess me again in a negotiation or disobey my order to abstain from violence, and I will use that sword to gut you."

Isela watched in horror, hand over her mouth, as Gregor folded on the floor, his chest a crumpled mass. He bowed his head in acknowledgment, and the whispered gargle of a single word escaped him, "*Jawohl.*"

Azrael stood, wiping his bloodied hand on his pants as he looked to Lysippe. "Take him away."

Lysippe crouched down to scoop up Gregor. She lifted him as easily as a child and with some of the same gentleness. The door slid shut silently behind them.

Isela opened her mouth and, just as quickly, closed it.

"I apologize for how you were brought here tonight," Azrael said. "Gregor should have maintained his discipline."

"Is he—" Isela fumbled for words.

Azrael shook his head. "He'll recover. He needed to be reminded of his role."

Isela let out a noise that might have been a sob—or a laugh. "I hope your PR team has a plan B, because Gregor's really going to hate me."

"He already does, Isela," Azrael said calmly. "At least what you do to him."

When her eyes turned on him, he saw pain and confusion. The burgeoning desire to protect her stoked a possessive fire in him.

"You have a way of bringing back the humanity in them," he said. "Lysippe is not afraid to care for you, but Gregor would prefer not to be reminded of what he once was."

"Once was," she echoed softly. "What is he now?"

"When he came to my service, I gave him his sword and my protection," Azrael explained. "In exchange, he entrusted me with his mortal soul."

Isela laughed, coughing. "You have—his soul—somewhere, like in a jar on a shelf or something?"

She wavered, but when he stretched out a hand to guide her to a chair, she moved away.

He sighed. "Are you going to continue to be frightened by everything that moves, or can we sit down and get the conversation out of the way so you can get to your shower?"

He watched her weigh her options. Finally she moved to the seat that he had abandoned by the fire.

Isela eased into it, keeping her right leg straight and resting on her left side. Now that he was aware, he could see how she held herself in ways to protect the injury but hide it from others. Interesting.

He went to the mahogany liquor cabinet next to the window overlooking the garden and poured two scotches—adding an extra finger's worth to his own. He sat opposite her, offering a glass, but she shook her head. He set it down on the armchair table between them, closing his eyes as he swirled the amber liquid restlessly in his glass.

Giving her information before had proved to calm her. He hoped it would again.

"It's the closest to immortality I can give them," he said. "And the least they deserve in return for what they must abandon, wouldn't you agree?"

"Their humanity," she murmured.

He opened one eye and lifted his glass in affirmation. "Death is not always unwelcome." He paused. "Tell me about what happened tonight."

"What happened?"

"This can go fast or slow, up to you."

Isela sat up a little straighter, reached for her glass, and took a long swallow. He winced as she coughed and sputtered, her eyes tearing as her throat burned.

"Sip, Little Bird."

"Don't call me that," she choked.

Azrael waited patiently.

"I was dancing," she said after she regained her breath. "And the light touched me."

"The light?"

"My shadow," she stammered. "I don't know what it is. It dances with me."

He listened as she explained with growing confidence, the presence that appeared first as a glimmer in the corner of her eye and later as a figure that mirrored her every move.

"It never touched me before," she said. "It shocked me. I thought my heart stopped, and I was aware of the room again. I knew something was wrong, that something bad was going to happen. I think it warned me—"

Warned her—or it had been distracting her in some way? Azrael thought of the gold blade Havel Zeman's contorted spirit had plunged into his chest. *Were they connected?*

He wondered if she noticed how her voice softened and her cheeks warmed when she described his command to run.

It was the only thing Azrael could think of in the moment. Isela hadn't been about to move, he realized now, not just out of fear but also a concern for him he still found bewildering. He'd bundled a precious burst of power and sent it into her, commanding her to run. But he could not have controlled what she did with it. He listened carefully as she related fleeing, in the car and on foot, and described the demons.

Not a warrior but with the heart of one, he thought of Lysippe's words, as she finished her story.

He wished he'd thought to extend Gregor's punishment. It would take a miracle to repair his relationship with the coven. And the wolves might never trust him. He had to hope taking better care of Isela from here on out would help.

"And do you see it now?" he asked when she grew quiet.

Isela looked at him blankly, and Azrael realized how exhausted she was. The well of her strength had been tapped dry.

"The light," he pressed quietly, setting down his glass.

Resting his elbows on his knees, he leaned forward slightly. When she didn't pull away, he knew it was time. She shook her head softly.

"No, it's gone," she said. "Like it never was."

Azrael cradled her fingertips, pleased she didn't pull away.

"Azrael," she said, the ragged tone of her voice stopped him in his tracks.

The memory of the sound of his name in her scream struck him still. The warning laced with terror. He heard it again in her voice: concern. This fragile human, with no reason to think him anything more than a monster, cared for him.

"Who is the Queen of Diamonds?" she asked.

Azrael went cold, drawing back, and Isela flinched.

"You whispered it," she said. "Before you—"

Isela finished the remnants of her glass, making a face. She flushed as his eyes settled knowingly on her.

"There's something in the research you sent," she said. "A necromancer and a dancer. They're mentioned a handful of times, then nothing. Is it her?"

Isela was too fast for her own good. It was the risk he'd taken when he'd given her information no human should know. She was too close to connecting pieces that would endanger her further.

"Something was missing from the room when we got there," Azrael said to distract her. "Yet I can't see it. Do you remember it?"

Isela closed her eyes, and he wondered if she was going to fall asleep. He started to read her memory, knowing that forcing her recollection might break the fragile peace they'd found, when he realized she had retreated into her own stillness. Fascinated, he waited for her mind to prepare the scene and slipped into her memory with her.

* * *

When Isela closed her eyes, she saw the room again—the bloodbath it had been even before demons had begun to manifest from the shadows.

"It's called an aedis," Azrael supplied, and in her mind's eye she stood beside him, surveying the space. "The room."

She remembered the sense of déjà vu that struck her upon entering her mother's hidden room behind the studio. It had been similar in so many ways: the long counter and shelves lined with jars and containers. And on the center island, a giant book on an angled pedestal Bebe referenced as she assembled contents in a small stone bowl.

Isela's memory took them back to Havel Zeman's little room again: the bloodied walls and bits of flesh scattered all around her. She turned a slow circle, extended fingers reaching to touch something that should have been there.

"The book," she said, stopping before the empty lectern.

Azrael murmured, "a grimoire."

The sense of him beside her in her memories vanished. When she opened her eyes, she was surprised to see him standing across the room. "What?"

"Grimoire," he said impatiently. "It's a book of spells. Necromancers collect them."

"You have one?"

Azrael dismissed the question with a wave. "I have several hundred. But I've been around for a while. I wasn't paying attention in the summoning. It was there on the counter. Old—much too old for a second-rate soul reader like Zeman. When we got there, it was gone."

Hundreds. Just how old was he?

"How long?" She asked before she could check herself.

Azrael looked at her blankly.

"How long have you been around?"

It seemed to take him a moment to realize what she'd asked. Azrael turned on one heel and studied her.

"I am *very* old," he said cautiously.

"How old?"

"I was born somewhere on the plains shadowed by the Caucus mountains," he said slowly. "Before the common era."

Isela jerked as her body made one more attempt to follow its most instinctive urge: flee.

"Christ," she muttered.

Azrael's mouth canted. "I never got to meet him."

"You're two thousand years old?"

"Plus or minus," he said. "The records weren't very good in those days, and once I stopped aging, it was easy to lose track."

"Stopped aging?" she said lightly. "That must be convenient."

She studied him again. The lines of his face felt familiar and yet somehow foreign. The truth was written in his bone structure and features, calling back to an earlier age of humanity.

"The grimoire was missing," he urged. "Anything else?"

Isela was trying to stay afloat, struggling to keep herself from falling into complete hysteria. The shaking started at her fingertips and worked its way into her shoulders. She gripped her elbows in an effort to keep still.

"I don't... remember." Isela gulped in air. "I don't... know. Why would someone steal an old book? And kill him for it."

"You know the answer to the second question," he said. "It was a distraction. To keep us from seeing what they were after. What she was after."

"The Queen of Diamonds," she surmised.

Azrael nodded. "You were right. She was a necromancer, one we thought succumbed to death or madness. Until tonight."

Her head jerked up.

"You're reading my mind," she said.

Azrael inclined his head with a little shrug. "It's that, or let you bait me into anger, as you did the last time we met. This was much more productive, don't you think?"

"I make you angry?" she asked in a tiny voice.

Azrael crossed the room to her, murmuring a geas to keep her from moving away. Isela was spent. If she tried to bolt, she would injure herself further. A small, high-pitched sound escaped her as he came within centimeters. He settled his index finger under her chin, drawing her eyes to his.

"I have spent the last thousand years learning to control my emotions," he admitted. "Yet I have never wanted to break a man so much as I did the first time Gregor put his hand on you. You destroy my quiet."

CHAPTER SIXTEEN

This time the silver, cat-eye shine in Azrael's eyes made Isela shiver for an entirely different reason. He lowered his head, his mouth hovering close enough to hers that she could feel the heat of his lips.

"Come," he murmured. "It's time to clean off this demon filth."

The breath left her in a long exhale, taking the last of her defiance with it. Azrael hadn't always been gentle. That was not his nature. But he trusted her with information and conferred with her to solve the mystery of the necromancer's murder. Whatever her brain said, the most essential part of her wanted him anyway.

It was hard to believe a few hours ago he had been bleeding out. Yet she saw the stiffness in his movement as he crossed the room.

She followed him mechanically as her bleary eyes drifted over the subtly masculine palette: grays with touches of cinnamon and chocolate. This was a bedroom, she realized belatedly at the sight of a four-poster affair so tall she might have to hop to get onto the mattress. It was done in tawny sheets and a gold-threaded comforter that picked up the light of the fireplace and sent it dancing. An abundance of pillows clustered at the headboard, encased in a wild variety of textures.

Azrael's hands cradled her shoulders from behind. He lowered his mouth to her ear. "You expected black satin and cuffs?"

It was too hard to breathe. His fingers squeezed, warm through her wrap.

"Inhale, dancer," he commanded, shaking her gently. "I'm afraid carrying you might be out of the question tonight."

The slight edge of rue in his voice brought her back to her body. Azrael was injured. Isela tried to face him, but he kept his hands firm on her shoulders, directing her past the bed to the bath beyond. The enormous, tiled expanse greeted them, the floor warm beneath her toes. She marveled at the pristine counters, the enormous glass-walled shower, and the in-floor bathtub beside the window overlooking the darkness of the garden.

His fingers deftly found the edges of her tattered wrap and tugged it off one shoulder, then the other.

Isela watched herself in the giant mirror over the countertop, as if seeing a stranger being undressed by a sculpture of a man. The flush rose in her chest and neck, under the bruises formed by the seat belt and the collision. Azrael's brows lowered as his fingertips skimmed the edge of one blooming over her collarbone. He turned her chin gently, as if appraising the damage.

"Your witches are powerful. You should be in much worse condition."

She opened her mouth to defend her family, but the words stuck at the troubled expression on his face. She shifted her weight and winced when her hip protested. Azrael lifted her off her feet, settling her on the countertop with her back to the mirror. Without taking his eyes from her bruises, he reached left of her hip to a stack of plush white towels.

Water splashed in the sink beside her. He wrung out one of the washcloths and brought it to her temple and her brow. With his scent flooding her and her own body's thrumming response, she barely felt the sting. It came away red.

"You're going to ruin…" she protested as he rinsed the cloth and began again.

After a third pass, his mouth canted upward. "A shower would be more efficient."

He left her on the counter, pacing to the glass door. Looking at him now, it was hard to imagine that only a few hours ago she feared for his life. Even with the tattered remains of his shirt revealing the bandage beneath, he looked vital, dangerous and, she admitted, unbelievably sexy.

There was nothing soft about him—from the unforgiving angles of his face, to the tight V of his waist disappearing into the black pants. As he leaned in to adjust the water, his thighs flexed, and his pants grew flatteringly snug.

When he returned, yanking the tails of his shirt over his head, she realized he didn't intend to leave her alone. "Oh."

His eyes flickered up, meeting hers. The bright silver eyes, shaded with tousled dark hair, gave an amused challenge.

Isela closed her eyes. She'd been chased by demons and wrecked a car. Sharing a hot shower with a necromancer didn't seem quite so outrageous.

Oh, what the hell.

She leaned forward, bracing herself to hop off the counter. Azrael caught her weight first, easing her to her feet. The bandage on his chest slid against the broken straps of her leotard, slivers of skin connecting in the gaps. Isela leaned into him, snaking one arm up to hook around the back of his neck. Her lower belly pressed snuggly against the junction of his thighs, and she felt his response to the contact.

Her mouth angled up expectantly. She gasped at the sudden coolness of the air when he drew away. Her brows knit in confusion. He tsked, shaking his head, and she caught sight of the upward curl of his lips as they slid away from her.

"Filthy," he said, clearly enjoying her surprise at being denied.

His fingernail slid under the remaining straps holding her leotard up, and he made a soft sound of regret at the deep imprints the material left on her skin. Hooking one hand in the top of her leggings, she watched his fingertips begin to glow as he bent his knees, dragging his hand down her leg. The heat on her skin was comfortable, but the fabric smoldered where he touched it, melting away until he was able to shake the remnants to the floor. On one knee, he tugged the ragged dancing slippers loose of her feet one at a time.

Azrael kept his eyes fixed on hers as he rose, sliding his fingertips over bare flesh until he was at his full height. His fingers danced at the edge of her underwear, hot again, and the scrap of fabric fell away with a slight burned smell.

"You know, washing machines," she murmured, one brow raised.

"Ruined," he disagreed, shaking his head.

Her fingertips lifted, going to buckle of his belt, but he trapped her hands. "Not yet. "

He stripped off the rest of his clothes, and the light caught the planes and hard angles of his back and legs. The male form was no mystery to her: she had grown up among the long lines and graceful strength of the male dancers at the Academy. Azrael was something new, or rather, much older. Broad chested and narrow hipped, his was a body built for the labor of survival, honed by two thousand years of life.

He returned to her with selfless confidence, as if unaware of his effect on her.

Isela tugged her eyes from the manhood straining upward. Her fingertips brushed the white bandages at his chest. "What about this?"

Azrael huffed and let her go for a long moment to fuss with the edge himself. Whoever had bandaged him had done it well. He struggled with it until she brushed away his hands, finding the tucked edge between his shoulder blades, and began to unravel it. He tried to hurry her, but she growled in response and took her time. Two could play this game. Plus it brought her close enough to admire the bronzed, sun-freckled skin of his chest. Pale, clean flesh appeared at last, and she paused as the bloody packing came off in her hands, revealing a puckered white line, just beginning to scar.

"But you—" she began.

"I heal quickly." He took the bandages from her.

"Does it still hurt?"

"Some," he said. "I have an excellent distraction."

Isela flushed again, taking the hand he offered and limping gingerly into the glass box. The water burned, and she flinched. He blocked the spray with his body and adjusted the temperature.

"I forget how sensitive humans are," he said absently, chiding himself.

"You forgot?"

Comfortably hot now, he led her under the spray. Before she could let inhibition overtake her, he drew her against his chest, running a hand down the small of her back to the dimples above her hips. His erection throbbed against her, but he seemed to be in no particular hurry to sheathe it.

"It's been centuries since I've met a human extraordinary enough to take as my lover," he said, as though it had been something of an intellectual pursuit.

The water stung cuts and abrasions she didn't know she had, plastering her hair to her head and her back. She glimpsed down at the drain and shuddered at the sight of her own muddy toes.

"Sit." Azrael pushed her hands aside, seating her on the little tile shelf under a hot stream of water that bathed her back and shoulders.

He retreated, filling his palms with a pale yellow liquid. He rubbed them together until the shower was filled with the aroma of chamomile, and he laid his hands on her shoulders. Stroking slow circles, he worked his way down, thumbs tracing the lines of her collarbones, sweeping under her arms and down to her fingertips. His palms circled her breasts but did not linger. He rubbed her ribcage under the arms, slipping his hands along the sides of her waist and the small of her back. He scooped her buttocks into his hands, fingers teasing the crease between her thighs before dropping to one knee to finish her legs and feet.

Isela closed her eyes and let her mind drift as arousal took a backseat to relaxation. She lost track of time and her own body, surrendering completely to the sensation.

He pulled her under the torrent of hot water and chased the last of the suds with his palms, occasionally brushing her body with his own.

When she opened her eyes, something in his made her lips part, a soft sigh escaping.

"Good," he smiled, satisfied. "Now your hair."

Isela protested, "It tangles—"

"Show me this time."

This time. Isela bit her lip, but he retreated into that immovable stillness that promised the water would run cold before he changed his mind.

"Conditioner?"

She kept her eyes on the tile at her feet as she worked, shy at first. From the thick waves near her face to deep-spiraled curls at the back of her neck, her hair had always confounded her lovers.

Azrael was so quiet she forgot about him as she parted it into sections and carefully worked the tangles free with her fingers. When she opened her eyes, he was watching her with the focus of a cat at a bird feeder.

"I have seen mermaids perch on rocks to sun themselves, combing the lengths of their hair like so and singing love songs," he said. "They drive sailors into the sea, mad with desire."

"Lucky for you, I can't sing." She breathed.

"You don't need to," he said, bracing his hands on either side of her hips and leaning in to brush her ear with his mouth. "Whisper my name and I'd leap."

Arousal kicked hard against her ribs, robbing her of breath. She focused on finishing the last section and winding the length into a knot at the back of her head.

From her perch, she could watch him attend to himself with businesslike efficiency, soaping and rinsing, shampooing and rinsing again until he was finished. He turned his face up and let the water run down his body, and she forgot entirely how to breathe.

When he opened his eyes to find her staring, there was a little shine of pride in his gaze.

"Stay." He turned off the water.

"I am not a dog," she said, surprised by the husky timbre of her own voice.

"I know," he remarked casually as he dried himself and wrapped a towel around his waist. "Dogs obey. You have the blood of wolves in your veins. I should have known it from the moment I met you."

Isela bridled a little until Azrael tucked a soft towel around her. He offered a second towel for her hair, but she grimaced. "Too rough."

She squeezed her hair out, trying to decide what to do with it now. She dreaded what it would look like after sex if she left it down.

After.

The one word was a cold splash on her libido. There were plenty of good reasons dancers did not get involved with their patrons. The fact that hers happened to be an immortal capable of controlling death was the best one of all.

His brows rose, but he nodded. "Come."

She pattered after him, ignoring the little voice that protested being bossed around. On the bed a platter was piled high with fruit and sweet delicacies. While she was admiring the way the strawberries had been carved into little stars, he returned with a butter-soft T-shirt.

The towel wrapped around his waist revealed enough chest to make her pause midbite, the pooch of chewed food in one cheek as she stared. He helped her onto the bed. The scent of him, clean and no longer tainted with death, warred with her hesitations.

"What is this?" she asked finally.

"In my day," he began, "the first time a woman came to the man she chose, she spent the day among her sisters." He squeezed the length of her hair through the shirt. "Like so?"

She nodded, dumbly.

"They bathed and dressed her," he murmured. "Perfumed her and rubbed her with oils."

His fingers brushed her hairline, and she trembled. "I guess being covered in demon blood and smelling like wolf isn't exactly the same?"

His unchecked laughter startled her.

She turned her head to him, braving his shining eyes. "I thought—"

"That I wanted to have my way with a battered woman who can barely stand on her own two feet and still resists me at every turn?" he finished, parting the damp mass of hair.

He leaned in and inhaled close enough to her ear to drive shivers into the most feminine part of her.

"In my world, words are power, and vows are law," he said, plating the long strands into a loose braid at her back. "Have you forgotten my promise?"

* * *

When she was done eating, Azrael removed the platter. Isela yawned, ducking her head as she tried to hide it from him.

She didn't resist when he splayed her on the bed face down, pillowing her cheek comfortably, but he felt the tension creep into her body. He slid a finger behind her ear, enjoying the way her body responded to a single touch with a long uncurling stretch.

He shook his head, sighing. So new to a world that had spun for so long before her.

Time had taught him many things. Patience had its gifts; intensifying gratification being one of the most satisfying. He savored the torment of her—skin damp and sweet smelling. The taut lines of her body, all muscle and tone and delicious curves. He had always been attracted to women who understood and used their bodies intentionally—warriors, courtesans, acrobats.

The thought of days to follow intensified the slow burn building in his own body. He could smell her now that the musk of wolf and the stench of demon had gone. Beneath the clean and the lightly scented oils, her natural aroma reached him. He knew without touching her that she was damp between the legs. So responsive, and he had barely begun the seduction.

Azrael's curiosity at what kind of lover Isela might be filled him with excitement. Already he suspected a few days would not be enough to satisfy his desire for her. A subtle melancholy drifted over him as he swept the velvet skin of her back with his fingers, feeling it warm beneath his touch. A beginning only meant the inevitable end. It had not troubled him before, and he wasn't sure why it bothered him now.

Brooding, he filled a palm with oil, warming it. She murmured when his hands settled on her shoulders, kneading the long muscles connecting to her neck with even pressure. He combined techniques he'd learned from another Amazon for soothing muscles after battle with the pressure and relaxation points taught by a Thai madam that had taken a shine to him as a young necromancer. He worked toward her hip, circling the surrounding muscles until they eased in his palms before plying his fingers to the tender area. She sighed when he reached the source of the discomfort.

Azrael worked her muscles at the base of her spine, listening to her breath slow and grow even. She knew how to breathe with his strokes, and he worked with the steady rhythm until, at last, her mind surrendered to sleep.

The ache in his own side was a memory by the time he felt the night retreating in his bones, but the drain it took to heal himself and the expense of his power in battle had taken its toll. The din of a city full of waking minds pressing against his own with their urges and fears was simply too much to bear.

Isela didn't stir when he dragged the comforter over them both and slid her body into the curve of his own. Azrael pillowed his head on his arm, buried his nose in the hair at the base of her neck, and closed his eyes. Sleep came on him as a thief, consciousness stolen like a forgotten coin from his pocket.

CHAPTER SEVENTEEN

"Come for me," Azrael whispered in her ear, breath hot and damp against the lobe. Response surged through her body, curling her toes and arching her back, as the pulse of release swept through her.

Isela woke with a gasp, alone in the enormous bed.

The sun was setting in the western window—she'd slept all day. Every nerve ending in her body sang with unsatisfied desire, yet she was utterly relaxed. The heat rose in her body as she remembered his hands all over her, first in the shower, then the bed. It should have ended in mind-numbing sex.

Instead, she had awakened at some point to find herself encircled; an arm thrown over her belly and a leg twined between her own. She'd stirred, shifting her hip to a better position, and he'd tightened around her. She'd gone back to sleep without a second thought.

She woke up more turned on than she'd been in her entire life —and alone.

Isela yawned, arching her body under the blankets. Even the sheets, which had seemed to whisper of silk the night before felt irritatingly raw against her skin. Her eyes swept the room for confirmation. She was well and truly alone. But she hadn't been for long. It seemed like she could still smell him on her skin.

She shivered, curling into a ball around his pillow and breathing him in.

You will beg for me before we are done.

Isela sat up. She had never begged a man for sex in her life, and she wasn't going to begin now. She wasn't the weak, exhausted thing Gregor had dragged in by the scruff the night before. She had to get back to the Academy—they would be worried about her—and call her family. Azrael had to track down the dead necromancer's missing grimoire—and survive the Queen of Diamonds.

And then?

She had to go back to her life. Back to being the Academy's premier godsdancer until she could no longer perform. Which, after last night, she feared was going to come sooner than she'd like to admit. Whatever the witches had done had helped but not eliminated the damage.

Everything had changed now, she couldn't deny it. Her brothers ran on four legs at night, and her mother and sisters-in-law had formed a coven. A Hessian solider wanted her dead. A glimmering gold light had decided to be her guardian angel. And she'd been seduced by a necromancer. Nothing would ever be the same.

Isela climbed out of bed, sliding to the floor. A silk robe lay across the footboard, and she slipped it on. It fell to her calves, open sleeves settling into folds around her arms. An explosion of red-tipped, blush-colored peonies graced the emerald panels, matching the thick scarlet border. She searched for a tag and found none.

In the bathroom, the light came on automatically, pleasantly even and perfectly flattering. Isela studied her face in the mirror. She looked thinner again but well rested. The tiny cuts on her face from running through the brush had almost disappeared. There was a new toothbrush and toothpaste next to the sink. She made use of them.

In the main room, she finally noticed the tray beside a renewed fire. On the chair was the bag Divya had sent with Gregor from the Academy. Inside were the clothes she'd worn from her parent's house to the summoning, freshly laundered and neatly folded. She slipped on underwear and Bebe's corduroy pants, delighted to find her phone, fully charged beside a carafe of coffee and a stack of sandwiches. On the platter beside the carafe, tucked under the plate was a folded notecard.

She unfolded the card, admiring the gold leaf border and the thick, heavy stock. In elegant script was his message:

Gone to track down the book. Expect you in bed when I return. Clothing not advised.

- A

P.S. The robe was a token of gratitude from an empress for helping solve her father's murder. You are the only woman who will ever wear it.

She fingered the silk and contemplated the likelihood that she had just brushed her teeth in a priceless antique. She didn't know a thing about silk, but one of the godsdancers she'd met in Tokyo had a thing for old kimonos. She had pieces that sold for more than Isela made in a year.

But if he expected her to sit around all night like a human fuck puppet, in a robe that belonged in a museum, he had another thing coming.

Isela picked up the phone. She'd missed calls from her mother, Bebe, and the Academy. Divya answered on the first ring, and the relief in her voice was palpable.

"Your mother called twice. I didn't know what to tell her." She spoke carefully. "I saw the report of Gregor's car being found in a ditch near Vysehrad."

"I'm fine," Isela said. "But I'm at the castle. Can you send a car soon? I need to come home."

Divya was all business again. "Niles will be there in less than twenty minutes."

Isela dressed, downing a cup of coffee and two sandwiches. She packed her bag, carefully folding the robe and adding it last. A gift was a gift. She grabbed a bottle of water and headed for the door. She cast one look back at the sumptuous room, closing her eyes and inhaling deeply so that she would always remember this moment. Her attraction to Azrael was a temptation she couldn't afford to give in to. Getting some semblance of her life back and protecting her family came first.

Focus, Vogel. Finish the job.

She grabbed the door handle and pulled. The damn thing

weighed a ton and a half. A startled, familiar young undead man waited on the other side. The doorman from the castle.

"Miss Vogel." He leaped from the chair beside the door as she moved down the stairs, bag over one shoulder. "My name is Tyler. I've been assigned to you during your stay at the palace. Like an attaché."

"I'm sorry," she muttered, heading for the elevator.

He tripped over his tongue and his feet. "But it's an honor, Miss Vogel. Is there anything I can get for you?"

"Azrael is gone for the day?"

Tyler paled at her casual use of his name. Had he fallen off the zombie turnip trunk yesterday? She'd just come out of his bedroom for gods' sakes. Did he expect her to address him as sir—or worse—master?

"The Lord is gone for the day." He nodded, slipping into the elevator with her before the doors closed.

"Gregor? Lysippe?"

"Accompanied him," the boy answered, flustered.

"Good," she said. She wouldn't have to worry about the Hessian trying to exact his revenge before she made it to the front door.

"I'm happy to bring you anything you need," he said. "You don't have to—"

"I need to stretch my legs," Isela said as the elevator opened. "Can you walk me back through the castle?"

"I would be happy to," he said, leading the way. "What did you want to see? We have an excellent collection of early twentieth-century work in the Basilica gallery, or if you like sculpture, the de Canova Psyche and Cupid has been installed in the stateroom. Mr. Schwarz mentioned your interest in the cathedral. The Mucha glass is quite incredible this time of day."

"Another time."

From the main building, Isela relied on her memory to guide her back to the front door. She left Tyler ticking off priceless works of art on his fingers. When he realized she was moving on, he hurried to catch up.

"Tyler, is it?" she asked. The castle seemed empty.

"Yes, Miss Vogel."

"It's just Isela, or Issy," she said. "Where is everybody?"

"Everybody?" he echoed. "Ah, Lord Azrael thought it would be a good idea for the others to remain low profile during your stay."

"Doesn't want to freak me out with a bunch of zombies wandering around, eh?" She winced at his stricken expression. "Sorry, Tyler. I was—that was rude of me—I apologize."

"It's no problem, Miss Issy," he prattled on. "I'm honored to be chosen to serve Lord Azrael."

"Of course," she said. As they passed through the doors into the courtyard, Isela saw the blue car waiting silently outside, and joy leaped in her chest.

Tyler looked stricken, darting into her path. "Miss—you aren't planning to—"

"I just have a few things to take care of, for him," she lied.

"But he left strict instructions," he began. "You're to be made comfortable *in* the castle."

Isela gave him her most gracious smile. He blinked, a goofy answering smile on his face. While he stammered, she hefted her bag onto her shoulder and slipped around him. "I really have to just take care of a few things at home."

Niles emerged from the sedan, moving quickly to the rear door. She could have kissed him.

"Wonderful to see you, Miss Vogel," he said as she slid inside before Tyler could catch up.

"Right back at you, Niles," she muttered as the door closed behind her. When he climbed inside, she clapped her hands with joy. "Take me home."

CHAPTER EIGHTEEN

Isela had never been so happy to see her apartment. Her father answered the phone when she called home.

"Hey, Little Bird," he said, rambling in the familiar way he did when he was walking through the flat. "Your mom is going to be happy to hear from you. We read about Gregor's car. I kept telling her the report said it was stolen, and you're fine, but you know how she is."

Lukas sounded bewildered, and Isela pitied him. From the sound of things, they were the only two normal people in the family.

"I know, Papa," she said. "But you shouldn't worry."

"I never worry about you," he said. "The boys give me gray hair, but you were born happy, and you brought happiness everywhere you went. Hmm, I can't find her. Maybe she's in the studio—do you want to call down—"

"No, Papa. I was hoping to talk to you for a while, if you aren't busy."

"Course not." He laughed, and she heard him settle into a chair. "How's that fellow of yours?"

"He's… ah…" she began. *Going to kill me at the next available opportunity.* "He's fine."

"Did I tell you what arrived today? A box, express delivery from his tailor in Leipzig. Your mother didn't want me to open it, but it was addressed to me for gods' sakes."

Isela found herself smiling at her father's stubbornness.

"It was a coat, like his, only in brown," he said a little awed. "It's a fine thing, Little Bird. I'd thank him personally, but I have no idea where to send the note."

"I'll let him know you liked it," she said over the knot in her chest.

Isela wasn't foolish enough to think the coat was part of Gregor's penance. That meant it had come from Azrael.

"Bring him to dinner soon," he said. "Your mom will warm up. She's always been protective of you, too much so, in my opinion. You have a good head on your shoulders."

She doubted very much that Beryl would *ever* warm to the Hessian. Or allow him in the building.

"Oh, here's Bebe. She wants to talk to you." He handed off the phone before she could say good-bye.

The sounds of footsteps retreating down the hall were accompanied by her sister-in-law's hushed voice. "God, Issy, we have been worried sick about you. Are you okay?"

She'd spent the night being seduced by a necromancer; she was definitely *not* okay. "Everything's fine."

"How could you go with him?" Bebe said. "We would have protected you—the boys—"

"Would have turned you all into widows," Isela said. *Now this was something she could talk about.* "I saw him fight those demons, Bebe. He's not human anymore. You ask me to live with knowing I got my whole family killed to prove a point to his boss?"

Bebe was silent for a long time. "Did he hurt you?"

"No," Isela assured her. "And he's been—reprimanded—for what he did last night."

"Reprimanded?"

Isela didn't think filling her sister-in-law in on the details was a good idea. "Trust me. He felt it."

"If you say so," Bebe murmured. "Look, before I met your brother, I'd been in a few doozies when it came to relationships. I know what it's like when you're attracted to someone, but you can't..."

"Don't worry, Beebs," Isela cut her off. "Something tells me we're done for good."

"Good." Bebe sighed. "Can you talk your father out of wearing that coat?"

"Is it safe?" Isela asked. "I mean was anything, you know—"

"Done to it?" Bebe finished. "Like a geas? No. Your mom checked it out, but I can't look at it without getting the heebie-jeebies."

"I'll do what I can," she said. "How are Mom and the boys?"

Bebe's sigh contained a world of meaning. Isela's throat clenched as she thought of Markus turning his back on her.

"Your mom understands, I think, but she's worried," Bebe said. "The boys… they'll come around. Male pride. They wanted a fight."

Isela's view of the Vltava from her window blurred with tears.

"I'm going to do what I have to in order to protect you guys," she said. "Even if they hate me for it."

"Oh, Issy." Bebe breathed, and Isela could picture her sister-in-law's heart-shaped face and pursed lips. "Just be careful. They love you more than you know."

"I will."

"I gotta go, I think Philip just shoved a crayon up his nose," Bebe said finally. Isela could hear screaming in the background.

"Tell Mom to call me," Isela said without much hope.

* * *

"Are you decent?"

Isela looked up from her reading to see Kyle peek over the divider between the stairs and the main room.

"Has that ever stopped you before?" she countered.

He contemplated that for half a second, then bounded up. "Nope. I came up to see if you're hungry. You missed dinner. Yana ordered in for carp, and I know you—"

"Hate fish," she finished. "I just can't get into the bashing a carp in the head on the street business."

"Neither can Yana. That's why she sends one of her dad's

cronies out to get it for her." Kyle's laughter was so welcome it brought tears to her eyes. "I hoped you hadn't changed and gotten all savage on me, hanging out with the necromancer's security hottie."

"Never," she said, getting up to greet him and help carry the brown paper bags. "What'd you get?"

The smells coming from the bag made her mouth water and her stomach grumble. Isela unloaded a series of paper boxes, a few with the beginnings of grease stains forming on the bottom. She glanced at the clock. It was well after midnight. After talking to her family, she'd buried herself in her research on Azrael's data, mostly to keep her mind occupied. She had a headache and a vaguely sour belly from lack of food.

"I thought we would cook something," he said. "But I danced earlier, and you know how lazy that makes me."

"Where did you find Chinese at this hour?"

He was in a brilliantly good mood as evidenced by the playful waltzing step of the *balance* he made across the kitchen to retrieve plates.

"Fucking ballerinas," she said, admiring the elegance that turned the simple step into something with breathtaking beauty and control. "Why are you so happy?"

Kyle winked. "I have my secrets."

"Your secrets are my secrets. Talk," she demanded.

He sealed his lips shut and blew her a kiss. They ate in companionable silence, passing cartons and stealing bits of food from each other's plates. She plucked a shrimp from his chopsticks halfway to his mouth.

"Shouldn't you be watching what you eat?" she teased.

"You're vicious," he snapped good-naturedly. "That's a beautiful yukata, by the way. They don't even make those in silk anymore—total antique. Where did you—" Kyle leaned over to admire the stitching and paused, glancing at her neck. "Vogel, what happened to you?"

He pushed the neckline open and blanched at the black-and-blue marks from her collarbones to her shoulder.

She brushed his hand away and tightened her robe. "You know the accident, with Gregor's car?"

His brows rocketed north, and he grinned. "So no third date?"

Isela laughed and offered her wineglass for a refill. "But on the upside, I have a new masseur."

Kyle froze midpour, his eyebrows up and a look of horror on his face. "Masseur is gendered and pretentious."

"Massage therapist." She stuck out her tongue. "I tell, you tell."

"Nothing to tell," he said with the most unbelievable mask of innocence she had ever seen.

"You little liar."

"You're one to talk." He sipped his wine in an attempt to hide a grin on his face. "I didn't bang the necromancer's head of security."

"I didn't..." she said, not waiting for him to register her words before moving on. "You and Jiří finally figured things out."

Kyle almost choked on his wine. "If you aren't fucking tall, dark, and Teutonic, who's giving you priceless silk robes?"

"You heard my offer." Isela sat back in her chair and crossed her legs primly.

"That's not fair," he said. "You know it was Jiří. You, on the other hand, are a wildcard."

"Come on, Kyle." She narrowed her eyes, tapping his knee with her big toe.

His eyes widened. "The necromancer?"

"Well, not exactly," she said. "But he's making a persuasive argument."

"Do you have a death wish?"

"That's one way to put it."

But the truth was, Isela had never felt so alive. At the Academy, her life had slipped into a familiar rhythm. She hadn't even noticed the touch of ennui beginning to creep in during the unchanging days. Now she was involved in more supernatural powers than she'd even known existed and was being seduced by a necromancer.

It wouldn't last forever, of course. Even if she survived this, he'd tire of her eventually. She'd enjoy it while it lasted and let go when it was done, as she always had. She felt a surprising little twinge of regret in her chest.

Oh, no you don't, Vogel. No attachments. Not to him.

"Does he give better massages than I do?" Kyle interrupted her thoughts.

"No way," she lied.

He sniffed. "Of course not. He's trying to get laid. I have pure intentions."

Isela reached forward to squeeze his hands. "Jiří's good, huh?"

"In more ways than one," he said.

Dirty jokes flew unrestrained as they cleared the table and did dishes.

On his way out the door, he called back up the stairs. "Oh, Yana says thanks for the new bag."

"New bag?"

"You sent one over, from Prada, to replace the one you scuffed up on your 'date' with Gregor." He drawled out the name. "She wasn't going to make a big deal of it, but… that was nice of you."

First the coat, now this purse. This devil certainly was into details.

Isela wondered if Azrael would be so detail oriented between the sheets. But she already knew that. He'd explored every inch of her body between the shower and the bed, except the ones that, by avoidance, made his purpose obvious: to make her beg.

She fidgeted restlessly, thinking of the tone of his note. She was not going to go run back to his bed. No way in hell.

* * *

ISELA DOZED until dawn but couldn't get comfortable in her own bed. When she admitted it, a dangerous, insatiable feeling had begun to grow. She was trapped. To go back would admit she was hungry for what he was offering. To stay away meant denying the need she hadn't known she possessed. She dragged herself out of bed and onto her mat to warm up her body and let the sunlight tickle her skin. It wasn't as satisfying as the stroke of Azrael's darkness.

Isela could have kicked herself. She thought about sending a message, but pride won out. He'd delivered a hell of a seduction, an invitation on a silver platter, *literally,* and she'd as much as declined by sneaking out like a petulant teenager. She consoled herself by remembering that the note had not been worded like an invitation. It was an order.

Isela refused to be bossed around. As Azrael had reminded her, she wasn't one of his people. And she still had a job to do. The allegiance had hired her to help Azrael find a killer. Identifying her was just the start. They still had to catch her.

She needed new choreography. She'd learned from the past she couldn't repeat a dance—it didn't work that way. Each one had to be unique, tailored to the specific request. It was time to get to work.

She thought of the gold shadow that danced with her. It seemed to want to help her. It had shocked her out of the dance in time to get to Azrael before the demon, maybe she could appeal to it for Azrael's protection when he faced the Queen of Diamonds.

Isela wondered if Azrael had told the rest of the allegiance who was responsible. She had reread every passage referencing the necromancer and the dancer. A few scanty mentions and then nothing. They had erased the Queen of Diamonds from the collective memory. What had she done?

"History is written by the victors," she murmured.

A flash of memory made her reach for her phone. What if the necromancers didn't have the only collective memory with information about the Queen of Diamonds? If necromancers and witches were somehow connected, maybe the coven knew something. She dialed her oldest sister-in-law, Evie. The phone went to voice mail on the second ring.

"I don't know if you're avoiding me too," she began her message. "I don't blame you. But I need to ask you something about the end of the war, something that might help me get out of this mess."

* * *

When Isela got back from the practice room, it was after dark and her muscles ached. Something was wrong with her choreography. She was missing a piece, and the gold flicker hadn't appeared once. Evie hadn't called back either, but perhaps Bebe could tell her something in the morning.

Frustrated and restless, she had a shower and then made herself go to bed. If Azrael called in the middle of the night, she needed to be rested and ready for—anything. Any murders, she corrected over the heat building in her body at the thought of what else the necromancer might require her for.

Idiot. He wasn't going to call. No, he'd send Gregor to drag her back to the castle by her hair. If he even still wanted her.

He was the necromancer, and one of the most alluring men she'd ever seen. If he needed a quick fuck, Azrael could avail himself of any one of the power-hungry women who made their interest in necromancers clear. And how dare he talk about wanting to break Gregor for touching her? No wonder Gregor was a homicidal maniac, working for a boss like that.

Isela shivered, thinking of the speed and intensity with which Azrael had struck Gregor, collapsing his chest like a paper bag. Maybe they were sitting around now, drinking that awful scotch and commiserating.

"No hard feelings, man." Azrael would laugh.

"Dicks before chicks." Gregor would remind him.

Furious at her own overactive imagination, Isela flung back the covers and leaped out of bed.

Into the arms of a masked man.

She didn't have time to scream. His hand closed over her wrist, twisting it to pin her arm to her back. He shoved her toward the bed. Isela went limp, rocking her weight sideways, and slammed his solar plexus with her free elbow.

A grunt and she was free. Unfortunately, he wasn't alone.

CHAPTER NINETEEN

Azrael peeled off his filthy coat, tossing it onto the nearest chair as he strode into the castle from the garage below. Shoes followed, he didn't want to track gods-only-knew-what over the priceless Berber rugs upstairs. Gregor and Lysippe remained below, dealing with the scum they'd apprehended in connection to the grimoire and the mess they'd made of the car. Usually Azrael would have stuck around, but he had other things on his mind.

The household was more active than he would have expected, given his orders. Then again, it had been almost twenty-four hours, and running a household this big took constant effort. He swore, thinking of the dawn that had come and passed in his absence, leaving his promise to Isela broken. If he had been particularly aggressive in his pursuit of the grimoire, it was because every hour that ticked past dawn reminded him he should be elsewhere at that moment—and otherwise occupied.

When Lysippe had woken him mentally with news of a lead, he'd had to pry Isela's body from his to leave the bed. The way she'd sleepily stroked him had almost made him call off the hunt for a few hours. But he wanted to enjoy her at his leisure, and there was no guarantee they would get another lead of this quality. He'd watched her curling into the warm space he'd left behind and walked away, counting the minutes until his return.

The aggression had served him. Their search had taken them through the seedy darkness of Prague's underground and all the way to Budapest tracking the last living link to Havel Zeman's unusual grimoire. But the creature got word of their coming and bolted, turning it into an all-out hunt through the Southern Alps to a small town on the Croatian coast. When they caught the creature, it was all Azrael could do not to expedite the process by killing it. Centuries had taught him the dead were much more cooperative than the living. But even if the creature hadn't been booby-trapped, there were other factors making death a more complicated option than usual.

Gregor seemed surprised at the command to secure him for transport back to Prague but, sagely, said nothing. The Hessian had regained Azrael's graces on this hunt; his origins as a member of the elite soldiering corps known as *Jaegers* made him ideal for operations like this. It was one reason he and Lysippe got along so well. The passion for tracking game of all kinds made them siblings of a sort. There had been a moment or two, while they were back-to-back facing a room full of undesirables, that Azrael had realized Gregor was enjoying himself, supremely. He and Lysippe had kept a running total of kills, bantering numbers back and forth on the ride home until Azrael put a geas on the car. He'd sketched the symbol for "silence" on the dashboard with one finger, and Lysippe's protest cut off midgroan under the magical command that barred sound. She crossed her arms over her chest in the backseat and raised her eyebrows in the rearview mirror. When he refused to lift it, she gave their captive a good kick with the heel of her boot in frustration.

He didn't have the patience for their chatter. His mind was where his body wanted to be: buried to the hilt between the lithe legs of a dancer who was currently warming his bed in eager anticipation.

Azrael mounted the stairs by threes, tugging at the remaining buttons of his shirt. He should shower first—perhaps he'd run them a bath in the big tub and splay her open on the warm tiles with the view of the snowy gardens stretched out beneath them.

The first sign that something was wrong was the empty chair beside the door where Tyler had been posted to attend to her. She'd possibly sequestered herself in the room and sent him on an errand. He knew the undead made her nervous.

But when he opened the door, the room was empty. The bed was made, a fire was going, a hot bath was prepared, but all signs of her presence had been eradicated. He sent a single thought to the household, a word and a command, as he swept the room. Even the smell of her had faded. She'd been gone for some time.

The boy appeared at the door. "My lord."

"Was I unclear?" Azrael banked his fury to a slow burn.

The boy flinched as if he'd been struck. Azrael had seen ghosts with better color.

"No, my lord," he said. "But she… she said she would be back. A few errands."

He was young and new to service but eager to please. Azrael thought he might be less off-putting to Isela—the newly dead were still so near to their humanity. Plus they had a common country of origin, and since Tyler had been voluntary, he'd been allowed to keep his memories and personality.

"And you believed her?" New and naïve.

"I tried to go to the Academy, but they wouldn't let me past the visitors' area," he said, evidently confused by the fact that being a messenger for the necromancer hadn't granted him an all-access pass. "I waited for hours, but she didn't come down."

Azrael should have known better. This was Isela. She was all stubborn pride and prickly independence. Even when her body wanted to be curled up against him, her mind adhered to her rigid code of their relationship as patron and artist and kept him at a distance. The same mind that had sparked her leap to his defense in a dark abattoir surrounded by demons. He had spent centuries collecting warriors brave enough to do such a thing.

If Isela thought he would be that easy to put aside, she was mistaken.

Azrael swore and smiled with a savage pleasure that made Tyler whimper. But the boy drew upright before him.

"I failed in my duties, my lord," he murmured. "I humbly submit to whatever punishment you see fit."

"Do you think I need you to *submit* to punishment?" Azrael growled.

Tyler quaked. But Azrael's fight wasn't with the boy. He wanted to get his hands on Isela. Obviously, she needed a reminder of exactly how thoroughly her body responded to him.

Azrael knew he should probably prove a point to Tyler. The boy needed to learn the import of a command if he was going to remain in Azrael's service. "Get to the garage. Gregor has his hands full."

Visibly trembling, Tyler collected himself enough to bow stiffly at the waist before disappearing down the hall. Azrael stalked into his room and slammed the door.

He reached for the phone, thought better of it, and put it down. He didn't want to give her any warning—she might take the opportunity to go hide under her mother's skirts, and he wasn't ready to deal with the coven. He knew where she'd be. He just had to retrieve her. This time he would go himself.

* * *

Out of the corner of his eye, Azrael caught a glimmer and paused, rubbing his drying hair absently with the towel. A hot shower had done worlds for his mood. He was almost humming as he prepared himself to hunt down his prize.

He knew better than to turn his head and look directly at it. Instead, he relaxed his vision and let his focus go soft. A familiar woman's figure contorted elegantly in postures he'd seen before: Isela. But there was a disjointed urgency to the movement. It was trying to communicate something to him.

Intrigued, he slowed his breathing, slipping into stillness between one heartbeat and the next. The glimmer touched the center of his chest. It hit him like a blow. And then he realized why. It was a blow—or the echo of one—Isela had just received. She wasn't dancing. She was fighting.

The touch formed a connection between them. He felt every blow as if it fell on his own body. A thickening, cloying sensation rose in the back of his throat. It had been centuries since he'd had any of his own, it took him a moment to realize what he was feeling: fear.

Azrael didn't stop to wonder at the sudden connection between them, arrowing a thought back to the source of the sensation.

Isela, say something.

A startled pause. Then, *Busy at the moment.*

The words were flippant, but he still tasted her fear as if it was his own.

Azrael dressed without thinking, cycling through his mental connections until he touched Lysippe's mind. *Car, front, now. Something is wrong with the dancer.*

Five minutes later, a black Porsche slid to a stop as Azrael ran to the curb. Gregor was still dressed as he had been for the hunt, and the hint of his sword hilt flickered like an afterimage between his shoulder blades.

Azrael frowned. "I called for Lysippe."

"The dancer is my… responsibility," he said as he whipped the car into the road.

Azrael's mind reached for the mental connection between them.

Isela, I'm almost there.

Better hurry. You'll miss all the fun.

Good, she was still joking, but the fear was there. Now he could also feel pain. Rage surged in him.

How many are there?

Two. My apartment. They're good. Fuck.

Another lash of pain, this time in his left hand. He slammed the fist into the dashboard, leaving a dent. Gregor downshifted, picking up speed as the engine roared.

This time her voice came after a sob. *Azrael?*

Yes, dancer.

Hurry if you can. Please. I don't think I can—

Silence. Azrael gripped the door as the car swung into a turn at an impossible speed. When he looked over, Gregor was smiling. For someone born before cars were invented, he'd taken to them with a natural affinity Azrael envied. He drove like he fought, all attack.

Dancer!

Stop shouting at me.

Answer me when I call you. He wanted her angry, fighting.

Weaker now. *I don't belong to you.*

Ah, but you do, he purred. *See what happens when you disobey me?*

You send a couple of thugs to kill me?

His chest clenched. *I favor diplomacy, as you know.*

I might approve of you punching a hole in these guys.

Leave them to me.

Might want to get a move on. The fear made her voice tremble.

If you let them harm you, I will turn you into a zombie. He felt the spike of her heart rate and thought he'd gone too far.

If you do, I'll spend my undead life trying to kill you.

Zombies can't kill their masters, he taunted.

Watch me.

Honking twice, Gregor plowed through the oncoming traffic, weaving through cars that too slow to get out of his way.

Isela?

Silence. Gregor slammed the brake, jerking the wheel, and the car swung 180 degrees, putting the passenger side closest to the Academy's front door. Azrael was out before the car had fully stopped. He glanced back once as Gregor emerged, the sword fully visible now. The Hessian nodded and, with a running start, began to scale the building's walls, heading for the roof.

Isela?

Nothing.

Answer me, godsdammit.

As Azrael drew power, the lights of the building flickered uncertainly. With a whispered word, he blew the door off the hinges. The night watchman leaped to his feet as Azrael charged up the stairs. Too startled to draw his weapon, he gaped openmouthed at the necromancer. Azrael rendered him unconscious with a flick of a wrist, unlocking doors ahead of him into the inner sanctum without slowing down.

Even at this hour, there were a few students roaming the halls. They stared at him; a few sinking to one knee as he passed. A petite Asian woman without an ounce of fear in her eye blocked his path.

Azrael scanned her mind—she was a friend of Isela's—and he grabbed the coordinates for her apartment as he dodged her. "Get your building's security director, and pray Isela isn't dead."

Her face drained of color, but she moved quickly in the opposite direction.

He splayed his hands at his side as he ran, calling power to him, and the halls succumbed to darkness before the emergency lighting flickered on. He sped his movements to a blur. He leaped two flights of stairs, ignoring the screams from those he surprised on the way.

Isela, answer me.

CHAPTER TWENTY

Isela, say something.

The first time she heard his voice in her head, her strength surged, as it had the night he had told her to run. It was clear the two assailants hadn't expected her to be as strong as she was. She used her flexibility and honed grace as her ally, dancing her way from them repeatedly. She had never been so grateful for Trinh's sparring matches; she'd managed to disarm both, twice breaking holds that should have forced her to surrender. But she was outmatched and outnumbered.

Isela had needed that second wind badly, and Azrael's continued baiting restored her determination.

She wasn't a fighter, and now her assailants were angry and growing desperate. It was only a matter of time before she made a mistake. She'd knocked the first one down by the couch but lost track of him in the shadows.

I might approve of you punching a hole in these guys. She made it to the kitchen, hoping to get to a weapon.

Isela took a risk, lunging too close to her opponent to get to a knife. He blocked her and grabbed her wrist. She tried to break the grip, but he held firm and swept her legs from beneath her. She hit the floor square on her back, her wrist wrenching painfully as she went down. She kicked up, catching him in the groin, but he was armored. He pinned his knees on either side of her chest. Her left hand yanked at the kitchen drawer level with his head. He stopped the motion by slamming it on her fingers.

The pain was exquisite. When his hands went around her neck, she surged, locking her elbow and aiming the heel of her left hand at his throat. He slumped with a choking gurgle, and she rolled him off, coughing as she dragged herself across the floor.

The second assailant slammed into her back while she was down. A thick cloth wrapped around her throat. She thrashed, struggling for air. If she was lucky, she had ten or fifteen seconds before she lost consciousness.

I'm not going to be strangled to death with my own kitchen towel.

Indignance fueled her struggles, but she failed repeatedly to break the hold. There was nothing left but surrender. She thought of her family, at home and at the Academy.

Niles would never forgive himself for allowing the breech. Her mother would never forgive the necromancer for involving her in this. The last thought before the blackness stole her vision was of Azrael; the silver shine in his eyes.

So much for no regrets. *I'm sorry.*

* * *

AZRAEL BLEW the apartment door open. A single burst of power knocked the black-clad figure off Isela's back. Gregor dropped through the window. As her assailant catapulted through the air between them, Gregor sliced the head from the body. He landed in a crouch before rising to meet any other threats as the head rolled across the floor. He sheathed his sword and slid a 9mm from beneath his coat, stalking around the apartment. But the space was still. The second assassin was on the floor, his windpipe shattered.

Azrael rolled Isela onto her back, untangling the cloth from her neck. The air wheezed softly in her throat.

Gregor returned with the silk robe hooked over his index finger. Azrael took it without looking, sliding the material around her body. He drew one arm under her knees, the other behind her shoulders, and lifted her off the floor.

Footsteps thumped on the stairs to the apartment, and

Gregor stalked across the room. Niles appeared in the doorway. Behind him was the Asian woman with a short, bladed staff in her hands.

When she saw Isela, a cry escaped her. "Is she—?"

Pushing up the stairs behind them was a tall blond man, a baseball bat on his shoulder.

Gregor slid between Azrael and the director's bodyguard, taking aim. All three took a step backward.

Put it away, Azrael commanded. *These are her cohorts.*

Gregor complied. Azrael hadn't mastered his rage. Only the knowledge that this was Isela's sanctuary kept him from tearing the room down around them. He turned cold eyes on the assembled mortals.

It was a look that had brought others to their knees, but this lot didn't back down from him. Their eyes were for her.

For Isela, Azrael made himself speak. She was so quiet in his arms. He remembered the taste of her fear in his throat.

"She'll live." His eyes found the Asian woman. "You should be proud. She fought well."

Tears sprang to the woman's eyes, but her nod was fierce. The taller blond man rested a hand on her shoulder, squeezing.

Niles swept the room with his eyes. He noted the two dead figures in black, he sheathed his weapon. "Lord Azrael, we had no alarm—"

"They were professionals." Gregor pulled the mask off the head, fastidiously avoiding blood. It was a woman. The man with the baseball bat turned a brackish shade of pale.

"Recognize her?" Azrael said.

They all shook their heads. Niles pulled the mask off the other. "I've never seen either one."

"I'd like a full security review," Azrael said. "I want to know how they got in undetected."

"You'll have it," Niles said angrily. "This should not have happened."

Azrael nodded. "Gregor, retrieve the bodies for interrogation."

Every mortal face in the room drained of blood, but they cleared a path for him as he walked down the stairs with Isela in his arms. Only the man, the bat now hanging at his side, moved to cross his path. Azrael controlled the urge to bare his teeth. The man was familiar with Isela. Loved her even. It was in his eyes.

"Issy—sir," he began over an audible lump of emotion. "What will you—"

"She's not safe here," Azrael said, a simple statement of fact. "I can protect her."

The man nodded. "If I pack some of her things—"

"I'll be sure she gets them," he replied, pushing past.

No one else dared to stop him on the way out of the building.

Isela's breath, coming in a gasping wheeze, was tenuous. Every few steps, he felt for her consciousness, but she stayed slack against him. Rory pulled up in the Land Rover as he cleared the front doors. Dory had the door before he'd reached the bottom step. It wasn't until Azrael slid into the backseat, never setting her down that her eyes opened and found his.

"If I'm a zombie—" she croaked as the door closed behind them.

"I know," he snarled, unable to smile. "You'll kill me."

A crooked smile rippled her cheek. One side of her face was going to bruise soon, but that little smile was full of life. That life made her seem bigger than the small form now curled in his arms.

"Where are we going?"

She'd almost been taken from him, so easily. It had been a long time since he'd cared for one of them. And he did, he realized, care for this mortal, who was so fierce and fragile at once. Azrael didn't realize he was squeezing her to his chest until she wriggled and grimaced. He forced himself to loosen his grip.

"Back where you belong."

Isela made a sound in her throat suspiciously like a laugh, and her eyelashes lowered, gray eyes on him. "And what makes you think I'll stay there this time?"

He lowered his lips to the top of her head. "I can be very persuasive."

She made a thoughtful, questioning sound. He could feel her breath on his neck and, so lightly he almost missed it, the first touch of her mouth.

"You underestimate me, Isela. I am not a boy that tires quickly in the pursuit of his interests."

Azrael kept his breath slow and regular as she tasted him again. Full lips just as luscious as he'd imagined, pressed against his collarbone through the open neck of his shirt. She snuggled deeper against him. He stiffened immediately, and she let out a raspy laugh that echoed with sex. He wanted to taste her, to feel those lips on his. The rage melted away, replaced with another heat.

Azrael wondered at her ability to turn his emotion so swiftly, tracing her hairline with one finger to the curve of her cheek. At the corner of her mouth, he stroked absently. She parted her lips, and her whole body trembled against him, inciting the most delicious heat in his groin.

"I know what I want," he said. "And I don't give up until I've had my fill."

When his parted lips met hers, it was no more than a brush of skin, but it held all the promise of what was to come.

Isela sighed into his mouth, content, and tucked her head against his collar. She stayed there the entire way back to the castle.

CHAPTER TWENTY-ONE

Isela listened to the beat of Azrael's heart, allowing the gentle rocking of the car to lull her into a state just below consciousness. The kiss lingered in her thoughts. She clung to it, keeping the memories at bay.

Not an hour ago, she was convinced she was going to die. With it came a suffocating sense that there was so much she hadn't done. It was as choking as the hold on her neck. And the first regret of many was Azrael.

He wasn't asking her to love him, to need him. He'd only acknowledged the current between them and been willing to pursue it. In his capacity as a necromancer, she may have been a tool, but Azrael was also a man and answered to the same demands her body placed on her. Judging by the danger they had been in so far, she might not be the only one with her life on the line.

When they arrived at the castle, she started to sit up, but his arm clamped down, holding her firm. She softened immediately. For a moment he didn't move. *Had she surprised him?*

Quiescent, Isela rested, saving her strength even as she savored his. Azrael climbed out of the car and strode into the castle with her in his arms. The heavy door of the bedroom fell back under his hand easily.

"Can you stand?" His voice was gruff, as though he was the one who had been recently strangled.

Isela nodded against his chest. When her legs held, he let go of her hips. Cupping her cheeks, Azrael turned her head left and right, and his thumbs stroked the bruised skin on her neck. She closed her eyes. She didn't want to think about it, now or ever. She wanted nothing more than to banish those thoughts with the reminder she was still alive.

"Are you going to keep playing nursemaid?" she taunted. "Or are you going to fuck me?"

When his eyes met hers, they were full of heat. Azrael smiled, as wicked and dangerous as ever, and Isela wondered briefly if she had overestimated his compassion for her.

"I didn't hear you beg."

Azrael took advantage of her parted lips, pressing his against the warmth of her mouth. The heat that had been building spilled down her body, pooling between her thighs and racing out her fingers and toes. When she opened her eyes again, she lay on the bed with no indication of how she'd gotten there.

Azrael stood above her, tugging the shirt over his head, his eyes never leaving hers. Isela scrambled out of the robe, wrenching the loose jersey tank top that served as her nightshirt over her head. His hands closed on her hips, yanking her toward him. When she tried to rise, he placed a palm in the center of her chest to pin her there.

The heat of his mouth left her raw and exposed as he worked his way down her neck to her collarbone. Stars raced behind her closed eyelids, exploding green and showering her in sparks. His mouth closed over her left nipple, swallowing the sensitive nerves in dark, wet heat.

From a life built on physical activity, she knew her body well; having an awareness of it was part of her job. Now that awareness had turned to intense pleasure, short-circuiting her ability to think, rationalize. And they hadn't even gotten to the main course. A note of panic tightened her back. This was more—much more—than she'd anticipated.

Sex with this man just might kill her.

"Surrender."

Isela whimpered as his free hand ran lazy circles around her navel, before drifting lower. "Let that busy brain rest, dancer."

Azrael joined their mouths again as he stroked her. Fingers met swollen flesh, slicked wet in anticipation. He groaned. When his fingers slid home, he swallowed her shout.

Her toes spasmed as his fingers curled against her inner walls. She clenched him hard, and her hips angled in invitation.

Every nerve ending in Isela's body sang with need, and Azrael keyed them into a harmony that threatened to push her over the edge. He could not be rushed—even the thoroughness with which he took her mouth resonated with control.

When she opened her eyes again, the smile that licked his lips was pure male desire. He knew what he was doing to her.

And he was enjoying every moment.

When his mouth replaced his fingers, Isela screamed—a hoarse, rending sound Azrael answered with a satisfied purr. A fierce liquid heat rushed to the junction of her thighs, threatening to overwhelm her. Her fingers tangled in his hair, but that only served to encourage his attention. His tongue flicked slow, easy strokes, as if he couldn't care less about the pleasure he inflicted.

Isela climaxed with a ragged wail, not recognizing the word embedded in it, until she looked down her body. Silver eyes were waiting for hers, alight with victory and a wicked grin of total masculine satisfaction.

"I'm sorry," he murmured, thumbing the last of the tremors from her body. "I didn't hear you."

Isela was beyond caring, beyond pride. Azrael had awakened something primal in her. There was only one thing she needed, and one word between her and it. Her own husky laugh startled her.

"Please," she repeated, drawing the word out.

His grin spread. "My pleasure."

He rose between her thighs, filling her in a slow, purposeful thrust. Her slick, swollen body expanded to contain all of him. When he seemed to think he could go no farther, she locked her legs around him and drew him deeper still. Desire pressed frenzy, and tremors shook him with the effort of maintaining control. He rocked his hips unwaveringly until she alternately pounded at his chest and urged him on with feverish insistence. By the time he started to stroke her with his cock, drawing and plunging in the same steady rhythm, her pleas dissolved into wordless cries.

Isela opened her eyes to find Azrael watching her, molten silver pools fixed on her face as though there were nothing else in the world that mattered.

That pushed her over the edge. This time he went with her, his body going so hard in hers the intensity of pleasure bordered on pain.

Snug between his forearms, she hauled in a long breath as he tasted the sweat on her brow. It was some comfort to her that his breath was ragged.

"Now," she panted. "I can die."

"Not so, dancer." Azrael's low, rumbling laughter made her belly quiver.

He flexed his hips, testing the slickness between them and evoking a groan from her heaving ribcage. This time, when her lips parted in anticipation, he took them greedily with his own, nibbling at her pleasure-swollen mouth until she hooked a hand around the back of his neck, drawing their bodies together fully.

His irises were thin bands of silver around the velvet darkness of his pupils when he met her eyes. "Did you think I would be satisfied with one taste of you?"

* * *

AFTER SHOWERING off soap and satisfaction, Isela retreated to the food tray that had appeared by the fire. Azrael followed lazily, enjoying the return of a deep calm that he hadn't known was missing.

The value of physical pleasure had declined as the centuries wore on. In the past, Azrael had considered it an evolution of sorts. There were necromancers who attributed the growth of their talents to their particular sexual prowess and tastes. He'd never given much stock to that theory.

Instead, he cultivated the stillness, the deep quiet that had captivated Isela. For a time, sick of the world he'd joined when he'd assumed his full powers, he'd fled from it. He spent a century in a monastery until the stillness came to him as easily as the power he wielded. After that, he'd rarely indulged himself in flesh.

Eschewing a chair, Isela folded herself onto the rug between the table and the fireplace. She started to wrap the towel around herself, but he made a sound of protest. She let it go without a thought. To compensate, he raised the temperature in the room until the rose-brown skin haloing her nipples bloomed soft again. He prowled the room for a moment before giving in to the pull to occupy the chair closest to her.

When Isela didn't resist, Azrael took over the task of squeezing the moisture from her hair. He rested in the silence between them absent of nervous pattering, more flirting or an anxious search for reassurance. Instead, she sighed, leaned back into his knee, and let him stroke her.

Arousal stirred in him at the thought of having her there; fire and sex slicking their skin with sweat.

Azrael chided himself. Isela needed to eat and sleep. He required little of either anymore. It was easy to envision spending the rest of the night inside her, listening to the sound of her pleasure until she was spent with release.

For all her stubborn resistance, Isela was an eager partner, confident enough in her own body to fully express her desire. It was a heady mix; for all her passion and fire, she remained somewhat inaccessible, challenging enough to keep all but the most determined away. Azrael wondered about those who came before him. An unfamiliar possessiveness urged him to mark her as his own.

The desire startled him. Craving, along with the urge to snap in half any man who touched her, didn't wane as it had with past partners, now that he'd taken her to his bed.

It wasn't just the sex. It was the effect she had on him. While he'd pursued her, she'd disturbed his peace. But now? Something about her—the shared pleasure of their bodies and the simple closeness of contact—settled the restless sensation in his chest that had always resisted stillness.

At last Azrael found himself breaking the silence to tell her about their pursuit of the grimoire. He avoided the worst bits—he healed so quickly there were not even scars to mark the wound or two he'd suffered. It wasn't until he got to the part about placing a geas for silence on the car, that he stopped to wonder why he was still talking. He wouldn't have bothered to give his own guard an accounting of his time. Yet here he was, obliquely explaining why he hadn't kept his word to her. After all, if he had, she might have never had to fight for her life in her own home. The knowledge unsettled him.

"And I thought you were just mad because I'd turned you down," she said, casting a mischievous look over her shoulder at him.

Azrael coughed lightly to cover a laugh. "Turned me down? My Little Bird, you weren't even playing hard to get."

* * *

ISELA STILLED, and the nickname hung between them.

Somehow it didn't seem as wrong coming from him as it did two days ago. She realized he was waiting, watching her intently from that stillness, for a reaction. "Did you have a silly nickname as a kid?"

She'd surprised him with the question. He laughed, and a smile crept up her lips before she could check it.

"My parents said I never stopped moving," she went on, unsure why she was telling him this, only that it felt right. "I guess I was always dancing around."

"Ah," he said. "I assumed it was due to your family name, Vogel."

"*Vögelchen.*" Isela flushed. "Yeah, that too. A little bird, flitting from branch to branch."

Azrael paused, seeming to retreat, and she bit her lower lip. What possessed her to think he even cared? He spoke a word in a language she had never heard before. It seemed distant, even for him. He repeated it with more certainty.

"Terror," he translated, with a touch of something she could only describe as rue. "That's what they called me."

"Gods," she said, horrified, before she could catch herself. She imagined tantrums with a child who could raise the dead. "Were you spinning your head around on your shoulders or something?"

Unbelievably, Azrael grinned. The shock of white teeth and the sudden ease in his face left her staring in wonder. "I was the youngest of six. Unexpected. My siblings were older, bigger, stronger. I had to be wilder, more daring. My mother called me the littlest terror."

"You had brothers too?" Isela relaxed, picking at the fruit tray again.

"Two," he admitted. "And three sisters who liked to dress me up and braid my hair."

She laughed and quickly covered her mouth. But he grabbed her hand, pulled her fingers away.

"That must not have made it any easier," she said. "Were they all—"she hesitated—"necromancers?"

It was his turn to laugh. Well, wonders never ceased. It was a beautiful sound, clear and ringing like a bell. "Gods forbid. No."

Azrael plucked the spent strawberry leaves from her fingers, sucking a final bit of red flesh from the root before discarding them in the fire. Isela chewed at her lower lip. "How did you become one?"

Something in his face closed.

"I was always different," he murmured, cutting off her apology. "But I did not come into my power until much later. Now, enough. You need rest to recover your strength."

Isela twisted her body around on the rug. Her breasts pressed against his knee, and her fingertips slid along his inner thigh. He caught her hand.

"There are many ways to recover," she said.

Isela took her lower lip between her teeth again, and he couldn't look away. He traced her mouth with his finger, and his body betrayed him beneath the towel. She smiled, and a wicked gleam filled her eye as her fingers went to the knot at his waist. "I think it's your turn to beg."

Azrael looked up sharply at a knock on the door, and Isela paused. The sound came again, louder, and he frowned with a little snarl of frustration.

"Unfortunately, it will have to wait." He lifted her hand to his mouth and sucked fruit juice from each of her fingertips. "Your neck must be attended to."

Azrael let her hand go as she pulled away to rise. When she had belted the robe around her waist, the door opened and his healer came in. He was, to Isela's relief, human. Isela wondered if Azrael was able to communicate with everyone, like he'd done with her at the Academy.

Azrael walked into the closet while the doctor finished examining her throat. When he emerged a few minutes later, he wore a pair of fitted, dark pants and a navy-blue T-shirt that hugged his chest and made his eyes particularly bright. She caught her breath, unable to look away. How could it be that sex only made her crave him more?

Azrael watched her, arms crossed over his chest, but his attention was elsewhere. She thought of the story of the grimoire and the person they'd retrieved for information. In bed, he seemed to care only for assuring their mutual pleasure, but he'd been tasked with finding an extraordinary killer. Sex was a diversion from his responsibilities. She was a diversion from his responsibilities. And a tool to be used to achieve his ends. She would be wise not to forget it.

Blowing off a little steam, Isela reminded herself, quieting the yammering voice in her chest that begged to be heard.

His healer attended her, puzzled by how quickly she'd already recovered. He departed after leaving a salve to apply to the bruising.

"What are you waiting for?" she asked quietly when the man was gone.

Azrael's shining eyes revealed his surprise.

Isela didn't expect him to massage her to sleep and hold her every night. The seduction had been achieved. She ignored the little stitch developing between her left ribs. It had been a difficult night, she told herself. She was overwrought and tired. That was the only reason she felt like begging him to stay.

"The two who attacked you must be interrogated," he said, striding to the bed. "The dead start to lose details and the ability to communicate if not handled quickly."

"But Tyler—"

"Because he is under a contract, he kept his memories and his personality."

"And the others?" she whispered, trying to convince herself that he wasn't what she wanted. "That's how you punish us humans, right? Turning us into *them*."

"That is a punishment for those who break the laws," he said. "They are stripped of anything but the knowledge that their service is atonement. It does not amuse me to turn humans into shambling idiots, but it does seem to serve as an effective warning."

"And the eyes," she said softly.

His eyebrows tilted in question.

"The ones you nailed to the door of that building?"

He frowned. "Some necromancers believe that power is gained through sacrifice and ritual. That one culled the old, and the infirm, and those who believed they had been called to the gods. He had made religion from their suffering. Enjoyed it, even."

He pulled down the comforter and the top sheet in invitation. She went.

"A summoning. Could I help? To dance?"

Azrael smiled, tucking her legs up under the comforter. "These are intact, fresh, and won't be spelled. If I can't summon them easily, I shouldn't call myself a necromancer. I need you rested for the next murder—if there is one."

"And you think the other man, the one you found in Croatia, knows what the Queen of Diamond intends to do with the grimoire?" Her words ended in a yawn.

"Maybe," he said. "A guard has been posted outside the door. You are safe here."

Isela blinked slowly. Safe. His hand settled on her cheek, tucking stray bits of hair behind her ear. His fingertip traced an intricate pattern on her cheekbone that could not have been random. Her eyelids felt weighted, impossible to keep open. She yawned again, drawing her knees close and her face into the pillow. As the realization struck her, she tried to sit up, but her limbs were too heavy. She glared at him, unable to hold it before another yawn broke her focus.

"What did you do," she said on the edge of consciousness, "to… me?"

CHAPTER TWENTY-TWO

Dory waited outside the door to his quarters.

"The geas should keep her down until I return," Azrael said. "But with the witch blood—"

"No worries," Dory said, his broad face alight with amusement. "I'm not a foolish boy."

"Not for the last hundred years or so, at least." Azrael's brow rose.

Dory slapped a palm against his ribs with a wounded expression. He bent over to inspect Azrael's face with a wily grin.

"What?" Azrael frowned.

His chest heaved with contained laughter. "Just checking for the ring she's got through your nose, Boss."

Azrael spared them both the illusion that Dory would stop speaking his mind anytime soon. "Speaking of foolish boys, what was Gregor's punishment for our young geneticist turned attaché?"

Dory grunted, acknowledging the subject change with a grin. "Waxing and buffing the car."

"Which one?"

"All of them."

The bodies had been laid out in his aedis, the same place that Isela had tried to dance for the first summoning. Some necromancers, like Havel Zeman, preferred practicing the old way—in the dark little hovels full of books and potions—but the modern age of fluorescent lighting and stainless steel had been a boon to Azrael. Why not evolve? His aedis was underground, as it should be. From there, it had little in common with those of his fellows; it resembled a modern morgue.

The attack disturbed him. Isela should have been safe at the Academy. Few people knew she was important to him—other allegiance necromancers and his own Aegis. He trusted his shield implicitly. The other necromancers were never to be trusted, and this would prove his suspicion that someone wanted them to fail.

Azrael began the ritual binding. It had been centuries since he'd required potions and lines on the floor that young necromancers used in their summonings. Even then, he knew it was more about focusing the mind than any power granted by symbols. The rituals created rhythm and sequencing.

These days he only needed the words. Spoken in a language ancient even to him, he began the summoning. Because the bodies were intact, he had no need to venture into the In Between. He yanked the soul back into the body easily.

The man came to with a gasp. His eyes rolled wildly. Azrael's summoning had included a block that stilled him physically so he could not try to escape. Not that it would do him any good. Once separated by death, mortals quickly began to forget how to use their physical forms. Most of his undead were made immediately after death, before the soul could leave the body. If not, they were shambling, drooling idiots for the first few hours, sometimes days, until they regained their control. But he didn't want to waste time watching the man thrash and groan like a Hollywood zombie. He placed a geas on the man's tongue, enabling him to speak with only a little slurring.

The man knew little. He'd been brought on by his partner—easy money, he'd claimed—kill a dancer. He had no idea who hired them or why. Only that they were supposed to make it look like an accident—although that was going to be hard since "…the bitch struggled so much."

Azrael snapped the man's mouth shut with a gesture. He began to wriggle on the table as he understood what he'd become and the first stirrings of fear overtook him. They all panicked eventually.

He focused his attention on the woman. Decapitated, her body twitched while her eyes rolled about wildly. He forced her to focus on his questions.

The woman who hired them had been "classy, old-school money-like," and spoke with an accent. The assassin assumed Isela had slept with the woman's husband or something. Azrael scoured her memory, raking through her thoughts for every scrap about the woman who'd ordered the hit. But there was an obscuring force on the hired killer. He caught only glimpses of hair that might have been strawberry blond under a blue silk scarf, and the flashy red soles of her high heels.

Azrael thought of both Vanka and the Queen of Diamonds. The former's grudge over a thrown knife wouldn't be enough to send her after Isela unless she truly was trying to undermine his effort.

The latter meant that she had read Zeman's mind when she took the book and knew Azrael and Isela were close. In either case, Isela would not be safe until this was over. And if they succeeded, would anyone on the allegiance forget her when they knew what her dancing had done for him?

By now the man was beginning to gurgle and weep as panic hit him. The woman's eyes switched rapidly, unable to turn her head but hearing her companion's terror. Finally she, too, began to gibber and wail. She pleaded for mercy.

Azrael thought of how forlorn Isela looked at the idea that Gregor might hate the humanity she brought out in him. She was so very human, full of compassion—and forgiveness. The fact that she'd come to his bed after everything she'd endured spoke to that.

It made her weak. The first thing any necromancer learned, if they hoped to survive, was to stifle fear and release the humanity that made any number of horrors seem inconceivable. In his time, he'd seen things that would leave her suffering nightmares forever. In his early days, he'd committed more than his share of violence.

Azrael now exercised force when necessary but no more than was required to accomplish his aim. And he'd let the rumors about him grow, knowing gossip and mystery would keep most in their place.

He knew he should make examples out of them, but he hesitated. There were other ways to protect Isela.

Wondering at his decision, Azrael released them instead, watching both bodies collapse on the table. He strode from the room, wanting to be as far from their true deaths as possible. Gregor was waiting. Azrael briefed him on what he'd learned.

"Send the heads to the underground," he said. "With the warning: Isela is mine. Anyone else who tries to take the job gets the same."

Gregor paused. "The heads, master?"

"Was I unclear?" Azrael went still, and Gregor looked away first.

Turning these two and delivering them as mindless undead was hardly necessary to send a message.

"Often the best demonstration of power is restraint," Azrael answered the unspoken question.

Savagery, for its own sake, had never been his way. As soon as he was powerful enough to defend himself and his servants, without brutalizing his enemies, he did so. Humans were more productive without living in terror. Keeping their lives calm and ordinary meant they could go about doing the things they did—brilliant, greedy, selfish, generous, petty—that kept his territory one of the most productive in the world.

"As you wish." Gregor hinged at the waist. "The other—the Rabbit?"

Azrael went still at the mention of the man they'd run down in the small coastal town in Croatia.

Summoning these two was one thing. Again, he thought of Isela. Azrael could not afford the same compassion that he had shown the two assassins. What he might have to do to get information from the man would horrify most mortals.

If the Queen of Diamonds was back, this was much bigger than the deaths of a few lower necromancers.

Isela's world had gotten more complicated, and now she was thoroughly entangled with him. That entanglement had already threatened her life. An idea had begun to form that any one of his contemporaries would say was a sign of his own weakness, or insanity. But it would be a way to protect her through this and—if anything happened to him—beyond.

To accept his offer, Isela had to know him fully. Azrael could not live with her looking at him with the innocence of those ashen eyes, welcoming him with her body, without knowing what he must be willing to do to keep her safe. He would not be able to shield himself from her forever. She must know the other side of the man she brought to her bed: the monster.

"Save him," he said to Gregor.

First he would go to her as the man she thought he was and allow himself to be that—for them both—just one more time. What happened after might change everything.

* * *

ISELA THRASHED awake in the canopied bed, gasping for breath as she fought the cloth around her neck. Azrael stirred beside her.

His hands closed over her wrists, preventing her hooked fingers from clawing at her own throat. Isela fought, but Azrael held firm. He chanted words until they became more than a jumble of sounds. "There is no rope. It's over."

The tension went out of her arms in a violent spasm.

As the specter of death closed over her, the night's memories washed away the fragile dam she'd built against sudden awareness of her own mortality. A rising tide of suffocating coldness caught in her throat until her breath hitched and gasped.

Azrael was there, in the dark, when fear and loneliness and the inevitability of death dragged her under. Strong arms closed around her, rocking, soothing. She wanted more, lifting her mouth to find his as though it held her next breath.

When they met, he found her salty and hungry with a need so great his body responded instantly. Their union was frenetic: a raging hunger that could only be satisfied by a feverish race to completion. Isela took from him until she felt alive again. When she came, marking him with her voice and her nails, Azrael rode her body hard enough to bruise until his own release thundered through him and pushed them both into oblivion.

CHAPTER TWENTY-THREE

The scent of agarwood and burned molasses tugged Isela from sleep. Azrael. Scraps of languid dreams faded with a tickle on her eyelids. She blinked her eyes open to take in sleep-spiked black hair on the pillow beside her own. Heat curled in her belly when he turned his head and the glowing silver pools of his eyes settled on her face. A sexy little smile licked at the corner of his mouth.

She yawned, detangling her arm from his body to cover her mouth, and caught a glimpse of her forearm. It was marked with a line of soot. She inhaled, frowning at the distinctive ashy flavor in the air.

"Who burned toast?" she asked.

Azrael propped himself up on one elbow beside her, freeing her up to scoot back toward the headboard and take in the surroundings.

"I… ah…" he began, glancing around them. "Overheated… a little."

They were on an island of intact bedding. The rest of the bed—what was left of it—was in ashes. Only chunks of melted metal poking out of the rubble suggested a frame. She clutched the singed sheet to her breasts.

"A little?" she echoed.

Azrael actually looked embarrassed—the smile going bigger in a way that was surprisingly boyish. Her heart did a backflip against her ribs.

No, she told it. *You do not fall for a necromancer whose orgasm sets the bed on fire.*

Isela remembered waking up after the nightmare with arms around her and then his body inside her. Phantom tremors shook her. She had wanted release, and a distraction, and he had burned the bed down around them.

Azrael searched for words. "You seem to have an unexpected effect on me."

"This doesn't happen… all the time?"

"All necromancers identify with one of the four elements," he explained. "Our ability to generate or control it is the first sign of what we are to become."

Isela's mind flicked back over the hot water, the room temperature, and now this—a bed turned to ash. "Yours is fire."

He nodded. "But loss of control is less common, as we age."

A lick of feminine pride rose in her. She wasn't the only one who had enjoyed herself beyond expectation. And even then, he'd kept her safe. Not so much as a blister or a burned hair. The rest of the room was untouched except for that faint lingering scent of burned toast. Her stomach rumbled.

Azrael licked a thumb and wiped at her cheekbone. It came away sooty.

"I guess I need another shower." Isela dropped the sheet mischievously and climbed out of bed to stand in the ashes.

At the sight of her, his eyes went hot again.

"After a shower and breakfast," she chided. "Lunch? Food. I'm starving."

Azrael leaped from the bed with catlike quickness, tossing her over his shoulder and striding into the tiled room. She admired the firm roundness of his bare backside, smiling at the sooty footprints he left on the floor. "Consider multitasking."

Well, as long as whatever it was between them lasted, it certainly wouldn't be boring.

* * *

Azrael sent a command to the kitchen as they finished drying off, and a few minutes later, there was a tap on the door. He tossed her the robe on his way to open it.

Gregor bore a platter and a large duffel bag.

Shutting the door behind Gregor, Azrael felt her surprise and a little bit of embarrassment as she purposefully avoided looking at the ruins of the bed. Gregor had no such compulsions. He took in the entire scene, and his mouth set in a long, thin line.

"I intercepted Tyler on his way up with these, and I have some information about the attack," Gregor said, depositing the tray on the fireside table. "Two birds, one stone."

"Later," Azrael said as Isela whispered, "Tell me."

As Gregor looked between them, she poured two cups of coffee and snagged a cookie. Gregor's gaze settled on Azrael, waiting for his command.

"I need to know." Isela met Azrael's eyes as she handed over the coffee.

Go ahead, Azrael commanded.

Gregor stalked to the window, his back to them.

"They exploited a gap in the system," he explained. "The head of Academy security found it. Then it was just a matter of timing to catch the blind spots in the sensors. It's being addressed."

"Do you know who hired them?" Isela said. "Was it her —the Queen?"

Gregor half turned, appraising her. "Do you doubt it?"

To her credit, Isela addressed the question without rising to the challenge inherent in Gregor's voice. "Maybe. But I was in that room with the allegiance. You'd be an idiot not to see the tension. What if bringing me in was just for show? What if they didn't expect us to get as close as we have? I'm the weak link, right? Get rid of me, and Azrael has to start all over again."

Azrael admired how collected she remained even as her pulse raced against the skin of her throat.

"Both are so powerful." Her voice cracked finally. "Why hire humans to kill me?"

"The Academy's security includes wards against the supernatural," Azrael said as Isela cleared her throat with a sip of coffee.

"Another necromancer would have triggered my alarms. We trusted the cameras and sensors to guard against human infraction."

She paled. "What about my family? My friends? If she can get to me—"

"I've sent word to your mother and assigned a few of my people to the Academy." Azrael said, addressing Gregor, "You made the delivery?"

Gregor nodded, looking pleased for the first time since he'd entered the room. Azrael could count on his gruesome warning of severed heads deterring any other attempts. Gregor had a way with theatrics. Azrael was sure he would hear about it from Lysippe.

"Until we know, or this is finished, I'm assigning a guard to you," Azrael said. "And you will stay here."

It wasn't a request, and he expected her to fight. He knew how much she valued her independence. But when she spoke, her voice was full of hard-fought resolve.

"I won't put the people I love in danger with my presence," Isela agreed.

Azrael sipped at his coffee to avoid taking her into his arms, startled by the impulse to comfort her. Between one breath and the next, her spine straightened.

"What do I need to do to help you finish this?" Her eyes were firm.

"Prepare yourself to dance again," he said.

Gregor set down the duffel bag. "Your cohorts at the Academy sent this for you. I presume you will find what you need here."

"The ballroom is yours," Azrael said. "If you need anything else, inform your attaché. He'll see it done."

* * *

THE BALLROOM WAS A LONG, rectangular space with soaring ceilings painted in vivid frescos over glossy wood floors. In one corner, a freestanding barre had been placed near the mirrored wall. The floor was taped to the dimensions of the Academy ring. The room was warmed to a comfortable temperature, and she inhaled the scent of cardamom and oranges.

He'd gotten everything right, she considered. Down to the smell.

Of course he would. Isela dismissed the little singing voice in her chest. It's not like he was giving her a key and a toothbrush. Well, a key.

What she had done in Havel Zeman's little room had been effective, regardless of the outcome. If he wanted more of the same, the effort he'd expended to keep her environment familiar was sensible.

Isela set down her bag and the pile of books she'd brought with her from the library. One of the twins that had been in the car the night before had been her silent shadow all morning. He now stood at the edge of the space, waiting.

She faced him, hands on hips. "I don't usually rehearse in front of others."

"I will be outside." He gestured to the door they had entered. "My brother waits at the other door." *In case you were having any bright ideas about escaping*—the unspoken conclusion to his sentence.

She remembered how the two men fought the demons in the bookstore with the sheer force and inexorability of tidal waves. The only weapon either of them needed was the four fingers and a thumb around the two dinner plate-size palms. The machetes were for efficiency.

Both were a handsome shade of polished teak, slabbed with muscle, and moved with incongruous grace and speed. Brothers yes, twins maybe, but they were not identical. Though neither had broken the stern expression in her presence, she had the impression this one did not laugh. His earlobes were punctured with smooth black discs, and his luscious, curly hair was bound at the nape of his neck.

"Thank you, Rory," she said, betting on her hunch though Azrael hadn't called him by name, and he hadn't offered.

Rory grunted and stalked away, but she was sure, for just a moment, she had seen the surprise on his face. That meant his brother was Dory.

Isela's body ached: she focused on her exercises at the barre and prolonged stretching before stepping lightly through the sequence she'd been crafting. She'd already worked out the big movements of the choreography; all that was left were the transitions, smoothing and shaping them to draw the whole dance together.

Isela was taking a break and checking her phone when the door opened. Nothing from her mother or Evie, but Bebe had called —twice.

"You have a guest," Rory said, standing aside.

Isela tossed her phone into her bag at the appearance of a dish-water-blond man with eyes that darted around the room in a combination of awe and terror. "Kyle."

When he saw her, his face broke into a smile of pure relief. And then she was in his arms. Kyle lifted her off her feet and spun her in a little circle before setting her down.

"You scared the bejesus out of us, Vogel," he muttered into her hair, dragging her away from his chest to look at her face. "Are you—"

"I'm fine," she said, furiously wiping at tears coursing down her cheeks.

"'Course you are," he said, but his voice was uneven.

Isela's eyes found Rory. "Is there somewhere outside we can take a walk?"

"Gardens," he grunted, staring ahead.

Isela passed Kyle a look of hopeless exasperation. He grinned, tucking her under his arm. "Look at you, commanding the troops."

Isela rolled her eyes, pressed her face into his coat, and breathed him in, picking up hints of arnica and wintergreen oil. Kyle squeezed her shoulders.

Tyler met them at the door to the north courtyard with a long coat and a thick stole of soft wool for Isela. "The Garden of Paradise," he announced as they walked through the doorway.

Even in the winter, the shapes of plants and trees looked elegant beneath a light dusting of snow.

"The kid, with the coat, is he…" Kyle began.

"Tyler," she nodded. "He's their attempt to get me used to being around them."

"He's not bad," Kyle said. "If it weren't for his eyes—"

"I know," she whispered. "And they have no smell. It's just wrong."

"You and your nose, Vogel," he said. "I bet your mom's got the bloodhound on her side of the family."

You'd be surprised, she wanted to say, thinking of them. Her mother *was* the fiercer one of the two, yet her mild-mannered father carried the wolf gene. Guess you never could tell.

"So how's things with lover boy?" he asked finally.

Azrael hardly fit the description, but the flush rose in her cheeks anyway, and Kyle cackled.

"How *are* things," she corrected.

"You totally hit that!"

Isela pressed her gloved hands to her cheeks in a vain attempt to stop the flush from spreading.

"Not that I blame you," he said. "Your necro is something. A terrifying something, but my gods, those eyes." Kyle glanced around. "And this isn't a bad setup: bodyguards, a zombie foot servant. What more could a girl ask for?"

"Her friends," Isela said plainly, squeezing his arm. She forced a laugh. "My necromancer. It's not even like that."

"Oh? What's it like?" he quipped. "You two playing tiddlywinks to pass the long, cold nights?"

"None of your business." Isela was unable to keep from grinning. "Anyway, he sleeps during the day—when he does."

Kyle's eyes widened. "Like a ghoul?"

She slapped his shoulder. "Shut up." She dropped her voice. "The walls have ears."

"So do I," he teased. "And I want details. He looks like he'd be a hurricane between the sheets."

"More like an inferno," she said, thinking of the bed they'd incinerated. "I can't believe we are talking about this here, of all places." She paused. "Speaking of places…"

Kyle must have heard the ache in her voice. "Niles had the windows boarded up, and the guys were working on the door when I packed your bag. I'll keep an eye on the place for you, promise."

"This will be over soon," she said, reassuring them both. "I'll be home soon."

Kyle sighed, and for a long while they stood in silence, breathing in the crisp winter air as the sunset cast faded golds and vivid magentas across the city below.

"It's good that you're here, Issy," Kyle said eventually. "You're safe here… from everything."

The skin crawled on the back of her neck. "What do you mean—"

He looked out over the city sprawled below the castle, teaming with people and activity in spite of the cold. His jaw worked in frustration.

"Kyle?"

When he looked at her, his eyes were full of tears. "People are idiots, Vogel."

Her chest clenched. "What's happened?"

He sighed, tucking his chin into his chest with a resigned shrug. "One of the paps got a picture of Azrael carrying you out of the Academy. It looks… Pictures lie, Issy, but you're in that robe and not much else, and you look… dead."

"Someone tried to kill me, Kyle," she said.

His eyes shown bright with tears. "I *know. We* know Issy. A brick was thrown through the window of the Academy this morning."

"Was anyone hurt?" Isela gasped.

He shook his head doggedly.

"What is it?"

"There's speculation," he said, hesitating.

"Speculation?" Isela tried to keep the desperation out of her voice. "What are they saying?"

"Zombie," he whispered. "Azrael turned you, for Gregor—or himself—or gods only know what. It's nonsense, Issy…"

It was foolish, and reasonable people might know better, but where necromancers were untouchable, godsdancers were human. They made accessible scapegoats for the uneasy human relationship with the gods.

"Azrael is right," he said resolutely. "I hate it, but you're safer here."

Isela swallowed the raw burn in the back of her throat. She pasted on a smile. It felt brittle as old glass. "I should get back. I have a lot of work to do. Thank you… for checking in on me."

As if on cue, the door opened and Tyler appeared, framed by light.

Kyle hesitated, searching for something to say. He must have guessed at the fragility of her control, because he sighed instead.

"Anytime, Vogel." Kyle hugged her once more. "Divya is waiting for a full report."

Isela stood at the wall for a long time after Kyle was gone until she could no longer feel her fingers. A sound from behind startled her into turning.

Rory waited in the growing twilight a few feet away. He was coatless, the thin gray T-shirt stretched over his chest and a dark brown cloth wrapped around his hips. He didn't seem cold in the slightest.

"How are you not freezing?" She impatiently wiped the last of the wetness from her cheeks. "How long were you standing there?"

He shrugged. "Long enough."

"It's guard *and* spy now?"

"I have no need to spy," he said. "The Matai sees all."

"Matai?" she said. "Is that Fijian?"

Rory grunted and crossed his arms over his chest.

"Brilliant," she muttered, striding around him back toward the door. "Taking Gregor's side, I see."

He moved so fast she only saw the blur of his passing. He held open the door for her. "You endanger him."

"Oh really?" she said, stalking past. "I thought I was the puny, fragile human."

"Our duty is to protect Azrael against threats even he cannot see."

Isela threw up her hands as she returned to the ballroom and shucked off her outerwear in the doorway.

"I'm a threat," she muttered, "to Azrael?"

"For whatever reason, he has decided to protect you. But he is more important than a single human life."

She scowled at the implication. "Thank you for reminding me of my place in the scheme of things."

He grinned, exposing a beautiful set of strong, white teeth. "You're welcome."

Isela slammed the door in his face.

She threw herself into dancing, pushing herself harder than she would have before Kyle's visit to keep her mind from wandering.

The door opened. Expecting Rory, she spun with a frown to see the Amazon.

"Lysippe," she said cautiously.

"Dancer." The woman did not smile, but there was no animosity in her gaze either. "Azrael would speak with you."

Isela hesitated just long enough to evoke a canted half smile from the Amazon.

"Not every battle must be fought."

"Am I that transparent?" Isela asked, grabbing a towel and the oversized sweater to keep her upper body warm.

The taller woman said nothing. Isela followed her into the hall. The chair Rory had occupied was empty.

"I, too, bridled at first," Lysippe admitted after a moment. "Where I came from, only a fool would follow a man into battle. But Azrael leads a worthy command."

Her stride was so long Isela had to half jog to keep up. Everything about her was pure warrior. "Where… do you… come from?"

"You mean, when?" the Amazon said.

"That too," Isela said.

"My homeland is known by a different name, and my sisters no longer ride," she said. "Everything changes."

"You call him Azrael," Isela said, suddenly realizing it. "Not master, or sir, or matey."

"Matai," Lysippe corrected, "is a Samoan title of honor and leadership. We choose the word that suits. Azrael only asks for the respect."

The way she said his name did hold a bit of resonance, as though it were more of a title.

"The word my people used translates roughly to honored aunt, or mother," she went on, raising an eyebrow. "Neither of which applies."

"Does he… have your soul too?"

The Amazon glanced at her, and her expression held mild surprise.

"I'm not supposed to know that, am I?" Isela asked, stricken.

"It's up to Azrael." Lysippe shrugged. "And yes. I entrusted my soul to him." A familiar, savage smile parted her lips. "In exchange,

I have seen civilizations rise and fall. No wound can touch me. What warrior wouldn't take that bargain?"

Isela thought about what that must be like; to watch humanity pass before timeless eyes until individual human lives became a blink. She thought about seeing her family and friends age and die while she remained unchanged. It made her shudder. No weapon or strength would make up for that loss. Not to mention being owned by a necromancer.

"You wouldn't," Lysippe assumed.

Isela's eyes darted to hers and then away.

The Amazon shrugged. "To each her own."

"Azrael must be—a tough person to spend an eternity working for," Isela said diplomatically.

The taller woman bared her teeth again in that smile, and Isela suddenly realized why she recognized it. Though their features bore no relation, something in its character reminded her of Azrael's smile.

"I suppose," Lysippe answered. "But he's my father. I'm used to it."

Isela was aware her jaw was hanging, but Lysippe had already moved ahead to open the door to Azrael's great study. She snapped her jaw shut with a clack of tooth on tooth and took a breath to quiet the deep sense of foreboding.

The door closed behind her, and she was plunged into the firelit darkness of the cavernous room.

* * *

"I DIDN'T KNOW necromancers had family," she began lightly.

Unable to see him as her eyes adjusted, Isela felt him as a sudden wave of heat at her back before she heard him. Her body had no qualms about responding to the heat rolling through her. The magnetic attraction of skin hovering just shy of touch tingled. She closed her eyes and angled her head sideways, exposing her neck.

"We don't have the gift of creating life." Azrael took the invitation, pressing fingertips to the braided hair at the base of her skull and lips to her nape.

"Nor do we create art," he murmured against her skin. "It's lost as we gain power over death. This is why we envy humans. We need you and loathe you at the same time."

"Is that like Gregor hating me for reminding me of his humanity?"

"Hate is a lower emotion, to be overcome. And there are many ways to make a family."

"So I guess we don't have to worry about protection," she said, her voice thick.

Isela had the physical memory of the sweeping heat of him swelling into her womb. Her breath hitched.

Azrael chuckled, and the length of him connected with her back. "No. And I am immune to the diseases of humanity."

She couldn't remember a conversation like this ever being so sexy.

Damn him for turning everything into foreplay. His fingers dusted the curve of her neck as his mouth moved toward her spine. When he inhaled, the fine hairs stood on end.

"You smell like the ocean after a storm," he said, "and the spice vendor in the market, and Isela."

Liquid heat made her thighs tremble. "I thought I had the wolf nose."

An arm snaked around her abdomen, locking her in place. She tensed, but when his palm opened at her waist, fingertips flexing, her body betrayed her again by softening. She groaned.

"Too hot," she breathed at his touch. Azrael laughed again, softly, and instantly the temperature of his skin dropped.

She surrendered her weight to him fully. He purred satisfaction.

The ridge of him pressed against the crease of her backside as he lifted her off her feet. Pinned to him, he carried her across the room to the broad desk. His hand returned to the nape of her neck, exerting a gentle, unmistakable pressure.

Isela angled her upper body toward the desk, pressing her hips into him.

Any worries she'd had coming into the room simply burned to ash in the fire between them. Whatever her primitive hindbrain said about the danger she was in, just breathing the same air as the necromancer, her body had no qualms about what it wanted.

The skin of her back prickled with gooseflesh as he bunched the sweater and traced his fingers under each of the delicate straps of the leotard crisscrossing her spine. The liquid heat of his mouth on the sensitized skin sent the blood pounding in her ears.

His voice rumbled against her ribcage. "You will become my consort."

"Your what?" Isela didn't want to think. It was energy wasted when there was so much to feel. "Is that like a chain-me-to-the-bedposts thing?"

His fingers brushed her most sensitive bundle of nerves through the thin leggings, teasing. "That can be arranged independently."

She braced herself on her elbows, pressing her fists into her closed eyes to force herself to focus. His hand slipped under the waistband of her leggings. When his fingers parted her body, she tried to clamp her thighs shut, but her legs refused to cooperate. Her hips tilted into his palm, urging him deeper.

"Are you asking me to marry you?"

That brought him upright. He withdrew his hand. Snorted.

"Marriage is a human ritual designed to secure property and wealth exchanges between families."

Isela slid away, tugging her sweater down as her senses came stumbling back. "Way to romance a girl."

She turned in time to see him pluck his two fingers out of his mouth as one eyebrow rose. His hair was mussed, and his expression screamed sex so dangerous it threatened to undo her completely.

His words were cold. "Is that what you want? Shall I ask your father's permission for your hand?"

She couldn't even mentally place her necromancer in Lukas Vogel's study. On top of that, Lukas would take the request as an insult to her sovereignty.

It was her turn to smile wickedly as she sat back against the desk, crossing her arms over her chest. "No, I'll stick with the bed-burning sex."

That earned her a flare of heat in his eyes and the hint of a smile that promised exquisite torment. She ignored the thrumming response of her body, trying to concentrate on the words. Azrael stalked forward, resting his hands on the desk edge on either side of her hips.

"You're the one with the fancy titles," she said warily, leaning back.

"To become my consort means you give yourself to me, completely," he said, one hand going to the braid that trailed down her back. "You share my bed, and you will take no other man to yours." The tie holding the end of her braid went up in a quick pop of flame. "And you will have the my protection of myself and that of my Aegis against any threat to you—body, mind, or soul."

Azrael slipped his fingers through the braid until her hair hung loose, brushing the desk. Her voice emerged, trembling.

"Does this mean you put my soul on the shelf beside Gregor's?"

"No." He buried his fist in the thick of her hair, using the pressure to expose her neck. It took a moment for her sticky, dry mouth to function as he tasted the flesh under her jaw.

"Do I at least get a cool sword?" she croaked.

"Gregor was right about your mouth when you're nervous," he said, brushing his lips against hers until electricity sparked between them.

"I have a strong sense of self-preservation," she said, lowering her chin.

He exhaled sharply and released her.

Isela pulled herself into a seat on the desk, bracing her weight on her hands. "What did you expect, Azrael? You're talking about something that sounds more serious than just taking a job for the allegiance. People already think I'm your cat's paw. I'm trying to understand what this means."

Azrael pulled back for a moment, and his eyes narrowed in consideration.

"As my Aegis, Gregor, Lysippe, and the others exchanged their souls for a portion of my power, for strength and longevity," he said. "They vowed allegiance, loyalty, and obedience. The weapon is the manifestation of their essence as warriors and a seal of our covenant."

She thought of Gregor's black sword, as unflinching as his demeanor but also something of striking beauty.

"They are my servants," he went on. "A consort is a bond; more than a lover, although that can be part of it. I cannot give you strength, or longevity. But by being mine you become untouchable and a penalty for harming you can be exacted." His eyes hooded. "And as a bonus, I can continue to burn down our bed as often as you desire."

Prickles of anticipation and anxiety raced from the nape of her neck to her low back.

"But your Aegis will protect me now, if you tell them to?" she said, forcing herself to think.

"Unless they perceive the danger to me as a greater threat," he said. "If I am wounded, or unconscious, I cannot enforce such protection."

She thought of Rory's words about guarding Azrael from threats he could not see and the look in Gregor's eyes when he thought she had stabbed Azrael. She understood what the power of that protection meant. "The night in Havel's bookstore, when you told me to run—"

"In my state, you would be secondary," he said. "And if I had fallen, their obligation to you would have ended."

Making her life meaningless to them.

"If I was your consort…" She struggled with the word and the stitch in her chest that developed at the image of him lifeless. "And you…"

Isela couldn't say it aloud. For a creature whose purview was death, she had never met someone so vibrantly full of passion. What kind of power would it take to rob him of that? She didn't want to know.

"They would defend you as my own flesh," he said. "If I fell, the Aegis would be yours until the end of your days."

She thought of Rory's open dislike, and Gregor's, thinly veiled. "And they would approve of this?"

Azrael gave a shrug that said exactly how little their approval mattered. "When they accepted me, they accepted my decisions. They will obey."

She snorted, thinking of how long Gregor would stick around after Azrael was dead—or how long it would take him to kill her to free himself from the bond.

"The moment they raised a hand against you, the covenant would be broken," he said quietly. "Their existences would be forfeit."

Something about the way he said it made her think that "forfeit" was a euphemism for something painful. Perhaps worse than death. She had no idea what held necromancers and their shields to an increasingly intricate code of honor, but it seemed more powerful than either of them. She was out of her depth, with no one to give a second opinion.

She asked the first thing that popped into her head: "What's the catch?"

It was his turn to echo in surprise. "Catch?"

"You know, the strings," she said. "I get bed-burning sex on demand and a personal bodyguard. Granted, I actually might need them because my new boyfriend probably has some pretty scary enemies. Besides that, you don't get something for nothing."

This time she could not mistake the heat in his eyes for desire. She fought the urge to capitulate. He was *asking*, after all, when he clearly could have commanded. This must be part of the code. He could not make her accept. She had a right to know, and he had the responsibility to tell her.

"I am…" he began.

He withdrew and she realized he was at a loss for words.

"I, alone, will see to your pleasure," he tried again, as if she had missed that part. "You will take no other man to your bed while we are in contract."

She stared. How on earth would any man ever have a chance, now that she'd had him? A glint of male satisfaction crossed his expression with uncanny timing. If she had known better, she would have thought—

"Are you reading my mind?"

Silence.

"You can't *do* that," she said, furious. "Stay out of my head, Azrael. It's not fair."

"Fair?" A savage look masquerading as a smile settled on his face. "You believe the world operates on rules of fairness after you've danced to put money into the accounts of businessmen?"

Heat rushed to her face, fueled by hurt and anger at his words.

"How can you expect me to be a partner," she said, "if I can't have the privacy to think my own thoughts and choose when I share them with you?"

Azrael held up a finger, the humorless smile still creasing his face. "First. A partnership implies equality. If you live to be a thousand years, we will never be equals.

"Second, everyone in this household is an open book to me."

Once again, her anger burned away diffidence. Isela rallied, pitching her upper body forward, raising her index finger to his face in response.

"First. Partnership implies equity, which is not exclusively equality," she said. "I may never be as powerful as you, and you may think you are giving me a great gift by allowing frail human me to become your consort. But I have something you *need.* And it's gotten me up to my eyeballs in demons and death threats. I think I deserve to be given a little bit of privacy to think about how sad my life is going to be when this is over."

"Second," she pressed. "What about *your* bed?"

Azrael inhaled sharply. "My bed?"

"Do you think I'm just going to sit back and let you fuck anything that catches your eye," she said. "While I'm under the 'necromancer only' clause?"

Azrael had too many teeth, she decided. And that smile was getting more predatory by the minute.

"Again, your mouth shows me a lack of respect, dancer," he murmured. "I offer you an honor which has never been extended to any human, and you throw it in my face with accusations of infidelity."

When he was a boy, his mother called him little Terror, the small voice in her chimed in. She remembered the way he'd faltered through the words and the distant look in his eyes. It wasn't a story many people had heard, no matter how long he'd been alive.

She reached out and lay a hand on his cheek, ignoring the burn of his skin against her palm. He inhaled deeply, and the heat abated.

"And what do you give me, as my consort?"

That caught him off guard. "My protection—"

"All you have to do is ask me what I'm thinking," she said to that deadly, beautiful face. "And maybe wait awhile, especially if I'm mad. It's hard for me to verbalize sometimes until I calm down. But I promise I will tell you."

His nostrils flared.

"And I will not share you. I don't think my heart could handle it."

"Your heart," he murmured.

"I'm not going to call you 'master,' so don't even think about it." She pushed on to cover the dangerous slip of words.

"I prefer Azrael," he said, "or 'my necromancer.'"

She flushed a little. "Were you spying on me in the garden? That was a private conversation."

"I can't assure your safety unless I know what's happening to you," he said.

"I was talking to Kyle," she said. "He's my best friend. He would never hurt me—"

She paused, and her head angled slightly.

"You're jealous," she said.

Maybe it was being so close to death, but she couldn't help it: she laughed. Only when she saw that his countenance didn't lighten, and he looked even more brooding and fierce, did she realize whatever this consort business was, it was very serious.

"I'm sorry," she said, biting down on a grin. "It's just… Kyle is taken."

"Some men do not think that is an obstacle in the pursuit of a new conquest," he spoke carefully.

"Yes, but the fact I have breasts is an enormous obstacle," she finished, changing the subject. "How long does the contract last?"

Again, Isela seemed to catch him by surprise in a way that pushed him toward anger. "So eager to be free of me?"

She sighed, weary now of the minefield that lay between them. "I'm sure your last consort understood the terms perfectly, but I need a little help."

"No." His hands closed on her hips, dragging her to the edge of the desk.

"No… what?" She suddenly had the urge to weep. How was it possible that one man could send her swinging between desire and frustration so quickly? "No help? How do you expect me—"

"No other consort," he said in that same emotionless tone. "I have never offered it to anyone before."

"Oh."

Azrael's hands settled on her legs. Warmth radiated into her from his palms. His thumbs pressed against the sensitive skin inside her knees, and without thinking, she spread them, creating a cradle for his body between her thighs.

The thin fabric of her leggings was a flimsy barrier between him and the most intimate part of herself. She quaked, and her thighs clenched reflexively against his hips. How quickly he took her from wanting to run away to craving his touch, and what a particular effect the transition had on her libido.

He grunted satisfaction as his hands slid to her waist, pulling her closer.

His pants strained against him. It looked painful. She slid her hands down the impossibly firm plane of his chest, under the thin T-shirt, to the waistband of his pants. He caught her fingers on a mission of mercy to his zipper. His mouth hovered over hers, breath a hot, cinnamon sweet wind on her lips.

"I'm going to have to think about it," she whispered, tongue darting out to lick his lower lip in invitation.

Isela felt his stillness, but her passion took her beyond fear. She nipped his lower lip, squeezing it between her teeth like ripe fruit.

"I mean, thank you. I'm flattered." She flattened her chest against his, craving the heat of his body. "And I will consider your offer—"

His hand slipped to her wrist, pinning it to the small of her back. He trapped the other hand before she could reach for him, joining it at her spine. She gasped, eyes blinking wide, but she was still too taken with her own arousal to protest.

Now his smile was a terrible thing, full of possession and lust. Isela wondered if it was possible to orgasm from a look.

"You will… consider," he said with a light tone that belied the thunder beneath it, "my offer?"

She strained against him, ignoring the discomfort, and pressed her lips to his jaw. The restraint only aided the arousal sharpening to a physical pain in her core.

Azrael had both her wrists in one long-fingered hand, the other pinched her chin in his fingers and drew her mouth away from him. His face hovered a few tantalizing inches from hers, but he kept her from touching him. He revealed a new edge to his smile, cruel in its sensuality, turning the lines of his face into stone.

"Perhaps you think me like one of your admirers from the Academy," he said. "To be toyed with."

He released her then, and pried her thighs from around him, crossing the room so swiftly Isela braced herself on the heels of her hands to keep from tumbling backward.

His name left her in a breath so full of longing she could see his shudder across the room. Instead of answering, she watched him retreat deeper into his stillness. The heat in his eyes was snuffed out. She shivered, and her arms slipped around her body, palms rubbing her biceps.

She snapped before she could catch herself. "You want me to hand myself over to you, to have my mind picked apart whenever you like, and my body—"

"I cannot be other than I am, Isela," he said. "You must accept that."

"And if I can't?"

His eyes, a quicksilver shine as deadly as any blade, were her answer.

CHAPTER TWENTY-FOUR

Isela took a break when her stomach grumbled. A tray had appeared as if by magic while she had been fixated on her dancing. As she cooled off, she nibbled at grilled veggies before dipping into a bowl of chicken soup with homemade dumplings. Satiated, she stretched out on the floor, moving into deeper stretches designed to release tension in her hip while she flipped through her notes and the information Azrael had given her.

Everything led to the words circled repeatedly in ink: Queen of Diamonds. Frustration made her switch tacks. If she couldn't find anything about the woman, maybe there was something about the book.

Grimoire was a blanket term for a book of magic. Though the word itself was French in origin, the concept went beyond borders, with roots in cultures all over the world. From carved walls and tablets, to papyrus scrolls and bound volumes, spells could be recorded and passed on in an impossible number of ways.

But magic was no more about potions and séances than lightning was the strike of an angry god thrown from a mountaintop. Magic was a flow of energy. Which made spells something like channels to direct it. The necromancer who had the most spells had a great deal of access to power, beyond his or her inherent abilities.

Isela thought back to the collection in Azrael's study. Hundreds, he'd admitted casually. She had seen no more than three books on the shelf in Havel Zeman's aedis, all with modern bindings. Azrael seemed to think the one Zeman had been working from when he was killed was much older—something that should have been beyond his reach to possess.

What if the Queen of Diamonds wasn't looking for the grimoire itself—but a spell it contained? And if they could somehow determine what spell she had been looking for, maybe they could find a way to stop her.

She rocketed off the floor. When she flung open the door, Rory looked up, ready to stop her.

"I need to see Azrael," she said.

"He's indisposed."

Isela ignored the sting. It had been two days since the conversation in the library, and she hadn't seen Azrael. It shouldn't have surprised her—it was a castle after all—but after their fresh intimacy, the loss was palpable. Worse, she had been installed in his private rooms, like the new wrought iron bed that appeared after the ruins of the old had been cleared. She was surrounded by him; the whole room carried his scent, from the closet full of clothes to the toiletries in the bathroom.

But Azrael must have had other rooms, other wardrobes and collections of deliciously scented soaps, because she had not heard so much as the echo of his voice in two days. In spite of being constantly shadowed by one of the four members of his Aegis who seemed closest to him, no one would respond to her questions about Azrael. Rory and Gregor seemed all too pleased to ignore them. At least Dory and Lysippe had the grace to be apologetic.

All because she hadn't jumped at the offer to become Azrael's love slave.

"Tell him it's urgent," she insisted. "I think I know why..."

Rory had already angled his head in that particular way that said there was mental communication happening. He dismissed her with his eyes.

"He'll call for you later," he said.

Call for you. She raged inwardly. This was the most bizarre sexual coercion she'd ever heard of. All because she hadn't been willing to give up everything she worked so hard for to become another one of his automatons.

It was fine if he wanted to deprive her of sex, but she was trying to do her job— the job the allegiance had brought her in for—and she would be damned if she would let his errant male pride stop her. She felt the roar building up inside her and then, surprisingly, a glimmer of gold she hadn't felt in days.

She and Azrael had communicated directly before. Why not now? She arrowed a thought to the image of him in her head. *This can't wait.*

Azrael's mental growl was just as threatening as the real thing. She fought off the goose bumps and the urge to be silent.

It's about the grimoire. She pressed. *I think I know what she was looking for.*

Silence.

"Let's go," Rory said.

She had to jog to keep up with him.

"I'm sorry I called you Fijian," she said.

He said nothing. They took an elevator down.

"I don't want to hurt him," she said. "I don't want to be his weak link. I just want to get this done so I can go home and get back to my life."

That earned her a sideways glance. She fought the deep ache the image of life without him brought with it. But she did want her family and friends safe. And she would give up Azrael, if that's what it took.

The elevator opened on the same floor as the morgue. Rory stepped out so quickly she almost missed his words. "It's too late for that now."

He led her down the hall to another room and opened the door. She took a big breath and went inside. The door shut behind her with a vacuum-sealed thud, and she found herself sharing a concrete-walled room, no bigger than a closet, with Gregor.

* * *

THE ROOM WAS SPARSELY FURNISHED: another door, a sink, and

the plain army surplus cot with wool blankets that bore signs of recent use.

"The dancer," Gregor purred, stalking across the room.

She dodged him, avoiding the sink next to the door opposite the one she had come in. Her attention went to the one-way mirror that filled the wall behind Gregor.

Beyond it, Azrael stood under hard, bright lighting, facing a man who had been chained by the wrists and suspended from the ceiling. Based on the limpness of his body and the lack of tension in his shoulders, they had been recently dislocated. The man was dressed in what had been a nice dress shirt and navy slacks. What was left of them were stained with blood and torn with holes. His head hung limp, chin sagging against his collarbones. Sweat and blood caked limp, graying hair.

In spite of the wreckage of his clothes, Isela noted that the skin beneath was unblemished. As she watched in horror, Azrael struck out with preternatural speed, his fist smashing into one of the man's upper arms.

The man's head flung back; the once-handsome face forming a mask of agony that made the blood freeze in her veins. She couldn't hear the scream.

She staggered backward into Gregor's chest and flung herself blindly to escape him. Her stomach clenched.

"Not again, dancer," Gregor said calmly. "And certainly not for this filth. He's hardly earned your empathy. Watch."

Isela turned back, hand over her mouth. The arm that had at once swollen and purpled was rapidly returning to flesh color. His shoulders seemed to reattach themselves as she watched.

"What—" she managed, finding Gregor's eyes in the dark.

He nodded at the window.

She looked back and now noted the floor was littered with human parts. His parts, she realized. But he had all his fingers and toes—and the nose and ears were also in their proper places.

"What the fuck?"

"Incubus," Gregor said as if that explained everything.

"They're immortal?" she said.

"Not quite." He shook his head. "They draw power from sexuality. This one trafficked females. He sold them to the highest bidder, although he kept quite a harem for himself. Human women were a particular specialty. He's quite old and has been gorged for some time. It's taken days to wear him down to this point."

Her mind stumbled over his words, trying to make sense of what she was seeing. Azrael didn't move his gaze from his captive, but she felt his attention shift, as if he had looked at her. That didn't stop him from what he did next.

An emerald blade materialized at his side, fisted in his hand. With a single stroke that was a blur to her eyes, the blade sliced up in an arc, severing the man's arms below the wrists. The incubus collapsed to the floor in a boneless heap. She looked up at his clenched fists sticking out over the top of the manacles and fought back a scream.

On the floor, the handless man thrashed. There was no blood. The heat of Azrael's blades had cauterized the wound instantly. The man made the mistake of trying to brace himself on one stump and collapsed, rolling in agony. Azrael took him by the back of the neck, lifting him off the floor. She didn't hear what he said, but in one smooth yank, he stripped the majority of the man's spinal column from his body. He tossed the ribbon of bone and tendrils of nerves across the room and spat on the twitching mass on the floor.

Isela didn't feel Gregor's hand on her shoulder as she heaved into the waste bucket he held under her face.

"The man is a parasite," he murmured. "He has no scruples and delivered anything for the right price. Worse, his own tastes had corrupted. Most incubi deliver pleasure as they take power. This one found pleasure only in inflicting pain."

Isela stumbled backward and let Gregor guide her onto the edge of the cot. It smelled strongest of Azrael here, and she saw a few fine black hairs on the pillow. Had he been here the whole time, sleeping on a barren cot a few feet away from the monster on the other side of the glass? While she swam in the enormous bed and fractiously resisted his offer of protection against a world that included creatures like this.

"Knowing this, still you pity him," Gregor said, interrupting her thoughts.

"I have never seen anyone tortured before."

"You did not see the females in his possession," he said. His voice held tension she had never heard before. "A quick death would have been a mercy he did not deserve."

She froze at the emotion she'd never thought cold, calculating Gregor capable of: grief.

"He broke Azrael's law," Gregor said, crouching beside her. "The enslavement of humans and breaking of females has been outlawed since Azrael took this territory. What message would a quick death send to others of his kind? An example must be made."

Isela shuddered, even as a righteous heat rose in her chest. The door to the inner room opened. She could not find the strength to look up, but Gregor stood and moved away immediately.

"Leave us," Azrael rumbled.

She heard the door close, and they were alone. On the other side of the glass, the twitching had stopped. Azrael cleaned his hands thoroughly in the sink beside the door, moving around the small room with the ease of familiarity.

"Is he dead?"

"No," Azrael said. "But it will cost him dearly to regenerate from this. And he will feel every bit of the pain."

She took a deep, steadying breath and looked up at him, gripping the cot's metal frame until her knuckles were white. She focused on the roughness of the blankets, the scent of him in the room, and refused to look through the glass again.

"Good," she said, and an image of Evie, bouncing Thyme on her hip, flashed to mind.

He looked surprised for just a moment, and his eyes steeled as he crouched beside her. "You know of someone who was abused by a man like this."

"You didn't read my mind?" Her voice was a ghost of its former defiance.

"I'm learning to ask."

"My oldest sister-in-law," she said. "She had to do things to survive after her family was killed. Things a man like this took advantage of her for."

He nodded solemnly. "Unfortunately, he is not unique. You see now why I bridled at the insinuation that I would have coerced you."

"I'm sorry."

She had the sense that the predator had been caged, but she trembled anyway.

Azrael rocked back on his heels. "You are frightened of me now."

She met his eyes. "You just ripped out a man's spine."

"And I will do it again before this is through," he said. "Perhaps next time you will wait, as I requested, instead of insisting to see me."

"You need to talk to Rory about what a request sounds like." Heat crept into her cheeks as she looked at her feet. "You have been avoiding me."

He reached out to touch the hair that had come loose from her bun, caught himself, and withdrew. "It seemed best to let you focus on your dancing while you made up your mind.

"But I'm glad you are here." He sighed. "I cannot protect you from this side of me. It is who I must be—to maintain that which I value in my territory."

"What is that?"

"Civilization," he said. "The world is a much more savage place than most humans would comprehend. I am the monster that keeps all others at bay. Do you understand?"

She nodded.

"Yet you are still frightened," he said.

She drew a hard breath and met his eyes.

"What is the price you pay?" she asked. "For maintaining the illusion that it is only gods and necromancers we must fear."

Again came that flare of surprise in his expression. He looked puzzled, and his eyes roved her face, searching for the answer to a question he didn't know how to ask.

"You came to tell me something," he said instead.

"The grimoire." Isela drew a breath, exhaled slowly, and returned her attention to her purpose.

"He acquired it from a woman who came into his possession," Azrael said, the word like a curse. "It was in her family for generations, but she did not know where it came from."

"Is she—"

The flash of silver gave her the answer. "Gone. She would not be broken, so he destroyed her. I have tried to summon her but with no success. He kept nothing of hers."

"How did it come to Havel?"

"Zeman was a well-known dealer," Azrael said. "And he was unafraid to dirty his hands. After the book was sold, this scum found someone else was looking for it. She paid him a visit, he gave up Zeman, and she let him be."

Isela turned the growing theory over in her mind one more time.

"What is it?"

"You said the grimoire was old," she began. "And that makes it valuable. Why?"

"The first necromancers were like scientists, experimenting with their powers to find what they were capable of, and where the limits were. What went wrong killed us. What we survived, we wrote down."

"The first grimoires," she said.

He shook his head. "Witches invented grimoires. We may be more powerful outright, but our distrust of one another makes us solitary, and vulnerable… Witches' strength is in numbers and sharing knowledge. We did not share as they did, but we learned from each other's mistakes and compiled our spells in their fashion. Over time, many of the oldest spells were abandoned because they were too dangerous. Those are rare."

"How many are there?" Isela demanded.

His brows rose in question.

"Spells so dangerous only a necromancer as powerful as she is would attempt to pull them off," Isela said, pausing. "There can't be many. Can there?"

Azrael rose with leonine grace, stalking back into the inner room. Gregor returned in time to catch her shoulders when she tried to follow Azrael inside. The door to the inner room swung open, and the broken incubus's ragged breaths echoed against the walls.

The necromancer crouched beside him, gripping a handful of sweat-soaked hair in his fist.

"What did she say to you?" There was an electricity in his voice that made sparks fly from the overhead lighting.

Isela gasped at the ozone charge in the air, ignoring Gregor's hands as she watched, transfixed. The apparently lifeless figure's eyes rolled open. His mouth began to move, but no words came out at first. Azrael sent another surge that stiffened his limbs.

Words escaped this time, garbled on his broken tongue. Azrael jolted him again. The lights flickered.

He howled, gibbering, but Azrael held him firm. "The fury of wings! Wings. The fury of wings."

He collapsed to the floor as the overhead lighting dimmed, then flared bright enough to shatter the bulbs and shower the room in sparks. In the darkness, Azrael swore and bit out a single word: "*Goetia*." A ball of glowing emerald hovered like a ghost light, illuminating the room. It floated in front of Azrael, and Gregor yanked Isela out of the way as he strode back through the door and toward the Aedis.

In the hall, Azrael dismissed the light with a wave. "Gregor, secure him. We may need him again when he's recovered."

"Goetia," Isela repeated, jogging after Azrael as he strode down the hall toward the elevator. Already dreading the answer, she asked, "What does that mean?"

"There are certain spells that are legend, even among necromancers," he said. "Their power so great—so destructive—it's a mercy they remain lost. This is one of them."

"This one?" They exited on the main floor. "You understood that?"

The warmth of success flushed her cheeks. She'd been right. She took her first deep breath since she'd followed Rory down into the bowels of the castle.

His chin dipped once. "She's going to summon an angel."

They returned to the study, and Azrael immediately began pulling books from the shelves, levitating them to the enormous desk at the end of the room.

Isela quit gaping long enough to ask, "Aren't angels the good guys?"

He spoke almost as an afterthought. "You're thinking like a human."

"I *am* human," she challenged. "Educate me."

"You've met demons," he said. "Demons are the power of death in form. They can be summoned and sent against an enemy. Angels are the opposite: life in its purest form. And they cannot be summoned or directed."

"I don't see—"

"Pure life is chaos." He interrupted. "Uncontrollable, transformative. The same chaos that started the universe in a bang and will contract it again into nothingness. The same chaos that brought oxygen and hydrogen together, that multiplied the first single-celled organisms. Death provides a balance, and between life and death, everything—order—is maintained."

Isela leaned on the desk. The scent of old books coated her nostrils: paper bound in leather, pages like skin, scrolls of a linen so fine it was almost translucent.

She looked over his shoulder at the book open before him. It was a Bible but one larger than she had ever seen, open to Revelations.

"The human book was not wrong," he said. "Mucked up by dogma is all. The world's ending will come on angel wings. The same chaos that created it is capable of its destruction."

Azrael stood back, shaking his head. "The murders were just a distraction to keep us busy chasing a killer when we should have been trying to stop her from unleashing an angel."

"Once she has the spell, what will she need to cast it?"

"An aedis," he said thoughtfully. "Like Zeman's hidden room or mine downstairs. Something large and located near water. Or a place of the dead would have the most potential energy. A spell that big would require an enormous amount of power—casting it at the right time would also help."

"Like a full moon?"

Azrael didn't laugh. "Power is energy. Water, gravity, the pull of planets on one another affects energy. In this case, a new moon would be better."

Isela looked up, remembering suddenly she'd been ready to ask her sister-in-law about the queen. "My phone. Bebe called twice, and maybe the coven can help find her. I have to call her back."

She ignored his expression, racing from the room. She'd left her phone on her bag in the ballroom. It was still there.

"My gods, Issy, we've been trying to get ahold of you." Bebe picked up the phone immediately.

She heard voices in the background, angry, conflicted.

"I'm sorry," she said. "I've been… insane the last couple of days. I—"

"You have to get down here," Bebe cut her off. "The doctor says he doesn't have much time now. You need to say good-bye—"

"Good-bye?"

Isela looked up at a noise to find Azrael standing in the doorway. She instinctively turned away from him, curling her body around the phone.

"Beebs, what are you talking about?" she said when she could manage a breath. "Bebe, *who*?"

"Your dad," Bebe said, and Isela heard the grief in her voice. "He's dying."

* * *

ISELA STUMBLED to her feet as the call disconnected. She spun, all thoughts of angels and apocalypse fading into a dull noise in the back of her head. She didn't feel Azrael's hands on her arms until she realized she was no longer spinning.

"You have to calm your breath," he instructed, black spots marking his face in her vision.

She had never seen him look so… concerned.

"Isela, if you hyperventilate, you won't get there in time," he snapped. "Dancer! Do it, or I will make you."

Azrael shook her once, gently, but her teeth clacked together anyway, and she bit her tongue. Pain shot through her, clarifying. She felt the air entering her lungs slowly and modulated her exhales to match. The black spots began to fade. But she couldn't feel anything.

"I have to go," she said, trying to free herself from his grip. "I have to go somewhere."

Azrael's eyes never left her face.

"Don't look at me like that," she said, struggling for her next breath. "You don't need me now. I just need to go out for a few…

awhile. I'll be back soon. You can send Rory with me. I won't try to get away."

For a long moment he said nothing as she tried to pry his fingers free. At once, without warning, he released her. She stumbled away.

"Wait in the courtyard," he ordered her. "I'll send the car around."

Isela bobbed her head, and gratitude made it difficult to hold back tears. She fled the room.

Tyler met her with a coat and a scarf. She didn't notice him helping her into it, tying the scarf around her neck.

"I'm sorry, Miss Vogel," he said, paler than usual.

She shook her head, unable to speak. But he did not leave her until the chili-red, two-door Tesla pulled up in front of the building. He opened the door as she stumbled forward. The cold should have been like a slap, but nothing registered. She was numb.

It wasn't until she climbed in that she realized it wasn't Rory at the wheel.

"What are you—"

"Lysippe can start the search without me," Azrael said, putting the car in gear. "Seat belt."

He whipped away from the curb. He was a more cautious driver than Gregor but only by a hair. Her eyes stayed on the road, open wide and seeing nothing. Gradually, she was aware that he was talking.

"...descended from a long line of Amazons who fought on the battlefield at Troy," he said. "After the city fell, they migrated south and were taken in by tribes of North Africa. Myrine, Lysippe's mother, saved my life when I was still young enough for ordinary weapons to be a threat. Even heavy with Lysippe, Myrine and her axe could match any man in combat.

"I put myself in her service, and she tolerated me." He smiled faintly. "Myrine's skill and reputation was such that no opportunity to repay the debt presented itself and, eventually, I asked her to be the beginning of my Aegis. She refused. When a plague swept the tribe, I could not save her. On her final day, she asked that the debt I owed her be passed to Lysippe. So, I raised her as my own. When

Lysippe became a warrior in her own right, she asked for the gift her mother had refused."

"Your daughter," she said softly. "She gave you her soul—to protect."

"And she has fought at my side," he said, pausing. "Except for one rebellious period around the turn of the century. She worked as a stunt rider for a traveling Wild West show in America. She's magnificent with horses."

"Do all necromancers have an Aegis like yours?" Isela stared at him and felt the first stirrings of sensation return to her own body.

It began in her chest, behind her ribcage and slightly to the left —a dull ache that grew with each breath, beginning to throb in rhythm. She balled up her hand, pounding the spot through her coat as though she could soothe the pain.

"Three or six, perhaps." Azrael captured her fist, forced her fingers apart, and slid his between. "It takes time before one is powerful enough to afford to give such a gift."

"How many are in your guard?"

"Nine," he said, again in that same emotionless tone.

The heat of his palm radiated into her arms and her chest. He let go only to get out of the car. As she climbed out, he waved a hand, and a curling emerald glow flared from his fingertips. She recognized it from the night in Zeman's little room. He'd formed weapons made of light fighting the demons. It had been in his palm when he pointed at her with the command to *run*. This was his power being used.

"Floor three, room one hundred and six," he murmured.

Isela stared at him, closing the door. "Did you read someone's mind?"

He paused, troubled. "Am I supposed to ask everyone now?"

They left the car at the curb. Walking into the hospital, they were greeted with such overwhelming silence that Isela drew up short. Everywhere people were asleep—sitting or standing. She looked back at Azrael, who lifted his shoulders innocently.

"I am a lord of death," he said. "What is sleep, if not a preview?"

"Why did you do that?"

"Humans find my presence disturbing in places like this."

"No kidding," she said. "Are they…"

"Fine. As soon as I lift the geas, they will go on exactly as they were."

They took the shoebox elevator to the third floor, and Isela tried to get her mind around how, with one wave of his hand, he'd sedated a few hundred people. It was the first time she had ever heard him refer to himself by the title "lord of death." It was no boast, and it wasn't spoken with any particular pride. Like admitting the size of his guard.

"Death and sleep," she mused softly.

His eyes met hers, and she saw a languorous flare of heat curl within. "Did you know that the French idiom for orgasm is *la petite morte*?"

In spite of everything, she felt a smile creep to her mouth. "The little death? Is that why you're so good in bed?"

Azrael spread his palms in a gesture of humble confession.

The elevator doors opened, and three snarling men barreled down the hall, midway through their transition to becoming full-blown wolves. Hair had begun to sprout densely from their arms and legs. Marcus's face was all snout and ears. Christof had teeth in a muzzle no human should possess.

Before Isela could cry out to stop them, Azrael stepped in front of her, lifting a hand. She heard the grunt of air leaving lungs as their bodies were flung sideways and thumped into the wall. She grabbed for Azrael's arm, trying to see around him, a plea for mercy on her lips.

"They are unharmed," Azrael said, holding her back as he addressed the three weres. "We are in a place of sanctuary. I call on the code of Raziel for a truce on neutral ground."

There was something about his voice, as though he were invoking something older and more powerful than he was. The snarling stopped. At the other end of the hallway, her mother and her sisters emerged from the room.

"Mom!" Isela started forward, but Azrael's hand was like iron.

She tugged at him, but he held firm. Silver eyes flicked to her face. "You must wait until permission is granted."

"I don't need permission from you," she snarled.

The corner of his mouth lifted. "Not from me, from her."

Isela looked down the hall at her mother. There was no mistaking it; their postures were protective ones. They were guarding the door, she realized.

"Mom?"

"You've cast your lot with death's hand, Little Bird," Beryl Vogel said, words of power. Finality.

"I vow no harm to you or your kin," Azrael said, none of the ancient import in it but with such dreadful formality. "I've brought your daughter here in peace, witch, to pay the proper respect to her sire."

Azrael made the word *witch* sound like a gracious title of respect.

"She can come, but you stay," Markus snarled, thrashing against the wall.

"I apologize for the behavior of my man at your last meeting, and I will make amends," he said, speaking only to Beryl. "But she is under my protection."

"No deal," Markus barked. "He doesn't get anywhere near Dad."

"Quiet." Beryl waved a hand, and Isela jumped as her brother's jaws snapped shut.

They were slowly turning human again: the fur receding, the faces becoming familiar.

"You will do no work in this room," Beryl said. "You will come, and depart, in peace."

Azrael nodded. Isela knew the bargain had been made when the three men slid down the wall to their feet, and Azrael released her arm. She ran to Chris first, who enfolded her. Mark kept his distance, and when she reached out to him, he jerked his arm away and would not meet her eyes. She heard the warning snarl in his chest.

Toby steered her toward the room. The Sisters broke from Beryl's side to hug and greet her. Bebe was sobbing openly, dragging Isela forward.

Only one person remained as she stood. Beryl Gilman-Vogel blocked the doorway, and this close, Isela could see the grief etched on her face. At last she opened her arms, and Isela went into them.

Her mother felt thin, and the tang of sorrow eroded her usual vibrant smell of lilac and honey.

"Why didn't you say anything?" Isela asked.

"He made us promise not to tell you," Beryl said. "He didn't want you to worry. Go."

Her father's withered body barely interrupted the blankets of the hospital bed. The sickness was visible in his face. He seemed to be sinking into himself: his skin stretched sallow and thin over his skull. His eyelashes fluttered against the purple circles beneath his eyes as he slept. Parched lips twitched faintly, but no sound emerged.

Tubes and monitors seemed to be the only thing keeping him attached to life. She noticed the monitors were off. His narrow chest rose and fell, rattling softly. He appeared to be sleeping peacefully.

"What happened?"

"A tumor." Evie spoke. "He finally went to the doctor six months ago when his eyesight was affected, but they think it's been growing for years. He tried to keep it from us, but the boys smelled something was off and told Mom. We begged him to tell you, Issy."

Isela could see her family had occupied this room together for days, the imprints of bodies on the spare beds, the tossed blankets and old cups of coffee. She ached knowing they had been here, as a family without her. The pain under her ribs came back with new force.

"Can't you do anything?" she asked, looking at the four women.

"We've made him comfortable, Issy," Bebe said. "But death must take its due when the time comes. He refused life support yesterday. We were going to take him home but…he's ready—he's just been waiting."

Isela shook her head, her eyes returning to her mother. "You stopped Gregor. You have the book—the grimoire—isn't there something in there you can use?"

Beryl looked over her shoulder at Azrael before she returned her focus to Isela. "We can create, but not alter, the course of life toward its end. To interfere with death would disrupt the balance. Create chaos."

Chaos, the word kept rearing up. But she also heard another

word that had come to mean more to her in the last few days than in her entire life: death. She spun on Azrael. "You can stop this."

* * *

Azrael felt the weight of all eyes turning to him, but his attention was on Isela. The pale, tormented face, eyes wide and stark with the kind of panic that only came when the realization of death was certain. He wanted to enfold her in his arms and cradle her. To assure her, in this case, the witches were right. Death could also be mercy—he knew that better than most. But he knew she would not accept it. Gray eyes swam in unshed tears as they bored into him.

He used their mental connection. *Not this. Don't ask it of me.*

"Azrael, please," she whispered.

"You don't want what you're asking for," he said.

"You can stop this. Change him. Make him one of your undead."

He heard the cries of protest, but he held his gaze steady. "He will not be the same."

A sob escaped her, stifled by the fist she pressed against her mouth. Spots of high color rose in her cheeks, and her eyes were feverish, desperate. The first tears began to streak down her face. "I'll do whatever you ask. I'll be your consort. I'll dance for you—whenever. You can use the power to boost yourself whenever you need it. I'll do it. I swear. Just don't…let him…go."

Azrael saw the horror on her mother's face. He didn't know whether it was watching her daughter beg or the mention of the word "consort" that did it. He crossed the distance between them before Isela could jerk away and caught her fists in his hands. She was trembling, and her strength had turned brittle.

Something cracked deep inside of him facing the knowledge that his power was useless here. Azrael struggled to draw his next breath.

His lungs filled with a desert heat as he remembered stepping onto a barren plain that had once teemed with life: grazing animals, tents and herds and families. His home. It had been a thousand years since he had seen it. He'd gone to his knees, digging his hands in the soil and feeling the bones of hundreds of thousands dissolved into earth. Nothing remained, and the loss had almost spent him.

Standing in the cramped hospital room, sterile and thick with the proximity of death, he realized it was not protection she needed. Nothing could protect her from the pain of this loss. She needed to know that she could survive it.

"Look at me," he said as her eyes grew unfocused with grief. "Your father has chosen release. If you love him, you will respect his wishes as your own. He is waiting for you. Sometimes the only thing to do is to let go."

He could feel the sobs in her, beginning to overtake the scraps of her control. He locked his arms around her and spoke for her ear alone.

"When you come to me, as my consort, you will do it from your own desire," he murmured. "Not as payment for a debt. You have the heart of a she-wolf, Isela Vogel. I will not take you sniffling and begging on your knees like a common cur."

His words found the prick against her pride he had counted on. He felt the breath she took, gathering every ounce of strength she had left, and let his arms fall.

Now send your father on his way, with the love and devotion of an heir, as is his due. Tonight I will hold you, and you can tear my skin and hair every night until your grief is spent. Azrael kept a hand at the base of her neck, sending heat into her skin to remind her of his presence and keep the tremors at bay.

When she met his eyes, the ash gray was ringed with red, her cheeks puffy and mouth swollen. He wanted to kiss her until nothing remained but the mindless, senseless release that overtook her in his arms. But he could not take this pain from her now.

Only when the hot flow of tears ceased did he lift the veil of sleep from the man on the bed so subtly that only Beryl, had she not been dulled with grief, would have sensed it.

"Little Bird?" Lukas Vogel blinked his way back to consciousness. "Isela?"

Azrael let her go and watched with increasing pride as she crossed the room, a smile blooming on her face.

"Caught you nappin'," she said lightly, through a throat raw with banked emotion.

The bony face broke into a smile that spoke of the quiet handsomeness the man had once possessed. Isela took his hand in her own. Beryl rose, leaving the room. As she passed, she laid a hand on Azrael's arm in gratitude. The touch left him shaken.

Witches were mortal; they honored life and bowed gracefully to death. He thought them weak for clinging to each other. Their families and their covens made them vulnerable. Now he understood the strength it took to make those bonds, knowing they could not last. They loved, in spite of the inevitability of loss. This was their strength: courage in the face of change.

You will have my fidelity, Isela Vogel, for as long as you live. At last he, too, turned, leaving Isela alone to say good-bye.

* * *

ISELA HEARD the click of the door shutting behind them, but her gaze was focused on her father's distant gray eyes. When he gestured, she slipped onto the bed and curled up beside him. She rested her head gingerly on his chest, and his free hand settled on her cheek.

"It's up to you to protect this family now."

She smiled, thinking of her coven-leading mother and three wolf-brothers.

"I'm serious," he chided. "And you know it. Those boys are all Gilman. You got the Vogel good sense."

She coughed a little laugh at the thought of where her good sense had landed her. "Papa—"

"I know you will," he said. "You and that nice man of yours."

Isela decided the time for untruths was gone. "Gregor is not—"

"You take me for a blind fool," he said impatiently. "The one you came in with pulls the strings all right. The coat, the book that arrived for your mother—why she would want some dusty old thing she can barely lift is beyond me."

His laugh turned into a wheeze and a long inhale. "Forgive me, Issy, for keeping this from you. And the truth about your brothers."

"You knew?"

"Your mother warned me about what she was," he said. "But

the boys were unexpected and their lives will always be different because of what they are. I wanted your life to be normal—as normal as possible, under the circumstances."

How could she judge, when she had lied for the same reasons. She thought about the long argument between her parents when she had been offered a scholarship to the Praha Academy. She could have continued to live at home while training to dance. But the resident program meant she would live in the dorms as other students who came from farther away, and she would have her regular education at the Academy in addition to dance training. Her mother had been reluctant, but her father had pushed. Though she was only a short distance away, the intensity of the education made trips home increasingly infrequent. Gradually the Academy took its place.

"I understand, Papa," she lied. "Can I get you anything?"

"Not a thing," he said.

"Let me get Mom and the boys." She started to rise, but he caught her hand.

"*Bleib bitte.*" *Stay, please.*

And she did, listening to the soft rattling of his chest and the quiet beating of his heart. The beats slowed until she strained to hear the next. He took a breath and, for a long moment, nothing, then exhaled. She waited. They came less and less frequently, the pauses between growing longer and longer.

"She's beautiful," he breathed at last.

"Who, Papa?"

"Your shadow."

A chill raced up her spine. "You see her?"

"She's waiting for me," he said. "But she has a message for you and your necromancer."

Another exhale, this one so final she was sure he was gone. He inhaled again, and the words were so soft she almost missed them.

"Find the place of the martyr's rest among the multitudes."

With that, Lukas Vogel was gone. She felt his departure as surely as she felt the touch of the golden shadow on her skin, comforting her as she realized she was alone in the room. She buried her face in his chest and sobbed until her voice gave out.

Isela rose slowly, the ache in her hip pronounced now, and

folded his hands on his chest. She would grieve later. They had a job to finish.

Outside, the family waited. They knew. Azrael stood slightly apart. She touched each of her sisters' hands, and hugged her mother. Christof could barely stand, Ofelia holding them both up, but he squeezed her so hard she thought her ribs would crack. Toby made a space for her head under his chin, as their father always had, and her control wavered. Mark paced, the hurt clear on his face. She reached out a hand, but he didn't meet it. Evie caught her fingers before she let them fall, gripping her hand.

Isela nodded, accepting this too, and turned to Azrael.

"We have to go," she said.

He didn't question. They were almost at the elevator when her mother's voice rang. "Necromancer."

Azrael turned.

"You have only to call," Beryl said. "And the Vogels will come to your aid."

He froze, and only Isela stood close enough to see the way his jaw clenched and jumped. He took a hard breath, and she recognized the husky edge of his tone.

"You have my thanks, Vogels." He bowed his head, a timeless gesture of an ancient system of honor. It spoke of respect earned and alliances newly formed. In the midst of her heartbreak, Isela could only wonder at what the future might bring.

"I think I know where the Queen of Diamonds will be casting her spell."

CHAPTER TWENTY-FIVE

"It's a trap," Gregor pronounced.

Isela rubbed the back of her neck with her palm, closing her eyes as the argument resumed. At some point on the ride back to the castle, she'd split herself in two. She'd cordoned off the raw, grieving ache in her chest with the promise that one day it would have its due. The rest of her owed it to everyone she loved to see this through.

It would not have been possible if she'd gone home with her family. There, in the building her father had turned into a home, his absence would have been inescapable. But high in the castle on the hill, among a conference of immortals, she could forget for a moment about the most human part of herself. Here, she was just a dancer, a tool to be used to stop a killer.

Except she wasn't *just* that anymore. Not under the constant, warming gaze of the necromancer. No matter where he was in the room, or where the conversation went, Isela felt the heat of him, pulsing quietly under the ache in her chest. Azrael's presence kept her heart from turning to ice when she would have allowed it to go so cold it might never thaw.

She forced herself back into the discussion. She owed it to her father—and the golden shadow that had come to ease his transition—to make the message heard. She'd repeated it twice for Azrael in the car, and again here, among the core members of his Aegis.

"She warned me in the bookstore," she said. "It was the only reason I got to Azrael before the demon did."

"A shimmering shadow of gold," Gregor repeated, nodding. "And the blade that stabbed him in the In Between was also gold. Who is to say she isn't playing both sides?"

Azrael shook his head. "The blade was like ice."

"The shadow isn't cold," Isela agreed. "Every time I've made contact, it's been warm."

"Róisín was—is—a creature of ice," Azrael said.

It was the first time Isela had heard her named. A shudder raced the length of her spine.

"Incidental." Gregor dismissed them with a hand.

"She knows we're right behind her," Rory said, shrugging his mountainous shoulders. "We can assume everything from here on out has barbs meant for you, Azrael."

"Is there a chance her dancer survived?" Lysippe asked carefully, without looking at Isela.

Azrael strode to the window. It was the first time she felt his heat waver. "He was sent to the final death."

"Her dancer?" Isela heard herself echo. "The one that helped her summon a god?"

The room was quiet for a long moment.

"We have two nights until the moon is new," Azrael said resolutely.

"You mean to wait." Lysippe looked dismayed. "Why not move now?"

"I won't be able to locate her until she begins to cast," he said. "It's luck and fate she's chosen to exact her revenge here. I can't risk her seeing us coming."

"That doesn't leave much room for error," Gregor said.

Azrael relented. "Two on surveillance, but do not be detected. If she goes to ground, we'll lose her."

Lysippe, at least, seemed pleased.

At last they were alone in the enormous study. Isela exhaled her body into the nearest chair. Her head had begun to throb. She looked up only when the door opened again, and Tyler entered bearing tea and a tray of food.

"Welcome home, Miss Vogel," he said before catching himself. "Back. Welcome back."

He set the tray down, retreating under Azrael's dark glare. When he was gone, Azrael dragged an ottoman into place in front of her. He offered a bowl that sent out aromas of garlic, onions, and tomatoes. She shook her head wearily, drawing her heels beneath her.

"You need your strength," he insisted. "It's almost done now."

"You like to give orders." She resisted, without heart. "Bossy."

"Eat."

The contents tasted as good as they smelled: little tender chunks of stewed meat and veggies dissolved on her tongue. She took the bowl and a hunk of bread when it was offered.

It turned out she was ravenous. She cleaned the last of the broth from the bowl before Azrael took it away. He handed her a cup of tea.

"How is your hip?" he asked, settling a hand there.

"It hurts," she confessed. "But I've been pushing harder than usual."

Isela sighed when heat soaked into the soreness. She bit her tongue on the knowledge that the pain had gotten exponentially worse in the past few days. Something had changed in the ache; it was growing sharper and more insistent every time she moved.

"I cannot fix this," he said.

"I don't feel it when I'm dancing, that's all that matters." She opened her eyes when he remained silent. "Dancing takes a toll on the body. I'm old for an active dancer. Most of the others have retired—gone into teaching or other performance."

"Old." His exhale betrayed his amusement. "At thirty years."

"In August," she said. "And after this job, I'll take a long vacation."

If they survived.

Azrael stroked her hips, the lengths of her thighs. She sensed the passion in him caged, contained in the same way he leashed the predator in her presence.

"Why do they call her the Queen of Diamonds?"

His silence deepened, and for a moment she thought he would try to change the subject again. But at last he spoke.

"Paolo called her that first." A wry smile twisted his mouth. "The Queen of Diamonds. Róisín was beautiful and hard. She was the most powerful of all of us. We came together under her hand to take over when you—when the godswar began. She rallied us.

"When it was discovered the dancers could boost our power, some necromancers cried for all the dancers to be slaughtered, to keep war from breaking out between us as it had among humans. Róisín was the one who figured out the key to manipulating the gods using dancers. She devised the bargain that would remove the power of gods from human hands and end the war."

"No one expected her to fall for her dancer," he finished. "They thought her blinded when her dancer joined with the god. It rocked the allegiance. It was so young, newly formed. They saw the possession as a threat to their own power, and they undermined her."

Isela's heart pounded against her ribs. "What happened?"

"She killed him, her dancer," Azrael finished. "It broke her mind." He paused, as though considering adding something, then thinking better of it. "Or so we believed. She abdicated the allegiance and was never heard from again. The allegiance scrubbed the memory of her union with the dancer from the records."

"Until now."

"She'd been missing for so long some were convinced she was dead."

"And she wants to make the whole world pay." Isela finalized.

"It was her union with the dancer that saved the world from the godswar," he said. "So destroying it would only be fitting."

"You said it's luck and fate she's here..."

"This was her territory, from the start," he said carefully. "Her absence left a void—Vanka wanted it, the others feared the advantage so much territory would grant her. I ascended to make sure that would never happen."

"How could they do that to her, Róisín," Isela said, shuddering. "How terrible."

"So human," he said, and for the first time, it held no derision. "So willing to empathize."

"And you don't?"

He shook his head. "Róisín was no innocent. She carved up the world with the rest of the allegiance. And when, out of their own fear, they began to whisper that her loyalty to him was a liability, she chose to listen. They convinced her that her dancer would one day become more powerful than she and she would lose herself to the god inside him."

He paused, searching her face. "Do you know where she killed him?"

Isela wanted to shake her head, to close her ears, but she had already gone too far. She had to know.

"In the bed they shared," he finished, his voice laced with disbelief. "There was no sign he struggled. He trusted her until the end. She violated her vow to him out of a craven desire to preserve her own power. If she had truly fallen, she would never have been capable of such betrayal. I won't let her take the world to flames out of an undeserved sense of revenge."

The resolute tone of his voice was the slam of a door.

Isela shivered, but she was not afraid. Not any longer. She knew him now. Not everything, but she could see the core of him. Azrael might act in ways that terrified her, but she would never fear him again. When their eyes met, his held a tinge of regret.

"That was a terrible bedtime story," he said, brushing a stray bit of hair from her brow.

His fingers trailed a hot path down her cheek, tracing the line of her jaw to her lip.

"Let me take you to bed." His voice was the hum of a fire dissolving fuel in heat so intense it lacked flames.

"The book. You sent my mother a book?"

The slow curl of his lips. "An old witch's grimoire I thought she might appreciate." He drew her to her feet. "Among the many 'threats' the allegiance neutralized when it stopped the godswar were the witches. Covens were broken, books stolen or destroyed. Most of the witches went into hiding. Your mother is the first High Priestess brave enough to exercise her coven, the only one strong enough to have a chance against one of us."

Isela couldn't help smiling at the thought of her mother in her bumblebee house shoes, facing down the Allegiance.

"When the other necromancers find out?" Isela let herself be led from the room.

Azrael made a sound that from another man would have been arrogance. But she knew what he was capable of. "This is my territory now. Let them dare."

* * *

ISELA WOKE IN A SWEAT. She'd been dreaming about a flickering gold glow and a woman who opened her chest and revealed an enormous chunk of fractured ice shaped like a broken heart. The woman screamed, but Isela recognized her own voice in the sound, and the shock brought her awake with a desperate gasp for breath.

Azrael's arms closed over her in the darkness, his body pressing the length of hers, calling her back into the world. His arousal pressed into the damp heat of her skin. Between heartbeats, the heat became a fire, molding them together.

Isela wrapped her legs around his hips, feeling him resist. His hands tangled in her hair, and the silver coins of his eyes were alight.

"Let me be your shield, Isela," he said, his voice a tenuous rasp in the darkness.

As the last cobwebs of sleep faded, she said the words she knew he needed to hear.

"I accept," she said. "I accept you."

Azrael plunged into her with a groan that tore her heart free from the restraints she'd placed it under. The gentleness was gone; he pinned her wrists above her head, maneuvering her thighs apart so that he could enter her fully. She matched him, stride for stride, straining off the bed and toward the fiery body claiming her own. When she came, it swept through her in a primal scream, leaving her sobbing and boneless beneath him.

"Don't fight it." He pinned her cheeks between his hands as their breath began to return to normal. Well, his breath slowed. Isela couldn't seem to stop gulping air between waves of emotion. "I'm here."

Grief rent her heart into pieces, and she only knew one way to drive it back. Steam rose from her cheeks where he kissed the tears with lips like brands. Her nails scored his arms, leaving tracks that healed moments later.

"Again," she said, twisting her hips against his. "Again."

* * *

THEY DIDN'T RISE until well after noon. Isela slipped from the bed first, relieved to find it still standing, although the metal frame *was* warm to the touch. She padded to the little square rug she had been using as a makeshift mat for her morning stretches. She lost herself in the simple rhythm of greeting the sun. She didn't see the glimmer of gold, but sensing its presence just outside of her vision soothed her. No matter what Gregor feared, she knew it was not a malevolent force. When she opened her eyes again, Azrael was sitting up against the headboard, watching her.

She knew the look in his eyes, and the recognition brought her a little thrill. This was it, the private language of lovers, and it was hers. Hers and Azrael's. She crossed the distance to the bed in a flurry of spins and a gracefully executed backflip that put her just out of his reach. She gave a little curtsey, a mischievous smile on her face. His eyes burned, the silver heated to molten pools. He held out a hand to her, beckoning.

"Come to me, my consort."

"You still don't get to order me around," she said.

Azrael bared his teeth in the dangerous smile that used to make her knees quiver with the urge to run. Now she saw the true nature of this side of the predator: desire. His movement blurred, and the next thing she knew, she was leaning into the bed over his chest with his hand fisted in her hair, pinning her close.

"If you will not obey." He bit her lower lip, snaking out his tongue to taste her flesh. "Then I must learn to make the lure irresistible."

Isela purred at the promise in those words. She just couldn't help it. The man *was* a lord of death, great and small.

When they emerged from Azrael's quarters, Isela feared she wouldn't be able to dance that afternoon. Her body ached in a hundred subtle hidden places from the fierceness of their congress. About to mention it, she stepped into the hall and came to a stop.

The heat of his body behind her flared. His forearm settled around her collarbones, drawing her close to his chest. She inhaled sharply.

The hall was lined with Azrael's Aegis. The four she knew and three others she did not. At the head of the line, Gregor's black sword was clearly visible. Beside him, the hint of a black bow and quiver crossed Lysippe's back. Rory and Dory needed no weapons, but their hands and shoulders seemed to emanate the same fearsome energy. The others all bore some semi opaque weapon—their visibility a message.

She tried to look back at Azrael, but he was too close. His hand settled on her hip, and his cheek brushed her temple as he nodded.

One by one, the guards went to one knee, faces as still and implacable as stone. All except Lysippe, who fought the knowing grin tugging at her mouth as she lowered. Gregor looked as though he wanted to kill something.

"What is this?" Isela breathed.

"It is an acknowledgment of your new status in my house," he said simply. "And their new responsibility. Two are absent on surveillance. They send their regards. Come."

His hand slipped around her own, and he released her from his chest. They walked down the hall, past the kneeling men and woman. Isela couldn't help herself. As they reached the elevator, she looked back. Gregor liberated his wallet as he rose with the others. Lysippe snapped the bill from his fingers with a wily grin.

Isela flushed, turning her attention to Azrael to find his eyes had never left her face. "There were bets on if—"

"When," he corrected. "Not if." He shrugged before she could decide to take offense. "Soldiers and wagering have gone together since the beginning of time."

"I suppose you'd know," she said lightly, as they entered the elevator. "Since you *were* there."

CHAPTER TWENTY-SIX

Isela snugged her warm-up sweater over leggings and her most serviceable black leotard as she came down the stairs from the bedroom. She'd forgone dancing slippers for a pair of comfortable running shoes and braided her hair tightly, pinning it to the back of her neck. Azrael looked up as he slid on his long midnight coat, the material of which she still couldn't name. Even its scent defied her nose—something spicy and vaguely reptilian, with the hint of old char. It should have been off-putting but was strangely intriguing instead.

He paused, watching her without comment. She buckled the leg holster and checked the pull on her knife. When she was ready, she looked at him. "I'm going with you."

"No."

Isela laughed. "You can't expect me to stay here. What if something happens?"

"Aleifr will remain behind," he said. "I've asked the witches to protect the city from any fallout. If I fail, he'll take you to your mother until the rest of the Aegis can regroup to get you all out of danger."

He started toward the door. She hurried to block his path, unable to speak for a moment over the flash of anger.

"I meant if something happens to you," she said. "Everything I studied says that the proximity is key. This kind of dancing doesn't work as well if I'm far away."

"This won't be like the other times," Azrael said. "I know what Róisín is capable of."

She followed him out of his apartment. Tyler waited attentively beside the door. She held up a hand as they passed.

"I've arranged to have the cathedral opened for you." Tyler called after her.

"Later, Ty," she said, ignoring the discomfort in her hip to hurry after Azrael.

When the elevator doors closed and they were alone again, she spun to face him. "She's the most powerful necromancer in the allegiance. That's what you said. And you have to stop her—alone."

"Róisín will be distracted by her spell, and we have surprise on our side."

"She's been ready for us at every turn," Isela argued. "I've been thinking about what happened at Zeman's, and I think I found a way to boost your defenses, along with the power transfer. But the closer I am to you the more effective it will be when you need it."

"I won't." Azrael said. "And you will remain here."

The door opened, and Gregor stood in the hallway, waiting. All warrior tonight, he wore black from head to toe; some kind of old-new amalgam of bodysuit and armored plates that resembled a lightweight, mobile version of old-fashioned armor.

"Dancer." It was a greeting and a dismissal as they stepped into the gallery hall.

"Aren't you supposed to be immortal? What's with the suit?"

"Cut me into enough pieces, and even I can't come back from that," Gregor said.

Knowing Gregor felt threatened enough to armor up didn't reassure her. Azrael caught her by the shoulders, drawing her eyes to his with a simple telepathic entreaty. *Consort, mine.*

I will not beg you. She grit her teeth.

I ask you not to.

"Please," she hissed anyway, ignoring Gregor.

Azrael's face lit with the shadow of a smile as his thumb settled in the corner of her downturned mouth. "I will be *your* shield. That is my vow."

"What about you—"

"That's what my Aegis is for," he said.

Isela wanted to resist, but it was useless against the wall of his resolve. She should have been relieved to be far away from the danger. Instead, the sense that she was going to lose him clutched her by the throat.

"Lysippe and the twins are en route," Gregor announced.

"It's almost sunset," Azrael said, dropping his hand. "The glass in the cathedral is beautiful this time of day."

"So I've heard," she said miserably.

He joined Gregor, and they walked away.

"Azrael!"

When he turned, she launched herself at him, wrapping her arms around his neck. It seemed to take him a moment to understand before his hands slid around her back. She pushed her face into his collar, drawing in a deep breath of his scent.

"Don't let your guard down, not even once," she demanded in a strangled whisper. "And kick her ass."

His laughter sent her heart stuttering unsteadily in her chest. "As my lady commands."

She stepped back when he let her go, clasping her hands together so she didn't reach for him again. Gregor cast a gimlet eye in her direction.

"Do your job," she growled at him. "Because you don't want me for a boss."

He angled his head, and the light caught the bright blue of his eyes. It was too much to think she might have actually made him laugh. "Indeed."

Tyler caught up while she stood in the empty hall. He puffed, out of breath. Behind him, the towering Nordic bruiser Aleifr kept a silent watch.

Tyler sucked in a breath to speak. "The cathedral?"

"Tyler, I don't give a shit about the windows," she said miserably.

* * *

Isela mentally reviewed the dance for the third time, marking the movements in abbreviated motion and mental notation. When the sequence was complete, she stretched before the windows overlooking the city. The last of the golden light bathed the red roofs and flared off gilded domes, spires of smoke rising from chimneys to soften the edges of everything.

She turned at the sound of a bell. The door opened and Tyler emerged, bearing a tray crowned with an evergreen wreath.

"What's this?"

"Something special the kitchen sent up," he said proudly. "It's the solstice. The shortest day of the year. It's practically sacred around here."

What had Azrael said about the effect of planetary energy on power? She shivered, though the room was warm enough. "The longest night."

Tyler nodded, setting the tray down. She scented molasses cookies and spicy ginger tea. She prowled the room, circling the table as he set out cups and poured. By the time she paused behind her chair, he was watching her strangely.

"What?" she asked.

"Your hands," he said, blushing. "It's like they're dancing for you."

She laughed, looking down at her still twitching fingers. "It's my way of marking choreography."

He nodded, as though she'd shared a great secret. The knot in her stomach eased. She sat down.

"It's just a kind of visualization," she said, letting the conversation distract her. "My friend Kyle, from the garden the other day, does this mini-marking thing with head and neck."

She imitated Kyle's head throws and shoulder shrugs with dramatic emphasis.

Tyler smiled. He relaxed visibly, joining her at the small table. "Is that how you memorize all the steps? I was at the fall gala, and it was amazing to watch the troupe all moving together."

"Ballet dancers have it much harder," she said. "They're memorizing choreography that's been given to them. I design my own. Still, the attack is the same. Break it down into small pieces, learn the section, and then layer section onto section until you know the whole thing without thinking about it."

"Chunking," he nodded. "I did a paper in undergrad on language acquisition. It's similar then."

Isela nodded, accepting the plate of cookies and the tea.

Tyler cleared his throat. "Is it warm enough in here? I could turn up the heat."

"It's fine, Tyler."

She waited, sensing he wasn't finished.

"You're not afraid," he blurted out. "Of all this."

Isela choked on her tea.

"When Lord Azrael called on you for the allegiance," he said. "You walked in… fearless. Even after—the demons—and Gregor… and I saw the car they brought that thing back in. An incubus, I mean…"

He took a deep breath, and his hand trembled so hard he set it down on his knee. She poured him more tea.

"But you don't show it," he said, "and you hold your ground with Gregor, and Lysippe likes you, *and* you can tell the twins apart. Twelve years, and I still mix them up."

"Dory laughs," she offered, sliding the plate of cookies his direction. "Twelve years, huh? Can I ask why you…"

"Became a zombie?"

She flushed.

"It's okay." He nibbled at a cookie. "I know that's what people call it. I get it. When I took the contract, all I could think of was my work. I just thought, this would be the best way to get the kind of long-term inheritance data geneticists dream about. Part of my obligation to Azrael includes applying my expertise to other services at his request. He asked me to help him analyze samples. Samples I didn't understand at first, they were so alien from human tissue. Things I couldn't explain. Creatures. I started… losing it."

"So you got banished to reception?"

"He thought I needed a break," Tyler said, deflated. "At least that's what I was told. Then you came."

"I'm a performer," Isela murmured. "I spent my whole life learning how to show the world what I want it to see."

Her laugh sounded strained, even to her own ear.

"Every time something weird happens, you just go with it."

"Have you met my family?" she asked. "My brothers? They're not exactly human."

"Actually they are." He pushed his glasses back up his nose, and she saw the confidence come back in a breath. "They're as human as you or I. What's curious is that the same isn't true when they're wolves. There are six key sequences…"

"There," she said, lifting her hand. "That's something you can understand. Start there, and add a little more, bit by bit."

He smiled faintly. "Chunking."

She lifted her teacup. "We're in this together…"

His cup rose in solidarity. A shock of gold touched her when the cup met her lips. She flung it away, staring after the broken pieces with wide eyes.

"What's wrong—" Tyler yelped. "Aleifr!"

The Viking burst through the doors with a grunt, sweeping the room as though expecting to thwart an attack with the force of his glare.

Isela kept her gaze unfocused as Azrael had advised, letting the gold flicker come to her. She gasped as pain lanced through her ribcage and down her leg. Isela pushed away from the chair, staggering to her feet. She touched her skin as the sensation faded like the aftereffect of a camera flash. The gold streaked across her vision, moving in erratic imitation of the dance she had prepared for tonight. She felt the tug of the connection that enabled her to communicate directly with Azrael the night of her attack.

"Get a car," she said. "Azrael's in trouble."

Aleifr crossed her path, silent and immobile.

"Yes, you can come," Isela said, her finger in his substantial chest. "But don't try to stop me."

His nostrils flared over the great, blond mustache, and the small bells and trinkets in his beard jingled. He jerked his head.

"Shouldn't I call Gregor or something?" Tyler asked as they ran to the garage. "Let him know we're…on our way?"

Isela shook her head. "They need to stay focused on protecting Azrael."

Rory's Land Rover was closest to the doors, but they all hesitated when Tyler held up the keys. Aleifr shrugged and climbed in the back.

"You don't drive?" Isela glared at him. "How is that possible?"

"He's set in his ways," Tyler muttered. "Hasn't said a word in the entire time I've known him, either."

"That explains the grunting," Isela said, glancing balefully at the keys.

Resolutely, Tyler gripped the keys and climbed into the driver's seat. "I'll drive."

As she pulled open the passenger door she noted he was paler than usual. "It's okay to stay here."

He swallowed hard but fixed his hands on the wheel.

"In this together," Tyler confirmed, grim but determined. "What's the plan?"

Isela jumped in and shut the door. "Drive."

Isela never thought she would long for Gregor's psychotically precise driving skills. Her phone rang as she gripped the dashboard against another hard turn and she opened it without checking the number.

"I can't talk long," Bebe said. "Evie says you're about to do something dangerous…"

"How did she—"

"That's Evie's knack," Bebe said, the hint of a shrug in her voice. "Mom's sending the boys your way, just...be careful Issy."

The call disconnected.

Tyler yanked the wheel, bumping over the curb toward the gates of the Olšany Cemetery.

"Stop!" Isela screamed as familiar flash of black fur caught in the headlights.

Tyler slammed on the brakes and the car slid to a stop. The black wolf lowered his head and growled at the brush guard. The grey and white wolves emerged from the brush, circling the car like cornered prey.

"Sorry," Tyler yelped.

Aleifr climbed out of the car, ignoring the wolves. As the Viking strode toward the cemetery gates, his open hands went to the small of his back. Two leather wrapped hilts solidified as his fingers closed over them. Twin axes materialized from the hilt up, the moonlight glinting off sharpened blades as he slid them free.

He glanced back at the car expectantly.

When Isela looked at Tyler, his hands shook as he stared into the vast darkness of the cemetery.

"Stay here," she said. "You did your part. Aleifr and the boys will get me the rest of the way."

The muscles in Tyler's jaw worked; protest warring with the relief knotting his brow. "But I…"

"That's an order." Leaning over to kiss his cheek she whispered, "Thank you."

She climbed out of the car after Aleifr. The three wolves bounded to her side. Tobias pushed his head under her palm. Christof reared up on his hind legs to swipe at her face with a long tongue. Markus wouldn't quit growling as he paced a small circle around them all.

Isela saluted Tyler then quickened her step after her guard. The wolves fell into loose formation around her as they left the living city behind and entered the realm of the dead.

Relying on her connection to Azrael, they left behind the well-tended graves heading northwest to the oldest section of the necropolis. There, the bushes grew thick between broken headstones. The reflective quality of the unbroken snow dimmed under the dense canopy of overgrown trees. Even bare for the winter, their tangled limbs turned vast swaths of shadow into a shattering darkness. Dilapidated tombs had surrendered to the steady assault of nature; many of their doors and barriers had crumbled to reveal glimpses of the interred beneath. The statues of angels and saints marking tombs seemed to follow their progress with faces eroded by time.

Róisín must have known she would be vulnerable once she began the spell and she wasn't relying on the sheer size of the largest cemetery in Prague to hide her. With an estimated two million interred over centuries at her disposal, even a fraction made a formidable army of undead. Most they encountered seemed little more than mindless shamblers, but others, runners, were sharp, agile, and battle-trained.

Aleifr handled most easily, his twin axes singing through the air.

The wolves took care of the stragglers. But when a wave of particularly rabid -looking zombies raced toward them, Isela drew her blades.

The Viking went swinging into the fray. There were too many, with desiccated, grasping fingers and sunken, blank faces. They pushed around him and Isela couldn't avoid the fight. The reek of rotted flesh and old earth made her gag even as brittle bones snapped easily under the impact of her blows. Every bit of Trinh's training served her well, but her blades were for personal defense, not beheading zombies. She stumbled backward on her bad hip and the wolves closed rank around her.

A familiar black-clad shape plunged into the fight with his blade bared.

"You couldn't—" Gregor grunted—"just—" two fell to his sword. A third zombie managed to get around him and dive for Isela—"stay put?"

He spun before she could reach for her blade and severed the emaciated head from a dirt-crusted body. A ball that was more skull than head rolled to a stop at her feet. Isela stared into the empty eye sockets and felt the bile rising in her throat.

"Not again," Gregor growled. He booted the skull into the bushes. "You are going to have to develop a stronger stomach, dancer."

She didn't know whether to thank him or take a swing at him. Consort or not, Isela still ranked about as high in Gregor's estimation as the mud on his boot. Some things would never change.

"Can you hold them?" Gregor barked at Alefir.

The Viking snorted assent.

Gregor grabbed Isela's arm and dragged her away from the melee. He'd been cut in a few places, burned in others.

"How did you know?" Isela panted, struggling to keep up.

Gregor waved a slim black rectangle before sliding it back into some unseen pocket in his armor. "Your attaché called when he left you at the gates."

Isela flushed. "I told him…I didn't want to distract you. Are those…bite marks?"

Gregor snarled, dabbing at the gaping tear in his neck. She tried to get a better look but he jerked away. It began sealing itself before her eyes.

"You are not supposed to be here," he barked.

"I won't distract him," she said. "I just need to be close enough for the power transfer."

From a space in the tombstones on her right came a runner in the tattered remains of a suit. Gregor spun, reaching for his sword. The black wolf lunged from the shadows to intercept it. The wolf caught the filthy, snarling corpse by the thigh, snapping its femur with a dull crack. Gregor sliced the head clean away. It collapsed immediately, lifeless again.

Gregor stepped across Isela's path and she was forced to look up to maintain eye contact. She closed the distance between them in a stride.

"You shouldn't be here," Gregor snapped. "Your job is done."

"It's not a job" Her voice cracked with cold and worry. "Not anymore."

Gregor stood, his breath coming much harder than it should have. Ignoring prudence, she reached out to him. When her fingertips touched his arm he flinched. She recalled Azrael's words about the protection of his Aegis extending to her as his consort. She hoped it included their obedience as well.

"I can feel him, right now, here." She pressed her fist to the center of her chest. "And sitting this one out isn't an option."

Isela latched on to that connection, using it to give her the courage to take the next step. She slipped around him, continuing into the dark. She didn't realize her whole body had been bracing for him to try to stop her until she released a ragged breath.

Emboldened, she lengthened her stride as Christof and Tobias fell in at either side. She glanced back to see Gregor, still standing, and Markus between them. The black wolf's jaws snapped shut, and he bared his teeth, daring Gregor to challenge.

"Are you coming?" she asked both males.

She never thought she'd see surprise on Gregor's face, but it was there, beneath the cold, practiced blankness. He swore and caught up to her in a few swift strides before moving into a ground-eating jog ahead of her. She took a big breath, and started to run. Her limp was more pronounced and the youngest wolf stayed at her hip. She leaned a hand on his withers. Tobias fell back to guard the rear. Markus remained on the perimeter, and she saw only flashes of black fur moving through the moonlight-dappled snow.

In the oldest part of the cemetery, Lysippe stood at the entrance to one of the mausoleums. The briefest flash of a smile creased her mouth when she saw Isela. "Good."

"What's happened?" Isela asked between breaths.

"She was ready for us," Lysippe replied grimly, stepping aside to let her pass down the stone stairway. "She drew him into the In Between."

Lysippe dropped to the rear guard as the darkness swallowed them.

The room was vast, much bigger than it should have been, given the aboveground terrain. A deep cold sank into her bones as they drew closer to the flickering light of a torch circle around a stone altar.

The grimoire from Havel Zeman's aedis rested on the altar beside a thing that resembled coalescing frost beginning to take human shape. Standing before the altar, Azrael faced a woman—Róisín. They were frozen in place. The stillness raised goose bumps on Isela's arms. The room was silent. Not even a twitch of the earth stirring above or a breath from either one of the frozen figures broke the tableau.

She recognized Azrael's stance, the casual feint before the strike, but the woman captured her attention.

The Queen of Diamonds looked as if carved from marble, her arms raised in welcome. But beneath her dense, pale brows, cerulean pupils shone with the sickly gleam of an oil slick and a savage smile twisted her face. The victory in her expression chilled Isela.

Between the firelit circle and the room's darkness, Gregor and Lysippe joined Rory and Dory to complete a second circle of Azrael's four. They had their weapons drawn, backs to the circle of fire, but there was no enemy to fight. She knew without being told they could not breach the light—not even with the weapons Azrael had given them.

Whatever was happening between the necromancers was happening somewhere *else*. She thought of the night in Zeman's aedis, how Azrael had seemed frozen in place before he'd collapsed, clutching a wound she hadn't seen inflicted. Whatever happened there, the consequences were real enough.

"Hurry," Dory said, and she saw the frost on his breath.

Isela shivered, nodding.

Her muscles contracted in the cold, and pain arched up her hip with every breath. She closed her eyes, clenching her teeth to keep them from chattering, and began to dance. Her body was tense with worry, but after a moment or two, training and muscle memory took over.

Isela didn't hold back, immersing herself fully in the expanding bubble she created. She flung herself into it, ignoring everything, and became the dance. The room warmed slightly. The air no longer burned her lungs with cold.

She heard a shout, as if at a great distance, and there was sound again, not just the pant of her own breath and the pounding of her heart. She found herself face-to-face with the golden shadow.

Though she couldn't make out facial features, Isela knew it was staring into her. It cocked its head, like a curious animal, darting closer.

She couldn't help herself: she smiled at it. It mirrored her face, smiling back, and then they were dancing together, and nothing else mattered. It grew closer, and her moves became an invitation. She spun, stamping, and when she looked again, the glittering shadow was close enough to touch. If Azrael was right, guardian angels didn't exist, not the way people talked about. This was no angel. This was a god. She spun with delight, and the god matched her movement perfectly.

The tearing sensation in her hip came first as if at a great distance. Pain brought it into immediate focus. Her step faltered as the raw burn shattered her concentration, cutting through adrenaline and endorphins. She heard a high, keening sound before she realized it was the sound of her own frustrated grief. Any second she would fall, and any good she might do Azrael would be lost. If she ever danced after tonight, it would be a miracle. If Azrael fell to the Queen, they would all die.

Time slowed as her shadow peered at her hip. She didn't need to explain. She had opened herself—become the conduit—it knew her well enough to see the truth. It understood her anguish and urgency. It offered itself up.

Isela didn't think about the ramifications of what she was about to do. All she could hear was Azrael's unchecked laughter when he told her his childhood nickname. She would give herself over a thousand times to hear that laugh again.

Isela reached out, touching the shadow for the first time. "Okay. I accept you."

The world rippled. She sealed her eyes against the burning light, tears streaming between her lashes. Her body fell away, left behind.

She was the shadow, and now she could see *everything*.

A battle was being waged in the shifting, windswept gray place she now understood was the In Between. Azrael and Róisín fought one part hand to hand, one part power.

Azrael bled from tiny slashes on his face and hands, as though he'd been hit with flying glass. Every time he scored a hit, shards of Róisín broke off; tiny pieces of ice or diamonds that glittered through the air, slicing anything they touched. In this place identical to the physical room it overlaid, the torchlight whipped in the heated wind that rolled off Azrael, and the room was bright with his fire.

As Isela watched, Róisín spun a long, bladed staff. Azrael lunged away, barely avoiding her. When he lunged forward again, he was bearing a long, double-bladed axe that became two when his hands parted.

In this place, Isela could clearly see the figure on the altar taking shape. A network of shining, translucent threads, like liquid diamonds, swiftly knitted itself into a humanoid form. Beneath the figure, spilling over the altar sides, was the first suggestion of wings.

"The angel," she breathed.

It begins here, but it must not be allowed to cross into the physical world. If it takes shape there, all is lost. The voice belonged to her shadow, only it came from within her chest now.

Azrael grunted. He went to one knee to block the force of a blow but moved too slowly to avoid the second sweep that sliced into his shoulder, opening his chest up.

Isela was running before she made the decision. *I need a weapon.*

The gold shadow was ahead of her, a smile in that glittering voice. *Look down.*

In her hands were the two small blades she always wore, but here, they were the length of stilettos and shining gold with a back edge holding a wicked curving arch. These weren't designed simply to slice but to open flesh and leave it bleeding. She aimed her gaze at the Queen of Diamonds and charged.

* * *

"HAD ENOUGH, AZRAEL?" Róisín inquired, as if offering seconds at a meal.

The Queen of Diamonds, taken by madness, was still stronger than he ever expected. He'd misjudged her and overestimated his ability to simultaneously fight a necromancer and undo the spell creating the nascent angel. He was running out of time. Soon the angel would be strong enough that destroying it would be impossible.

"Sorry, majesty, we've only just begun." Azrael spread his arms, giving a little courtly bow.

A terrible scream tore from her, and he had just enough time to move sideways before her blow struck. "You mock me, little goat boy. When the devil bred you on your mother, she begged him for more."

"Is that the best you can do?" Azrael said, baring his teeth. "After all these years?"

He'd blocked pain long ago, but the wounds he acquired here affected his body on the physical plane. His ability to heal himself would draw power he needed to fight her. Enough injury would weaken him past the point of no return.

She spun away, alternately laughing and howling like a moon-struck banshee. The sound made the hairs on his neck stand on end. That such a madwoman held power like hers was beyond belief.

At once, she stopped, but she never let him get closer to the altar, keeping herself between him and it the entire time. *So not fully mad*, he thought. There was something left of her old self, cunning and ruthless.

And broken.

She began to sob, shrieks becoming thin wails as she let go of the staff with one hand to beat at her chest. He heard the hollow booming like icebergs calving from a glacier with each strike.

"They took him from me, Azrael. My dancer," she said. Her eyes met his, naked with sorrow and bottomless pain.

"You killed him, Róisín." Azrael kept his eyes from moving to the altar as he edged sideways.

"But he was a threat," she pleaded, tears crackling into shards that flaked from her cheeks. "He would have taken my power. He and that god, conspiring against me and joining together."

"Is that what Paolo told you," he asked. "Or Vanka? Those two should never be trusted. You taught me that."

For the sheerest instant, he felt pity. Perhaps it was what Isela brought out in him—the ability to see the broken thing she had become and to empathize. He remembered who she was just in time.

Azrael narrowly avoided a swipe of Róisín's bladed staff that would have opened him from gut to gullet. He rolled, suddenly infused with power, and struck out. The blow ripped through her from shoulder to waist, tearing her open and exposing the glistening organs beneath. She screamed with uninhibited rage.

And still she fought, the wound sealing as she struck back.

Azrael countered her attack with a new strength, realizing it came from Isela dancing. For him. Heat surged in him, and he radiated it out. The ice tracks on Róisín's cheeks melted and steamed, and her blade dripped.

The resurgent power gave him a new gambit. He may not have been able to undo the spell, but he could strike against the angel while it was too weak to defend itself. The backlash from contact with the angel would cost him his mind. If he was lucky, the shell of him would survive to absorb Róisín's rage while Gregor and Lysippe protected Isela and escaped with the grimoire. Beryl would know how to destroy the book so the spell could never be used again. He sent the plan to his four.

Neither looked up from the demons they battled, but he felt

the acknowledgment, and Azrael had never been more proud of the four finest members of his Aegis. They were warriors; they understood what needed to be done. Isela would understand too, in time.

A bolt of ice shot into his leg, and he felt the wound drive to the bone. The agony of it, muscles and nerve endings electrified with pain, knocked him back. He barely held off the attack, and both of Róisín's blades took payment in flesh from him as they struck. He only needed to hold her off a moment longer.

Out of the corner of his eye, he caught a flash of gold moving faster than any living thing should move.

* * *

ISELA AIMED for Róisín's blind spot. She dropped into a slide, blades up. Róisín moved fast but not fast enough to avoid the cut that opened up the back of her thigh and sent her to her knee. Isela rolled as the diamond blade struck her bicep, and pain lanced up her arm. Wherever they were, the wounds were real enough.

The Queen of Diamonds snarled as Isela rebounded to her feet, but her eyes widened. For a moment Isela saw recognition in the madness.

Azrael was also looking at Isela, trying to make sense of something, but it was as if he couldn't recognize her. Impossibly, Róisín attacked.

Whatever the nature of Isela's shadow, it was a warrior. It rode her form like a second skin, driving her into moves and combat techniques she had never seen, never mind executed. But it was her. Each move came from the dancer's skill; a performance turned deadly. Some giddy part of her huddled in the back of her brain, watching herself under the control of this golden creature that turned her body into a deadly weapon.

Between Azrael and Isela, the Queen of Diamonds began to falter. Now Róisín was on the defensive, and as they demanded more of her attention, the formation of the figure on the altar began to slow.

The voice of the golden shadow echoed as if at a distance. *Now while she's weak. Leave her to Azrael. We must kill it.*

Isela waited until the queen was occupied with Azrael, then she made her move.

Azrael and Róisín realized where Isela was headed at the same time. Forgetting Azrael, Róisín lunged after Isela with an animal howl. Azrael had his opening.

* * *

As THE GOLD figure drew Róisín's attack, Azrael swept the physical room with his gaze. Demons were beginning to bleed through the walls, and his four met them without hesitation. Only Gregor stayed close to the pale wolf. Something was wrong with the wolf. As it fought, it—and the Hessian—stayed in a tight formation around an object lying in a crumpled heap on the floor. He recognized the spill of braided hair, the long line of hip and thigh, and a hand, open and limp, palm up.

His eyes went back to the gold figure dodging Róisín's blades, knowing now why it had been so familiar to him. *The golden thing has her shape*, he thought. He even saw the shadow of gray in its gilded eyes.

The angel's wings began to beat, stirring the In Between into a whirling mass of non-air.

He had to stop her.

He leapt after Róisín as she followed the golden shadow. Azrael slammed into Róisín from behind, knocking her to the ground. She kicked his legs out from beneath him. Róisín's blade darted between his ribs, just missing the heart, as it split bone like blades of grass. She staggered to her feet.

A battle cry in a long-dead language tore from Azrael's throat as he yanked the staff deeper into his chest to drag Róisín off balance. He dropped, dragging her down as she struggled to free her blade from his body.

Isela reached the altar, but her first blow must have missed. The angel howled, but there was no blinding light. Azrael still had a chance to stop her.

Róisín hesitated, stunned that Azrael kept coming. His hand snagged her wounded thigh, and he dug his fingers into the bleeding gash. She buckled, screaming. He manifested a blade of his own power with the next breath. He drove the blade up, under her ribs, and it hit something hard that reverberated an icy cold pain up his arm.

She began to laugh. "I haven't had a heart for millennia, Azrael."

It gave him enough time to summon a second blade to his now-free hand. He sliced her head from her neck before the shock could register on her face.

It was not finished. There was a chance she could still regenerate herself. He gathered the last of his power and pumped fire into her, shielding the others in the room to contain the flame so hot it burned no color at all.

When it was done, all that remained was the ashy imprint of her body on the ground. In the center, rocking faintly, was a diamond the size of his fist in the shape of a human heart. He took a breath and dragged the staff blade from his chest.

His vision swam as consciousness began to fail. Still, he struggled onward.

The golden figure had a knife clenched in both hands now. The angel crouched at the foot of the altar, keening.

Azrael could barely hold his eyes open to watch Isela's golden blade plunge into the angel's chest, and the world became a blaze of light.

* * *

ISELA APPROACHED THE ALTAR, swept along by the intensity of the figure before her. It was a vortex, sucking in everything that came too close while giving out an incredible amount of its own power. For a moment she was stunned into stillness. It was more humanlike than ever now but also more alien. Its body was too long, face too narrow.

A wing brushed her as they began to beat, and she felt chaos sweep through her. If not for the golden presence driving her body, Isela would have been lost to madness. As it was, she could not lift the knife. She began to weep.

The angel opened its eyes.

Pure black, without an iris, the eyes took up half its narrow face. In them, she saw nothing—and everything—the cosmos born and dying, in endless sequence. She knew what she must do. Its hand shot up to her wrist. She twisted, spinning and dragging the thing off the altar onto the floor. It was still weak physically—and she was able to get her hand and the blade free.

The blade sang through the air twice, and the angel let out a shriek. It fell back onto the floor. It left severed wings behind, trailing diamond threads like droplets of blood. It backed into the altar, mouth open mutely now, and Isela drove the knife home.

The world went white.

CHAPTER TWENTY-SEVEN

Why haven't you spoken to me before?

None of us possess the ability of speech unless we take possession of a human.

Isela was having a telepathic conversation with her shadow. The god. All around her was darkness and stillness so profound she felt it must have always been and would never end.

She tried not to think about how strange this all was.

Who—what are you? she asked.

I loved her once, in the body of another mortal. I tried to warn him, but he was lost to her.

You were the god that possessed her dancer, Luther Voss.

A sensation of assent. *We have never been gods, Isela. You named us that.*

The light was not uniform. A soft-edged glow pulsed in the distance like a dying star. She was moving toward it now, though her body was still. What a strange dream this was.

But I thought you were female.

A laugh so gentle filled the air it made her want to smile. *Gender is a human trait, Isela. It is enough to say that I am.*

Are all—of them—like you?

Are all leaves the same—even from the same tree?

Isela considered it for a moment. *Why do you care? About us?*

You fascinate us. Your short lives are ruled by your physical presence. We have neither. We find humans intoxicating.

You let us think you were gods.

Why not? We like your gods. There are so many to choose from and each with its own relationship to your race.

Isela thought of the war that had almost ended the world. *Why did you help us try to destroy one another?*

Don't mistake fascination for regard, the voice chided. *Some of us hate our addiction and would see you perish.*

Yes, she was definitely moving. Or the light was drawing closer. *Where are we going?*

I don't know, I've never followed a mortal this far before.

This far?

Into death.

Isela would have gasped had she had lungs. Instead, she found she could control her movements, and she spun, running back the way they had come, but it was impossible to tell if the distance shortened. When she turned, the light was larger. Brighter.

No, she shook her head. *I can't be dead. I can't.*

No mortal can survive an angel's touch. Even one not fully formed.

"Little Bird? Is that you?"

A sob stuck in her throat, and she turned back to the light to see her father emerging. He looked as he hadn't in twenty years, and it was clear how much his illness had cost him at the end. She ran into his arms. He smelled the same, felt the same. In that moment, she was seven again, and he was pushing her on the swing set in the park.

When she opened her eyes, they were in Vysehrad Park on an autumn day. The leaves were shades of flame and ember, the air so crisp it stung her lungs.

Lukas Vogel laughed. "You're much better at this than I am."

I'm dead?

Yes and no, the golden voice said.

What does that mean?

If death were a train ride away, you're in the station waiting to board. Your dad is real though. He hasn't moved on.

Isela collapsed into the nearest swing, kicking her feet in the leaves and sand beneath.

"What's the matter, Little Bird?" Lukas Vogel grasped the chain links on either side of her hands and began, gently, to push.

"Dad, we're dead," she whispered around the tightening in her throat.

Lukas Vogel sat in the swing beside her, stretching out a hand to catch hers. "I know. I didn't expect to see you here so soon."

All the unspoken regrets rose in her. That she would never feel Azrael's heat racing through her body again or wake up in a pile of smoldering sheets. She would not get to know her family for who they truly were and see her nieces and nephews grow up.

You did what had to be done. You made a great sacrifice. She couldn't be allowed to succeed.

But Azrael. Her desire drew her back to the room below ground in the cemetery.

Isela hovered above the mess: the remnants of angel wings, hardening pewter dull, and the fading demons, melting into shadows once again. Outside the circle of light, she recognized the familiar dark head of hair and broad shoulders, crouched on the floor with a limp body in his arms. Around him, his four were down on one knee, heads bowed. The pale wolf, his pelt sticky with blood and demon gore, sat back on his haunches and loosed a skull-tingling howl. The rest of the pack came down into the darkness to join their brother in mourning.

Her. She realized. They were calling for her. And Azrael was sitting on the floor, bleeding from a hundred different wounds with her body cradled in his arms. He was rocking, she realized, and saying something she could not quite make out.

Isela was standing outside the circle, and no one could see her. She looked at her father beside her, his face full of pain.

"You don't belong here, Little Bird."

What if there was a loophole between life and death, a way back, would you take it?

Isela would have stopped breathing, but that was already status quo. She went still and silent. Waiting.

I can't bring you back to life, but I can take you with me.

I don't understand.

You accepted me once. Do it again, Isela. Only this time make it permanent. Share your body with me.

Horror crept through her. Possessed by a god. It was no better than becoming a zombie, a slave at the whim of a more powerful entity.

I don't want to control you, to make you anything other than you are. I like *you, Isela.*

What's the catch?

The gold shimmer laughed. *I experienced physical form once for such a short while. I want to be alive again. And I can be helpful, you'll see. I know things that even necromancers don't.*

Isela heard a wink in that voice. She closed her eyes, unable to watch Azrael grieving any longer. She felt her hand encased in a larger one, warmth spreading up her arms. Once again, she was being asked to give up everything she'd ever known for something she'd never known she wanted.

"I want to go home, Papa."

"I know," he said, pressing his lips to her temple. "I know."

* * *

LOSING to Róisín couldn't have felt worse than this. Azrael had won; his Aegis was whole. He would recover, even increase his power in time. Defeating another necromancer always strengthened the victor.

Yet he had never felt this hollow. The emptiness cut deeper because he had so recently known fullness to the point of bursting in Isela's arms. Grief crumbled a thousand years of world-weariness like waves drawing sand under his feet.

His sight began to return as his corneas healed. He'd felt his way to her, crawling across the floor until he could put his fingers on her face. He wanted to believe he saw the rise of her ribcage and the flicker of her eyelashes against her cheek.

But he knew better. From the first days of his power, he could sense the death that each mortal held, like the blemish of a bruise on a ripe fruit. In some, it was small; in others, large and imminent. But it was always there. In those that death had taken, the mark covered them head to toe. Isela was a darkness, an absence of all light and warmth. He barely registered the hand on his shoulder.

"Bring her back," Rory said, a gravel-toned command.

It had been his first instinct, to reach into the In Between and call her soul back into her body. He should do it. She belonged to him. His dancer; her human body too frail to serve the wolf heart it caged.

It had been a thousand years since he'd known grief. More since the realization he would outlive everyone he loved and their children's children, for an eternity. It had taken him decades to rise up out of the ennui caused by that kind of loss. He wanted to hate Isela for stripping away the walls that he'd cultivated. Gregor was right to reject his humanity, to protect himself from the damage it could wreak.

He should bring her back. It would serve her right. She would have no choice but to obey. As the summoned dead, she would be a servant to his will. And she would never forgive him for it.

Azrael shook his head, unable to speak.

Anguish and rage swelled in the emptiness. As Isela would have said, it simply was not fair. He'd done everything he could to protect her. And she had walked into her own death with open arms. To help him. To preserve a world that would be dimmer for the loss of her presence.

Azrael curled the empty body in his arms, feeling the heat from his skin flow into hers. In the silence, the voices of the wolves called into the night in tones richer than any human song.

"I will build you monuments," he promised her at last, preparing himself to give her one last gift. "Everyone will know what Isela Vogel did for humanity."

He would burn her body. With no physical remains, she could not be summoned. She would never be forced back into this plane against her will. It was the least he could do to protect the life he had cherished. He let the heat flow into her, prepared to hold her until the last of her became ash.

The youngest wolf stopped midhowl. He slunk forward on his belly to put a paw on Isela's leg. He whined, and Azrael met his gaze. The too-human glaucous eyes looked unsure.

Azrael wondered how much they understood as animals. The young wolf nudged his arm where it rested against her chest. Again the whine, questioning. *Should he try to explain?*

The howling stopped abruptly.

"Monuments, Azrael?" A weak voice murmured from under his collarbone. "Let's not get ahead of ourselves."

Azrael felt her body beginning to stir as life crept into the darkness, chasing away the shadow of death. Hope, raw and unbidden unfurled in his chest. It filled the hollowed-out space and expanded, making his ribs ache. She was alive. He crushed her against his chest, determined not to let her go.

"Why is it so hot in here?"

Azrael recoiled the heat as quickly as he could as the sweat began to bead on her skin.

A wolf tongue flicked out, bathing her face from chin to temple.

"Chris, gross!" Her nose wrinkled in disgust.

The gray's jaws opened in a canine grin. She laughed, and Azrael watched a thread of gold streak through her irises. He took her chin in his bloody hands, turning her face toward him. Her expression changed, the helpless smile sliding slowly away as she saw the realization in his face.

"Isela," he breathed. "What have you done?"

Before his eyes, the ashen gray was slowly overtaken by shining gold.

* * *

WHEN ISELA EMERGED from the tomb in Gregor's arms, something about the sight of desecrated graves and still-twitching corpses in dawn's rosy sunlight undid her. Behind Gregor, Rory supported Azrael's weight, while Lysippe bore the wrapped grimoire and Róisín's broken heart.

From the time Isela and her brothers had been children, their mother always said the solstice was a time for strengthening bonds and taking stock of the past to move forward into the future. Flanked by three wolves and surrounded by Azrael's inhuman guard, she had the distinct impression the Isela who had walked into that tomb had been left behind. And it wasn't just the goddess inside her now. The dancer she had been—naïve of the true world

—was gone. She didn't know the woman who emerged, but there was time enough to find out. She began to sob, for no other reason than she would live to see the days grow longer again.

Gregor grit his teeth and produced a handkerchief.

The coven had done its job well—minimizing the damage outside the cemetery to the equivalent of a minor earthquake. Azrael's people would be busy for weeks maintaining the cover story while the work was done to repair the damage done by Róisín's attempted revenge.

The local police and the undead servants of the necromancer had cordoned off the cemetery. A series of black vehicles with tinted glass was waved through to meet them. Lysippe helped Azrael inside a Mercedes van.

She could see Azrael's power now, as though an extra layer of sight had been added to her eyes. It curled and roiled around his edges like sun flares. Even the members of his Aegis bore faint traces of it.

Gregor slid her inside with more gentleness than she knew he possessed, before snarling at her to put on her own seat belt.

"Hi, Miss Vogel," Tyler said from behind the wheel. His aura was an absence of light. She wondered if that was because he was dead and if so, what she looked like. "Glad to see you're all right."

"You too," she said, meaning it.

The wolves sulked, clearly unsure of how to deal with their sudden exposure to daylight in the middle of the city. Gregor opened the tailgate. Markus growled, ears flat. Tobias looked between Isela and their brother.

Christof decided, leaping in with a wag of his plumed tail. Tobias came next, almost missing his landing when his injured leg buckled. Gregor hooked him under the hind legs, boosting him the rest of the way.

Still bristling, Markus made the easy jump, staying far away from the Hessian. The Sprinter's rear springs sagged alarmingly.

"Suit yourself, fleabag," Gregor said cheerily, slamming the door shut.

Isela smiled at the sight of the three panting werewolves. She patted Tobias, and Christof took another long swipe at her face with a big pink tongue. "Quit that."

Markus growled uneasily, and she reached a hand to reassure him, but he darted away. Isela settled in her seat, ignoring the ache of his rejection. She watched Rory hoist the bag holding the remnants of the angel wings. Dory took the cloth-wrapped grimoire from Lysippe.

"Is it dead?" Isela asked.

Azrael shook his head. "It was too close to being complete. But it has no physical form, and you prevented it from acquiring its full power. It fled, without a trace, but the Aegis will continue to hunt for it."

Gregor climbed into the passenger seat as the rest of the guard filed into the other vehicles. When she looked away from the window, Azrael was watching her.

"It can't hurt anyone can it?" Isela said, a tangle of emotion in her throat.

"Not as it is," Azrael said. "And with the grimoire under my control, the spell cannot be completed."

"Can't you just let it be then?" She avoiding meeting his eyes as tears blurred the scenery outside. "Do you have to—kill it?"

Azrael sighed. "You are still human enough, so quick to empathize."

She thought about the bargain she'd made. How much would the goddess change her?

"I can't read you anymore," Azrael said quietly.

Isela hesitated, knowing he saw exactly what she was. Her throat was a tight knot. She remembered the arrogant confidence of his statement that everyone in his household was an open book. Even if he had been trying to respect her boundaries, it was a choice. That had been taken from him. Fear of the unknown had undone Róisín, made her susceptible to the suspicions of the other necromancers.

"Is that the only thing that's changed?" She was happy she managed to sound calm as her chest clenched.

"It's gone," he said. "The kernel of death that all humans hold. I've scanned you, three, four times since we left the tomb. It's gone."

Isela turned her attention inward, alarm growing.

Can you hear me?

Of course. The golden voice came sluggish and distant, as if it were curling up for a long sleep.

Does that mean—

You can still be killed, Isela. It will be a while before you are strong enough to resist blade and spell. But disease, illness, or age cannot touch you. Consider it a side effect.

What am I now?

Same as you've ever been, the golden voice answered. *Just with a few—tweaks. Shh, I didn't know it would be so tiring—being born this way.*

Azrael was waiting in that patient stillness when her attention returned to the car.

"I just wanted to come back," she said bluntly. "I wasn't ready to leave you. Now I don't know who—*what*—I am anymore."

She felt it first—the long tendrils of heat that curled away from his body and encircled hers. They beckoned, when his arms were too weak, and she went willingly.

She thought of what the golden shadow had said about warning Luther Voss. She understood now how Róisín's lover would have gone to her bed anyway, knowing she would be his end.

Isela couldn't have made herself run from Azrael if she wanted to.

In spite of her own terror, the golden shadow seemed quiescent in her chest. Azrael waited until she was curled up against his least-damaged side, tangled his fingers in the mess of her hair, and drew her face to his.

"You are Isela Vogel," he said. "Kin to witches and wolves. Vessel of a god. And my consort."

Azrael named her, and claimed her, in a single breath. And she knew whatever happened next, she was home.

CHAPTER TWENTY-EIGHT

Even with her own army of undead, pulling off a dream wedding on New Year's Day took more work than Isela would have imagined. With Azrael healing, Lysippe was charged with handling his official business, including the fallout from Róisín's attack on the city. That left Gregor to be Isela's right hand.

The more things changed, the more they stayed the same, she thought. Gregor snarled at the catering assistant lingering too long in the sculpture hall, transfixed by Michelangelo's *David*.

Thank goodness she had a little help.

Kyle stepped between the Hessian and the cowering man. "It's fine, just head into the dining room."

When the man was gone, Kyle tilted his head, staring fearlessly into the scowling face of the necromancer's enforcer. "Cool it, handsome. You're scaring the help… again."

He patted the taller man's shoulder and started down the hall.

Isela laughed. Of all her friends, Kyle handled the changes the best. As he told her the first morning Azrael had allowed anyone in the castle, "You're still my friend, Vogel. Even if your *new* friends are a little—frightening."

"Mistress, the narrow chap with the funny hat would like to know the desired placement for the groom's cake," said a rusty voice behind her.

She turned to see the Nordic bruiser, Aleifr. They were the first words she'd ever heard him utter. "Aleifr, it's just Isela. Or Issy."

He grunted assent. She sighed.

"Chuck the damn thing in the garden," she said, knowing she was fighting a losing battle. "Or the stag moat. At the bottom of the Vltava. I don't know."

Her brothers had volunteered to be in charge of the groom's cake. In all the chaos, they'd managed to keep it from her until that morning. Smart move on their part: she would have put the kibosh on a cake shaped like the stag in Gregor's family crest, done in red velvet so that when sliced, it appeared to bleed. The Vogel boys. Young wolves, all.

"And for gods' sakes, keep it from Gregor until the last possible minute," she called after him.

She caught the wily grin cast over the Viking's shoulder and knew she had been right to lay down the command. Undoubtedly the rest of the Aegis who had caught on were having their fun with it.

"Tell the others too," she thought to add before he was out of earshot, muttering under her breath. "I want this to be a wedding, not a funeral."

"There you are."

Beryl Gilman-Vogel came down the hall in flowing purple robes, looking a bit like a goddess herself. If anyone had told Isela that her mother, as High Priestess of Prague's first official coven, would have been wandering down the halls of the necromancer's castle a year ago, she would have suggested they avoid the hallucinogens.

"The Sisters are looking for you," Beryl said. "It's time to get dressed."

"Already?"

"Time waits for no immortal," Beryl said, her smile taking on a hint of sadness. "Even a newly born one. They're so golden today."

Isela understood her surprise; she still hadn't gotten used to seeing her own reflection in the mirror. Some days her eyes were still an earthy gray. Others, they glowed like sunlight rippling on water. She let her mother hug her for a moment.

"I'll be right there," she said. "I just have a few things to check on."

Isela sprinted down the hall. It was old habit to favor her hip and move with slow, steady control to avoid aggravating it. But the throbs of pain she'd grown accustomed to had been gone since emerging from the tomb: another one of the goddess's tweaks.

She skidded to a stop in the dining room. The theme was a winter garden, and all week exotic plants had been arriving by the truckload. The settings were silver and gold, with white runners and snowflake lace so fragile she was afraid to touch most of it. A group of the silent undead moved around the last of the decorating. Isela couldn't say she was entirely comfortable in their presence, but she was trying. She cleared her throat. The leader, the one she was beginning to think of as Azrael's version of Niles, looked up from arranging a delicate explosion of peonies and ivy in the center of a table, and his empty eyes fell on her. She gritted her teeth to keep from shuddering.

"Everything good?" she called.

He folded at the waist and resumed his task. Assuming that was affirmation, she grimaced and moved on.

Her last stop was the wedding site itself. Azrael had picked the garden of paradise, and in spite of her objections to him using his power for something so trivial, he'd heated the whole space. Ever the green thumb, Bebe had coaxed verdant grass around the cleared paving stones, framed in turn by a fresh dusting of snow. On the bare stone, lines of chairs in white and silver angled toward a long aisle carpeted in green. The weak winter light was boosted with torches glowing with something she knew was too rich to be fire-light alone. At the front of the isle was an altar so simple and elegant it stole her breath.

Tyler escorted a final group of arriving guests to the reception area. He looked handsome in a slate-gray suit, complete with tails.

"Looking good, Ty," she said.

"Thank you, Issy." He bowed slightly.

Isela turned her attention to the guests.

It was a small affair, but she suspected this was the first time the castle had so many human visitors in some time. A few expressed surprise to see her, and she greeted everyone with smiles. Divya hugged her so tightly her ribs ached.

"We expect you back at the Academy," she informed her, brushing dampness from her cheeks. "There is a teaching position opening up in the spring."

"We'll see."

What she would do now was still an open debate, although Azrael assumed it had been closed when he made the decision that his consort would not continue as a godsdancer. She agreed it wouldn't be right to dance for patrons any longer, but dance was her life and the Academy her family. Not even a necromancer's power could keep her from that. Azrael would realize eventually.

"Niles," she addressed the suited man at the director's shoulder.

"Miss Vogel." He inclined his head, surprised when she threw her arms around him.

"Issy!" Bebe leaned out the window of a room above the courtyard. "Hurry up!"

"Gotta go."

Isela ran. Not because she had to, though Bebe had sounded out of patience, but because she *could*. She gloried in the freedom and strength of her body. Repairing the damage to her hip has been only the beginning. She was faster and stronger now than ever before. She had begun training with the Aegis, because the god seemed content to honor her word and remain an observer.

The suite designated for the bridal party was a flurry of hairspray, silk, and flowers. Isela closed the door behind her and hurried into the melee. Bebe snapped her fingers and the last dress left on a hanger drifted obediently across the room. Isela sneezed at a whiff of Ofelia's perfume—a heavy bouquet of mixed blooms dusted in honey—and collided with the levitating garment. She swore, tangled in lengths of fabric.

"You are going to be the death of me," Bebe said, exasperated as she rescued the delicate material from Isela's flailing limbs.

Isela kissed her sister-in-law's cheek and flung off her clothes. "Dying has worked out OK so far."

"That's not funny." Evie chided as she put the finishing touches on her lipstick. "Either of you."

Bebe rolled her eyes and Isela stuck out her tongue. Evie glared at them in the mirror before glancing at her reflection. When she pursed her lips critically, the color of her lipstick shifted to a more flattering shade.

"Nice trick," Isela said, ducking her head as Bebe helped her into her dress.

"I taught her that," Ofelia chimed proudly.

Isela sat patiently as her hair was piled into a simple upsweep off the back of her neck, fixed with the garnet clasp that had been a present from Azrael. Tiny tendrils slipped loose almost immediately, and no amount of hairspray would hold them. Bebe focused on makeup next. She spun Isela's chair to face the mirror. "There."

Isela looked into the face staring back and, for the first time, saw the familiar before the changes. The makeup was simple: soft, neutral lips, the hint of blush and a deep brown eyeliner that made her eyes—freshly minted gold today—stand out beneath the long, dark lashes.

"Ready?" Kyle poked his head in the door and sighed dramatically, one palm flattened against his chest at the sight of the four women. "Stunning. It's go time, ladies."

"Let's get this over with before I start puking again." Ofelia sighed, one hand on the tiny mound of her belly.

* * *

ISELA CAME down the aisle at a stately walk, cupping a blooming peony in her palms. As the petals unfurled over her fingertips, sparks of gold flickered down her hands and cascaded to the floor. It was a startlingly easy bit of illusion that had taken a single afternoon of Bebe's careful tutoring to master. The effect, each woman treading on the previous' trail of light as she passed, was worth the effort. The afternoon sun had turned the garden golden, and with the heat radiating off the tiles, she barely felt the cold in the sleeveless crimson gown.

At the altar, her mother waited. The boys were lined up on the groom's side, looking spectacularly handsome in charcoal suits with Markus, composed and watchful, at the end. Toby, his left arm still in a sling, adjusted his glasses and tried not to fidget. Chris, roguish as always, winked at her from Azrael's side. She scanned the assembly, familiar faces, friends, family, and her heart ached for a beat at the one face that was missing.

She caught a glimmer out of the corner of her eye as she reached the front. A chair had been set aside, but it was not quite empty: it held the suggestion of a body not fully formed. Her ribs expanded painfully as she fought the urge to let a tear escape. A tendril of warmth reached out to her across the aisle, and shining silver eyes met damp gold. She nodded recognition and moved to stand beside Bebe, turning to face the aisle.

The music changed, the long, low, resonate tone of the cello before the melody. Isela had insisted on a real string quartet. If they'd left it to Fifi, it would have been speakers thumping a dubstep wedding march remix. The gathered rose.

Ofelia came down the aisle. In spite of her nerves and nausea, she looked radiant. A single spill of bone-white satin draped her body flatteringly and turned her swelling belly into an homage to fertility. She'd forgone a veil, and when her eyes locked on Chris's, Isela heard her brother's breath catch.

Isela smiled at the word Azrael murmured to him. "Steady."

She had promised herself she would not cry. But at some point during the rings, or Chris' vows, she felt the first tears and the handkerchief Bebe pressed into her fingers.

It had surprised everyone when Azrael offered to hold the wedding at the castle. Isela suspected it was a gesture of good faith and thanks. Lysippe claimed it was an act of strategic alliance forming with the coven. Gregor blamed it on creeping insanity.

Fifi had been unable to contain herself. If not for Chris's hold on her, she might have just hugged the necromancer. The boys came around to the idea eventually, mostly through Beryl's intervention.

Now if only she could keep the peace through the cake cutting, Isela thought, this might be real progress.

When it was over, Azrael wrapped his arm around her shoulders vaporizing the last of her tears with the heat of his mouth. He still moved stiffly, suggesting the depth of the wounds from which he was still healing. From the edge of the garden, they watched Chris and Fifi receiving their guests on the way into the reception hall.

"Antiquated human ritual, eh?" she challenged, pressing her nose into his collar for a deep whiff of the agarwood and toasted cinnamon coated in molasses she'd come to love.

"It has its merits." He traced her bare bicep with a finger.

"Consort has a much nicer ring to it." She hooded her golden eyes and gave him her best come hither glance. "Sounds more dangerous."

A feral smile licked the corners of his mouth and sent curling heat into the pit of her belly. "You'll break a man with that look."

"Good thing you aren't a man."

"Good thing," he echoed. "Come, consort, your guests are waiting."

"Just a minute," she said, glancing back at the empty chairs.

He let her go.

She walked to the chair at the front. The light flickered around the suggestion of a human shape. She sat down next to it, not sure this wasn't part of her longing for the impossible.

"We miss you, Papa," she whispered. "But I promise, I'll take good care of them."

She stayed until the sense of him was gone. When she turned to the hall, Azrael was waiting, silver eyes warm.

"I hoped you'd do that soon," he said quietly, slipping an arm around her waist. "A necromancer with a haunted house? I'd never live it down."

Her questioning eyes met his.

"A necromancer's purpose is not only to summon the dead," he affirmed. "We have the responsibility to release them when they're stuck. Mostly, they just need to be told it's all right to go," Azrael said, pausing to touch her damp cheek. "Don't do *that.* You'll give Gregor an aneurism."

"Might be worth it," she said shakily, wiping her cheeks.

Azrael took her hand. "We have one more hurdle to face. Are you ready, consort?"

Isela drew a hard breath and felt the god stir under her breastbone like a second heart beginning to pump.

They had been waiting for this moment. She shouldn't have been surprised it would come now—when the allegiance would undoubtedly think Azrael was at his most vulnerable.

She nodded and laced their fingers together.

* * *

AZRAEL FELT them as the celebration began to wind down and most of the human party had departed. He mentally prepared his Aegis and sent a tendril of warning to Beryl, testing her resistance to mental communication. Unlike her daughter, she had no qualms about accepting his connection—and the warning. She would prepare the others.

By the time he and Isela stepped into the banquet hall, the remaining guests were silent, resting at their tables face down, fast asleep. All except his own warriors and the wedding party.

This part of the plan Gregor had agreed on with bared teeth. It was only a matter of time before word of Azrael's success would reach the allegiance, and the rumors of how he had achieved it—and his unorthodox allies—would surely follow. Necromancers had placed themselves above all other creatures when they took over, ruling with tight fists. That Azrael would allow witches to practice, and ally with wolves, would be seen as a threat even if it was in his own territory.

Rather than waiting and reacting to whatever action they might take, Azrael proposed they force the conversation. What better way than to lure the allegiance into the open. What better way to bait the trap than offer the opportunity to confront Azrael and his new allies at once, with their guard down.

Or so they would expect.

The wedding party and his Aegis fell in behind Azrael and Isela, leaving the banquet behind to enter the great hall, just as the enormous front doors blew open and seven shrouded figures entered. Behind them came their respective guards, no one's equal to Azrael's, but in combination a force to be reckoned with.

"They do have a flair for the dramatic," Isela said lightly as Azrael closed all doors to the room with a flick of a finger.

He thought about squeezing her fingers to caution prudence, but this was his Isela. A low growl sounded from his left. The Vogel boys lined up beside Gregor. The growl came from Markus, of course. The inhuman sound left no doubt that they were more than human.

The seven figures formed a long line on the other side of the room, shoulder to shoulder. They wore ceremonial shrouds, he noted, the same worn in appearances during the takeover and division of the countries. He thought of his own, packed away with the things from the old days. Some of them had continued to embrace their fearsome otherworldly image, but he'd long ago given up the need. He would be savage when required, but he would never hide his face. His Aegis and undead would know whom they served, and the humans would know the face of the one they answered to.

But in choosing to wear the shrouds, the allegiance was making a statement clearer than any words. He had transgressed and must be brought to heel. He wondered briefly if this was how they had come for Róisín. Or had they worked on her slowly, one-on-one, convincing her everything she held was threatened by her lover.

Yes. They would know better than to try that with him. They had come to see their will done by force if necessary.

* * *

"To WHAT DO we owe this pleasure?" Azrael addressed the allegiance as calmly as the wedding guests.

Isela almost smiled.

Having a god inside her was like having another sense. This one tuned to power of all kinds. Now, as well as feeling his total and complete stillness, she was aware of the power amassing within him. This close, it made her tremble.

But the tremors were no longer fear. She tasted a gritty eagerness as the power in her rose to full awareness, perhaps sensing the threat—or opportunity.

"Many goings on in your territory are being spoken of Azrael." Paolo brushed back his hood, and the others followed. "Disturbing rumors."

She had no doubt these were not projections as they had been the first time she saw them assembled. The power from the collected line swelled across the distance. At once, it seemed to dwarf Azrael, and her own golden strength flickered like a candle.

"You came a long way for rumors," Azrael said, voice still light but edged with something darker. "Into my territory, unbidden and uninvited. Surely you have not forgotten the rules of our allegiance?"

"You speak of rules, and yet you piss on them," Vanka snapped, her green eyes flashing. A sneer curled her upper lip. "Consorting with wolves and witches."

Markus's growl gained a new depth.

"I have but one consort, Vanka," Azrael corrected. "But you insult my allies."

"Allies," Kadijah spat. "He allies with dogs."

"Watch how you speak about my brothers," Isela said, bristling as Toby's growl rose in chorus with Marcus's.

"It's true," the Japanese necromancer said, taking Isela in with a breath of surprise. "You've committed the great offense that caused Róisín to be cast out."

"Cast out?" Azrael sneered. "You deceived her, convinced her to break her vow to her own consort. You know the price of breaking the contract with violence: she paid for your meddling with her sanity. I call that a betrayal."

Isela froze. It should have been obvious. The dancer channeled the god. Róisín made the dancer her consort. And she and Azrael had repeated the cycle. Despair surged in her. How could they hope for a different outcome?

You seem to doubt the strength of what lies between us, said Azrael's voice in her head. *I am not weak as she was, Isela.*

I thought you couldn't read me. She wanted to weep.

Perhaps, he admitted. *But your body is mine. I feel your heartbeat. I hear your breath.*

The chill in her was too deep to be put aside with heated words.

They won't let us succeed, she thought frantically. *They have an eternity to work at us. They won't let us win.*

We don't need their permission to be what we are, he assured her. *And I fight for what I love.*

The heat that surged in her was part him but mostly her own

heart. She knew in that moment they were bound together, rise or fall, succeed or fail.

She wouldn't have it any other way.

Azrael loosed the tethers of his powers, and his increased strength swept into the space between them and the allegiance. She sent her own power down her fingers, intertwining with his. Gold and green flared, and the lights threw sparks as electricity surged through the building.

Now you're getting the hang of it, the golden voice said.

Behind them, protected by the Vogel boys and Azrael's own guard, her mother and the Sisters stood shoulder to shoulder, power curling off them. Lilac and sunlight warm, it pushed at her back like supportive hands.

"Let me tell you how this ends." The Sur American spoke, his voice cast in a heavy sadness that rang hollow. "You will give her your heart. And the goddess in her will destroy you. The world will be cast into chaos and war again."

"War and chaos, that's what you wanted when you set Róisín after the goetic spell, wasn't it?" Azrael said lightly. "You have always been good at spinning words. Róisín counted on it when she recruited you to the allegiance. Do the others know you used it to destroy her?"

Isela watched the eyes of the allegiance, noting the first flickers of uncertainty at the mention of the ancient spell that was legend among them. Others looked less convinced in their purpose here. So this was not unilateral agreement. She could see the fractures in their alliance.

"Róisín's talent was finding things and people," Azrael mused, as if reminding them of an old memory. "She saw the power in me and made it her duty to teach me our ways. She was the one who found the spell to bar the gods from humanity. She found each of you when the time was right."

Necromancers did not have children, which meant they were born to normal people. Róisín must have been the first to identify herself to him and teach him what he was. He would have known her skills best and she his, making them more than a match for each other. That's why he had been charged with finding her.

Azrael inclined his head with an unspoken command.

From the line beside him, Gregor tossed something wrapped in cloth into the center of the room. It rolled across the floor, shedding the black fabric as it went to reveal an object the size of a fist and roughly the shape of a human heart. An icy vapor rose from it, staining the floor with a creeping black frost.

"This was never about revenge," Azrael said. "Róisín didn't have a heart left to seek it. It was about power. You send her to flush out the book, I die trying to stop her, and you sweep in to claim her loyalty—and the spell to raise angels. No need for an allegiance then, is there? Not when you hold the power to destroy the entire world."

Even Vanka's glare went to Paolo, green glass in her gaze. "He speaks the truth?"

"A clever lie," Paolo snapped. "Now he has the book and a god. We cannot let him regain his strength."

The allegiance's power snapped together again. But Azrael threw back his head and laughed. It shook the building, the strength of that laugh. It swept through the room. The power behind it battered his enemies with hot desert air that scalded the flesh from more than a few lips and cheekbones, but left his own allies untouched.

"The book is no more," he said. "The spell died with it. But a half-formed angel is now loose in the world, and it will take all my strength, and the god in her, to stop it if it ever comes to its senses and realizes what it is."

They broke in that instant: a thousand waves against the rock that was Azrael's strength united with the god in Isela. The unified wall of power began to retreat, each necromancer hastily absorbing his or her own strength, not trusting the others. Combined with his allies, Azrael's blazed brighter. So vivid and fierce Isela wanted to laugh. How could she have ever thought them in danger? That the allegiance had a chance? She exhaled a long breath she hadn't known she'd been holding.

About time you had a little faith in me, dancer. Such warmth in that voice.

Forgive me, my lord—a little tease in the title. *I will never doubt your sincerity again.*

Never is a long time, love. And I will prove it to you as often as it takes. His tone changed, edged with humor. *I'm happy to see you finally paying me the respect I am due. Although I prefer "master."*

Don't press your luck.

"Let *me* tell *you* how this ends," Azrael boomed to the intruders. "I will allow you to return to your respective territories. If you—individually or as a whole—encroach on my territory without permission, you will remain as corpses. If you make a move against my consort or the one she holds, I will shred your flesh from bone with my bare hands and hang you still breathing from the walls of the city as a warning to others. If you harm my allies, wolf or witch, I will come for you in the darkness like a pestilence and take your strength, leaving you husks for the things that prowl the night."

Azrael the Monster was terrible to behold. But she did not look away. He was her monster. The goddess in her affirmed their union with a surge of electricity.

"I will make no bid for any of your holdings so long as I am respected," Azrael finished. "If not, I will not rest until every last one of you is in chains, and I smash the souls of your Aegises into the final death."

She saw more than one throat bob. The warriors behind their necromancers shifted restlessly.

"Now, you have interrupted a joyous day for my consort's family and our allies," Azrael said quietly, with a formality deadlier than any of his previous words. "I bid you take your leave and wish you swift journey on your way."

They retreated, cloaked in the mists of their arrival but departing in cars real enough to form a convoy of vehicles. Azrael's people erupted into cries of victory that rang to the ceiling.

Azrael gave direction to his Aegis. "I want them tracked, and confirm when they clear the borders." He paused, surveying the rest of his guard. "And Gregor…"

"*Jawohl.*" Gregor came to attention, the black sword reforming and ready for the hunt.

Markus surged eagerly at his side, ready for a fight, his ears already beginning to come to black-furred points.

"Go eat some cake," Azrael said. His tone lightened. "I hear they're serving Schwarz Hirsch at the groom's table."

The look of horror on Gregor's face was priceless. Isela pressed her hand to her lips to catch the laugh. She started forward, ready to get between Gregor and her brothers if it came to blows. But Mark grinned as the wolf retreated from his features, and with all the confidence of a young groom, Chris pounded Gregor on the back companionably.

"Come on. It's red velvet. An American specialty. You'll love it." Chris laughed.

Gregor's nostrils flared, but he sheathed his sword. He shook off the younger man's arm, tugging at his lapels, and followed the still-laughing pack into the reception hall.

One arm around Isela's shoulders, Azrael offered his free hand to Beryl Gilman-Vogel. She clasped it briefly. "You've sanctioned witchcraft again. You must know we're not the only coven. Others will come here, seeking sanctuary."

"And they will be permitted to practice under your supervision," he said, shaking his head when she began to protest. "They cannot practice in freedom yet. I need to be able to protect us all until this settles. We'll work out a way to coexist. In the meantime, I expect you will be busy supervising them."

Azrael and Isela trailed the celebratory party into the banquet hall where guests were stirring as he lifted the geas. He moved slowly, the display in the hall had taken more of him than he was willing to let anyone see. When he wavered unsteadily, she was there, leaning into his side, lending him her strength.

"I will be your shield," she murmured. "This is my vow."

Azrael pulled her hand to his mouth. "All that I am is yours. This is my vow."

His finger slid down to her wrist, over the skin twisted and blackened by the angel's touch.

"How is it today?" he asked.

"Not bad," she said, wiggling her fingers.

For the first few nights, it burned insistently, and neither witch's potion nor Azrael's geas could ease it. Occasionally, pain sprinted into the nerves in her hand. But gradually the pain abated.

Still she pled for mercy. If the angel caused trouble, they would take care of it. Marked by its touch, she would always have a way to sense it. Azrael kept the wings and the grimoire under lock and spell in his aedis. They would need both if it came down to it.

He kissed her fingertips one by one, sending heat through them and into her body.

"Tonight?" she whispered.

She had been patient, knowing he needed to recover, but she hungered for him nonetheless.

A wicked smile full of sensual promise curled his lips. "Are you so eager for my touch, dancer?"

The bloom of heat in her chest was no longer just passion to be satiated but something deeper. An eternity awaited them. They would explore it together.

"Come, necromancer." She led the way into the banquet hall and cast a mischievous, golden-eyed glance over her shoulder. "Don't make me beg."

COMING SOON

Turn the page for a sneak peek at the sequel to Death's Dancer!

Coming 2018

DANCER'S FLAME

GRACE BLOODS #2

A goddess tilted her face up to the sky, drinking in the sight of the stars and the distant moon and her own thin breath and wondering what greater magic there was than this. Her skin prickled in the cold. She relished the sensation of gooseflesh and the tickling of hair on her shoulder blades and breasts.

The other stirred fitfully in the back of her mind. *Sleep, little one,* she bade, stroking it tenderly. *Tonight is for me.*

Then she lifted her arms, bathed in the moonlight, and began to dance.

* * *

Azrael woke alone in the dark. His fingers stretched out, reaching for Isela without thought. The sheets where she should be were rumpled but cool. He sat up in the bed.

Father?

Lysippe, he responded after a quick scan of the room determined Isela was gone.

The garden. Her telepathic voice was terse, worried.

Azrael leaped from the bed, tugging on the pair of pants he'd discarded hours ago when Isela showed him her own version of the dance of seven veils. He had lost his head, in a manner of speaking, in the best way. Returning arousal at the memory was immediately dampened by concern. He might not be able to read Isela's mind any longer, but even when she turned restlessly in her dreams he had awareness of her. That she had slipped out, unnoticed, was wrong somehow.

Barefoot, he jogged down the stairs into the main room of his quarters. The door to the garden was wide open. He hadn't heard that either. Rory stood on the other side, scowling.

Azrael frowned. "Where is she?"

"Thought it best for Lysippe to keep an eye on her until you got here," Rory grunted, thrusting a bit of fabric at him.

He took a moment to recognize the heavy silk in his hand. Isela's robe. He looked at Rory again. The bigger man shrugged, articulating his opinion without words. *Your choice, your problem, mate.*

Azrael followed tracks through the snow-dusted garden. He recognized Lysippe's but not Isela's. Something with the placement was wrong. He stepped over a crumpled length of familiar cotton jersey. Isela's nightshirt. How many times had he teased it off her, amused that she clung to the old thin fabric instead the more obviously seductive items he'd filled her wardrobe with.

He emerged beside Lysippe where the trees circled an enormous fountain. The shadow of the old winter palace, long ago closed up, loomed in the background. Without a word, he followed her gaze.

Isela danced in the moonlight, clothed only in the spill of her sleep-tousled hair. She'd been in the fountain; water curled the ends of her hair into tighter spirals and dappled over the velvet expanse of her brown skin. The pale moonlight caught in droplets and glittered like jewels. Her muscles bunched and lengthened as she swept through wild, uncoordinated movements.

Arousal jetted through him even as the hair on his arms stood on end.

Rory was on patrol, Lysippe said. *She said nothing on her way out, refused to respond to him at all. He called me when she started—*

Her brow rose. Isela cartwheeled, missed the landing, and tumbled into the snow, laughing. Snow clumped in her hair, mud on her elbows and knees. He'd seen her perform more acrobatic maneuvers—she was as sure on her hands as her feet. She didn't *fall.* Something was not right.

Thank you, he said.

Lysippe dropped back into the shadow of the trees. Azrael turned his attention to his consort.

"Little wolf," he called softly.

She didn't respond. He stepped forward. She was on her feet again, dancing. The movements were uncontrolled and uncoordinated, like a child's.

"Isela."

She froze, deerlike, and turned to him. He shivered. He'd followed the contours of her face a hundred times with his fingertips. Fast asleep or in the throes of passion, he knew it. Whatever was looking out at him wore her features like a mask.

He switched to the oldest tongue, the one he used to summon the dead and command the pure strength of his powers. It was said gods had no language before humans danced for them, but that wasn't entirely true. Most humans had just forgotten it by then.

"Goddess," he said.

Eyes the color of molten gold fixed on him. "Begone, death dealer. This night is mine."

"Where is she?"

"Her heart was heavy; I offered to lighten it." The goddess curled around herself as if cradling a baby to her breasts. "She sleeps. Safe as a babe."

"This was not the agreement you made."

The goddess flung out her arms as she stalked toward him. Her mouth curved, teasing. "How do you know what bargain was made between her and me, O lord of death?"

She slid against him. Her nipples, pebbled with cold, brushed his chest as her frozen arms wrapped around his neck. His body responded and she smiled knowingly.

"I know Isela," he said into the brilliant gilded pools of her eyes. "She would not want this."

"She wanted you so badly she would have agreed to anything." Her mouth brushed his, tongue darting out to lick his lips. "Now I know why." She ground her hips into his.

His arousal throbbed, painful. She danced her fingertips down his chest, nails leaving tracks as they went.

"Come, death dealer," she whispered. "Let this night be ours. Do you think you can bring a goddess to her knees?"

* * *

Subscribe to the newsletter at www.jasminesilvera.com for new release information!

ACKNOWLEDGMENTS

No writer becomes an author without a lot of help. In my case, I should start with the fourth grade teacher who praised my first short story about a sentient Christmas Tree, and include every barista who caffeinated me, friends who waited patiently as I tried to answer "what's the book about?" in the tidiest ramble I could muster and, finally you, the reader, who took a chance on the book. I cannot thank you enough for being part of this journey. As far as Death's Dancer goes, there are a few specifics I have to acknowledge with gratitude:

To Beth Green, NaNoWriMo buddy extraordinaire, for teaching me how to pronounce "tea" in Czech and encouraging me to write the "fun" one.

To author and dancer, Camille Griep, for doing her damnedest to keep the dancing honest. Any liberties taken are my own.

To draft warriors: Amy, Sandra, Lucie, Kam, and Esha, for smart, and occasionally hilarious, critiques and words of encouragement.

To Mom, for taking me seriously and being the most incredible grandmother.

To Dad, for introducing me to the writing of Octavia Butler.

To Clarion West, for giving me the opportunity to meet her.

To the city of Prague: I have taken significant artistic liberties with your treasured landmarks and buildings, and I humbly beg your pardon.

To the mamas and papas of Someone Just Pooped. Thanks for letting me join the club.

To OG, there's nothing like a due date for a deadline.

And my husband, Oliver, who is always up for a murderous game of gin rummy and can finish my sentences with song lyrics. You knew I could do it, even when I had doubts. There aren't enough words to thank you for your patience, persistence, and support; so please accept my heart instead.

ABOUT THE AUTHOR

Jasmine Silvera spent her impressionable years sneaking "kissing books" between comics and fantasy movies. She's been mixing them up in her writing ever since. A semi-retired yoga teacher and amateur dancer, she lives in the Pacific Northwest. A semi-retired yoga teacher and amateur dancer, she lives in the Pacific Northwest with her partner-in-crime and their small, opinionated, human charge.

Connect with Jasmine at www.JasmineSilvera.com or on Facebook at www.facebook.com/JasSilvera/

THANKS FOR READING

Reviews help other readers find their next favorite book. Please consider leaving a review on Amazon, Goodreads or your favorite source for book recommendations.

* * *

Interested in more from Isela, Azrael and company? Be the first to find out about new releases by subscribing to the mailing list at www.jasminesilvera.com where you can also find deleted scenes, extras, and other goodies!

CPSIA information can be obtained
at www.ICGtesting.com
Printed in the USA
LVHW04s2315090518
576669LV00001B/173/P